Guardians
of the
Sacred Moon
A Solstice Coven Novel

Wendy Hewlett

Guardians of the Sacred Moon
Wendy Hewlett
Copyright © 2020 Wendy Hewlett
All rights reserved.
ISBN-13: 9781999262648
ISBN: 9781999262631(eBook)

To Andrew ~
Light of my life.

Chapter 1

The spring rains painted the area a brilliant green. Raven Bowen walked down the open field, her father at her side and her six-month-old daughter in her arms. Despite each being a generation apart, they were the spit of each other with their jet-black hair, ice-blue eyes, and delicate yet strong features. Raven and Kiran were both tall and muscular, but she was lithe and ripped, whereas he was bulkier. The years of running and hitting the weights in her home gym were evident in her black tank top and cut off blue jeans.

The trees to her right were full and lush, the leaves whispering in the breeze. To her left, the jagged cliffs of the Canadian Shield gave way to the sparkling blue waters of Fairy Lake. She'd grown up here on the land owned by generations of Bowen women, but she didn't consider it home. The old Victorian house standing regal on its hill held too many horrific memories for her to regard this as a place of sanctuary.

After her mother's passing over a year ago, the house and the land came to Raven. But, it was Kiran who resided in the Bowen homestead, which was about to be overridden by vendors and witches from around the globe. Each year, a coven from somewhere on the planet hosted the Pagan Festival. This year, it fell to the Solstice Coven. Ena Bowen,

Raven's mother, had done most of the groundwork before her passing. Raven and Kiran turned it into a tribute to Ena and the work she did over her lifetime.

"The vendors' tents will be lined up on either side of this clearing," Kiran said. "Leaving a walkway down the middle." He pointed ahead to the end of the field where the forest began. "The stage will be set up there."

It seemed pretty straight forward to Raven. In a few days, the place would be crawling with bodies and that thought made her cringe. She felt like they were about to be invaded. "And the gathering?" At the end of the festival, the Solstice Coven would host a massive celebration of the Summer Solstice known as the Wiccan Sabbat Litha or Midsummer.

"Our usual place." Kiran stretched his arms out and relieved Raven of Indigo. She snuggled into her Grandda's shoulder and started sucking on his neck. Kiran's eyes lit up as he smiled down at her. "I think she may be hungry, aye?"

"I just fed her before I left the house." The clearing in the woods where the Solstice Coven met was sacred ground. Raven wasn't so sure she wanted a bunch of strangers tramping around it. "You think they'll all fit?"

"Oh, aye. Maybe it's time you started feeding her pablum."

Raven laughed, something she was doing more and more of lately. "I tried that yesterday and ended up wearing most of it." She'd had to bathe Indigo then take a shower. She reached into the diaper bag that seemed to have taken up residence on her shoulder and pulled out a baby cookie. "You might want to hand her back, or you'll be wearing most of this."

"Better on me, I suppose. You don't want to go to your appointment wearing baby cookie goo." Kiran took the cookie from Raven, shifted Indigo in his arms and held the cookie to her mouth. Indigo grabbed onto it and started gumming it for all it was worth. "She's definitely hungry,

Rave."

"Or teething." She hadn't cut a tooth yet, but her cheeks were flushed, and she was forever gnawing on anything she could get to her mouth. "I've weaned her off the breast milk. I don't want her anywhere near me once she cuts a few teeth."

Kiran raised an eyebrow and grinned. "A bit sensitive, are you, darling?"

Not a conversation she wanted to have with her father. Raven inherited her mother's insatiable appetite for sex and any hint of her sexuality had a knowing grin forming on her father's face. It was a bit disturbing. Besides, she hadn't had sex in over a year. It wasn't that she didn't want to. She was still working on putting her past trauma behind her and becoming the kind of person that Riley, her ex-girlfriend, deserved. She wanted to be worthy of Riley's love before they got back together. "I'll be going back to work soon, so I figured it was better if she was weaned before that happens."

"You've still got six months' maternity time, don't you?"

"Yeah, but I thought I'd go back in September." It was still over two months away. She'd become a planner since giving birth to her daughter. She couldn't leave the house without taking into consideration everything Indigo would need, planning for any mishap or eventuality.

"Do you miss it then?"

Odd, but she missed her job as a police detective a lot less than she'd imagined when she first went off on maternity leave. "Some." What she missed was the adult interaction which was so not her and perhaps a sign that she was finally healing. "I thought the event planner was supposed to meet us here."

"Aye. She must be running late." Kiran rocked back and forth from foot to foot and held Indigo's hand while she sucked on the cookie. "I'll wait for her if you want to get to your appointment."

Raven took out her cell phone and checked the time. She was going to have to leave in the next five minutes or be late. "You sure you'll be alright with Indi?"

"We'll be fine, love."

"I left a couple of bottles in the fridge, and there's a box of that pablum in her diaper bag if you want to give it a try."

"Okay."

Why was it she nearly had an anxiety attack every time she left Indi in someone else's care? She leaned in and pressed a kiss to Indigo's cheek. The cookie came out of her mouth and she graced her mother with a toothless grin. Raven laughed. "Be good for your Grandda."

* * *

Dr. Kirsten Shoal's office was on the third floor of the Solstice Hospital. Raven entered through the admitting area to avoid running into Riley in the ER. She didn't want to cause Riley any more pain than she already had, and it seemed like it was hurting Riley that Raven was taking so long to heal her wounds.

"Rave?"

Well, so much for that bright idea. Raven turned as Riley rushed down the hallway, her tightly restrained red hair giving her a studious look. The bright, cartoon filled scrub shirt had the opposite effect. It hurt Raven's heart to see the dark circles under Riley's pale green eyes. "Hey? Everything okay?"

"Yeah. I wanted to catch you before you went in to see Dr. Shoal."

She supposed she shouldn't be surprised Riley knew she had an appointment with Shoal. She worked in the hospital. It would be easy enough for her to check with Shoal's secretary. "What's up?"

"I wondered if I could see her with you."

"Why?"

Riley stuck her hands in the pockets of her scrub shirt and shifted from foot to foot. "It's been six months, Rave."

"And you're getting tired of waiting." She couldn't blame Riley. She was asking a lot of her to wait around until she got her head together. "I'm sorry."

"You're sorry as in no, or you're sorry that it's been six months?"

One of Riley's complaints about their relationship had been that Raven was closed off. She didn't want to shut Riley out anymore, and that made the decision easy. "You're welcome to come as long as it's okay with Dr. Shoal."

Riley's shoulders dropped, like air being let out of a balloon. "Thank you." They walked to the elevators together and Riley hit the up button. "How's Indi?"

"Great. Kiran thinks she's not getting enough to eat. We're trying her on pablum." She could picture Kiran and Indigo now, both of them covered in the ivory paste. Raven grinned. "Trouble is, I don't think she realizes she's supposed to swallow it." Raven thought Riley would laugh, but it was a forced smile she gave. It certainly didn't reach her eyes. Raven wrapped her hand around Riley's. "What's wrong, Ri?"

"Sorry. I'm happy for you, Rave. I just wish I was there to experience her changing, too."

"You know you're welcome at my place anytime."

"I know."

As the elevator doors opened, Raven released Riley's hand. They didn't speak on the short ride up to the third floor. Raven wasn't sure what to say that wouldn't make Riley feel worse. She wasn't sure if it was because of her or because Riley delivered Indigo that she felt such a deep connection with her daughter. Riley came over to visit now and then, but it only seemed to make her sadder.

Dr. Kirsten Shoal's office was a throwback to the eighties.

An old metal desk sat in front of a window overlooking the parking lot below. The light blue, plush love seat and chairs surrounding a scarred coffee table were worn and dated. Several diplomas hung on the wall next to a Robert Bateman print of snow-covered evergreens in the moonlight. If you looked closely at the painting, you could see several wolves in the background. It was calming, serene.

"I hope you don't mind me crashing your session, Kirsten," Riley said as she took a seat on the comfy, plush couch.

Raven sat next to her, waiting for Riley to explain.

"I wondered if you could give us an idea of how much longer it will be before Raven is ready for a relationship."

"Ah." Kirsten raised her eyebrows at Raven, a warm smile on her face. "Perhaps this is a conversation the two of you should have."

Raven turned to Riley and retook her hand. "I just want to make sure I'm worthy of you and can give you what you need in the relationship."

"Why do you feel you're not worthy, Rave?" Kirsten asked.

"I don't know. I was completely closed off the first time around. I still feel guilty for hurting her the way I did."

"That wasn't your fault, Rave," Riley said. "I understand that now. If you want to blame someone for that, blame Adara."

"Why don't you tell us your concerns, Riley?" Kirsten picked up a legal pad from the coffee table, set it on her lap, then made a few quick scratches with her pen.

"I can't stand waiting. I feel like I'm not living. I'm just in a holding pattern, hoping, praying that Rave will get where she needs to be."

Raven felt even worse. The past six months, she'd been enjoying watching her daughter grow and sharing that with Indi's father, Jaxon, and Kiran. "What do you need from me to make this better, Ri?"

"You." Riley slid off the love seat, sinking to one knee, her hands clasping Raven's thighs. "Marry me. Spend the rest of your life with me. We can work through all of this together."

Raven always thought she'd be the one to pop the question. She closed her eyes, pictured her view of Fairy Lake from her isolated cottage and took a deep breath. She opened her eyes, gazing into Riley's. "Can we take it a little slower? Start with dinner at my place tonight?"

The dullness faded from Riley's eyes, a bit of their sparkle returning. She grinned up at Raven. "Yeah. That sounds perfect."

* * *

Raven answered the door with a cranky baby on her hip and a tea towel in her hand. "Hey. Come on in. I'm just trying to get dinner ready."

"With one hand?" Riley asked, a sheepish grin on her face.

"I think Miss Cranky Pants is cutting a tooth." Raven headed back into the kitchen where she was trying to assemble a salad. "I tried putting her down, but she just wailed."

"Let me wash my hands, and I'll take her." Riley hooked her purse over a chair at the kitchen island and went off to the powder room.

"There, there," Raven whispered to Indigo, brushing a kiss over her silky hair. She picked up the knife sitting beside the cutting board and took another go at slicing the tomato with one hand. It wasn't going well.

Riley came back in, took Indigo from Raven's arms and stuck her pinky in Indigo's mouth. Indigo gnawed on it vigorously. "Oh, it's right there at the surface. Her first tooth!"

"Where?" Raven put the knife down and leaned in for a look in Indi's mouth.

"On the bottom."

Riley removed her finger and Indi wailed, but Raven got a good look at the tooth just below the surface of her gums. She buttered Indi's cheeks with kisses. "Stick your finger back in there. Quick."

As soon as Riley complied, Indigo stopped crying and began gnawing again. "Aww, poor baby."

"You're so good with her, Ri." Raven finished slicing the tomato, tossed it into the salad, then washed her hands at the sink. "I just have to check on the steak and potatoes on the barbecue."

By the time she came back in with a plate, Indigo was asleep on Riley's shoulder. Raven settled her into her crib, and they sat out on the deck with the baby monitor to eat dinner.

"So, tell me what you've been up to." Riley cut into the steak, put it in her mouth, then closed her eyes. "Oh, my God. That's heavenly."

Raven laughed. One thing she could do was barbecue. "I've been looking after Indi and getting ready for this Pagan Festival."

"You know, I've been studying Wicca for the past year."

Raven's eyes darted up from her plate to meet Riley's. "What? Studying or practicing?"

"Both. After I saw you heal yourself, I was drawn to it."

"You should've told me. I would have helped you."

"I'm telling you now. I want to become a member of the coven."

"Riley," Raven grinned and reached across the table for Riley's hand. "That's awesome."" She should have known Riley would resonate with Wicca. She was as connected with nature as Raven was. "Speaking of the coven, Kiran found a photo of that woman you remind him of. I think you need to see it, Ri. If I hadn't known better, I would have sworn it was you."

"You think she may be my birth mother?"

"If not, she has to be related."

Riley took a deep breath, staring out over the lake. "Does he remember her name?"

"Just her first name. Jenny. He thinks she was sixteen or seventeen when he left to go back to Scotland." Kiran had left Solstice just after Raven was conceived, and it had broken Ena's heart. Her mother suffered those years that Kiran was gone from her life, and it affected Raven's youth. Which was one of the reasons she still had a lot of work to do on herself.

"Jenny," Riley whispered as if trying the name out on her tongue. "Do you think he'd bring it over so I could see it?"

Chapter 2

Kiran stepped up onto the deck, joining Raven and Riley at the table. The dishes had been cleared away and Riley sipped on a glass of wine while Raven had a beer. Raven got up to get one for Kiran.

Kiran placed a photograph on the table in front of Riley. "Her name is Jenny. I don't remember her last name, but Simone may."

Riley stared down at the photo and gasped. Raven had been right. If she didn't know better herself, she'd swear it was her standing next to Ena with Ena's hand on her shoulder. "I need to talk to Simone."

Raven set a beer in front of Kiran and sat down next to Riley, taking her hand. "You okay?"

"She has to be my birth mother. Don't you think?"

"Trouble is finding her," Kiran said. "She left the coven not long after I did and hasn't been heard from since as far as I know."

"But, if Simone remembers her surname, there's a chance."

"Aye," Kiran said.

Raven noted the flash of worry in Kiran's eyes. "Will you call Simone?"

He got up from the table, pulling out his cell phone and walked around to the side of the house.

"This is upsetting you." Raven held tight to Riley's hand, searching her pale green eyes.

"I've wanted to find her for so long and never got closer than the fact that I was born in Huntsville. This is the first real lead I've had and I'm afraid to get my hopes up, but I can't help it. Raven…" She touched her finger to the young woman in the picture. "This could be my mom."

Kiran stepped back up onto the deck. "Simone remembers her magical surname, Dragonfly."

Riley deflated into her chair. "That won't be much help."

Kiran smiled. "Oh, I don't know. Simone also reminded me that Ena kept records of all the coven members. The boxes are in the attic, all labeled by date. It shouldn't be too hard to find the period Jenny was a member of the coven."

Riley sat up straight, squeezing Raven's hand, her eyes locked on Kiran's. "Can we go check? Now?"

Kiran laughed, his ice-blue eyes sparkling. "Aye. Of course."

* * *

For an attic, it was surprisingly dust-free and tidy. Ena's boxes of records were stacked in one corner and ruthlessly organized. Kiran pulled out the box labelled with the year before Riley's birth, the year he'd left Ena and returned to Scotland, and took it downstairs.

They'd just settled into the great room when Simone entered through the kitchen door. "I thought maybe I could help," she said as she crossed the room.

Kiran and Raven sat on the floor and sifted through the files in the box.

"You remember her?" Riley asked Simone, her eyes wide.

"When Kiran told me, I did, yes." She sat down next to Riley on the couch and placed a hand on her forearm. "We've had a lot of members over the years, and Jenny was with us for such a short time. She was young and, if I remember correctly, alone."

"What else do you remember about her?"

Simone tilted her head up, staring off into the past. "She had some powers, but she was still learning and developing them."

"What kind of powers?"

"I believe she was developing her psychic powers, but she was a born healer."

Raven snorted out a laugh. "That fits."

"Here," Kiran announced, pulling a folder out of the box. "Jennifer Dragonfly, aka Jennifer Lochleigh Gallagher."

"Gallagher? But that's my adoptive name?" With a shaking hand, Riley accepted the folder from Kiran and opened it on her lap.

Raven sat down next to her and peered over her shoulder. There was very little on the one sheet of paper inside the folder. Jenny's magical name, her real name, birth date, and an address in downtown Solstice followed by a phone number. "She was fifteen the year she was in the coven."

"So young to be out on her own," Riley whispered. She whipped her head up to Raven. "Sorry, that was insensitive of me."

"I wasn't alone. I had Adara." Despite Adara using and betraying her, she had taken Raven in and cared for her. Raven pulled out her cell phone and dialled Constable McHaela Warren's number.

"Hey," she said when Mick answered, "I need a favour. Can you run a Jennifer Lochleigh Gallagher for me?" She gave Mick the birthdate and then ended the call.

"Lochleigh," Kiran said. "I know that name. There was a couple in my mother's coven when I was a lad with that name. Janet and Randall Lochleigh."

"Did they have kids?" Riley asked.

"Aye, I believe so, but I never met them. I could call my

mother in the morning. It's the middle of the night over there now."

Riley turned to Simone. "Do you remember if Jenny had an accent?"

"She was a quiet girl. I didn't talk to her much, but if she did have an accent, it was slight."

Riley dropped her face into her hands and Raven scooched closer to her, wrapping an arm around her shoulders. When her cell phone rang, Riley flinched in her arms. "Hey," Raven answered. "Nothing in Ontario? Can you go Canada-wide? Yeah, thanks. Get back to me." She disconnected the call. "No record of her in Ontario. Mick's extending the search."

"I shouldn't be disappointed. I've learned more in the past hour than I have in the past fourteen years." She'd been fourteen when her parents passed away, and she found her certificate of adoption amongst their paperwork. She'd been searching for answers ever since. When she graduated from nursing school, she went to Huntsville and was drawn to Solstice.

"There's no reason to be disappointed, love," Kiran said softly. "We've only begun."

"If she still practices Wicca," Simone began. "She may very well attend the Pagan Festival."

Riley straightened. "Do you think?"

Simone smiled and ran her hand down Riley's back. "It's certainly possible. If I had the ties to this area that she seems to have, I'd want to come back."

"Do you remember if she was seeing someone? A boyfriend?"

"I don't remember her being with anyone, but I didn't know her that well. Ena would have known her better than any of us. She would have looked out for her, knowing she was so young and alone."

The hair on the back of Raven's neck stood up. She

motioned to the box sitting on the floor. "Would you mind if I took that home for the night?" She wanted to know who the members of the coven were when Jenny was a member.

"Aye, of course. They're more yours than mine, love."

Raven and Riley took Indigo back to her place. While Riley got her out of her car seat, Raven went into the kitchen to heat a bottle. She put a pot of water on the stove, turned it on, then retrieved a bottle from the fridge.

"You're not breastfeeding anymore?" Riley stood at the entrance to the kitchen with Indigo curled into her shoulder.

Raven kept her back to Riley. "I thought I better wean her off it in case I go back to work soon."

"In case you go back to work soon? I thought you weren't planning on doing that until at least the fall."

Raven turned then, not wanting to admit the real reason she'd put Indigo on formula. Open and honest. That's what she needed to be for this relationship to work. "I, um …" Her gaze fell to the floor. "My breast milk dried up."

"And how long have you been keeping that little secret?"

Raven's eyes flicked up to Riley at the warm sound of her voice. She suppressed a smile, light dancing in her eyes. "A couple of weeks."

"Why?"

Open and honest, she reminded herself again. "Because I feel like I'm failing her." Tears burned her eyes, but she didn't let them fall.

"Oh, Rave. You're not failing her. You're doing an awesome job with her. Can't you see that?"

She turned back to the stove, removed the bottle from the water and gave it a shake before testing the temperature on her wrist. Perfect. "I hope I'm a good mother. I want to give her that more than anything."

"But, you doubt yourself because of your difficult childhood." Riley took the bottle from Raven and walked out to the living room, settling on the couch with Indigo. "If anything, Rave, I think what you went through will make you a better mom." She nestled Indi in the crook of her arm, brushed the nipple of the bottle over her pert little lips and Indi clamped onto it.

Raven sat beside Riley, watching her nurturing lover doting on her daughter. "This feels so right, doesn't it?"

Riley grinned and leaned over to kiss Raven. A soft brushing of lips. "Yes. So right."

* * *

Raven let Riley change Indigo and settle her into her crib. It made Riley so happy, given her nurturing soul. She couldn't help but think that Riley was made for motherhood. The baby's room was painted a soft sage green with dark wood furniture. The crib was a work of art with moons and stars carved into the headboard and footboard. The matching dresser and change table lined the opposite wall with a comfy, sage green rocker under the window. Raven often sat there rocking her daughter and looking out over the lake.

"You could stay the night," Raven whispered. She leaned on the door jamb, watching the two people she loved most in the world.

Riley walked to her, smiling and leaned in, brushing her lips over Raven's. "I thought we were going to take this slow."

The edges of Raven's mouth curled up until dimples appeared on her cheeks, and her ice-blue eyes sparkled. "I can manage slow."

Riley giggled, wrapping her arms around Raven's neck and pressing her body along Raven's. "Oh, I know you can." Just the thought of Raven making slow love to her was enough to fire up her libido and it had been far too long since she'd experienced it first hand. "But, it's been an emotional evening, and I need to process everything that's happened."

Raven's arms encircled Riley's waist and held her close. "I'm here if you need me. You know that, right?"

Riley leaned back, placing her palms on Raven's cheeks. "Thank you for that. It means everything to me."

"These past six months, did you think I wasn't available to you? Is that why you've been scarce?"

"No." Riley shook her head. "Well, maybe some. I felt like an outsider, I guess. It hurt to see you and Jax with Indigo and I so wanted to be a part of that. Of her."

Raven dropped her forehead to Riley's. "I'm sorry for that. I never meant for you to feel that way. I want you to be part of her life as much as I want you to be part of mine."

With tears forming in her eyes, Riley closed her mouth over Raven's.

Raven tilted her head, taking her fill as red hot desire shot to her core. Her hands slid up Riley's back, beneath the soft, worn t-shirt. She'd missed this so much. Just holding her, touching her smooth skin over tight muscles.

Riley broke the kiss and stepped back, sliding her hands down Raven's arms until she captured her hands. "Slow, remember," she said with a warm smile.

"Didn't you get down on your knees and ask me to marry you just a few hours ago?"

They both laughed, and Riley stepped back in, hugging Raven fiercely. "I love this new you even more than I loved you before. But, you were right about taking it slow, I think. Besides, I have to work early tomorrow morning."

Raven pressed her nose into Riley's fiery curls and inhaled the scent of her shampoo - lavender and a hint of something else she couldn't identify. "Will you come over tomorrow after work?"

"Wild horses couldn't keep me away."

* * *

Raven set the file box she'd brought home on the coffee

table in the living room and flipped the lid open. The first few folders were ones she expected - Ena, Kiran, Adara, and Simone. There were several other familiar names. Some were still members of the coven today. It was near the back where she came upon the file she had feared would be among the rest - Gregor Paigo - the man who'd molested Raven as a child over the two years he'd been dating Ena.

When she'd sat listening to Simone describe Jenny Gallagher - young, shy, alone - the hair on the back of her neck stood up. Simone didn't remember her having a boyfriend and she disappeared from the coven, never to be heard from again. Her daughter ended up being adopted, seemingly by a family member, yet Jenny never had any contact with her. It made complete sense to her that Jenny Gallagher may have not wanted anything to do with her daughter because she was a horrible reminder of how she was conceived.

Chapter 3

Raven lifted Indigo from her bath and wrapped her in a soft towel, carrying her through to her changing table. She rubbed her, head to toe, softly with the towel and drew a diaper from the stack on the shelf. Leaning over, she blew a raspberry on Indigo's belly and delighted in her laughter. "You're feeling better this morning, aren't you?"

She looked up at Indigo's gaping smile and saw a flash of white on her bottom gums. Pulling down on Indigo's lip, she stared at the tiny white tooth peeking through the pink flesh. "Indi. You've got your first tooth." She picked her up, held her to her shoulder, and spun in a circle, laughing with tears in her eyes. "Come on. Let's get you dressed and go show Grandda."

Raven climbed the porch stairs at Kiran's within half an hour with a diaper bag over her shoulder and Indigo snuggled into her car seat. She found Kiran in the kitchen over a bowl of oatmeal. "Hey, Grandda. Indigo has something to show you."

"Oh, aye?" Kiran got up from the table and walked over to take Indigo out of the car seat. "Good morning, love. What have you got to show me?" He lifted her and gave her a little toss in the air, sending her into fits of laughter. He grinned at her giggles, two deep dimples forming on his cheeks. "You're a happy wee thing this morning, aye?"

"Notice anything in her mouth?" Raven asked, grinning ear to ear, her dimples matching Kiran's.

Kiran started laughing. "Oh, you've cut your first tooth." He gave her another little toss. "What will we do to celebrate? You're too young for champagne."

Raven pulled the box of pablum from her diaper bag. "How about we try this again? You seem to have more luck with it than I do."

"Would you like some pablum, wee one? Aye? Oh, yes. Let's give it a go."

While Raven mixed the pablum with some warm formula, Kiran strapped Indigo into her highchair and tied a bib to her. Indigo slapped her hands on the highchair's table, babbling away in baby talk.

"Oh, you've a story to tell, have you?" He kissed her forehead and pulled a chair up to the highchair. "Will you be seeing Riley today?"

"She's at work, but she's coming over to my place afterward."

"What time does she finish?"

"Three."

"I'll come over then. I've some news."

"You talked to Rauri?"

"Aye, but I think it's for Riley to hear first. Did you hear anything from Mick?"

"Mmm. Nothing on the Canada-wide search." She handed the bowl of pablum and a baby spoon to Kiran. "Would you like a bib, too?"

Kiran laughed. "I think I'll manage." He dipped the spoon in the pablum and touched it to his upper lip to test the temperature then spooned it into Indigo's mouth. She grinned then blew a raspberry sending pablum flying. Kiran looked down at his t-shirt and laughed. "Maybe the bib was a good idea."

"Told ya," Raven snorted.

Kiran slipped another spoonful into Indigo's mouth and leaned back out of reach, but she didn't fire this one out at him. Her fingers found her mouth, then spread pablum across her face and into her hair.

Raven grabbed Indigo's hand and wiped it with the cloth she had at the ready. "Geez, I just gave her a bath."

"You may as well wait until we're done here. I've a feeling it's going to get messier. What are you up to today, love?"

"I've got to go to Mystique to pick up a few things. I thought I'd take Indigo with me."

"Are you going on your first trip to the Mystique Boutique then?" he asked Indigo and she grinned at him. He shovelled another spoonful of pablum into her mouth. "You know Alana will spoil her rotten, Rave."

"She's been bugging me to bring her in for months."

Kiran's eyes met Raven's. "Have a care, aye? Witches have already begun pouring into Solstice."

Raven slid her hand over Kiran's shoulder and squeezed. "We're protected." Her free hand covered the talisman hanging between her collar bones. She'd also done a protection ritual that morning and had a protection sachet in her pocket, and one tucked into Indigo's diaper.

"Should I come with you?"

Raven patted his shoulder. "Not necessary. Besides, don't you have people coming to set up the vendor tents today?"

"Aye. I'm beginning to wish this whole thing was over." He leaned in to give Indigo a quick peck just as she blew a raspberry and splatted pablum all over his face. All three of them burst out laughing.

* * *

Raven walked into Mystique with Indigo in her arms, surprised at the number of people crowded into the little shop. Alana was behind the counter helping a couple of ladies, so Raven went straight to the aisle with the aromatherapy oils. She picked out a bottle of patchouli oil. It had been one of Ena's favourites, but it was also great for protection. A little dab on her and Indigo and she'd feel less anxious with all these strangers coming to town.

"You don't need to bother with these little touches of protection when you're surrounded by a bloody forcefield. See?" Alana took a step towards Raven and bumped into an invisible shield that Raven hadn't even realized she'd erected.

"Wow, sorry."

Alana raised her arms towards Indigo. "Can you at least include me in it? If I can't hold this baby, I'm going to cry." She lowered her voice to a whisper. "I'm only sensing positive energy in the shop. You're safe here."

Raven blushed, but as she glanced around the shop, everyone's eyes were either on her or Indigo. A few people glanced away when she met their gaze, but most of them continued staring. Still, there didn't seem to be any negativity in the stares. Was she overprotective? The protective shield vanished, and she passed Indigo to Alana.

"Hello, sweetie. Let's see what pretty things we can find."

Alana wandered off with Indigo while Raven clutched her chest and struggled to control her breathing. She shouldn't feel this anxious over a friend taking her baby a few feet away, should she? Being a mother was more difficult than Raven expected and for totally different reasons than imagined. She picked up a bottle of sandalwood oil then moved to the incense, keeping a close eye on Alana and Indigo.

A bell jingled and a cool breeze brushed the back of her neck. Raven glanced over her shoulder at the air conditioner over the door, blowing out frigid air, and then her gaze lowered to the striking emerald green eyes that were locked on hers. The woman had a golden tan, platinum blond hair that stuck straight up in short spikes, and sharp features. Tall and lithe with dangly earrings, a red silk sleeveless top, and a gauzy purple skirt. She was beautiful.

Raven tore her eyes away to search the shop for Indigo. Alana walked towards her with Indigo in her arms, waving a silk scarf that was a kaleidoscope of bright colours - red, purple, orange, and yellow. Indi stuffed it in her mouth. Raven reached for the scarf. "Sorry, she just cut her first tooth. Everything within reach ends up in her mouth."

Alana waved her hand away. "It's hers. She picked it out herself." She held Indigo out to Raven. "I've got some customers to take care of."

Raven took Indi and perched her on her left hip. "Are you sure about the scarf? I can pay for it."

With laughter in her eyes, Alana said, "I'm sure you can, but it's a gift." She turned and headed for the counter at the back of the store.

Raven bounced Indi on her hip. "Got her wrapped around your little finger, don't you?" Indi pulled the scarf from her mouth and babbled then stuffed it back in. When Raven turned around, she nearly bumped into the woman with the emerald eyes. "Oh, sorry."

"No, my fault. I wanted to introduce myself. I'm Jade Storm, third-degree priestess of the Shadowmoon Coven."

She didn't offer her hand, which suited Raven. She didn't want to shake it. "Raven Bowen." She shifted to her left, moving Indigo away from the stranger.

A musical laugh rang out. "Oh, I know who you are. The rumour mill has been buzzing with news of a Bowen-Hayes offspring for the past year. You can't deny the Hayes in your blood, can you? You're his spit."

"You know Kiran Hayes?" Kiran's words kept repeating through Raven's mind - *Have a care, aye?*

"I've met him from time to time. I enjoy attending Pagan Festivals. I think the last time I met him was at the festival in Scotland a few years back. Your mother was with him, but no one ever mentioned they had a daughter."

Raven wasn't about to explain why no one had known about her and her parentage.

"And who's this little cutie? She's gorgeous."

Jade reached a hand out to Indigo and Raven shifter her out of reach. "It was nice to meet you, Jade."

She stepped around the woman and went to pay for her oils and incense, then she took Indigo out and got her settled into her car seat in the Range Rover she bought when she went off on maternity leave. She wasn't going to have her police vehicle, so she needed her own. Once she got Indi squared away, she got in the driver's seat and turned the car on to run the air conditioning while she watched the door of Mystique. When Jade exited, she noted the vehicle she got into and the licence plate number. Then she called Mick.

"Hey. I need another favour."

* * *

The Solstice OPP Detachment was pretty much deserted this time of day. It was nearly noon, and Raven needed to get Indigo home, fed, and down for a nap, but she needed to get some information first. She found Mick in the squad room, pouring a cup of coffee, waves of blonde hair flowing down her back despite being in her dark blue uniform.

"Oh, I'll take one of those."

"Yay! You brought Indi." Mick set her cup down and reached for the baby on Raven's hip. Indigo lifted her arms and snuggled into Mick's shoulder. "Aww, sweetie. I love you."

Mick spent quite a bit of time with Raven's daughter since she was dating Indigo's father, Jax. Indi loved her and Mick was great with her. "She's probably going to get cranky any minute now. She needs a diaper change."

"I'll change her. You grab yourself a cup of coffee." Mick took the diaper bag from Raven's shoulder and set up a makeshift change station on one of the tables. She laid Indigo down on a changing pad and removed her shorts and diaper. "Hey, what's this?" She picked up the little sachet Raven had stuck in her diaper and held it up.

Raven turned to Mick, blowing into her steaming coffee. "Oh, it's a protection spell."

"In her diaper?"

"She doesn't have pockets."

Mick shook her head, but she was grinning. "What's she doing to you, sweetie?"

Indigo scrunched up her little nose and laughed.

"Oh, Indi's got a tooth!"

"Yeah. She cut it during the night."

"You'll have to write it in her baby book." She dropped her head and tickled Indigo's belly with her hair, then popped her head up and grinned at her. "This is a special day, isn't it? Wait till your Daddy hears you got your first tooth."

Should she have called him? Raven wondered. *Shit.* "Would you watch her for a sec while I run a plate?"

"Yeah, sure. Is this about Jennifer Gallagher?"

"No, just someone I met today who gave me her magical name. I wanted to check her out."

"You're getting nervous with all of these witches coming into town."

Raven shrugged. "Just being careful." She went to her desk in the bullpen and booted up her computer. It probably hadn't been started since she went on maternity leave nearly seven months ago. She logged on and entered the plate number. She figured it was going to be a rental car and she wasn't wrong. She called the rental company, introduced herself as Detective Constable Bowen of the Ontario

Provincial Police and asked for the renter's information. Pulling a notepad from her desk drawer, she scribbled down the details as Mick stepped up beside her.

"Elizabeth Jane Thompson from Lake Louise, Alberta," Raven said when she disconnected the call.

"What name did she give you?" Mick set the diaper bag on Raven's desk and bounced Indigo on her hip.

"Jade Storm."

""Well, that's much sexier than Elizabeth Jane Thompson. Was she cute?"

"Hot." Raven grinned. "Not that I was looking."

"Hey, looking never hurts."

Indigo reached for Raven and Raven took her from Mick, hugging her to her chest. Indi burrowed her face into Raven's neck then moved lower, searching for her breast. "I think someone's hungry. I better get her home."

"You can feed her right here if you want. No one's around."

Raven still hadn't told Jax about the formula or why she was giving it to Indi. She didn't think it would be right for Mick to be the one to inform him. "Ah, that's okay. It'll only take a few minutes to get home." Raven got to her feet and slung the diaper bag over her shoulder. When she started towards the door, Mick called after her.

"Hey, Rave? If you've got any names or plates to run, just text them to me."

Raven walked back and gave Mick a quick hug. "Thank you."

Chapter 4

Raven sat on her deck feeding Indigo a bottle. Or trying to. Indi kept pulling the bottle out to grin at her like she was showing off her new tooth. "Silly girl," Raven laughed, dropping a kiss on Indigo's forehead.

"Hello," Kiran called out as he stepped up onto the deck.

Raven glanced over her shoulder to see Kiran and Simone side by side and hand in hand. Simone, wearing a siren red, tight-fitting sundress, dropped her hand from Kiran's and blushed.

"Hello, Raven. Indi." Simone kissed Raven's cheek then leaned over to give Indigo a peck. Indigo pulled the bottle from her mouth and grinned. "Oh, look at you. You've got a pretty new tooth." She ran her fingers through Indigo's soft hair.

"Do you want to feed her?" Raven got to her feet and offered her child to Simone.

"Love to." Simone took Indigo and lowered herself into one of the deck chairs, cuddling Indi in the crook of her arm.

"Riley's on her way over. Can I get you two something to drink?"

"I'll get it, love," Kiran said. "Would you like a beer?"

"I'm good, thanks."

Kiran went through the sliding glass door into the house as

Raven sat next to Simone. "You know that Ena wanted him to move on, right?"

"Yes, of course."

"Then what are you afraid of?"

Simone kept her gaze on Indigo. "That you'll think I'm moving in on Ena's territory."

Raven took Simone's hand, looking into warm brown eyes. "I want him to be happy. And … I want you to be happy, Simone."

Simone's eyes glassed over and she squeezed Raven's hand. "Oh, Raven. I want that, too. I'm afraid I've fallen in love with him."

"Nice." Raven leaned back in her chair and closed her eyes, enjoying the warmth of the sun and the soft breeze on her face. "That's … nice."

Kiran stepped out of the sliding glass door, followed by Riley.

"Hey," Riley said. She went straight to Raven and gave her a chaste kiss on the lips, drawing back just enough to gaze into Raven's eyes. "Hi."

"Hi. How was your day?"

"Busy. Yours?"

"Interesting." She didn't elaborate. There would be time for that later.

"Do you know someone from the Shadowmoon Coven in Lake Louise? Tall, blonde, named Jade Storm?" Raven asked Kiran as he sat next to Simone.

"Doesn't ring a bell," he said.

"She says she met you a few times at annual Pagan Festivals, the last time a few years ago in Scotland."

Kiran took a swig of his beer and stared up at the sky. "Jade Storm?"

"Her real name is Elizabeth Thompson."

"No, I don't remember anyone by those names. Doesn't

mean I haven't met her, though. I've met a lot of people at different festivals over the years."

Even though that made sense, Raven figured he'd remember a woman as beautiful as Jade Storm. She put it out of her mind. "So, you talked to Rauri this morning?"

"Aye."

Riley sat on the arm of Raven's chair, linking her fingers with Raven's, her eyes glued to Kiran.

"Rauri remembers the Lochleigh's very well. Randall Lochleigh passed away shortly after I left home, and Janet moved to Canada with their two wee ones. A girl, Jennifer, and a boy, Graeme. She remarried a man named Gordon Gallagher who adopted her children. Rauri lost touch with them after that."

Riley lost all the colour from her face, her hand gripping Raven's so tightly Raven's fingers turned red. "Graeme Gallagher was my adoptive father's name. He wasn't just my adoptive father, was he? He was my uncle."

"Aye, I think maybe he was." Kiran took another swig of his beer then set it on the arm of his chair. "There's more."

Riley nodded.

"Jennifer Lochleigh Gallagher returned to Inverness the year after you were born. She lives there still and is a member of the Highlands Dragonfly Coven."

"The Highlands Dragonfly Coven?"

"Aye, my mother's coven."

Riley's free hand shot up to cover her mouth as tears glistened in her eyes. "You found her?"

Raven pulled Riley onto her lap and wrapped her arms around her.

"Aye. Rauri is coming tomorrow for the Pagan Festival, bringing most of the coven with her."

"My mother's coming here? Tomorrow?"

"Aye. She is."

"Does she know about me?"

Kiran shook his head. "No, and I've asked Rauri not to say anything. It's between you and your mum."

Riley nodded her head, her hand still covering her mouth and tears sliding down her face. "Thank you," she croaked.

Kiran downed the rest of his beer, then went to Riley and dropped a kiss on her cheek. "You're welcome. Come by the house tomorrow evening for dinner if you like. You don't have to say anything to her if you're not ready, but I imagine she'll take one look at you and know." He reached over and took the baby from Simone. "We'll be off then." He gave Indigo a quick smooch before handing her off to Raven. "Give us a call in the morning, love."

"Yeah. Thanks, Dad."

Kiran put his hand on Riley's shoulder for a moment before taking Simone's hand as they walked away. Raven watched them go with a smile, then she cupped the back of Riley's head and drew her into her shoulder.

"Sorry," Riley sobbed. "I shouldn't be blubbering all over you."

"It's alright," Raven whispered. "I've had worse all over me in the past six months."

Riley hiccupped a short laugh. "I've wanted this so much for so long, but now that it's within reach, I'm scared shitless."

"Shhh. I don't want Indigo's first word to be shitless."

Riley pushed off of Raven's shoulder and gave her a sad smile. "You've developed a sense of humour lately, haven't you?"

"I think it's been there all along. It was just buried under the walls I had up."

"Well, I'm glad they're starting to come down."

"Me, too. Jaxon is coming over to spend some time with Indi. When he gets here, you and I are going for a walk."

"Are we?"

"Yeah. I think a little nature ritual will do you wonders."

* * *

The small clearing in the woods was surrounded by lush vegetation, towering pines, maples, poplars, elms, and birch. Raven led Riley by the hand to the centre and turned in a circle, admiring every inch of earth, grass, and plant. The view of Fairy Lake through the trees was spectacular with the late afternoon sun gleaming on its surface. A chipmunk raced across the clearing and dashed under a low-lying plant. Birds chirped all around them. The wash of waves upon the shore whooshed every few seconds while the soft breeze rustled the leaves in the trees. This was Raven's happy place.

"Can you feel the energy?" Raven asked.

Riley closed her eyes and tilted her head towards the sun. "I think so."

"Have you done a nature ritual before?"

"I've meditated out here."

"Okay. It's very similar. Find a place to sit and then just try to tune in to nature and the animals until all you are aware of is the natural energy that surrounds you."

Riley sat at the base of a maple tree, crossing her legs in front of her.

"You can close your eyes if you want, but it's better if you pick a tree or a plant that resonates with you and focus on that." Raven took her favourite spot in the centre of the clearing facing the lake with the sun beaming down on her. "Breathe deeply as you would in meditation and think of yourself as an integral part of all of nature."

Raven took several deep breaths, soaking up the energy all around her. "Feel the energy in the earth beneath you. In the plants and trees. In the animals and birds. In the lake and marine life. In the sun and sky." She spoke softly and slowly taking time for deep breaths between her words. "Feel yourself as a being resting on this specific part of the planet. Experience the planet as Mother Earth holding you lovingly to her bosom." She stopped talking, forgot all about Riley as she focused on the energy of nature and her place in it. When she came back to herself, she had no idea how much time had passed. "We thank the earth and the natural world for all of its blessings. Thank you to the nature spirits who guide us. Blessed be."

She took a few more deep breaths then glanced over her shoulder to check on Riley. She sat there, at the base of the tree, dappled sunlight setting her hair on fire, her eyes on Raven and a glimmer of a smile gracing her face. "Okay?" Raven asked.

Riley gave one short nod. "Good. I feel … energized."

Raven laughed as she got to her feet and went over to help Riley up. "That's the benefit, I guess. The purpose is to develop a greater awareness of nature's life energy."

"It took me a while, but I felt it." She leaned in and kissed Raven. "Thank you for sharing that with me."

"It's more of a solitary ritual, but I wanted to show you. The more you practice it, the better. It teaches you to love and respect the nature around you, to love and respect Mother Earth." She twined her fingers with Riley's and began the short trek back to her cottage.

"Why haven't you taken over as High Priestess of the coven yet?" Riley asked. "I thought that was the plan."

"I will. Eventually."

"Eventually? You're qualified as a third-degree priestess, aren't you?"

"I was initiated as a third-degree, but I'm not adept."

"I don't understand."

Raven stepped over a fallen log and turned to ensure Riley got over it safely. "A big part of the Wiccan religion is personal development. Being adept is essentially mastering your personal development. I'm not there yet."

"But, I thought Ena taught you everything you needed to know."

"She did, but all those walls I had up prevented me from growing on a personal level."

"I see."

The back of Raven's cottage came into view and Jax, Mick, and Indigo were up on the deck. "He's good with her," Raven said and had Riley looking up to the deck. "They're both good with her."

"So are you."

Raven smiled at Riley. "Thank you for that." She leaned in, pressing her mouth to Riley's. It started innocently and deepened until Raven thought the top of her head was going to blow off.

"Hey, you two. You're going to set the beach on fire down there," Jax called out.

Raven glanced up at Jaxon leaning over the railing smirking at them.

"There's plenty of water down here to put it out." She felt like jumping into the lake to cool off her raging libido. Her gaze fell on Riley's beet-red face and she grinned. "Are you working tomorrow?"

Riley shook her head.

"Will you stay tonight?" When Riley hesitated with her answer, Raven lowered her forehead to hers. "I've missed you so much. I miss us."

"You're the one who wanted to go slow, and I'm the one who's holding back. I'm sorry."

"There's no rush. We've got the rest of our lives together, Ri."

Riley's eyes pooled. "Do you mean that? I'm not forcing this by what I did in Kirsten's office?"

"Is that what's worrying you?"

"It's part of it, I guess."

"I wouldn't ask you to stay if I didn't want you to, Ri. What if you stayed and just let me hold you?" Goddess help her. She didn't know if she could keep her hands off Riley if they shared a bed.

Riley threaded her arms around Raven's neck and whispered in her ear. "I have an overnight bag in the car."

* * *

They had dinner with Jax and Mick then put Indigo to bed together once they left.

"I could get used to this," Riley said as she settled onto the couch with a glass of wine. "The routine of putting her down then relaxing together, knowing she's safe and snug in her bed."

Raven laid down on the couch with her head in Riley's lap. Days ago, she would never have thought she was ready for this, but having Riley around the past couple of days felt so right she never wanted her to leave. "Then move in."

Riley choked on her wine and very nearly spewed it out over Raven's face. Raven bolted up to get out of the way then patted Riley's back like she would Indigo's. "Are you okay? I thought that's what you wanted."

"I do. I just wasn't expecting you to ask. When we were together before, you were adamant about having your own space."

That was before Riley left her and a gaping hole took up residence inside her. "My space means nothing without you in it."

"Geez, you have changed, haven't you?"

"Losing you changed me, Ri."

Riley placed her wine glass on the coffee table and scooted closer to Raven. Her smile started slow and spread to a broad, beaming grin. "When can I move in?"

"Is now too soon?"

Chapter 5

For the first time in over a year, when Raven reached for Riley in the night, she was right there in her arms, and it was glorious. She'd kept her word and just held Riley close, awakening to the scent of Riley's shampoo and nuzzling her nose into Riley's hair. The front of her body pressed to Riley's back with Riley's bottom cradled in her pelvis and their legs entwined. Her arm draped over Riley's waist, her hand lightly cupping her breast. If this was a dream, she never wanted to wake up.

"I can't believe you made it through the night without jumping me."

Raven snorted out a laugh. "I told you I'd just hold you. I kept my promise."

"Mmm. Pity."

Raven pulled on Riley's shoulder until she was on her back then rolled on top of her. "Is that so?" Riley circled her hips and Raven was pretty sure that her eyes crossed as her vision went blurry. Her lips met Riley's, diving deep, savouring her sweet taste.

The baby monitor squealed out an ear-piercing wail.

"Oh, shit." Raven launched herself out of the bed and ran through to the baby's room wearing nothing but the silver pentacle necklace Kiran had given her for protection.

Indigo was at the foot of her crib with her face pressed against the rails, screaming bloody murder. Jet, Raven's black cat, crouched at Indi's side, purring and nudging her side with her nose. Raven lifted Indigo out of the crib and hugged her to her chest.

"How did you get way down there?" She rocked back and forth, whispering soothingly. "You're okay, angel mine. I've got you."

"She okay?" Riley asked from the doorway, wearing a faded t-shirt.

Jet jumped out of the crib and put her front paws on Raven's leg, staring up at them. Raven reached down and picked her up. "She's alright, see?" Jet nudged Indigo's cheek with her forehead, rubbing and purring. "Somehow, she made it down to the bottom of the crib and got jammed against the rails."

Riley grinned. "She must have rolled her way down there. She worried Jet."

"She's Indi's little protector." Indigo's sobs quieted to hiccupped gasps with Jet's affection. Raven set Jet down and lifted Indigo to look at her face. There was a red mark on her cheek, but she didn't think it was bruised. She pressed a kiss to the mark and hugged her to her chest again. "I'll get her changed and warm a bottle."

"As much as I love seeing you naked, how about I change her and you throw something on."

It was going to take some getting used to, having someone around to help in the mornings. Raven smiled, kissed Riley quickly, and handed Indigo over. "I'll be right back."

She threw on a pair of sweatpants and an old OPP t-shirt and went through to the kitchen to start heating a bottle. Riley came in with Indigo in her arms, a smile on her face, and Jet trailing after her. Jet wasn't taking her eyes off the baby. Raven just stared at Riley for a few moments. She was glowing. Her eyes sparkled and her face was a healthy golden tan, an explosion of freckles dotting her nose. "Motherhood looks good on you."

The grin dropped from Riley's face. "You say the most beautiful things."

"It's the truth." Riley had always been a nurturing soul. When it came to kids, it was doubly so. "You were made to be a mother, I think."

"Shut up. You're going to make me cry."

"You know, if you wanted to take some time off work when I go back, you could. I'd rather you to take care of Indi than put her in daycare or get a nanny."

"Rave."

"It's just something to think about, and only if that's what you want."

Riley came around the counter and pecked Raven's cheek. "I'll think about it. What are you up to today?"

"The family should be arriving this afternoon. We've still got some work to do to get ready for the festival, too. The event planners are doing the setup, but I need to be there to organize the vendors and make sure there are no problems."

"Is it alright if I come with you? Maybe I could help."

"I'd like that. Are you worried about meeting your mother?"

"I don't know. I've felt … peaceful about it since we did that nature ritual. I just hope she doesn't freak out when she sees me. I mean, she gave me up and never contacted me, even after her brother passed away."

"I'll be right there by your side. If you need anything, I'm there for you."

"Have I told you yet today how much I love this new you?"

Raven laughed and bumped Riley's hip with hers. "Charmer."

* * *

Kiran's was a madhouse with vendors setting up their stalls, work crews putting together the stage and sound system, planning staff trying to organize the loading in of vendors' goods and food trucks, and guests arriving to set up in the campgrounds on the property. The Bowen house and land belonged to Raven, but it was Kiran's home. One day it would be Indigo's and Raven was good with that. She had her home and her land on Fairy Lake. It wasn't as enormous or as majestic as this property with its high cliffs bordering the lake, but it was secluded and suited her.

They entered the house through the kitchen door and found Kiran and Simone sitting at the kitchen island with a book of figures in front of them. "I need a bloody accountant to keep track of all this," Kiran huffed and threw his pen down on the counter.

"Then hire one," Raven said. She hefted Indigo in her car seat up onto the kitchen island. Simone began undoing the straps and lifted her out to cuddle her.

Riley set the diaper bag on the floor against the island. "I work with a nurse whose husband is an accountant. He works from home. I'm sure he'd be happy to help. I can call and ask if he's available to come over."

"I think you better," Simone said. "Before he tears all of his hair out. I'm quite partial to that hair." She ran her fingers through Indigo's thick hair. "Have you just had a nap? Mummy didn't comb your hair."

"I combed it," Raven defended herself. "It just does what it wants."

"It's exactly like Raven's," Riley laughed. She ran her fingers through Raven's unruly black locks.

Raven sucked in a sharp breath and narrowed her eyes at Riley. "Careful. You know what that does to me." Riley just had to touch the tip of her finger anywhere on Raven's body to set her on fire. After this morning's near-miss in bed, she was close to the edge, like a tightly wound harp string waiting to be plucked.

Kiran coughed and Riley drew her fingers out of Raven's hair, her face flushing a beautiful shade of rose. She smiled demurely and took a step back.

"I've got a busload of house guests arriving any minute. My mother and father will be staying here, as well as my brother, Alec and his wife, Helen, their kids, Caleb and Elly, my sister, Jasmine, her husband, Michael, their daughter, Kelly, and Jennifer Gallagher with her partner, Rebecca Jordan."

Riley's brows shot up. "Her partner?"

"Aye, my mother didn't say what kind of partner, but I'm assuming she's gay."

Riley dropped into a chair at the island, a gust of air shooting out of her lungs. "Well, I guess I don't have to worry about coming out to her."

"Honey," Simone began. "You're surrounded by Wiccans. You don't have to worry about coming out to anyone."

"Riley's Wiccan herself," Raven announced. "She's been studying and practicing Wicca for the past year and would like to join the coven."

Simone reached over and squeezed Riley's hand. Kiran turned to her and wrapped her in a hug. "Welcome to the family," he said. "To our Wiccan family and the Hayes family. If you need anything, all you need do is ask."

With tears in her eyes, Riley thanked Kiran. Her parents passed away when she was fourteen, and even with a foster family, she'd been on her own.

"Okay, enough with the mushy stuff," Raven said before she got emotional, too. "What do you need us to help with? Where are you putting the rest of the busload from Scotland?"

"The rest are going to the campground. I've rented several RVs for them. They'll need help to drive their luggage over to the sites and get them settled in. I've invited everyone back here for dinner at six o'clock."

"Riley and I could do that in my Range Rover and your SUV. Will you look after Indigo?"

"I will," Simone said with an ear to ear smile. "Kiran can get his family settled in here."

"You better bring her out to the driveway for a few minutes, Simone. The bus is pulling in and the first thing Rauri will want to see is her great-granddaughter." He grabbed Raven's hand. "And the second thing she'll want to see is her granddaughter."

Raven felt like they were all being herded out to be put on display. She leaned over and whispered to Riley, "You don't have to come out if you're not ready. You can wait in here if you like."

"Yeah. I think … I'll just … wait … here." She stared out the window at the bus in the driveway as she spoke, her face paling to ivory.

Raven wanted to wrap Riley in her arms, but Kiran tugged her out the door. She mouthed, "Love you."

* * *

Half a dozen people were outside the bus, unloading luggage from the storage compartments along its side. Rauri stood, tall and majestic, directing them. She had Kiran, Raven, and Indigo's jet black hair, but her eyes were a warm brown. It was William, Kiran's father, who had the ice blue eyes. His hair was dark brown, threaded with silver.

Rauri turned as Kiran called out a greeting then charged for him. "Son, how are you, love?"

Rauri embraced Kiran in a fierce hug and Raven stopped in her tracks, worried she was next. She wasn't a fan of physical contact except when it came to Riley, Indigo, or Jet. She was still trying to get used to Kiran hugging her after over a year of knowing him.

"Where's my great-granddaughter?" Rauri roared. When she spotted Indigo in Simone's arms, she held out her arms and strode to Simone. "Oh, Great Goddess, let me look at you. Well, aren't you the double of your mum and your granddad? Oh, Kiran, she's perfect."

She lifted Indigo from Simone's arms and Raven wanted to run over and snatch her back. Irrational, because she knew Rauri was full of love for her kin.

Kiran put a hand on Raven's shoulder. "She's fine, love. My mother hasn't hurt any of us yet."

"Raven, love. There you are." Rauri dashed over with Indigo bouncing on her hip. Raven winced as Rauri's free arm came around her. "How are you then? Is motherhood agreeing with you?"

"Hi, Gran. I'm great, and yes, I'm loving being Indi's mother."

"Indi. Yes, it suits her, doesn't it? She's precious, Rave. I don't think I'll be able to keep my hands off her while I'm here. You just tell me if I'm overstepping, aye?"

"Fair enough," Raven answered. "How was the flight?"

"Long. You'd think there'd be a faster way to get across the pond by now. Whatever happened to the Concorde and three-hour transatlantic flights?"

Raven shrugged. She had no idea what the Concord was. Out of the corner of her eye, she caught sight of a woman descending from the bus with waves of curly red hair cascading down her back, nearly reaching her waist. She wore a hunter green t-shirt, faded blue jeans, and black Doc Marten boots. Raven had to do a double-take. She looked exactly like Riley except her hair was longer and she was a couple of inches shorter. With her eyes cast down, she turned away to sort through the luggage. Another woman descended right behind her, took a deep breath of the fresh air and looked all around before trailing after Jenny. She had short, dark brown hair and a handsome face with pink-tinged cheeks and deep blue eyes.

"I should check on Riley," Raven said.

Kiran rested a hand on Raven's shoulder. His eyes were focused on the red-haired woman pulling a suitcase from the pile beside the bus. "Aye, love. You go ahead. We'll sort this out and let you know when we're ready to transport the lot to the campgrounds."

"You'll keep an eye on Indi?" She was in Kiran's sister Jasmine's arms now, giggling at the stuffed bear in a kilt that Jasmine held in front of her. Jasmine had her father's dark brown hair, hanging down her back in shiny reams, and eerily light grey eyes.

"Aye, not to worry, love. She's in good hands."

Raven sighed. It was going to be a long day and her little angel was going to be cranky by the end of it from being passed around like a hot potato. She turned to see Riley standing at the end of the driveway, pale and staring towards the bus like she was in a daze. Her mouth gaped and her hands clenched at her sides. Raven started towards her at the same time Riley began walking, with short hesitant steps.

"Ri? You okay?"

Riley's gaze never strayed from the woman she was focused on next to the bus. "I don't know. I ... I ..."

Raven glanced back down the driveway. Kiran stood speaking to Jenny and Rebecca. Kiran's hand was on Jenny's shoulder, but it was Rebecca who was doing the talking. Kiran waved his hand towards the front door and Rebecca looked up towards the house. Her eyes drifted over Raven and Riley and narrowed. She said something to Kiran, then leaned over and whispered in Jenny's ear. Jenny's head jerked up, her eyes locking on Riley and the two of them stood frozen, gaping at each other.

Raven wrapped her arm around Riley's waist and held her close as Rebecca took Jenny's arm and led her up the driveway towards Riley. They stopped a few feet in front of her.

"Hello, Riley," Jenny said in a whisper quiet voice.

"Hi."

"We have a lot to talk about, but it's been a long journey. I need to rest." She dropped her gaze back to the ground and Rebecca led her into the house.

"Is it just me, or was that weird?" Riley asked, leaning into Raven.

"Totally weird."

"You alright, love?" Kiran asked, putting a hand on Riley's shoulder.

"I have no idea." She huffed out a laugh, but there were tears in her eyes.

"Rebecca said Jenny wasn't feeling well after the long trip and she needed to lie down," Kiran said. "Please don't be upset."

"No," Riley shook her head. "I'm okay. It's just that it was like she expected me to be here. She wasn't surprised to see me and it sounded like she was prepared for the talk we need to have."

"Aye, well, she's clairvoyant. Perhaps she had a vision of meeting you if she came here."

Riley pulled away from Raven and gave Kiran a quick hug. "Thank you." She stepped back with a hint of a smile on her face and took Raven's hand. "We'll help get luggage loaded into the SUVs and get the rest of your guests settled in."

"You sure you're up for it?" Raven asked.

"Yeah, keeping busy is what I need."

* * *

Delivery trucks and people continued to arrive and depart

randomly, blocking the road in front of the house and slowing traffic as people seemed to be wandering with no apparent destination. Raven was frustrated when she pulled into the driveway behind Riley. She hadn't had an opportunity to talk to her as they drove separate vehicles and tried to organize who went into which RV. She was glad to get back to the house to check on both Indigo and Riley.

Riley slipped out of Kiran's SUV as Raven approached.

"How are you holding up?"

Riley brushed a lock of hair behind her ear and shrugged. "I felt better after Kiran said that Jenny was clairvoyant. It made me feel like maybe she came here because of me, but the more I thought about it, the more upset I got. My mother didn't show any emotion towards me, Rave. She just gave her excuse and walked away. I don't know, but if I just ran into my daughter after not seeing her since birth, I don't think that would be my reaction."

Raven slid her arms around Riley's waist and hugged her close, resting her cheek against the side of Riley's head. "We don't know what she's been through, why she gave you up to her brother and never saw you. Maybe it's best to wait it out and see what she has to say."

Riley pushed away from Raven and stared into her eyes. "What's your gut telling you about Jenny Gallagher?"

"I don't trust my gut."

"But you trust it enough to believe us being back together is right?"

Raven shook her head. "No, I don't trust it. But I trust that I love you, that I've been in love with you since we met." She laid her hand over Riley's heart. "I trust that you're the most beautiful, kind, caring, nurturing soul that I've ever met."

Moisture pooled in Riley's pale green eyes, making her lashes look like they were dusted with diamonds in the sunlight. "Then respect me enough to be honest with me about what your gut's telling you."

Open and honest. "You want me to tell you a hunch that I have no proof of. A hunch that might hurt you. A hunch that may very well be wrong. How can I do that?" The backs of her fingers brushed down Riley's cheek. "You're asking me to hurt you."

"I'm asking you to trust me to be able to handle it. I need to know the truth, no matter how much it hurts."

"I don't know that it is the truth."

Riley sighed and closed her eyes, forcing a fat tear to slide down her cheek. She splayed her fingers over Raven's belly and opened her eyes. "*I* trust your gut."

Raven's hand covered Riley's on her belly. Open and honest, but Goddess, it was hard when she knew it would tear Riley apart.

"You took that box home the other night, Rave. Why? What were you looking for?"

"I was … playing a hunch."

"And what did you find?"

Now would be an excellent time for the earth to open up and swallow her whole. Goddess help her. She didn't want to do this. "I found that Gregor Paigo was a member of the coven at the same time Jenny was there."

"Oh, Jesus!" Riley's brows drew together, her mouth agape. "You think he raped her? Oh, my God. You think Gregor Paigo is my biological father."

Raven grabbed Riley around the waist and held her tight. Riley collapsed into her and wept. "It's just a theory. I could be way off base. The things I went through in my childhood could be screwing with my perception. Oh, God, I'm sorry, Ri. I'm so sorry. Please don't cry, baby."

"I feel sick," Riley whispered into Raven's neck. "Rave, I'm going to be sick."

Raven reached an arm under Riley's knees, scooped her

up, and ran into the house. She got to the powder room door, but it was closed and locked. "Shit." She turned and rushed up the stairs as Riley's chest heaved and she covered her mouth with her hand. Raven took Riley straight into the en suite in the master bedroom and deposited her in front of the toilet, gathering her hair and holding it for her as Riley emptied her stomach.

Riley reached up and flushed the toilet. "I'm sorry," she murmured, her voice echoing into the bowl.

"Shhh. You've got nothing to be sorry for." Raven was the one who was sorry. She never should have voiced her concerns, not when it hurt Riley so much.

Simone knocked on the open bathroom door. "The way you ran through the house with Riley, we thought you may need a doctor."

"I'm fine," Riley croaked.

At Raven's nod, Simone walked away, leaving them alone.

Riley pushed up off the floor, leaned over the sink, and splashed cold water over her face.

Raven passed her a towel. She'd never felt more helpless in her life.

"Could you drive me home, Rave?"

"Yeah, sure. Let me get Indi and we'll go."

"No. I just need you to drop me off at my place. I need to be alone for a while."

"Ri?" The horrible pain that had been absent from her chest the last few days came back with a vengeance and Raven pressed her fist to it. "Please don't shut me out. Please don't let this hurt you. Not until we figure out the truth."

Riley reached out and took Raven's hand. "I'm not. I promise. I just need some time. You have to admit that it fits. It explains why she wouldn't want to see me. I'd just be a reminder of what happened. What it doesn't explain is why she's here now. Why would she come back here and stir up those memories?"

"We don't know that's what happened, Ri."

Riley leaned into Raven. "Thank you for telling me. I love you all the more for you doing that, knowing how it would make me feel because I asked you to."

"I can't stand to see you hurting like this."

"I know. That's why I love you for it."

Chapter 6

As soon as Raven got back to Kiran's, she went looking for Indigo. It felt like days since she'd seen her. She found the entire Hayes clan in the great room. Indi sat between Kiran's legs, her little hands banging away on a tribal drum.

Raven lifted her and hugged her to her chest. Indigo smushed her face into the curve of Raven's neck before popping her head up, scrunching her nose and rapidly sniffing in and out. She roared with laughter as the whole room broke out in hysterics.

"Oh, that's lovely. Who taught you that?"

"Sorry, love," Rauri said. "You've our Caleb to blame for that one. Wait until you see the face her Grandda taught her."

Kiran shot Rauri a narrow-eyed stare. "Look at you, throwing everyone under the bus. You're not innocent in this, Rauri Hayes."

At that, Indigo raised her black, perfectly arched brows, and her little mouth formed a tiny o. "That's definitely a Rauri face," Raven said, giving Rauri a hard stare herself. But Indi was laughing a full out belly laugh, and Raven couldn't keep a straight face. "What am I going to do with the lot of you? You need more supervision than Indi."

The only one in the room who wasn't laughing was Jenny Gallagher. She sat stiffly next to Rebecca on a love seat, staring off into space. Raven had an urge to go over and slap her. The woman needed to pull herself together.

"I've got to take a walk," Raven said. "I need to check on the vendors loading in."

"You can leave Indi here if you like," Kiran said.

"That's okay." She'd missed her daughter and wanted to spend some time with her before the Hayes clan monopolized her again. And she was worried about what else they might teach her. "The fresh air will do her good. I'll get her a bottle when I get back."

She walked over to the rows of vendor tents with Indigo in her arms, walking tent to tent, asking if they had everything they needed. She got halfway down the aisle when she spotted Jade Storm setting up a jewelry display in one of the tents. She wasn't sure what it was, but something about Jade Storm didn't sit right with her.

"Hey," she said as she walked up to the tent, scanning the silver and gold jewelry fitted with crystals and stones of every variety. "Everything going okay?"

"Raven. How nice to see you again."

"You didn't mention you were one of the vendors."

"I make jewelry for a living and the Pagan Festivals are my highest revenue earners. See anything you like?"

"I'm not much into jewelry."

"Really? That pendant around your neck says different."

Raven touched her fingers to the silver pentagram. "It was a gift."

"If it's protection you're looking for, I have several pieces that may suit."

Raven's right eyebrow shot up. "I get the impression you're a great salesperson."

Jade laughed. "Point taken. I'll stop pushing my wares on you."

"Let me know if there's anything you need," Raven said as

she walked away, pulling out her cell phone. She hugged Indigo in one arm and texted Kiran with her free hand, asking him to come and meet her by the vendor tents.

She visited three more tents by the time Kiran caught up to her. "Walk with me," she said and walked in the opposite direction of Jade's tent. "There's a tent behind us with a sign that says Jewelry by Storm. Let's take a casual walk past and tell me if you recognize the woman there."

"This is the woman you were concerned about."

"Yeah, Jade Storm."

Kiran nodded as they changed direction. "I looked up the Shadowmoon Coven. There isn't one by that name in Lake Louise."

"Isn't that interesting?"

Jade stood behind the table displaying her jewelry, taking a swig from a bottle of water. She lowered the bottle and smiled at Kiran and Raven as they walked by. Raven waved and continued on. "Recognize her?"

"No, I don't think so. She's … striking. I think I'd remember that face. What is it that's bothering you about her?"

Raven glanced over her shoulder. Jade was staring straight at her. She turned around again, pressing a kiss to Indigo's head. "I don't know. I can't put my finger on it."

"Have you tried using your psychic powers?"

Raven shook her head. She didn't like hearing people's thoughts, but she'd use it if she had to. "Let's just keep an eye on her for now."

* * *

The carpet in front of the living room window wore down as Raven paced back and forth. Half a dozen calls to Riley went unanswered. She understood Riley wanted some time alone, but she was worried sick. She was about to drive over to check on her when there was a knock at the door.

She opened it to find Riley leaning against the doorjamb, one edge of her lip curled up. "Hey."

She extended her hand and pulled Riley into her embrace. Riley burrowed her face into Raven's shoulder. "I was so worried about you. You okay?"

Riley shook her head and wept. "I was lying in bed, feeling miserable and sick and sorry for myself when it occurred to me how selfish I was being."

"You, Riley Gallagher, have never had a selfish moment in your life."

"Raven, I never took into account how all of this would make you feel. That man hurt you, too."

"Oh, Ri. This isn't about me."

"If Jenny Gallagher can't stand to be around me because I remind her of what he did, how could you?"

Raven lifted her head and framed Riley's face with her hands. "Look at me." She waited for Riley to lift her red-rimmed eyes. "I love you for who you are." She placed her hand over Riley's heart. "In here. That's what matters to me."

Riley's eyes filled.

"Well, that and the supreme sex."

Riley shoved Raven's shoulder and laughed. "Nymph."

"Only when it comes to you."

* * *

Raven woke in the night, reaching for Riley. When she was met with empty, cold sheets, her heart sped up, her chest constricting, and she sat bolt upright in bed. Riley was silhouetted by the moonlight streaming in the sliding glass door, her arms wrapped around her middle. Raven slid out of bed and went to her, wrapping her arms around Riley's. "I'm so sorry I hurt you."

Riley leaned back into Raven's warm, muscled body and Raven's breaths sped up, shooting out in warm caresses over Riley's neck.

"You didn't hurt me, Rave. I needed to know the truth."

"We don't know that-"

"No," Riley cut her off. "You may not trust your intuition, Rave, but I do. Besides, it makes too much sense not to be true."

With a long sigh, Raven nuzzled Riley's neck just below her ear with her nose, glorying when Riley shuddered against her.

"If that monster is my father, what does that make me?" Riley's shudders turned to sobs.

Raven turned her in her arms, hugging her tight. Her hand cradled the back of Riley's head and held her to her shoulder. "You're not him. You're nothing like him." She'd hated Gregor Paigo for a long time, but never had she wanted to rip him to pieces as she did now. She could tell Riley a million times that she wasn't her father, but she knew in her heart that Riley would always despise that connection to him. She wondered just how many lives Gregor's depravity had affected and how many she could have prevented if she'd only reported his abuse of her. Tears formed in her own eyes. "I'm sorry." She wasn't sure if she was whispering those words to Riley or to the unknown innocents out there who had been hurt by the same monster who hurt her. Goddess, forgive her for staying silent for so long.

They wept in each other's arms until Raven finally led Riley back to bed. Riley curled into her side, resting her head on Raven's shoulder, and sighed, exhaustion finally taking her under.

Raven closed her eyes and pressed her lips into Riley's curls. They had to be at Kiran's early in the morning, but she had a stop to make first. One that was years overdue.

Chapter 7

The Solstice OPP Detachment was in the middle of shift change when Raven and Riley walked in with Indigo in her car seat. Raven figured she'd be passed around enough by the Hayes crew over the day, so she kept her in the chair while the officers coming and going cooed and awed over her. They slowly made their way to Detective Sergeant Grayson LaCroix's office and found him sipping a cup of coffee. He stood when they appeared in the doorway. "Rave, it's about time you brought her in." He leaned over the car seat and smiled. "Hello, cutie." When he straightened, he was wearing a wide smile. "Hey, Riley."

"Gray."

"So." He waved a hand between Raven and Riley. "You two back together then?"

They answered, "Yes," in unison.

"Good," Grayson grinned. "I'm happy for you both."

Raven's fingers sliced through her hair, leaving whisps standing up on end. "I dropped by because I want you to take my statement."

His brows shot up. "On?"

"Gregor Paigo."

His smile turned into pursed lips as he studied Raven, then he waved towards the chairs in front of his desk. "Why don't you take a seat?"

Raven sat, setting the car seat on her lap. Indigo gripped a ring of primary-coloured plastic keys in her little hand, shaking it vigorously. Raven took Riley's hand as Riley settled into the seat next to her.

LaCroix took his seat and clasped his hands in front of him on the desk. "Why now, Rave?"

Raven blew out a breath, but it did nothing to relax her. "Because we think we may have found a woman he raped nearly thirty years ago and I couldn't help but think if she'd just reported it ..."

LaCroix was silent while he waited for Raven to continue. When she didn't, he said, "And that got you thinking that if you'd reported him, you may have saved others from the same fate as you?"

Raven closed her eyes and nodded in short, jerky movements.

"Raven." LaCroix released a loud sigh and leaned back in his chair. "When that story broke on the news about Paigo sexually assaulting you as a child, women began to come forward and report their experiences with Paigo. An investigation began at that time."

Raven shot to her feet, cradling the car seat in her arms. "What? Why wasn't I told?"

LaCroix's hand shot out, palm out. "Sit down and hear me out."

Raven huffed then lowered herself back into her chair, muscles tensed and back straight. Indigo fussed, so she undid the buckles, lifted her out of the seat, and sat her on her lap, handing her the plastic keys. Indi settled again, waving her colourful toy.

"I had strict orders from the chief of police that you were not to be involved in the investigation. The only way I could ensure that was if you didn't know about it."

Raven huffed again, but she knew he was right.

"Paigo has been charged with thirty-two counts of rape of a minor and child molestation to date, the oldest incident going back twenty-five years. If you know of someone who was assaulted by him nearly thirty years ago, she hasn't reported it to us. Do you think she'll talk to us?"

"I'm not even sure he raped her. It's only a hunch at this point."

LaCroix took a business card from a holder on his desk and handed it over to Raven. "Give her this and tell her I'll have a female officer speak to her if she's willing."

Raven took the card and slid it into her back pocket. "What about my statement?"

"I'll have Mick meet you in the interview room."

"Why don't I take Indi for a walk?" Riley squeezed Raven's hand. "You can text me when you're done."

"Her stroller is in the back of the car." Raven handed Riley her car keys and buckled Indigo back into her car seat.

* * *

They were ushered to a buffet line in the kitchen when they arrived at Kiran's. Someone had been busy making bacon, sausages, eggs, pancakes, and home fries. There was enough to feed an army, which Raven supposed is almost what they had when she entered the great room and saw them all sitting around the room, some balancing plates on their laps and some sipping tea or coffee.

Jennifer Gallagher sat in the corner of the love seat again, still stiff and withdrawn, while Rebecca sat next to her. Raven leaned against the wall with a cup of coffee. She wasn't hungry after giving her statement to Mick. She wasn't sure if she was going to be able to keep the coffee down. Riley must have felt the same. All she'd taken from the kitchen was a cup of herbal tea.

Indigo bounced on Rauri's lap, giggling away. Despite how

sick she felt, Raven smiled at the sight.

William, Kiran's father, pushed himself out of a leather recliner and cleared his throat. "Now that we're all here, we've some business to discuss, aye?"

All eyes fell on him.

"We all know the risks facing Raven. With witches coming from all over the world in droves, her safety is of the utmost importance."

"I'm protected," Raven said. And she could damn well protect herself. She didn't need all these people freaking out and putting constraints on her because they were worried about her safety.

"We know, love," Rauri said. "But, we've got more than double the normal attendance numbers for this festival. We believe it's because the curious are coming to see you for themselves. However, not all of them are coming out of curiosity."

Raven narrowed her eyes. "Do you know of a threat?"

"There have been rumours," William said.

"I don't put a lot of stock into rumours."

"There hasn't been a witch with your potential powers in decades," Rauri said. "As time goes on, the bloodlines are growing weaker, not stronger. Many covet your powers, Raven Sage."

She'd be damned if she let anyone use her like that again. Adara had soaked up her powers for years without Raven having an inkling she was doing it. She wasn't going to let that happen again. She knew how to protect herself now.

"They can covet all they want. No one is going to take advantage of me." Not this time. Not ever again.

"It wouldn't hurt to take some precautions, would it?" Riley said.

Raven's gaze fell on Riley, her eyes wide and glassy, her teacup clutched to her chest. Raven's heart did a slow somersault. Why was it she kept hurting the person she loved the most? "No, it wouldn't."

William nodded, a small smile forming on his weathered face. "You're wearing your great gran's pentacle, that's a good start."

Raven's fingers glazed the medallion on her chest, feeling its power.

Kiran shifted forward in his seat, resting his elbows on his knees. "Don't forget, the very thing that attracts unwanted attention to my daughter is the thing that will keep her safe. Her own powers."

"You're so sure of her power?" William countered.

"Aye. I've seen Raven protect our entire coven with my own eyes, father."

"Against one woman. A woman with weak bloodlines."

"A woman using Raven's powers against her."

Raven pushed off the wall. "Debating whether my powers are what they're rumoured to be isn't helpful."

"Aye, you're right," Kiran said. "We have a couple of clairvoyants in the room. Has anyone had any visions?"

"I'll spend some time this morning with my crystal ball," Jasmine offered.

Several eyes drifted to Jenny, but she stared out the window like she was ignoring them all. Rebecca's hand slid onto her thigh and squeezed, but Jenny didn't acknowledge it.

"Fair enough," Rauri said. "We'll meet back here for lunch and continue this conversation."

The opening ceremonies were set to begin mid-afternoon, followed by a concert in the evening. Raven needed to check that all of the vendors were loaded in and that the stage was ready. She headed over to Rauri, reaching for Indi.

"Why don't you leave her with us while you see about your business, love?"

Raven hesitated and Rauri drew to her feet, hugging Indigo to her chest and wrapping an arm around Raven. She whispered, "Don't worry, love. I'll take good care of her, aye? She doesn't often get to see her great gran."

"Yeah, sure." She raked her fingers through her hair then dropped her hand to her side.

Riley linked her arm through Raven's. "Come on. I'll accompany you to the festival grounds."

As they turned to leave, they came face to face with Rebecca, blocking their path. "Jenny would like to speak with you now," she said to Riley. "I'll take you into the office."

Raven and Riley looked at each other and Riley gave a short nod. When Raven followed along behind Riley, Rebecca stopped and shot her a cold glare. "Jenny would like some privacy."

"If you're going in to support Jenny, I'm going to be there to support Riley."

Rebecca's lips formed a tight white line, but she nodded and continued into the office. Jenny was standing at the window, her arms crossed over her breasts, staring off into the distance. Her face was pale, but Raven wasn't sure if that was her usual colour or not. Rebecca took up a position at her side.

Raven slid her hand into Riley's and linked their fingers.

"What is she doing here?" Jenny asked without turning from the window. The way she spoke made Raven sound like the vilest thing roaming the planet. "I want a private conversation with Riley, Ms. Bowen."

"No, problem," Raven answered. "I'll leave with *Ms.* Jordan."

Jenny turned then, her gaze meeting Rebecca's before throwing Raven a death stare. "Very well." She faced Riley with her arms still crossed over her chest.

"What the hell is wrong with you?" Riley asked with a

scowl. "You're staying on Raven's land, in Raven's house. You have no right to be so rude to her. You don't even know her."

"I came here to warn you, Riley. The woman you're choosing to share your bed with has a challenging path ahead of her. You'd do well to steer clear of her."

Riley's face turned a bright shade of red. Her hand squeezed Raven's until Raven was sure the blood flow was cut off. "That's it? You came here to warn me away from Raven? Well, that's great. You've done what you came for. Now you can go the hell back to where you came from."

She spun around and started out of the room, pulling Raven with her.

"Riley!" Jenny shouted.

Riley stopped in her tracks and turned back.

"Do. Not. Defy. Me."

Snorting out a laugh, Riley gazed up at Raven. "Oh, this is freaking brilliant." She turned a narrow-eyed glare on Jenny. "Don't defy you? Go to hell. You gave up the right to tell me what to do twenty-eight years ago." She tugged on Raven's hand and stormed out of the room, straight to the front door and out into the sunshine before taking a deep breath.

"So…that went well," Raven said.

"Who the hell does she think she is? Arrogant, prissy, stuck up bitch!"

Raven wrapped her arms around Riley from behind and brushed her lips back and forth over the thundering pulse point in Riley's neck. "Breathe, babe."

She breathed, but it was like that of a bull preparing to charge. "She's been hanging around here like a starched cardboard cutout with a stick up its ass. What the hell is her problem?"

"I don't know, but she isn't impressed with me."

"That says a lot right there. She must be stark raving mad."

"Why, lover, that's the sweetest thing you've said to me in a long time."

Riley laughed and turned to face Raven, wrapping her arms around Raven's neck. She burrowed her face in Raven's shoulder. "I don't know what she's seen, but nothing could keep me from loving you, from being with you."

Raven leaned her cheek into Riley's hair. "Maybe you should hear her out."

Jerking back, Riley glared up at Raven. "Now, *you* sound crazy. She's a raving lunatic. Nothing she says could convince me to leave you."

Raven sighed and touched her forehead to Riley's. "It would kill me if you left me again, but she's a clairvoyant. Something made her come all this way when it's probably the last place on earth she wants to be."

"You saw how she was. You can't have a conversation with someone like that. It's like she expects everyone to obey her orders, jump when she says to jump."

"Well, maybe Rebecca needs to mediate."

Riley drew in a breath, her shoulders dropping on a heavy exhale. "I know you're trying to be reasonable, but I don't want anything to do with that bitch."

Raven couldn't blame her.

* * *

Hand in hand, they strolled down the centre aisle between the vendors' tents. Raven spotted Jade Storm coming out from behind her tent and two men strolling off in the opposite direction. They both wore aviator sunglasses, black jeans, black t-shirts, and big black biker boots. One had straight, sandy brown hair and the other had curly, dark brown hair to his shoulders and a thin mustache. She walked straight over to Jade, who wore a purple tie-dyed scarf wrapped around her head, the tail hanging down behind her right ear. It matched the purple silk shirt she wore above a white flowy gauze skirt.

"Good morning. Who're your friends?" Raven nodded to the two men hightailing it towards the parking lot.

Jade glanced over her shoulder at them. "Oh, just a couple of guys who lugged over some boxes of supplies for me." She nodded towards Riley. "Who's your friend."

"Riley Gallagher, Jade Storm," Raven said.

"Nice to meet you, Riley," Jade cooed, her eyes never leaving Raven.

"Pleasure," Riley said coolly.

"I'd heard you were single, Raven."

"Nope." Raven pecked Riley's temple. "If you'll excuse us." She kept her eyes on Riley and walked away.

"She's beautiful," Riley said.

"Is she?"

"Don't tell me you didn't notice. It's impossible not to. She certainly noticed you. She wants you, Rave."

"I only have eyes for you."

Riley snorted and bumped Raven with her shoulder. "Who's the charmer now?"

Raven led Riley away from Jade's stall then cut in behind the tents. There were no boxes behind Jade's. She turned back and headed for the parking lot.

"What are we doing?" Riley doubled stepped to keep up with Raven.

"Looking for those two guys."

"Why?"

"Because I don't trust Jade Storm." She stepped into the parking lot as a black Lexus drove by carrying the two men. She memorized the licence plate.

"That's them," Riley said.

"Yep."

"What are you going to do?"

"Run their plate." She texted the plate number to Mick.

Chapter 8

By the time they made it back to the house, Raven had sorted out three disputes between vendors fighting over their territory and averted chaos with a band who were freaking out that their equipment wasn't going to arrive on time. Raven simply called the shipping company and was assured the delivery would be made before noon and was able to calm the band down.

Raven found Indigo in her highchair wearing pablum all over her face and in her hair. Her hands were covered in it. As was Rauri. Raven found a clean spot on Indi's head and dropped a kiss onto it. "Having fun?"

Rauri roared out a laugh. "Oh, aye."

Indigo scrunched up her nose and sniffed in and out, spraying more pablum everywhere then giggled, slapping her hands on the tabletop.

"Geez, you're a riot, kiddo," Raven laughed. She went to the sink and ran a washcloth under warm water then cleaned her daughter up as best she could. "Someone's going to need a bath."

"Oh, aye, I do," Rauri said and roared again. "I'm sure most of it's in my hair."

"Where is everyone?" Raven asked as she lifted Indigo out of the highchair.

"They're having hamburgers and hot dogs out on the deck. That'll be a Canadian tradition, I suppose."

"I guess," Raven said. "We love to barbecue." She sat down at the table across from Rauri, sitting Indi in her lap. "What do you know about Jenny Gallagher?"

Rauri raised an eyebrow and Raven wasn't so sure she would answer the question.

"She's harmless, our Jenny. Although, she's been behaving strangely since we arrived here. You're worried about your … partner?"

"Partner, lover, girlfriend. Whatever you prefer."

"You know, you're the first lesbian we've had in the Hayes clan." Her eyes twinkled and she smirked. "That I know of."

"Nice deflection, but I still want to know about Jenny."

"What is it that's bothering you, love?"

"Jenny says she came here to warn Riley away from me."

"Did she say why?"

"Only that I have a difficult path ahead of me, and Riley would do well to steer clear of me."

Rauri's brows drew together and she lowered her gaze. When she looked up again, she patted the table lightly. "Would you wait here for a minute?"

Raven nodded.

Rising from her chair, pablum still stuck to her face and hair, Rauri said, "I'll be right back."

Raven stood Indigo up in her lap and grinned at her. Indi's little legs pistoned up and down like she was on a trampoline. Raven gasped, exclaimed, "Kisses!" then peppered kisses all over Indigo's face sending her into fits of giggles. She repeated the routine three times before Rauri came back into the kitchen with Jasmine in tow. She sat Indi in her lap again, giving her the washcloth to play with.

"Jasmine is clairvoyant," Rauri said. "I wonder if you'll allow her to see if she can answer your questions?"

"Okay." Raven didn't have a lot of experience with clairvoyants. Ena had been clairvoyant, but her psychic powers were never her priority. She was more focused on her intuition than visions. Raven was clairaudient and Kiran was an empath.

"Why don't you start by telling Jasmine what you told me?"

Raven repeated what she'd told Rauri about Jenny.

"Before we do anything else," Jasmine began. "Can I tell you my impressions."

"Sure."

"Up until the last day or so, talk of a Bowen-Hayes offspring were just rumours. Word is already spreading through the Wiccan community that the rumours were true. Even if you don't possess extraordinary powers, you will be a target for those looking to increase their own."

"Which will make my road challenging," Raven said.

"Aye, to say the least. You'll always need to have your guard up and those around you will need constant protection."

Raven knew that much already. Her untrusting nature and cop instincts would help her there. She was suspicious of everyone anyway.

Indi pressed her little fist to her eye and rubbed then launched the washcloth across the table. Rauri caught it effortlessly and set it down next to her.

"Will you take my hand?" Jasmine held out her hand to Raven.

"Wait a minute. I wanted to know about Jenny. Why would you need to read me?"

"If Jenny feels strongly enough to come here just to warn Riley away from you, I'd like to see if I can determine why."

All kinds of horrible scenes flashed through Raven's mind of Riley being hurt or, worse, killed because someone was trying to get to her for her powers. "I-I'd rather not."

"Alright." Jasmine drew her hand back to her lap.

"Do you have any idea why Jenny's been acting so strange since she got here?"

"No." Rauri's voice was devoid of its usual bubbliness. "But, you do."

Raven immediately threw up the shields that blocked people from reading her mind. "I don't, actually." It was the truth. She had no proof. Only assumptions.

"I think you do," Jenny said from the doorway. "The same man raped you."

Rauri and Jasmine sat with their mouths agape, wide eyes flickering between Raven and Jenny.

Raven got to her feet and lifted Indigo to her shoulder, rubbing her back as Indi snuggled into her. "If you'll excuse me, I need to put my daughter down for a nap."

Rauri reached out and clasped onto her arm. "Raven?"

Jenny Gallagher was really starting to piss Raven off. She had no right to blubber that out in front of her aunt and grandmother. The last thing Raven wanted was Kiran's family looking at her like a victim. "This is not a topic that's open for discussion." She pulled her arm from Rauri's grasp and started to nudge by Jenny in the doorway. Stopping herself, she pulled Grayson's card out of her back pocket. "If you find the courage to report what he did to you, call this man. There's an ongoing investigation into the girls he abused. Maybe if you'd reported it way back then, there wouldn't be such a long list of victims." Jenny flinched at her words. Raven shoved the card into her hand and fled up the stairs. She'd been petty, lashing out at Jenny, but the bitch deserved to be taken down a notch.

* * *

Odd that the room she retreated to was the same room that Gregor Paigo had abused her in all those years ago. Gone were the candy-pink walls and the canopy bed, thanks to Kiran. He'd painted the room a pale yellow and decorated it with baby furniture, made it into a soothing and peaceful space for her daughter. Raven sat in the rocker with her head back and Indigo sleeping contentedly in her arms.

A hypocrite was what she was. She hadn't been brave enough to report Paigo, and how many had suffered because of it? She squeezed her eyes closed against the tears.

"Hey."

Raven opened her eyes and took in Riley leaning against the doorjamb. She looked identical to Jenny, yet she was so much more beautiful and, Raven supposed, that came from the beauty on the inside - the massive heart and nurturing nature.

"You didn't have lunch."

Raven shook her head. "Not hungry. I just wanted to spend some time with my daughter."

Riley crossed the room, kneeling at Raven's feet. She placed her forearms on either side of Raven's hips and leaned over her and Indigo. "Something's bothering you."

"Do you ever not like yourself?"

"Sometimes, I guess."

"I wasn't very nice to Jenny."

Riley huffed out a short laugh. "That I can totally forgive you for. She probably deserved it."

Raven cupped Riley's cheek and brushed her thumb back and forth over Riley's temple. "She confirmed that she was raped by Gregor Paigo."

Riley's eyes shut tightly, forming lines around her eyes, and she dropped her head to Raven's lap. A fist gripped Raven's heart and squeezed. "I'm sorry, Ri. I'm so sorry."

"What did she say?"

"She just said that I was raped by the same man."

"Oh, Rave. My screwed up parentage is stirring up your

trauma. I'm sorry for that."

Raven's fingers slid into Riley's hair at the nape of her neck and massaged the tight muscles. "You've got nothing to be sorry for. I'm fine."

Riley raised her head and searched Raven's eyes. Raven just stared back, her heart swelling with the love she felt for this woman. She leaned forward and kissed the tip of Riley's nose. "I'm fine. If it hadn't been for the work I've done with Kirsten over the past year, I don't think I could have given my statement about Gregor. I'm in a better place now, a much better place. I look at it from a different perspective and think of myself more of a survivor than a victim. He couldn't break me. I won't allow him to continue to haunt me."

"It just makes me sick that my father was the one who did that to you."

"No." Raven cupped Riley's jaw. "He's not your father. There's nothing of him in your kind and loving soul. You're you, despite who's sperm and eggs made you, and you're beautiful right down to the core of your being."

"Oh, damn, you're going to make me cry again."

Raven wrapped her arm around Riley's shoulders and hugged her in close.

"I'm sorry to interrupt." Rauri popped her head in the doorway. "Riley, would you give me a few minutes with Raven?"

Riley began to sit back, and Raven tightened her arm. "Anything you want to say to me, you can say in front of Riley. She knows my history. And she knows her own."

Rauri took a tentative step inside the room and hugged her middle. "Firstly, are you both alright?"

"Yeah."

Riley leaned back onto her haunches, keeping a hand resting on Raven's thigh. Her eyes were wet and red-rimmed, but she offered Rauri a weak smile.

"Would you tell me about this man?" Rauri asked.

"No. I told you it wasn't open for discussion."

"I'm not asking you to tell me what he did, but I would like to know if he's still a danger to you."

Raven shook her head. "No, he's in prison."

Rauri nodded her head. "What you said to Jenny down there about her not reporting him to the authorities-"

"Even if she'd told Ena, Ena would have ousted him from the coven. She certainly wouldn't have dated the man, giving him access to our home ... and to me." As soon as the words were out of her mouth, she felt like the world's biggest hypocrite again. What if Paigo had made the same kind of threats to Jenny about her telling anyone? What if she wanted to, but couldn't because she feared for Ena's safety or her brother's?

A gust of air shot out of Rauri's lungs. "Dear Goddess, Raven. How old were you?"

It would all be a matter of public record within a day or two and Raven had a sudden thought that once it was, the media would pick up on her name being added to the list of Paigo's victims. She could only hope that it wouldn't happen until after the festival. Still, she was reluctant to tell Rauri any details. All it would do is hurt her, thinking of what her granddaughter suffered through. She shook her head, closed her eyes and pressed her lips to Indigo's hair. Riley's hand squeezed her thigh and Raven covered it with her own.

"I'm sorry." Rauri moved further into the room. "Not open for discussion. But, maybe if you told Jenny that this man was in prison, she would feel a bit better."

"Pfff." Indigo's short hair blew with Raven's exhale. She wasn't feeling a lot of sympathy towards Jenny Gallagher, but she had Riley to consider. If Jenny were to relax a bit, maybe she and Riley would have a heart to heart and begin to heal. "I'll let her know."

"Thank you, love." Rauri turned to leave then turned back. "You know, the three of you make a lovely picture sitting there. A bonnie wee family."

* * *

The afternoon sun shone down on the deck at the back of the Bowen house, overlooking the rock cliffs and Fairy Lake. Raven breathed in the fresh, lake air and closed her eyes. She was content just sitting with Riley next to her, their hands joined. Most of the Hayes clan had gone down to the beach for a swim. They weren't used to the heat and humidity.

William came out onto the deck and took a chair next to Raven. She missed his lunchtime meeting and had wondered how long it would be before he cornered her. She kept her eyes closed, soaking up the warmth of the sun on her face. "Hello, Granddad."

"Hello, Raven. Riley." He leaned forward and nodded a greeting around Raven.

"Mr. Hayes."

"Oh, please. Call me William or Granddad. You're family."

Raven opened her eyes and smiled at Riley.

"I wanted to speak to you about this threat."

"What threat is that exactly?" Raven asked. "What's worrying you, Granddad?"

"Both Jasmine and Rauri sense some negative energy. They feel more than one source of ill-intention. What we're concerned about, specifically, is a kidnapping."

It was something that Raven had already considered after the extents that Adara went through to keep her close. It wouldn't be much of a stretch for someone to plan to abduct her and cage her up somewhere so they could tap into her powers at will. What they may not realize was that Raven was now able to prevent anyone from stealing her powers. "I'm vigilant and well protected. What else would you have me do?"

"Ideally, leave this place until after the festival."

Raven's mouth dropped open as they stared into each other's ice-blue eyes. "That's not going to happen."

"It was worth a shot." His eyes twinkled. "Just promise me you won't go anywhere alone and be mindful of who and what's around you."

"You have my word."

Chapter 9

As darkness descended upon Solstice, hundreds of witches and druids from around the world descended upon the Bowen lands. Many of the women dressed in colourful, flowy skirts with circlets of flowers in their hair. Men dressed in robes carried staffs decorated with charms, crystals, and feathers. Everywhere you looked, people expressed their individuality in their dress, in tattoos and piercings, flashy jewelry, and even face paint.

The majority of people gathered in front of the stage where three men sat cross-legged with tribal drums between their knees while a woman with long golden curls in a flowing white gown led the crowd in a chant.

Raven, her hand clasped in Riley's, danced as she chanted the 'o' sound that was more of a vibration in her throat. Hundreds of voices joined together. Raven closed her eyes, feeling the energy, and let herself drift until there was only the energy, the vibration of those chanting around her. She floated. She was the energy, the vibration, connected to the earth, the air, the water, the fire ... connected to spirit.

The beating of the drums came to a sudden halt and the chanting followed. Raven took several deep breaths, becoming aware of her surroundings - the bodies surrounding her, the laboured breathing, the slight breeze, the grass under her bare feet. When she opened her eyes, all she saw was Riley, eyes still closed and a wide grin on her face as she swayed back and forth. Raven felt connected to Riley from the moment they met, but never this deeply, right down to the core of her soul. Raven leaned in, her mouth finding Riley's with all of the energy she'd soaked up in the chanting. Riley's arms came around her holding their bodies together. Everyone around them fell away and the only thing that mattered was showing Riley just how much she loved her.

"Riley!"

Riley's body jerked in Raven's arms. She pushed back, looking over her shoulder. Jenny stood a few feet away, her pale green eyes narrowed, her lips scowling.

Riley grabbed Raven's hand. "I'm sensing negative energy here. Let's go somewhere else." She pulled Raven along until they entered the forest just behind the stage. When she stopped and turned back to Raven, her face was glowing. "That was amazing. I've never felt anything like that in my life." She flung herself into Raven's arms.

Raven spun her around and placed her gently against a tree, pressing their bodies together. Her belly quivered with the contact. With quick, short breaths, she whispered into Riley's ear, "This is going to be quick."

"Yes!" Riley gasped.

It was as if the energy flowing through them desperately needed a release and what better way than loving each other, pleasuring each other. Their hands, mouths, and bodies moved together in a dance of souls joined by love, a symphony of whimpers, gasps, and groans building to a crescendo until they collapsed in each others' arms, gasping for air.

"Holy shit." Riley panted into Raven's neck.

"Sorry," Raven said when she regained the ability to speak.

"My finesse went right out the window." She'd also completely lost herself for the second time in the last hour. She couldn't afford to do that.

"Who needs finesse? That was earth-shattering."

Raven laughed and nudged her nose into Riley's neck. A stick snapping in the woods behind her had every muscle in her body tensing. She looked over her shoulder and saw only the darkness, but the hairs on the back of her neck stood on end. "We should get going."

"Yeah." Riley straightened her clothes, her eyes darting back and forth over Raven's shoulder. "I wouldn't mind a stroll around the vendor's area."

Raven took her hand and led them out of the woods. A folk band played on the stage. The crowd in front had thinned out a bit, but there were still hundreds of people milling about. She supposed she should be happy the festival was off to a successful start, but she'd be more so when all these people were off her land.

* * *

Many of the vendor's tents were lit with fairy lights, some with candles or fancy table lamps, casting the whole area in a mystical glow. They browsed the clothing, dream catchers, crystals, wands, cloaks, and mystical wares of all types. A crystal ball the size of a volleyball sat at the side of one vendor's table. Riley walked to it, hovering her hands over the crystal as Raven watched the elegant movement of her hands.

"It calls to you," Raven said.

The crystal ball's copper base was forged into flames, licking up the side of the crystal. "It's ... beautiful."

"Can you feel its energy?"

Riley nodded. "I thought for a second there I saw us in it. Ha," she laughed, but her brow was drawn in and she wasn't smiling. "It must have been a reflection."

"Don't be so sure. You may have your mother's gift of clairvoyance."

Riley stared up at Raven as she waved to the vendor.

"We'll take this."

"Oh, Rave, you can't." She pointed to the price tag.

Raven laughed. "Yes, I can." She gave the woman with a circlet of daisies capping her long dark hair her credit card, then picked up a purple, velvet cloth and added it to her purchase. "If you cover the crystal ball with the cloth when it's not in use, it will keep its energy within and keep it charged."

Riley only nodded. When they walked away from the stall, she asked, "Just how much money did your mother leave you?"

Raven looked into Riley's eyes. "A lot." She hadn't received her inheritance until a few months ago, once Ena's taxes had been paid. It still blew her away just how many figures were in the final amount.

"What are you going to do with it all?"

Raven shrugged. "I'm still working that out. There's more money than I know what to do with. I'm looking at charities and I've spent some of it buying more land around my cottage."

"How much land?"

Raven tugged on Riley's hand until she stopped walking and faced her. "It's a problem for you? The money?"

"No, I guess I'm just a bit surprised. You've always been very frugal with money, then you just bought that crystal ball on a whim. I didn't realize Ena left you a lot of money."

"I've struggled all of my adult life financially," Raven explained. "All along, I had a trust fund I didn't know about. The way I felt about Ena at the time, I didn't want anything to do with it. But now, I feel like she's left me a legacy and there's something important I should be doing with it. I'm just not sure what that is yet."

Riley smiled, leaned in and pressed a chaste kiss to Raven's lips. "That's a beautiful way of looking at it."

"Yeah." The hair on the back of Raven's neck stood up again and she glanced around her. There were too many people for her to get a sense of what caused her sudden unease. She reached out with her psychic powers, searching for thoughts of a negative nature and found only lightheartedness. Most people focused on shopping or lingering thoughts of the chanting and folk music. Her eyes met Jade Storm's. She stood in her booth on the other side of the aisle and waved her fingers.

"That woman wants you, Rave," Riley said.

Raven started walking again. "She wants something. I haven't quite figured out what that is yet, either." With a smile, she added, "Maybe you'll see it in your crystal ball."

* * *

Kiran, Rauri, William, Jasmine, Rebecca, and Jenny were gathered in the great room when Raven and Riley got back to the house. Jenny stood by the window with her arms crossed over her chest and a scowl on her red face. Everyone else looked weary.

"What's going on?" Raven wasn't sure she wanted to know. She felt like a teenager sneaking in late and finding her parents waiting up for her.

"You!" Jenny stabbed her finger at Raven. "Anything could have happened to Riley out there. You were lost to the chant and she was left unprotected."

Raven felt like that finger had been a fist to her chest. She took a step back as her palm flattened over her heart. "Excuse me?" Even when she'd let herself drift, she was connected to Riley in a way that any stress Riley may have felt would have alerted her immediately. Still, it may not have been enough. If anything had happened, it would have been all her fault. She was beginning to understand that being a powerful, hereditary witch came with a lot more responsibility than she realized. She couldn't just lose herself in a celebration and enjoy it like everyone else.

"I was never unprotected," Riley said. "You don't have any idea what you're talking about and you certainly don't have any right to question Raven about my safety. You've got no right to come here and pretend to give a shit about my welfare."

The colour in Jenny's face darkened with each word Riley spoke until it looked almost purple. The colour of Riley's face wasn't far off it.

"That's enough," Rebecca said. "You're upsetting Jenny."

"Well, poor fucking Jenny." Riley's entire body vibrated, her fists clenched tightly at her sides. "I'm getting a little sick of seeing her standing with her nose in the air like she's better than everyone else and dictating what I should do with my life. She's about twenty-eight years too late to show up here feigning concern and trying to be my mother."

Jenny flinched like she'd been slapped in the face.

"Okay," Raven said gently. She put her arm around Riley's shoulders. "Why don't we get Indigo and go home?" She put pressure on Riley's shoulders to turn her and lead her from the room.

"I didn't come here to be your mother. I came here to warn you away from that woman."

Riley spun out of Raven's grip. "*That woman* is the love of my life, my soul mate. I don't care how challenging a path she may face in the future. It'll be less difficult because we'll be forging it together, helping each other through it. Is that concept so difficult for you to understand?"

Jenny just stared at Riley. Riley slipped her arm around Raven's waist and headed for the stairs. "Let's go. I don't want to see *that woman* again."

"What did you mean when you said you were never unprotected?" Raven whispered as they climbed the stairs.

"I'm capable of performing a few protection spells of my own, Rave. It's not just your responsibility to keep me safe."

"I'm the reason you're in danger, so it is my responsibility. But I'm glad you're using your own protection spells, too." She leaned over and kissed Riley's temple. "We should work on your psychic abilities as well."

"I don't know if I'm psychic, Rave, but I felt something out there. In the woods and again when we were talking by the vendors' tents." Riley shuddered. "Something didn't feel right."

"If you feel anything like that again, let me know." She didn't say that she'd felt something at those same times. There was no need to freak Riley out any more than she probably already was. "Do you have to work tomorrow?"

"No, I booked off for the festival. I've never attended a Pagan festival or a gathering of witches. I wanted to be able to enjoy it."

Raven reached for Riley's hand and squeezed. "Seeing you hurting like this, I don't know what I'd do if I couldn't be here for you. What you said downstairs about our path being easier because we'd be forging it together, that's what relationships are about, aren't they? It made me realize that I was wrong to hold you away while I worked on my crap. I'm sorry for that."

"We're here for each other now," Riley said with a slow smile. "That's what matters."

"Yeah." But she'd hurt Riley once again by keeping her away. Raven packed Indigo's things into her diaper bag, then gently lifted her from her crib and buckled her into the car seat, covering her with a light blanket.

"You really can't let your guard down like that, love," Kiran said from the doorway.

Raven rolled her eyes. The last thing she wanted or needed was a fatherly lecture. "I'm aware there's someone out there, watching me. I just can't pinpoint who it is with all the people around."

Kiran's icy blue eyes darkened, his lips pursed to a flat white line. "I don't like this, love. Maybe William's right and you should leave for a few days."

"I'm not going to run every time there's a threat. Besides, if we ride this out and show people that I'm not an easy target, it may go a long way to deterring future problems."

Kiran's shoulders relaxed fractionally and he sighed, shoving his fingers through his hair. "Aye, you're right, of course."

"There's something else I thought might help," Raven said. "One of the reasons I haven't been able to pinpoint a source is the number of people around. Most of the witches here are true to the Wiccan Rede. They would harm no one. We could spread word through the Wiccan community that there is a threat and to be on the lookout for anyone harbouring ill will."

A smile formed on Kiran's face, deep dimples appearing on his cheeks. "Aye, you're a clever girl, Rave. I'll see that it's done."

* * *

Indi was awake and fussy by the time they got to Raven's cottage. Raven set a pot on the stove to heat a bottle as Riley mixed up some salt and water and used it to cleanse her crystal ball. She carried it through to the living room, set it in the centre of the coffee table, then sat down on the couch to admire it.

Raven sat next to Riley with Indigo nestled in the crook of her arm. She placed the nipple of the bottle at Indi's lips. Her little hands circled the bottle, pulling it into her mouth and she began sucking vigorously.

Jet jumped up onto the arm of the couch and sat, watching over Indigo like a sentry.

"You know that thing you do with the golden light?" Riley asked, still gazing at the crystal ball. "Is that something that you learned or is it something that you just do?"

Riley had walked in on her when Raven had conjured a golden ball of energy and used it to heal her wounds. "It's just something I've always been able to do. According to Ena, I was just a baby when I first started doing it."

Riley turned and looked Raven in the eye. "Will you show me?"

Smiling, Raven held up her palm. A hazy golden light appeared, hovering just above her hand. It swirled until it formed a glowing ball, lighting up the room.

"It's beautiful," Riley said.

The bottle popped out of Indi's mouth as she stretched her arm towards the glowing orb and pointed her tiny finger. Raven slid her hand a little further away. A frustrated cry escaped Indi's little bow mouth. She turned her palm up and a soft white light swirled, forming into a ball much like Raven's. Jet reached out a paw and batted the orb. It floated over to the crystal ball, engulfing it before fading away. An image appeared in the crystal ball of Riley and Raven facing each other, reaching for each other, their faces seeped in distress as an unseen force pulled them apart.

"Holy shit!" Raven gasped. The golden orb in her hand faded to nothing and the room dimmed. "Is that the image you saw when you were looking into the crystal ball at the festival?"

Riley nodded, her mouth open, her eyes bulging.

"It could just be a reflection of Jenny trying to pull us apart."

Riley nodded again. "Do you recognize where we were there? We were surrounded by trees and bush with flames behind us."

"No. It could be any forest." Trouble was, they were surrounded by natural forests in this part of Ontario. Forests and lakes. And bonfires were a staple in the Wicca religion.

Indigo pulled the bottle back into her mouth and suckled as if nothing had happened. Raven stared down at her in awe. "So, it begins my magickal little one. What great powers do you possess?"

Indi pulled the bottle from her mouth and grinned up at her mother.

Chapter 10

The sun crested the horizon as Raven sat cross-legged on her beach, eyes closed and hands resting on her knees, the pads of her thumbs and middle fingers touching. The waves whooshed softly into the shore just inches in front of her. The soft breeze flickered through her hair and caressed her face and the exposed skin on her arms and legs. Birds chirped their morning greetings and rustling in the underbrush alerted her to the presence of a chipmunk or squirrel darting around.

Light footsteps padded towards her through the woods to her right, but Raven kept her eyes closed, recognizing the energy of the woman approaching. She thought about reaching out with her psychic abilities, but the last time she'd done that, she opened herself for an attack. And she didn't sense a threat at the moment.

The footsteps stopped at the edge of the woods, about eight feet from where Raven was sitting. "Good morning, Jade."

If she was surprised, she didn't show it. "Good morning, Raven."

"You're trespassing on private property." Sneaking around her property in the dark is what she'd been doing.

"Oh, you're not going to hold that against me, are you,

detective? I just wanted a peek at where the queen of Wicca resided. You live quite modestly for someone of your net worth."

Raven glanced over at Jade. She leaned against a tree with her platinum hair sticking straight up, a purple silk scarf wrapped around her head and a flowing white dress. Her feet were bare. "What would you know about my net worth?"

"It's not like Ena's wealth was a secret. Surely you inherited the bulk of it?"

Raven hadn't known how much Ena was worth until after her death, but she supposed it wasn't a stretch that the Wiccan community would have an idea of her financial status. It occurred to her then that, in addition to her powers, the money may draw unwanted attention.

Jade wandered over to Raven and sat on the beach next to her. "You intrigue me, Raven. If it wasn't for your girlfriend, I'd make a play for you."

"Would you?"

"Don't sound so surprised. You're a beautiful woman. I'm sure you've got a long line of interested suitors."

"Not really." Obviously, Jade Storm didn't appreciate small-town life or the fact that Raven had been somewhat reclusive since her mother's passing. Or perhaps Raven just wasn't tuned in to anyone being attracted to her. Her only focus when it came to her heart, or her sexual desires, was Riley. "What are you doing here, Jade?"

Jade's laugh was low and musical. "You don't mix words, do you? I suppose I'm being nosy. I wanted to see where you lived and I have to say I'm surprised. I expected a sprawling mansion or a modern piece of architectural art. But I think this place suits you." She glanced up the slow, rising slope to the cottage behind her. Riley stood at the deck railing, glaring down at her. "Oh, your girlfriend doesn't look pleased to see me."

"Is that why you're here? To cause some doubt in my lover's mind?" Raven laughed. "You'd have to do much better than that." Rising, she dusted the sand from her behind. "I'm sure you can find your way out."

She climbed the slope to her deck and joined Riley at the railing. Jade continued to sit on the beach, smiling up at them. Raven brushed her palms over Riley's cheeks, sinking her fingers into her glorious red hair, and fused their mouths. It had begun as a show for Jade, but it wasn't long before Raven completely forgot about her presence below. Her heart sped up, her breaths ragged and short, her body moulded to Riley's. "I need a shower before Indi wakes up," she whispered into Riley's ear. "Care to join me?" She leaned back to search Riley's eyes. The pale green was rimmed with a darker shade, a forest green. Her pert nose was speckled with golden freckles and her lips, parted as she huffed in and out, were rosy and plump from their kiss.

"What about your guest?"

"What guest?"

Riley laughed, circled her arms around Raven's neck and leaped into her arms, wrapping her legs around Raven's waist.

"I'll take that as a yes." Raven carried Riley through the sliding glass door, closing and locking it behind her.

* * *

"I'll spoon it into her mouth if you hold her hands," Raven said. Indi sat strapped into her highchair as Raven held a bowl of pablum out of her reach.

"You can't tie her down to feed her," Riley laughed. "You just have to teach her not to play with it."

Raven frowned up at Riley, who stood at the counter, making oatmeal. "How am I supposed to do that?"

"Here." Riley pulled up a chair and sat holding her bowl of oatmeal. "Give her a mouthful."

As Raven spooned a mouthful of pablum into Indigo's mouth, Riley spooned oatmeal into her own then leaned forward, getting Indi's attention. "Mmmmm…num, num, num." She exaggerated her chewing, then swallowed and grinned at Indi. "Yum, yum."

Indi's lips smacked open and closed. She grinned back at Riley, displaying her mouthful of pablum. Raven laughed as Indi blew a raspberry, spraying pablum all over Riley and Raven. "Good job, Ri," Raven laughed again.

"Yeah," Riley said with a grin. "We're going to need another shower." Her eyebrows shot up and down.

"That would be wonderful, but we have to get over to Kiran's soon before he sends out a search party."

The smile dropped from Riley's face. "I'm not going to go over to Kiran's today, Rave. I don't want to see that woman again."

Raven dropped the spoon into the pablum bowl, but Indi's whining had her spooning another mouthful into Indigo's eager, open mouth. "Okay, we'll have a lazy morning here."

"No, you don't have to stay behind because of me, Rave. I'll go over to my apartment and pack a few things. I'll meet you at the festival this afternoon."

"I'm not leaving you alone, Ri. It's too much of a risk right now. There's a threat out there and I have no idea what someone is planning. You could very well be the target." Especially if it was about the money, she thought. "I'll call Kiran and let him know we won't be at the festival until this afternoon."

"But, you're a big part of the festival, Rave. You need to be there."

Raven spooned another mouthful into Indigo then leaned over and kissed Riley. "Wasn't it just last night you said we'd forge our path together? I'm not leaving you unprotected."

Once Indi was fed and cleaned up, Raven called Kiran.

"I've got some news, love," he said before she could explain she wasn't coming over until later. "I've something I need to show you."

"What's going on?"

"It's something you need to see, Rave. I was out for a walk this morning and discovered something in the woods. I've also called your sergeant and requested some pay duty officers to patrol the grounds until the end of the festival."

Raven blew out a breath and looked into Riley's eyes. Riley stood holding Indi by the window, rocking back and forth and singing a soft lullaby while Jet sat next to them, her tail switching back and forth. "Okay, I'll see you in a few minutes."

Riley's eyebrow shot up.

Ending the call, Raven strode over to Riley, easing an arm around her waist and staring out the window. "Something's up at the house. I have to go, but I don't want to leave you on your own." She turned her gaze to Riley. "Will you come? You don't have to go into the house. Kiran wants to show me something in the woods."

Leaning her head onto Raven's shoulder, Riley released a long sigh. "Alright, but I'm bringing my car in case I need to escape." When Raven started to protest, Riley added, "I'll take Mick or someone with me if I leave."

"Fair enough."

* * *

Kiran, William, and Jasmine waited on the porch as Raven pulled into the driveway with Riley right behind her. She caught a glance of Jenny standing stiffly in the window with a scowl on her face before she backed away into the shadows.

Raven got out and removed Indigo from her car seat before walking to the bottom of the porch steps. "What's up?"

"Good morning," Kiran said with a glimmer in his eyes. He descended the steps and reached for his granddaughter.

Indigo's arms stretched out to him.

"Morning," Raven said, a slight blush forming on her cheeks as she passed her daughter to her father. "What's up?"

Kiran laughed, bouncing Indigo in his arms as she giggled.

"Careful," Raven warned. "She just ate."

Kiran slowed his movements. He knew from experience not to jostle her too much when she'd just eaten. "Let's go for a walk, shall we."

Raven glanced over her shoulder to Riley, who leaned against the front of her little red SUV. She nodded and Riley pushed off the hood, wandering over to join them with her hands stuffed into the pockets of her shorts. As a group, they rounded the side of the house and headed for the festival grounds. It was quiet. The odd vendor had arrived to prepare for the day, but for the most part, the grounds were deserted. Peaceful, Raven thought.

Kiran led them down the centre of the vendors' tents and veered off into the woods at the back of the stage. Riley's hand slid into Raven's and held her back. She whispered, "This is getting a bit eerie." Kiran was leading them to the spot in the woods where they'd made love against a tree. At that exact tree, a photograph was nailed into the bark. A picture of Raven holding Indigo.

"Don't touch anything," Raven ordered. "I'll get Grayson to send a forensics unit out. I want everyone to go back out to the clearing. Try to follow the same path you came in on."

"But, I need to touch the picture," Jasmine said.

Raven met Jasmine's eyes and shook her head. "It needs to be dusted for fingerprints and we need to search this area for evidence. I need all of you out of here. Now."

"You know there aren't going to be any fingerprints on it. I could get a vision from it and identify the person who put it here."

Even though she knew the chances of them finding prints

on the photograph were slim to none, everything inside Raven screamed at her to follow procedure. "After we get it printed, you can-"

"It will be too late then," Jasmine said. "The energy of the fingerprinter will be in it. I won't get a clear vision." She stood unmoving, her big grey eyes pleading with Raven. "I'll just touch the edge."

Raven blew out a breath and threw her hands in the air. They fell to her sides, slapping her thighs. She couldn't believe she was about to do this. "Fine. Just the edge."

Jasmine nodded and took a careful step forward. The pads of her fingers touched the very edge of the photo. She tilted her head back, closing her eyes. "Two men, dressed in black. Tall. Muscular. Their faces are covered by black hoods. They're watching you. From the woods. You and Riley." She let out a little gasp and her face flushed. "Yes, well. You and Riley." She opened her eyes and looked at Raven with her head lowered so she was looking up through her thick, dark lashes. "You really enjoyed the festival last night, didn't you?"

"Great," Raven huffed. "You get a clear picture of that, but not what these two guys look like."

"When was this picture taken?" Kiran asked.

Raven studied it from where she was. She could see part of one of the vendor's tents in the background, but it was still vacant. The vendor hadn't loaded in yet. She was wearing cut off jeans and a blue tank top and Indi was wearing a white sundress with pink flowers. "The first day of the vendor load-ins," Raven said. She'd walked the area with Indi in her arms. She couldn't get a read on what angle the photo was taken from. There wasn't enough showing in the background to give her an idea of the direction of the photographer.

They all walked back out to the clearing in single file and Raven pulled her cell phone out of her pocket. She called

Detective Sergeant Grayson LaCroix and requested a forensic unit. Her face felt too hot and she was sure there was steam coming out of her ears.

"What do you think it means?" Riley asked Raven as they began the walk back to the house.

"I think they want us to know that they're watching us."

"You and Indi."

"Based on where he left that picture, I'd say they want us to know they're watching the three of us."

Riley's face paled. "I feel … violated."

Raven took her hand and pressed her lips to her palm. "I know. I'm sorry."

"You weren't the only one in the woods last night, Rave. I wanted you as much as you wanted me. It just … I don't know. It was an extraordinary and private moment. That someone was watching us makes it feel …"

"Spoiled," Raven finished for her.

"Close enough."

"You know they're going to want to watch over us every minute now." Raven nodded ahead to Kiran, Jasmine, and William.

As if he'd heard her, Kiran slowed his steps and waited for Raven and Riley to catch up. "The two men you saw coming out from behind Jade Storm's tent, they were dressed in black, aye?"

"Yeah, but it doesn't mean it's the same two guys."

"Mick ran their number plate?"

"Black Lexus. Registered to a Kyle Langley out of Barrie. He works for a delivery company and was on a run delivering goods for one of the vendors."

"In a Lexus?"

"Yeah. It was a last-minute rush. The vendor left a couple of boxes in her store that she needed here."

"So, on the surface, he checks out?"

Raven nodded. "On the surface."

* * *

Within thirty minutes, LaCroix was pulling into the driveway with two constables and two crime scene techs in tow. PC Gayle Trewelyn had been Raven's training officer. Her silver hair was pulled back in a tight ponytail and her deep brown eyes smiled at Raven. Raven nodded her greeting. The uniform at her side was another silver fox, yet he looked too young to be grey.

"This is PC Devon Cartwright," LaCroix said. "Cartwright, Detective Constable Raven Bowen."

"A pleasure," Cartwright smiled, his hazel eyes gleaming, and extended his hand to Raven. "Your reputation precedes you."

Raven raised her brows, shaking his hand. "I'm afraid you have me at a disadvantage."

He leaned in and whispered. "I replaced Darren Tate. Not the best tag line, but it's all I've got."

Charming, Raven thought. He was a vast improvement on the nasty Darren Tate, who was now sitting in the penitentiary, convicted of multiple counts of abduction, forcible confinement, rape, and murder. He wouldn't be wearing a uniform again in his miserable life. Tate was Gregor Paigo's son. Whether or not he was another product of Paigo's preying on girls, she had no idea. "Well, welcome to Solstice. Where are you from?"

"Born and raised in Toronto, but I've spent the last few years up at the Moosonee Detachment."

"What did you do to deserve that?"

Cartwright laughed. "I requested it. I wanted to experience the north. Now I'm ready for city life."

"In Solstice?"

"Compared to Moosonee, I'm sure it will be booming, especially in the summer."

He was right there. Cottages and tourists swelled the population to bursting in the summer months.

"Where's this photograph, Rave?" LaCroix asked, his eyes squinting at her and his mouth pressed into a taut line.

He probably wasn't used to her being so chatty. She wasn't sure if it was the work she'd been doing with the therapist or from being at home with a baby for the past six months, but that was probably the first time in her life, that Raven could remember, she'd made small talk with a new acquaintance. "Yeah, sorry, Sarge. It's in the back by the stage. I'll take you down."

They followed the same path into the woods that she had with Kiran, William, Jasmine, and Riley, careful not to disturb anything that may be evidence. Raven waved her hand towards the photo nailed to the tree. "I'd like to fan out and search the area."

LaCroix stood with his hands resting on his duty belt, studying the photograph and the nail holding it in place. "This spot have any significance for you, Rave?"

Heat bloomed up her neck and her face flushed. She hoped to hell no one noticed. "Ah, Riley and I hung out here to wind down after dancing last night." She turned to the direction where she'd heard a stick snap in the woods. "We heard a noise from over there and left."

LaCroix gazed off in the direction she'd indicated. "Why don't you and Trewelyn have a look while Cheryl and Dan process the scene here?" The two crime scene techs dressed in dark blue BDUs and matching polo shirts set down their cases and went to work.

Raven wandered into the bush with Trewelyn. "Hanging out or hanging on?" Trewelyn asked.

"There may have been a lot of groping involved."

"Oh, Rave. I'm sorry."

"Someone was watching us, Gayle. The hair on the back of

my neck stood up when I heard that stick snap." They walked slowly and carefully, side by side, scanning every inch of ground in front of them and the trees, bushes, and branches around them. The hard-packed earth was covered in pine needles, making it difficult, if not impossible, to see tracks. It had been a few weeks since they'd had any rain.

"Could be worse, I guess. It could have been a picture of you and Riley together."

"Too dark," Raven answered absently. She stared down at a freshly snapped stick.

"We're headed in the right direction."

"Right direction for what?"

"Good question."

They continued, finding nothing of value. Whoever had watched Raven and Riley may have just followed them into the woods and left after they did. She was about to give up when she spotted a dark patch in the clearing ahead.

"Looks like someone's been camping out here," Trewelyn said.

Raven took a cautious step into the clearing, noting the square of tamped down grass and ash-filled fire pit that someone had dug into the ground and surrounded with rocks. She crouched by the fire and splayed her hand out over the ashes. Still warm. "Let's get the forensic techs in here."

"It's not exactly a crime scene, Rave."

Raven blew out an exasperated breath. Trewelyn was right. Other than trespassing, no crime had been committed. So, she'd search on her own. She grabbed a stick and began sifting through the ashes in the pit, wishing she had her crime scene kit on hand when she found a cigarette butt intact against one of the rocks.

"I'll go back and borrow some gloves and evidence bags from Cheryl," Trewelyn said and headed back in the direction they'd come from.

Raven spent the next few hours combing every inch of the area. She found several cigarette butts, two different brands. They would provide DNA, but the chances of the DNA profiles being in the database weren't high. A discarded bottle of lighter fluid held more promise. She'd found it in the bushes behind the square of tamped down grass and was hopeful they'd get fingerprints from it.

By the time she got back to the house, Indigo was down for her nap. Raven found Riley snoozing in the rocking chair next to her crib. Her eyes fluttered open when Raven walked into the room.

"Sorry," she whispered. "I know you didn't want to be here, Ri. Thank you for staying." She hadn't given her much choice. She couldn't let her leave on her own, knowing someone was watching them.

"It's alright. I've managed to avoid Jenny so far."

"By hiding in Indi's room."

"Indi and I went for a walk with Jasmine and her daughter, Kelly. She's an interesting kid. She's studying Earth Science at the University of Edinburgh."

"What the heck do you do with a degree in Earth Science?" Raven asked.

Riley snickered. "I haven't got a clue, but she seems to enjoy it."

"I bet she loved to play in the dirt when she was a kid. Maybe she still does."

"I thought it had more to do with her Wiccan roots. I mean, it's an earth-based religion, right?"

"Right. We honour Mother Earth and all things living and growing on it."

"I don't understand why a witch or Wiccan would target another witch, threaten those close to you. Doesn't that go against everything you believe in?"

"It didn't stop Adara." Raven plopped herself down on the

floor in front of Riley. "Sorry. I guess I'm still bitter."

"You have every right to be." Riley raked her fingers through Raven's hair. "Is that what you think is going on here? Someone's greedy for power, so they're putting their core beliefs aside to get what they want?"

"I don't know. Anyone who would steal someone else's powers against their will isn't Wiccan. They may be a witch, but not Wiccan."

"Adara was Wiccan."

Raven leaned her head back against Riley's thigh, enjoying Riley's fingers running through her hair and massaging her scalp. "Adara may have thought she wasn't harming anyone by soaking up my powers, but she hurt both Ena and me by keeping us apart. She would have had to lie to hide her newfound power, and one lie leads to another. Before you know it, she was willing to do the unimaginable to gain what she wanted."

"I still can't believe some of the things she did. It was more than greed for power. She had to be more than a little insane. Who kills their best friend thinking they can take over their lives, including their husband?" Riley winced. "Sorry, babe."

"It's fine. It's true."

"Yeah, but you still blame yourself for not being able to prevent Ena's death, don't you?"

Raven sighed. "I know that it's not my fault per se, but I regret not being there for my mom and knowing that I could have healed her, even when the doctors couldn't have, makes me ill. If only I had known, if I'd been tuned in to my psychic powers or not been too stubborn to make up with my mom, she'd be here today."

"Maybe," Riley said. "But, you might not have Indigo."

Raven turned her head and looked over at the crib as Indi stirred. She couldn't imagine not having her now. Her little girl was the best thing that had happened in her life. "I just wish I could have both. Ena would have loved her granddaughter."

"How do you know she's not enjoying watching her grow and learn every day?"

Raven tilted her head back and smiled up at Riley. "I love you."

"Ditto."

Chapter 11

Raven, Riley, and Indigo spent the late afternoon and early evening with Jaxon and Mick at the festival. Then Raven gave their excuses to Kiran and they went home to Raven's cottage for a quiet evening.

When they walked in the door, Jet sat regally on the floor in the foyer, meowing nonstop while staring at Raven. "What? Are you upset that we've left you alone too much over the past few days? Well, I'm sorry. Aren't cats supposed to be solitary animals?"

Jet continued to meow at her. Raven handed Indigo off to Riley and went to check Jet's food and water bowl. When those were fine, she checked her litter and scooped it out. Jet continued to meow. She picked her up to pet her and Jet placed a paw gently on her cheek, staring into her eyes, meowing.

"I don't know what you want."

"You're clairaudient, aren't you? Can't you read her thoughts."

"I can read people's thoughts. I've never heard an animal's." But, she gave it a try. She reached out with her mind, focusing on Jet, and got an image of Indigo in her crib through a smoky haze. "Are you worried about Indi?" She scratched behind Jet's ears and kissed the top of her head before putting her down again. "Me, too, but I promise I'll take good care of her. Okay?"

Jet meowed.

They put Indigo to bed then Raven collapsed on the couch. Riley brought her a beer and sat next to her with a glass of white wine. Jet prowled back and forth in front of the sliding glass doors, meowing every few minutes.

"Something's bothering her," Riley said.

"I know. I've set the alarm and checked all the door locks. The windows are all closed and locked. And I've got so many protection spells going that I don't remember half of them. What else am I supposed to do?"

"Maybe you just need to relax. Why don't you turn a bit and I'll massage your shoulders?" Riley set her glass of wine on the coffee table.

After a few minutes of Riley massaging her tense muscles, Raven's eyelids were growing heavy. "If I don't go through to bed, I'm going to end up sleeping right here."

"We could let Indi sleep with us tonight."

"I don't want to become one of those parents who have their kid sleeping in their bed until they're sixteen years old."

Riley snorted out a laugh. "I doubt one night will cause an issue. Besides, it will ease both our minds."

She would feel a lot better if Indi was right there with them. Raven got up and padded down the hall to pick up her sleeping angel. She got her settled in the middle of the bed before stripping down and putting on a worn t-shirt. Riley and Raven brushed their teeth together then gave each other a minty kiss before climbing into bed with Indi between them.

Jet jumped up on the bed and pushed her way next to Indi, curled up, and rested her head on Indi's chest, watching her sleep.

"Such a protector," Riley said. She stroked a hand down

Jet's back and her tail switched.

"Mmmm." Raven never felt so content in her life, with her family wrapped in her arms and her cat purring madly. She could easily spend the rest of her life snuggling in bed with them. She drifted off to sleep with a smile on her face.

* * *

Raven woke to Jet meowing in her ear and batting her face with a paw. "Jet," she moaned, pushing her away. Raven inhaled and got a lung full of smoke. Coughing, she bolted upright in bed. "Shit! The house is on fire!" She reached over Indi and shoved Riley's shoulder.

Riley jolted up and began coughing.

An orange glow filtered into the room through a haze of thick smoke.

"Quick! Get dressed." Raven launched out of bed, threw the sheet over Indi's head, and grabbed a couple of pairs of sweat pants. She threw one pair at Riley and danced around on one leg as she tried to get them on as fast as possible. She yanked them up and lifted Indigo into her arms, pressing her face into her shoulder. "Stay with me," she said to Riley. "Do you understand? I need us all to stay together."

Riley scooped up Jet, both of them hacking. "I'm sticking to you like glue." Her free arm wrapped around Raven's waist.

The living room was aglow, one wall fully engulfed in flames, as was the hallway to Indi's bedroom. Thank the Goddess Riley had suggested Indi sleep with them. "We need to go out the sliding door in the bedroom." Raven turned back into the room, guiding all of them over to the door. She flipped the switch to unlock it and pulled it open. Flames, red and orange and yellow, burst into the bedroom from the hallway. They'd just stepped out onto the deck when Riley turned and ran back into the bedroom.

"Riley!" Raven's heart jumped into her throat as she

watched Riley dart into the room and disappear into the smoke. A moment later, she flew back out with her cell phone in hand. Riley called 911 as they descended the steps to the back yard with the lake below them.

A dark figure lunged at them from the darkness. Raven instinctively turned her body to protect Indi, but the figure bounced off the protective shield she'd surrounded them in. Another figure rounded the house from the opposite direction and charged at them. Riley yelled into the phone, clutching Jet to her breast. Indi screamed bloody murder, her little face red as a Valentine rose, her bottom lip quivering as she took a breath before wailing again. Raven concentrated on the two men dressed in black with black hoods covering their heads. If she engaged with them, she'd have to drop the shield. That was a risk she couldn't take. The second man bounced off the protective shell and fell backward, rolling down the incline towards the water. The first man was on his feet again and drew a knife from his belt.

"Stay with me," she called to Riley over the roar of the enraged fire behind them and the cackle of their hacking coughs. "As long as we stay together, we're safe." The heat of the flames licked her back as she faced the man with the knife. She hugged Indi to her chest and pulled Riley in front of her to protect them from the scorching heat.

He came at them slowly this time, waving the knife in front of him as his partner climbed back up the hill looking none too impressed. They had nowhere to go but closer to the flames.

Riley's terrified scream crackled with her raw throat as the knifeman lunged at her. Raven let go of Riley's waist, released a primal war cry, and thrust her hand out at him. Sparks the colour of a blue flame shot out, hitting the man solidly in the mid-chest. He flew up into the air and landed a good ten feet into the lake. The second man watched him splash into the water, then turned and ran.

"Jesus fucking Christ!" Riley screamed. She turned into Raven, sandwiching Jet and Indigo between them. Raven nearly had to lift her to get herself away from the flames at her back. "We need to get to safer ground." She led Riley out to the street, trying to console Indi, but she continued to wail between hacking coughs. Sirens sounded in the distance as Raven turned to look at her cottage. She'd put so much sweat and muscle into fixing it up and helping with the addition. It was engulfed. A complete loss. Her little sanctuary on the lake … gone. She hugged Indigo to her chest, bouncing her up and down, cooing to her, rubbing her lips back and forth over her temple while tears poured down her cheeks. Riley clung to her with her face buried in Raven's shoulder. *Those bastards!* What right did they have to destroy her home and nearly kill her child, her lover … her cat?

She couldn't take her eyes off the destruction happening before her. A loud groan, as if the building was crying out in pain, sounded before the roof slowly folded in on itself, sending a waft of embers shooting above the roaring flames.

The first emergency vehicle to arrive was LaCroix's, followed by the first fire truck. LaCroix jumped out of his SUV and rushed towards them. He grabbed for Raven's arms and hit the shield. "What the hell?" He rubbed the spot on his forehead that had collided with the invisible barrier. "Rave?"

She couldn't risk lowering the shield. Not yet. Not when one of the men was still out there, somewhere. "I need an ambulance for Indi and Riley," she croaked.

Jet growled out a hacking cough of her own.

"Your cat, too," LaCroix said.

"That cat saved our lives." That had another thought stirring in Raven's head. "The smoke detectors didn't go off, Gray."

LaCroix's eyes narrowed, his gaze fixed on the inferno as

well, like some morbid scene that you just couldn't help looking at. Their faces glowed in the flickering light of the flames.

"There's a man in the lake."

Jerking his head to face Raven, LaCroix asked, "What?"

"Two men attacked us when we came out of the house. One of them is in the lake. The other took off."

"Descriptions?" He called out the question, but he was already running towards the lake.

Her first thought was to answer, *he'll be wet,* and she had an insane urge to laugh. She shook her head, calling after him. "They wore black hoods, black clothing. Big. Maybe six-two. Muscular." She had no idea if he heard her. Her voice kept cracking and was barely more than a whisper.

The firemen pumped water into the flames, but it was far too late. Her little cottage had gone up like it had been soaked in fuel. An image of the small red container of lighter fluid she'd found at the campsite in the woods popped into her head. "Bastards!" she wept as her cottage groaned in agony and an entire wall collapsed.

Riley hugged her tighter. "I'm so sorry, babe."

Raven pressed her lips to Riley's brow and squeezed her eyes shut. She had to hold it together. The police, firemen, and EMS personnel showing up were all people Raven knew and worked with. She couldn't fall apart despite how much she wanted to sink to her knees and sob.

"You got the keys to those vehicles?" Mike Flaherty, one of the firemen, asked, hiking a thumb over his shoulder at Riley's little red SUV and Raven's black Range Rover. The Rover was closer to the house, closer to the flames. Raven shook her head. "They're in the house."

He stared at her a moment through the lens of his breathing apparatus. "Shame," he said and turned away. But he grabbed another fireman and they jimmied the door on

Riley's vehicle then pushed it up the driveway before going back for the Rover. Someone yelled out a warning and the two firemen jogged back up the driveway as the side wall collapsed with a loud creaking groan and landed on the Rover. Raven turned her head and wept. Not for the vehicle. That could be replaced. She mourned for the things that couldn't be replaced. The dreams she had for raising her daughter in that cottage with its gorgeous, calming view. Of spending the rest of her life with Riley there. The things that Kiran had given her that had belonged to her mother. And for some reason, she kept seeing Riley's crystal ball. That beautiful orb with the exquisite copper stand that Riley had been so drawn to. Gone.

* * *

The firemen continued to fight the blaze as Raven and Riley sat huddled together on the tailgate of an ambulance. Raven cradled Indigo in her arms, holding a little oxygen mask over her nose and mouth as she slept. Jet curled up in Riley's lap, resting after having her dose of oxygen. Every time there was a creaking groan and more of the building collapsed, Raven cringed. She couldn't look back at her little cottage again, at the flames hungrily devouring her home. That her sanctuary was being eaten alive by one of the very elements worshipped in Wicca made her sick.

She caught sight of Kiran racing up the road with Simone at his side, their hands clasped together. The lights of the emergency vehicles lit them up in flashes of white, blue, and red. Kiran's beautiful blue eyes scanned wildly, his face set in a grim, tight grimace. Raven's breath hitched, her shoulders heaved. She tried to keep it together, but the sight of Kiran made it impossible. His eyes found her and he let out a cry of his own, a pained primal howl that sounded more animal than human.

He dropped Simone's hand and rushed to Raven. Despite

the tension in his body, he gently wrapped an arm around Raven's shoulders and cupped Riley's head with his hand. He pressed his cheek to Raven's hair when she collapsed into him. "Is everyone okay?"

Raven couldn't answer. She couldn't stop the heaving of her chest, the gasping, hiccuping breaths, the tears flowing from her eyes.

"We're alright," Riley answered. "Minor smoke inhalation and Raven has some burns on her back."

Kiran stiffened, and Raven managed a croaked, "I'm okay."

"You'll stay at the house, for now, aye?"

"We've got my apartment," Riley said.

"Riley, love." His hand brushed over her hair before cupping her cheek. "I understand why you don't want to stay at our place, but it's the safest place for the lot of you. You're family. I need to make sure you're all safe."

"He's right," Raven rasped. "And if Jenny so much as looks at you wrong, she'll have me to deal with."

Riley covered Kiran's hand with her own and closed her eyes, forcing a fat tear to slide down her cheek, leaving a trail through the grimy soot. "Okay."

Simone squeezed in, pressing a kiss to Raven's cheek. "I'm so happy you're all okay." She leaned over and gently kissed Indigo, then bussed Riley's cheek."

"Who called you?" Raven asked. She should have called Kiran herself, but she hadn't even thought of it. She could have saved him and Simone a lot of angst.

"Grayson," Kiran answered. "He told us you were okay, but I had to see for myself, aye?"

"I'll take a look at all of you when we get back to the house," Simone said.

Raven nodded, but Simone checking them out wasn't necessary. As soon as they got away from this crowd, she'd heal all of them, starting with Indi's raspy little lungs and then Jet's.

LaCroix approached, giving Kiran a slight nod before addressing Raven. "No body in the lake, but there's footprints in the sand leading into the woods. I had the K-9 officer follow the trail, but they lost the scent about half a kilometre down the road."

"Had a car waiting," Raven said. They would have been gone before the first emergency vehicle arrived.

LaCroix nodded and patted Raven's shoulder.

* * *

When they walked into the house, Raven was surprised to find nearly the whole household up and waiting for them in the great room. Some wore pyjamas or bathrobes, and some had thrown on comfy clothes.

When she spotted Riley, Jenny jerked to her feet. "I told you. She nearly got you killed."

"That's enough." Kiran stepped in front of Riley, his ice-blue eyes like daggers. "I'm trying to be a gracious host, but you're staying in Raven's house, in my home, campaigning against my daughter and hurting your own. You may not consider Riley family, but I do, and I'll not have her or my daughter disrespected in my own home. They've been through enough tonight without having to deal with your bullshit."

Jenny's face flushed bright red, her nostrils flared, her eyes like a spooked horse's. Rebecca stood and placed her hand gently on Jenny's forearm. Jenny tugged her arm away, glaring around the room as everyone stared at her. "I've only tried to help you, Riley. But, if you don't want that help, fine. You're on your own."

"I always have been," Riley said quietly as Jenny stomped by.

Jenny stopped in her tracks and whirled around. "You had my brother and his wife," she spat.

"They passed away when I was fourteen. You didn't come to the funerals. You didn't contact me."

"You were safe."

That was true. Riley went into the foster care system and the family who took her in was kind and supportive. They didn't love her, but they took care of her until she turned eighteen. "No thanks to you."

Jenny stormed up the stairs with Rebecca close on her heels.

Riley took a deep breath, hugging Jet to her chest, and leaned into Raven.

"I'm sorry," Raven whispered.

"Not your fault."

"I'll apologize, too," Rauri said, crossing the room to embrace Riley. "If I'd known she was going to behave like this, I wouldn't have brought her. I'm sorry, love." She scratched Jet behind the ears. Jet attempted to purr and ended up hacking.

"Not your fault, either."

Rauri leaned back and smiled. "I hope you listened to Kiran. You're family, Riley Gallagher. You're not alone anymore." She kissed Riley's cheek then held her arms out for Indigo.

"Would you give us a few moments, first?" Raven asked. "I need to do a healing."

"Aye, love. You go ahead."

The front door opened behind them. Raven turned to see Mick and Jaxon coming in with their arms full - formula, diapers, bottles, and several bags. Where they'd gotten them in the middle of the night, she had no idea. "Where-"

Mick cut her off with a grin. "People have been showing up at the detachment for the past hour, dropping off donations."

Raven just stared at them open-mouthed. News travelled

fast in their small town, but in the middle of the night?

"There's more in the car," Mick continued. "Toiletries and some clothes for you and Riley."

Tears burned her eyes. Dear Goddess, don't let her cry again. "I don't know what to say."

"There's no need to say anything, love," Rauri smiled. "You go, heal your family and get cleaned up. We'll get a bottle ready for Indigo." She waved Raven and Riley off.

Raven took Riley, Indi, and Jet into the office and closed the door. "Can you believe that?"

"Not all people are self-serving bitches." Riley blushed at Raven's wide-eyed glance. "Sorry, I just don't get Jenny Gallagher."

"No, neither do I. But, you've got us, Ri. You don't need her."

"I know," Riley forced a smile. "I love you, and your father and grandmother are the sweetest for including me in their family."

"They love you, too." Raven sat in the chair in the corner that Ena used to curl up in to read a book by the fire. She supported Indigo in her lap and, since she was sleeping peacefully, she conjured her ball of golden light and healed Jet's rasping lungs first. She was immediately more energetic and jumped down from Riley's lap to explore the office.

Raven started the ball of healing energy towards Riley and Riley held up her hands. "Indi first. Please." There were tears in Riley's eyes, so Raven nodded and directed the light towards the sleeping babe in her arms.

Indi's eyes flickered open. She offered a one-toothed grin to her mother as the golden light surrounded her, then Indi conjured her bright white ball of energy. She sent it sailing to Raven, immersing her in energy so pure, so lovely, it was … blissful. Raven gasped, shuddered. Every muscle in her body relaxed and she experienced a sense of calm that she'd never encountered before. Her breathing eased and the rawness in her throat disappeared. "Holy crap, kiddo." She leaned back in the chair, wondering at her daughter's power at such a young age.

"That was … beautiful." Riley sighed, her eyes pooling. "What I wouldn't give for the ability to heal like that."

"Come here." Raven patted the seat next to her and Riley curled up at her side while Indi snuggled into her chest. "Let me heal your lungs."

"I'm fine until morning."

There was no way Raven was going to leave Riley rasping until morning. She lifted her palm and the room brightened. Golden energy swirled until it formed a beautiful, glowing orb. Raven sent it washing over Riley. Riley's body tensed then relaxed with a whoosh of air leaving her lungs. She shuddered, then leaned up and closed her mouth over Raven's. Raven's shudder matched Riley's but for entirely different reasons. She deepened the kiss, ignoring the thump on the chair until Riley started laughing with their mouths still fused. She opened one eye to see Jet staring back at her, perched on Riley's thigh. She snorted, staring back at Jet. "Thank you," she said and meant it from the bottom of her heart. "For saving our lives."

Jet meowed, threw her back leg up in the air and began washing it.

"I think she's still trying to tell us something," Riley said. "We all stink like smoke."

Chapter 12

Sleeping bags on the floor of Indigo's room wasn't Raven's idea of comfort, but at least they had a place to sleep where they felt safe. She'd spent the past year in therapy working on feeling safe and, in one night, two bastards had undone much of that work. She was scared shitless for Indigo. She tossed and turned, images of not being able to get to Indi's room through the wall of flames repeating over and over again in her mind. She didn't just have Jet to thank for their lives. She had Riley.

The other thing she kept rolling around in her head over the past year was if she hadn't suppressed her powers, she may have been able to save Ena. If she had just made up with her mother, she'd still be alive today. With the early morning light shining in the room, she couldn't help thinking what would have happened if Riley hadn't come back to her; if Riley hadn't been with them last night. If Riley hadn't suggested they take Indi to bed with them. So much of life and death seemed to balance on chance. Or was it fate? Was everything happening the way it was supposed to? If Adara hadn't put a spell on her that forced her to sleep with Jaxon, she wouldn't even have Indigo.

She huffed out a breath as she stared up at the ceiling. She should just be grateful that she had Indi and Riley and Jet.

She could build a new house and start a new life together with Riley. A home that would be theirs, not hers. A new beginning rising out of the ashes, literally.

Indi stirred in her crib and Raven gently slid out of the sleeping bag, careful not to wake Riley. She picked up her baby and hugged her to her chest. "Good morning, sunshine. I love you so much," she whispered. Indigo curled up and burrowed into Raven, sending Raven's heart soaring. "Let's get you changed, little angel."

She changed Indi's diaper then dressed in faded blue jeans that were a little loose and a tad short and a black tank top that someone had donated. She didn't even have underwear. Or shoes. And she hated shopping with a passion.

In the kitchen, she put a pot on to boil to heat up a bottle. Someone had prepared several bottles and left them in the fridge. Bless them. Once the bottle was warm, she carried Indigo into the great room to sit by the window and feed her. She came to a halt just inside the room when she spotted Jenny staring out over the cliffs to the lake beyond. "Sorry," she said and began to back out of the room.

"No, please. Come in."

It was the first time Jenny had been halfway polite to her. And the first time she'd seen her without Rebecca hovering over her shoulder. She shrugged, took a seat by the window next to Jenny, and settled Indi into the crook of her arm. Indi grabbed hold of the bottle and shoved it into her mouth. "Hungry, are we?" Raven asked with a laugh.

"She's lovely," Jenny said and had Raven lifting an eyebrow at her. "I suppose I owe you an apology."

Raven said nothing, wondering when the other shoe was going to drop. Jet padded in and hopped up on the window sill, sitting to watch over Indigo.

Jenny tugged on the tissue in her lap. It was then that Raven realized her eyes were red-rimmed and puffy.

"She hates me. Riley."

"Maybe you just need to have a conversation with her instead of dictating to her."

Jenny's gaze drifted back to the window and Raven rolled her eyes. "Do you even want a relationship with your daughter?"

Silence ensued and then Raven was surprised when Jenny answered. "I thought not," she said in a quiet voice as if she was speaking only to herself. "I thought seeing her would just be a reminder of that night. But, I don't see any of him in her at all."

"There isn't any of him in her. She has the most beautiful soul."

Jenny's gaze flicked back to Raven and her head cocked to the side. "They tell me you arrested him. Last year. Was that for rape?"

"Attempted murder of a police officer."

"You?"

"Yes. And another officer I was working with."

"Will you tell me, has he been charged with what he did to you?"

"Yes." She'd given her statement several days ago. The charges should have been filed against him by now.

"At the time that he hurt you?"

Busted. Now Raven really felt like a hypocrite. "No. He threatened to kill my mother if I said anything, so I was scared to death to tell anyone."

"Yet, you hold it against me that I didn't report what he did to me at the time."

"If it makes you feel any better, I blame myself for everyone he hurt after me."

Jenny sat silently for a moment. "It doesn't."

"No, I guess not."

"It was hard for me to come back here. I've had a difficult

life since I lived here, since that night. It was Rebecca who convinced me to come. She said if I thought Riley was in danger, I should warn her. She's not very happy with me for how I've gone about it and, to tell you the truth, I'm ashamed of myself. I didn't want Riley to have a difficult life, too. I thought that meant getting her away from you. Perhaps, I was wrong."

"You would have made it more difficult if she'd given up on our relationship because it was what you wanted. You can't dictate how she lives her life and not expect her to resent you."

"She's much stronger than I ever was."

There was a creak in the floorboards above them. Jenny looked up at the ceiling then rose from her chair. "Thank you for chatting with me. You didn't have to show me that kindness after the way I've treated you. Blessed be."

"Blessed be," Raven repeated as she watched Jenny walk away. Whatever Rebecca had said to her must have really hit home. Jenny Gallagher was like a completely different person this morning.

She feathered her fingers through Indi's thick, inky hair and watched her drain her bottle. Indi pulled it from her mouth, staring up into her mother's eyes. Raven wondered what she was thinking. The expression on her little face was serene, content. The trauma of the night before nowhere to be seen on that angelic little face. Thank the Goddess. "I'm sorry for what I put you through last night, angel mine," she whispered. "It's not going to be an easy life for either of us, is it? I'll do my best to keep you safe. I promise."

Indi babbled something back as if they were having a conversation, and Raven smiled. "I know. You'll keep me safe, too. Thank you." She brushed her knuckles over Indi's chubby cheek.

"Morning." Riley crossed the room and leaned over the

back of Raven's chair, brushing her lips up the back of her neck.

Raven shivered. "Morning." She wondered if the reason Jenny got up and left was that it was Riley stirring upstairs.

"I missed waking up next to you."

Raven craned her neck and caught Riley's lips with her own. She kissed her slowly, a greeting, a welcoming. "I didn't want to disturb you. You were sleeping so peacefully."

"And you didn't sleep a wink, did you?"

"Sorry, did I disturb your sleep?"

"No, I was down for the count. It's the dark circles under your eyes that gave you away." She rounded the chair and rested a hip on the armrest, sliding her arm around Raven's shoulders. "Good morning, Indi."

Indi grinned and babbled something that sounded very serious and important.

"Is that so?" Riley laughed. "Do you ever read her? I'd love to know what she's trying to say."

Raven shook her head. She'd promised herself never to invade her daughter's privacy in that way. "No. Everyone's entitled to their own private thoughts."

"So, what? You never use your psychic ability?"

"I'll use it if I have to." She reached for Riley's hand and gazed into her eyes. "I had a chat with Jenny this morning."

Riley stiffened and started to rise, but Raven tugged her back down again. "I think Rebecca may have convinced her of the error of her ways. She may be ready for a civilized conversation."

"Yeah, well, we'll see about that."

She couldn't blame Riley for being wary, knowing she was protecting herself from further hurt. "Whether you decide to talk to her or not, I'm here for you."

Riley leaned in and touched her brow to Raven's. "Have I told you yet today how much I love you?"

"If you have, I'm not opposed to hearing it again. And again." They both laughed and Indi joined in, clapping her hands as if she was cheering them on.

* * *

An unencumbered view of the lake from the roadway accentuated the gaping hole in the landscape where Raven's cottage should have been. The trees were scorched black and all that remained of her beloved home was a pile of ashes and soot. Her Range Rover sat crushed and burned to a grey skeleton of its former self in the driveway.

A man in a white shirt, navy slacks, and high black rubber boots crouched at the edge of the debris. His cropped chestnut brown hair waved in the breeze as he examined some piece of evidence that would tell him the story of how the fire started and spread.

Raven stood sandwiched between Riley and Kiran, wearing a pair of crocks that had belonged to Ena. Mick had run Riley home to pack a bag and pick up her extra set of keys, so at least she had clothes and shoes that fit. Raven was getting annoyed with having to hike up her jeans every few minutes.

She wanted to sift through the debris, see if there was anything salvageable, although it was doubtful. All she could think about was a list of the things that were lost. Indi's favourite blanket, the one she liked to grip in her fist and hold against her upper lip as she drifted off to sleep; Riley's beautiful crystal ball; her Book of Shadows. She'd made the first entry when she was five years old and was learning how to print and spell. Twenty-three years worth of spells and rituals that were personal and yet so connected with Ena that it was like losing another piece of her mother. Her chest ached, her eyes burned, and she told herself there must be residual smoke in the air.

The fire inspector rose from his crouched position and

waved them over. Raven jerked forward.

"Easy, love. Those shoes probably aren't very suitable for this." Kiran gently wrapped his hand around Raven's elbow.

She glanced down at the stupid crocks. They were the only shoes of Ena's that fit. Suitable or not, they were all she had.

"Thanks for coming out, DC Bowen. Inspector Nick Stokes." He extended his hand, held hers firmly then continued to Kiran and Riley. "I just have a couple of questions for you." He gestured to the woods on the far side of what used to be Raven's cottage. "If you don't mind, we could start over there."

Why he had questions that needed to be answered in the woods seemed a bit weird, but Raven knew evidence could be scattered and thought of her barbecue exploding. Goddess knew where it had ended up. They followed him like a row of ducks into the tree line and continued on for about twenty feet. He came to a stop and pointed ahead of him. "Those belong to you?"

Raven peered over his shoulder at six plastic, red gas canisters with bright yellow nozzles. "No. I should call out a forensics team. We need to fingerprint them."

Stokes raised an eyebrow at her. "I'll take care of that."

"Right." Not her investigation. *Crap.* She took a step back and shoved her hands in her pockets. Careless of them to leave these behind, but they'd left in a hell of a hurry. "Isn't six gallons a little overkill?"

"They doused the house. Every inch of it, except your bedroom."

Son of a bitch. "They wanted to flush us out the bedroom door. One of them was waiting there when we came out." Had they known Indi was in bed with them? Or were they not concerned if Indi lived or died? Raven's belly clenched and roiled. She glanced over at the bushes to her left, praying that she wasn't going to have to use them to empty the limited contents of her stomach.

Stokes led them back out of the woods and started down the lawn towards the water. He stopped halfway down the slope and waited for everyone to gather around. "How about this? This yours?"

He pointed to a spot in the grass and Raven crouched down for a closer look. Glinting up at her was a silver disc attached to a silver serpentine chain, the clasp broken. She leaned in closer. A compass with a centre circle and eight triangular spokes joining it to an outer ring. A fleur-de-lis graced the upper spoke, an S on the bottom, W on the left, and E on the right. Numbers had been engraved around the outer ring - zero to nine and then back down to zero, repeating itself twice in the circumference of the circle with the zeros positioned at North and South, the nines at East and West. The top of the disc, near the fleur-de-lis, appeared to be scorched. A result of her zapping one of their attackers or a result of the fire? She couldn't be sure.

What she was sure of was this medallion held power. She could feel the energy emitting from it as if it had been electrically charged.

"A traveller's protection," Kiran said.

He would know, Raven thought. Being a sailor and all. Without taking her eyes off the medallion, she said, "Not mine. There may be DNA on this."

Stokes smiled tightly. "I'll take care of it. I'll be in touch to let you know when we've cleared the scene."

Raven's eyes fell on the pile of ash and debris. "Do you think there will be anything we can salvage?"

His lips pressed together and he tilted his head. "I'm sorry. It's a total loss."

Stokes headed back up the slope as Raven turned to Riley. "I need your phone." She extended wiggling fingers. Riley pulled her phone from her pocket and held it out. Raven snatched it up and bent over the medallion, snapping a picture before Stokes could catch her.

"Do you feel it?" Raven asked Kiran.

"Oh, aye. It holds powerful energy."

"I'll talk to Grayson. We need to make sure it's well protected."

* * *

They stopped in at the local Walmart before going back to Kiran's. Nothing like one-stop shopping. Raven quickly filled a cart, despite Riley nagging at her to try everything on. Why, Raven wondered, when you could just bring them back if they didn't fit?

She dumped all the bags in Kiran's kitchen and took Riley out to the vendor's area and straight to Jade Storm's tent.

"Morning," Jade said with a cocky grin, her eyes taking a long journey up and down the length of Raven's body.

Raven couldn't imagine she was much to look at. She hiked up the loose jeans and glanced down at the butt ugly crocs on her feet. Maybe that's why Jade had the cocky grin. "Hey." Raven leaned over the display table at the front of the tent and began searching every piece of jewelry.

"Looking for something in particular?" Jade asked.

"Yep." Most of Jade's pieces were crystals entwined in silver, gold, or copper wire, gemstones set in silver or gold. Natural shapes turned into works of art. There were no silver pendants and no compasses that she could see, but she had to check.

"These are beautiful," Riley said. "You're very talented."

"Thank you. You might consider one of my amber pieces. They're a powerful source of protection."

Raven raised a brow. "And you think she needs protection, Jade?"

"Doesn't she?" She smiled demurely then turned serious. "I heard about your cottage burning down. I'm terribly sorry.

I can't imagine how horrible that must be."

Raven stared into Jade's green eyes, searching for … something. A hint that she knew about the fire first hand. A touch of guilt. Remorse. Anything. All she got was a bit of empathy. Whether it was genuine or not was another matter. "Good news travels fast."

"Bad faster." Jade shrugged. "It's all anyone's talking about this morning. Was it an electrical problem?"

"No," Raven answered, giving no more of an explanation. "You want to explain to me how you knew where I lived, Jade?"

The colour in Jade's cheeks flushed. "I may have followed you home the other day."

"Why?"

Jade huffed out a laugh, her eyes turning to Riley. "Is she serious?"

Riley just stared her down.

"You really have no idea how attractive you are, do you?" she said to Raven. "And I'm not just talking about your looks. Dear Goddess, you've got this … I don't know. Like a mystical magnetism. Your presence alone has every head turning to take you in." She turned back to Riley. "You know what I'm talking about."

"Careful," Riley warned, her eyes narrowed. "You're walking a fine line here."

Jade waved her hand from high to low. "Like you've got anything to worry about. If you think she'd stray on you, you're very wrong."

Raven's pulse sped up. She had strayed on Riley. Only because of a spell Adara conjured, but she'd strayed and the guilt stayed with her. She'd hurt Riley and very nearly destroyed their relationship. Having Jade remind her wasn't pleasant. She took Riley's hand in hers. "Nice chat," she said and turned away.

She led Riley up and down the vendors' area, checking every stall for pendants resembling the compass. There were pentacle pendants of every description, hundreds of crystals dangling from chains, but nothing resembling the rough yet elegant design of the compass. When she'd exhausted the search, she went back to the stall where they'd purchased Riley's crystal ball.

"Hello," Raven said.

In her dark hair, the woman wore a circlet of flowers - bits of lavender and bright gerbera daisies weaved together. She turned at Raven's voice and smiled. "Hello, again. I didn't realize who you were when you were here before. Please accept my apologies, Raven of the Solstice Coven. I'm Mara, priestess of the Glowing Moon Coven in Salem, Massachusetts."

"Salem?" Raven raised a brow. "That must be an interesting place to live, given its history."

"Yes, well, thankfully, they stopped burning us at the stake years ago." A slow smile spread across her face before she broke out in a musical laugh. "Sorry, I shouldn't make light of it."

"Not at all." Those days weren't something to laugh about, but humour had a way of helping people deal with the unimaginable. Maybe one day, Raven would be able to laugh about her cottage. "I was wondering if you had any more crystal balls like the one we bought the other day."

Mara's brow wrinkled, her eyes drooped. "No, I'm sorry. It was one of a kind. I'd be happy to give you the artist's contact information though." She reached out a hand and gently clasped Raven's wrist. "It was lost in the fire?"

Jade had been right about lousy news travelling fast. Raven nodded.

"I'm so sorry." Mara circled her other hand around Riley's wrist. "You had such a connection to it like it was made for you. It gave me great joy to see it go to you." She turned and picked up one of her business cards then pulled a pen from her pocket and wrote a name and number on the back. "Celeste Bishop. I'm sure she'd do a custom piece for you, especially once she hears what happened to the original."

"Bishop?"

Mara smiled. "You know your history. Yes, she's a descendant of Bridget Bishop and High Priestess of the Glowing Moon Coven."

Every witch had heard of Bridget Bishop, the first witch to be executed for witchcraft during the Salem Witch Trials. "Thank you, Mara." Raven held the card between her first and second fingers and waved it. "I'll give her a call." She wondered who Mara's ancestors were because this woman was a powerful hereditary witch in her own right. As they walked away, she studied the card - Mara Proctor. The surname was familiar. She couldn't place it precisely, but she was sure it was a prominent name in witch history. She glanced over her shoulder. Mara met her eyes, a knowing smile on her face.

Chapter 13

Between the things Jade said about her mystical magnetism and what Mara said about not realizing who she was, Raven was feeling a little uneasy. She knew people talked about the Bowen-Hayes offspring as if she were some kind of Wicca royalty, but she didn't feel like it. If she'd been asked to describe herself, she probably would have started with, *I'm a cop*. As if that would explain who she was.

Since Ena's passing, she'd reconnected with her Wiccan roots, but at her core, she still felt like a cop first and foremost. Maybe that was just habit. She'd changed over the past year, dedicating herself more to the craft and to the coven.

When they got back to the house, she dropped into one of the deck chairs and buried her face in her hands, thinking about the loss of her Book of Shadows. It wasn't something you could just replace. It was years of training, learning, trying different things to come up with her own unique spells and rituals. Losing it was like losing a part of herself. Out of everything she'd lost in the fire, her Book of Shadows hurt the most. It wasn't just her own soul, her own spirit that was woven into that book. It was Ena's and every Bowen ancestor who had passed knowledge down from daughter to daughter. And now it was just ashes, mixed in amongst the remains of what had been her sanctuary. Her breath hitched and Riley's arm came around her.

"What is it, Rave?"

"Sorry," she hiccupped. "Just feeling sorry for myself, I guess."

"You're entitled." Riley's lips, soft and sweet, brushed over her temple.

Comforted by the simple gesture, Raven fought back against the tears and the quivering of her lower lip, telling herself to get it together. "I define myself as a cop," she said. "But, it's not the loss of my badge or my police ID that I'm grieving. It's the loss of my Book of Shadows."

Riley sighed and leaned her head against Raven's shoulder. "Well, maybe it's time to update your definition."

"Yeah." Raven's voice cracked as she stared out over Fairy Lake. Who the heck is Raven Bowen? Definitely not the same woman she'd been a year ago. Back then, she'd only been the cop. Now she was mother, lover, daughter, witch, and cop. And, if she was honest with herself, she was even beginning to like the person she was now. But, was she the things Jade and Mara seemed to see? She figured maybe the Wiccan community just needed someone to look up to, someone to give them hope. Although, she was pretty sure it was a fictional character they admired.

Riley's head lifted from her shoulder. "It's not just your Book of Shadows that you're grieving, is it? I mean, your home was your happy place."

She sighed, her thoughts turning to her little cottage - scraping to save up enough money for the down payment; spending months fixing it up in her spare time until it was finally habitable and her hands were rough and callused; the peace she felt there with her own private view of the lake. "Yeah, it was." She smiled at Riley. It was nice having someone who knew her so well. Riley had always been that person for her, even when she was closed off. "I guess we'll just have to build a new place. One that's our happy place, not just mine."

"Oh, Rave." Riley leaned her head against Raven's shoulder again. "That sounds beautiful."

She pressed her lips to Riley's soft curls picturing a new sanctuary rising from the ashes. Maybe everything did happen for a reason. Perhaps they were meant to start fresh with a new home meant for the two of them. They could certainly use more room. "Start thinking about what you want in our new home. The sky's the limit."

Riley laughed. "I can't picture you in a place that's over the top."

"No, nothing over the top, but a place where we're comfortable and happy, connected to the nature around us."

"I think you should make all the decisions. It sounds like you have it well in hand."

"That would make it my place. That's not what I want, Ri."

Riley lifted her head and pressed her lips to Raven's in a quick, chaste kiss. "Point taken. I love you, Rave."

She couldn't help the grin that spread over her face. She may have lost her home and everything in it, but she had Riley and Indi, and that was everything. "We should go in. I need to check on Indi and we need to prepare for the Summer Solstice."

Riley pressed a hand to her belly and blew out. "I'm a little nervous. I don't want to screw up and make a fool of myself, or you, the first time I attend a coven gathering."

Raven stood and pulled Riley up into her arms. "It's not like you're going to be judged or anything. There will be so many people there. No one will even notice us."

"Yeah, right."

They entered the house and found Jet sitting on the arm of the couch, her golden eyes focused on Rauri, who was feeding Indi. Raven laughed as she crossed the room to them.

"I'm afraid what she might do if I make a mistake," Rauri said with a glint in her eye.

Raven picked up Jet, hugged her to her chest. Jet rubbed her cheek against Raven's. She rubbed back as Jet purred like a diesel engine. "Thank you for watching over my angel." She petted Jet then set her back on her post.

"How are you faring?" Rauri asked, her eyes dark and severe. "It was a terrible thing that happened last night."

"We're okay. We're alive and well and that's what matters."

"Aye. I'm proud of you, Raven Sage."

The glint was back in those warm eyes and Raven's heart swelled. When was the last time anyone had said they were proud of her? She couldn't remember. "Why?" She wished she could swallow back the question as soon as it was out of her mouth, afraid that the answer would diminish the warm feeling that washed through her at Rauri's words.

"For protecting your family and for knowing what's truly important."

"Thank you." Rauri's answer hadn't been the disappointment she was expecting. She felt ten feet tall and indestructible.

Jenny stepped into the room wearing a long, gauzy dress that matched the pale colour of her green eyes. "Riley, I owe you an apology for my abysmal behaviour. Would you sit down with me for a few minutes to talk?"

Riley glanced at Raven, who nodded with a slight smile.

"I'll be right here if you need me."

"Right. Okay." She took a deep breath and followed Jenny to the office, the door closing gently behind them.

"I'd like a moment with you while they're talking," Rebecca said from the doorway.

Rauri handed Indigo up to Raven. "I'll be off to get ready for the gathering. You two can have your wee chin wag in here." She kissed Raven's cheek and wandered away, humming a cheerful tune.

* * *

Raven took the spot on the couch that Rauri had just vacated and snugged Indigo into the crook of her arm. The bottle was nearly finished, but Indi continued to suckle.

Rebecca sat next to Raven, extending her long legs out in front of her. She wore white Capri pants and a blue and white striped t-shirt, looking very nautical. "I'm not a hereditary witch, but I'm Wiccan through and through. I don't enjoy seeing harm come to anyone. I know that Jenny's behaviour has hurt Riley, and for that, I'd like to apologize."

"No need. It wasn't your doing."

"I convinced Jenny to come here because I thought it may begin her healing. She's never gotten over what happened to her or processed it. She has so many walls up and protections in place. It's hard to get close to her. It's hard to be with her."

"Yet, you're still with her."

"I love her."

"When you first arrived, I thought you were doting. Then I thought you were following orders. I'm still not sure what to make of your relationship."

Rebecca threw her head back and roared. "I could say the same of you and Riley. You're fiercely protective."

"Maybe I need to be."

"Can't say I blame you after last night. I'm sorry for everything you lost. Your father and his family are fiercely protective, as well. You're safe here."

"Why is it that Jenny was so adamant Riley stay away from me?"

"I think you know," Rebecca smiled a cat-like smirk. "If the last few days haven't given you a taste of what life will be like now that everyone knows of your powers, I don't know what will."

Indigo popped the empty bottle from her mouth and Raven lifted her to her shoulder, patting her back softly. Surely everything would return to normal when the festival was over, wouldn't it? "You think people will always be after my powers?"

"Don't you? There are a lot of power-hungry, greedy individuals out there who would do anything to get ahead. You literally have to be very careful of who you let close to you for the rest of your life."

It wasn't as if that was news to Raven. Ena had expressed her concerns through letters she'd written before her death. Raven hadn't taken it all that seriously until people began arriving for the festival.

Indigo burped, then scrunched up her little body and snuggled her face into the curve of Raven's neck. Raven loved it when Indi did this, as if she couldn't get close enough.

"Anyway, what I wanted to say is that I'm sorry for the hurt we've caused and I assure you that it won't happen again."

Again Raven wondered what Rebecca had said to Jenny to cause the one hundred and eighty-degree turn in her behaviour. "So sure?"

"As I said, I don't enjoy seeing people hurting, but to get Jenny to see the error of her ways, I had to do just that." The slight wrinkles at the corners of Rebecca's eyes deepened. "I'm not proud of myself for it, but I'm happy with the result."

She still didn't know what Rebecca had said to Jenny, but she had a good idea. She figured Rebecca had to make Jenny see herself as everyone else was experiencing her and that couldn't have been pretty.

* * *

Raven tried to amuse Indigo with a plush toy while she

waited for Riley to emerge from the office. The house was eerily quiet, considering there were so many people staying in it. But, even in the silence, she couldn't hear the conversation that must be going on in the office. The longer the door remained closed, the more she worried.

Kiran stepped through the door off the deck, his hair sticking up in all directions. He spotted Raven and grinned, reaching his arms out for Indi as he crossed the room. "There's my love." He lifted her from Raven's lap and shot her in the air.

"She just …"

White liquid spurted out of Indi's mouth and down the front of Kiran's shirt.

"Ate," Raven finished.

Kiran laughed and settled Indi on his hip. "One of these days, I'll learn my lesson, aye?"

"I'm not so sure about that." She had to laugh at him. He didn't care about the baby puke on his shirt, only about the little bundle on his hip. And that was one of the reasons she loved him so much. "What have you been up to? Where is everyone?"

"Oh, here and there." He picked the plush toy up and handed it to Indi, who stuffed it in her mouth. "I've postponed the gathering."

"What? Why?"

"Just until seven this evening. There's … things that need to be taken care of."

"What things?"

The door to the office opened and Jenny walked out. She nodded at them and continued on up the stairs, her expression blank. Raven couldn't get a read on her. She stood and reached her arms out for Indi. "I need to go speak to Riley, but I'll find you afterward. I want to know what things need to be taken care of."

"Oh, aye. Of course."

Raven peeked her head into the office. Riley sat reclined in the comfy chair in the corner with her eyes closed. "Hey," Raven said quietly. She crossed the room and settled on the chair at Riley's side.

Riley's eyes opened slowly, as if they were too heavy to lift. "Hey."

"Everything okay?"

"Better, I guess."

Raven threaded her fingers through Riley's and waited, knowing she'd say what she wanted to say when she was ready.

"She apologized for the way she's treated me, but she wanted me to know that coming here, seeing me, is very difficult for her. It reminds her of a horrible time in her life that she doesn't want to relive." Riley sighed and closed her eyes again. "Seeing me reminds her of what he did."

"I'm sorry, Ri. There's none of him in you."

Her eyes opened a fraction and Riley smiled weakly. "Thank you for that."

"It's the truth."

"I may need you to keep reminding me."

"Whatever you need." She squeezed Riley's hand and dropped a kiss on her forehead. "What did you say to her?"

Riley huffed, half-sigh and half-laugh. "I told her that if she continued to use that excuse, that fear, to dictate her life, she'd never heal."

Raven grinned. "I don't suppose she took too kindly to that."

"I don't know. I think it got Jenny thinking. I think she wants to heal, Rave. I think she's tired and fed up with carrying all that around with her."

"And it hurts you to see her hurting." Her nurturing lover couldn't stand to see anyone suffering, even though she put herself through that every day at her job in the emergency room. If someone was hurting, she was compelled to do whatever she could to ease their pain.

"How did you do it?" Jenny asked from just inside the office door with Rebecca standing right behind her. "You live in Solstice. You're staying in the house where he hurt you. How did you get past it?"

Raven had no desire to discuss this with anyone, never mind Jenny Gallagher. But, one look at the pain in Riley's eyes and she couldn't endure it. Maybe she was the one who could begin Jenny's healing process and that would be a gift to Riley. "I can assure you that this house has been thoroughly cleansed and purified of his negative energy. And Kiran completely changed my old room, making it into a peaceful sanctuary for my daughter."

"But, I can't cleanse Solstice."

Raven raised a brow. "Why not? There are enough of us that we could manage it."

Jenny's palm flattened against her chest with a slap. "You would do that? For me? Cleanse an entire town?"

"Sure, why not? We just send people to the four corners of the town, north, south, west, and east and communicate by conference call. We could do it tomorrow morning if you want."

Jenny just nodded, reaching for Rebecca's hand. Riley sat up a little in her chair and Indi extended her arms to her. Riley's eyes popped open and she grinned. Lifting Indi, she pressed a kiss to her brow then settled her on her lap before turning her attention to Jenny. "It's not just about cleansing the area though. For many years, Raven did what you're doing. She suppressed the pain and kept herself very closed off. I know she was just trying to protect herself, but it wasn't healthy. For her or for our relationship. She began seeing a therapist a year ago and the changes in her are phenomenal."

Riley's eyes widened then met Raven's as she whispered, "I'm sorry. That wasn't my story to tell."

"It's fine." Raven weaved her fingers through Riley's again then brought their joined hands to her lips, pressing a kiss to Riley's knuckles. "If it helps her, you can tell her what you want."

Riley's eyes softened as a slow smile spread up from the edges of her mouth.

"You think I need to see a therapist?" Jenny asked.

"Not just a therapist," Raven said. "Someone you're comfortable with. Someone you feel safe with."

"You feel safe with your therapist?"

Raven nodded.

"Do you think she would see me? I don't have a clue how to find someone that I'd be comfortable with."

"I could ask her, but it would be better if you found someone at home. It's not going to be a quick fix and you have to build the trust, build your relationship with the therapist."

Jenny turned to Rebecca and they stared at each other for a moment before Rebecca smiled and nodded.

"If we were to stay here for a few months so that I could get to know my daughter, do you think she'd see me?"

Riley's mouth dropped open. "I thought ..."

"I want to get to know you, Riley. I've spent my life running from you, what I thought you represented, but I'm beginning to believe I was wrong. I hope that you'll give me a chance to try and have patience with me when I screw up."

"Yes." Riley's eyes pooled, a fat tear teetering on her lash. Indigo made a gurgling sound and flapped her arms like she was trying to fly. "Yes, I'd like that very much." She lifted Indi to a standing position in her lap and Indi's legs pistoned up and down. A wet, juicy fart reverberated through the room and Riley extended her arms, handing Indi to her mother.

Raven laughed and lifted Indi carefully into her arms, knowing this was going to be a messy one. She screwed up her nose as the warm, fetid odour breached her nostrils. "Yeah, thanks a lot, Ri."

Chapter 14

It required a bath and a change of clothes to get Indigo cleaned up, but Raven didn't mind. It gave her some much needed alone time with her baby. It felt like she'd only seen her in passing over the past few days and she couldn't wait for life to get back to a regular routine. Except, it wouldn't, she thought. They wouldn't be going back to her little cottage and settling back into her quiet life. There would be so much to do just to get the plot of land cleaned up and ready to rebuild, not to mention insurance companies to deal with. She still hadn't replaced her cell phone and she was going to need a new car sooner rather than later. A list was what she needed. She was going to need a long freaking list.

As she got to the bottom of the stairs, someone blew a short, sharp whistle, startling Indi. She looked down the hall. Seeing no one, she continued on into the kitchen while she soothed Indi. There was a full pot of coffee on the counter, one of the benefits of having a house full of people, she supposed. You didn't have to do everything for yourself. She poured herself a generous cup and was about to sit at the kitchen island when Riley walked in.

"Could you come with me for a moment?"

"Sure. Why?" Raven raised a brow as she sipped her coffee.

Riley grinned and nodded her head towards the great room. "There's something you need to see." She hopped back and forth from foot to foot, her energy nearly visible in its intensity.

Raven narrowed her eyes. "What's going on?"

"Come see!" Riley danced over to her, wrapped an arm around her waist, and led her towards the great room.

As soon as they crossed through, the room erupted in a loud, synced shout. "Happy birthday!"

Indi startled in her arms and began to wail. Raven hugged her closer, but with her coffee in one hand, it was like she was bound. Bound and cornered. Her heart raced as heat bloomed up from her chest and exploded over her face. People surged toward her and, although they were familiar faces, her breath caught in her throat. She couldn't breathe. Her pulse pounded in her ears and she took a step back, only to bump into the wall. Cornered. Nowhere to go. Her eyes darted around, searching for an escape as more people crowded in.

"Happy birthday, darling," Kiran said. He kissed her cheek and reached for Indi. Raven turned, placing her body between Indi and Kiran, protecting her baby.

"Okay, everyone back up. Give Raven a minute." Riley pushed between the bodies lining up to greet Raven. "It's a bit overwhelming. Please, everyone, just take a seat."

Kiran's fingers brushed Raven's cheek and she met his gaze. "I'm sorry, love. I didn't think this through. I should have considered a surprise may be a bit startling."

Her face was on fire. She'd reacted like a spooked horse, making a complete fool of herself in front of Kiran's family. She sucked in a deep breath and leaned back into the wall. "It's okay. It's just I didn't … I've never …"

"You've never had a surprise party?" Kiran asked.

She hadn't celebrated her birthday since she was fifteen and, even then, it was usually just a quiet celebration with

Ena. She shook her head. "No."

"We were going to wait until tonight, but I thought with everything that happened last night, sooner was better. I should have told you and not sprung this on you."

"It's okay. I'm fine now. It just caught me off guard." Indi continued to cry into her shoulder, her little body curled into a ball. "Caught us both off guard."

"Aye, poor wee lass." He reached his arms out to Indi again. "May I?"

Raven nodded and let her father take the baby from her arms. Kiran hugged Indi to his chest. "There, there, love." He rubbed her back and brushed his lips over her temple until her wailing became stuttered breaths. "That's better, aye?" He took Raven's hand in his. "Come. We've some presents for you."

"Presents." Dear Goddess, the last thing she wanted to do was sit there in front of everyone and open presents. "You shouldn't have done that."

"We missed your first twenty-seven birthdays, love. You can't deny us this one." His ice-blue eyes twinkled, his dimples deepening with his smile. He led her to a chair decorated in purple and white balloons and streamers. Raven sat with everyone in the room staring at her.

Riley perched herself on the arm of the chair and slid her arm around Raven's shoulders. "Try not to look so terrified," she whispered.

"Why not? I am."

Kelly, Jasmine's fourteen-year-old daughter, approached with a flowery gift bag. "This is from my parents and me." She held the bag out to Raven. "Happy birthday, cousin."

"Thanks." Raven took the bag because she didn't have any other choice. It was either that or look like an ungrateful idiot. She'd never opened presents with a crowd of people watching her. It was more than a little uncomfortable. She pulled the purple and orange tissue paper out and peeked inside the bag. Great. There was a royal blue box inside. She pulled it out and set it on her lap, placing the gift bag on the floor next to her. Kelly stood at her side, waiting patiently. Raven flipped open the lid and set on a velvet background were two silver broaches in an intricate Celtic knot with amethysts at their centres.

"This one's yours," Kelly explained, pointing to the broach on the left, although they were identical. "And this one is Indigo's. It's a Hayes clan tradition when we have new additions to the family. Only we didn't know about you until last year, so yours is a little late." She shrugged and her cheeks flushed. "We've all got one. It's a symbol of our unity and love, and it provides powerful protection to the wearer."

"They're beautiful. Thank you." She leaned over and kissed Kelly's cheek, causing her to blush a deep red.

"You're welcome." She rushed to her mother's side, grinning.

"Thanks, Jasmine. Michael."

"Our pleasure, Raven," Jasmine said.

For the next twenty minutes, Raven opened present after present. It seemed like it would never end. Many gifts were Wicca or witchcraft-related and would come in handy since all of her supplies went up in smoke. When she'd opened the last present, she leaned back in her chair and exhaled in relief.

"There's one more, love," Kiran said. "Only it's not really a present as it belongs to you." He'd already given her a new Book of Shadows. It saddened her that she was going to have to start it over, but there was nothing she could do about it.

Kiran walked over to a cabinet sand opened it. He crouched down and lifted out a massive, leather-bound book and brought it over to the coffee table, setting it down in front of Raven. "This is the Bowen Family Grimoire. In it are all of the spells, rites, and potions of the Bowen women going back nearly two hundred years or so. Ena's entries are in these pages." His eyes met Raven's. "As are yours."

A faint memory surfaced - Ena standing next to her as she wrote in this book. Raven rebelled against witchcraft and Wicca in her early teens. But Ena continued to train her, coming to her in dreams. Leaning forward, Raven ran her hand over the surface of the worn leather cover. A beautiful energy seeped into her and the memories came flooding back. Every spell and ritual she'd fine-tuned or created, every spell she'd written in her own Book of Shadows, had been repeated in this book to preserve it for the generations of Bowens to come. All was not lost. She could recreate her Book of Shadows using the Bowen Grimoire. Her teary eyes floated up from the book in front of her to her father's smiling eyes. "Dad." Her voice cracked.

"Aye, it's all there, love."

She rose and fell into his arms. Goddess, she loved this man with his tremendous heart. "Thank you." There were no words to express just how grateful she was.

"The book was always yours. I just hadn't been ready to give it up yet."

Because it held a piece of Ena that he wasn't ready to let go. He'd grieved quietly over the past year, but profoundly. Her arms tightened around him. "I love you. So much." When she pulled back to kiss him, there were tears in his eyes.

"You forgive me for terrifying you with the surprise party then?"

Raven laughed. "You're forgiven. Just don't let it happen again. I don't celebrate my birthday."

* * *

Indigo babbled to Jet in her crib while Raven searched through the bags of clothes that had been donated for an outfit suitable to wear to the Summer Solstice celebration.

Frustrated, she tossed the bags back into the closet, turning in time to see Indi lean forward so that her face was right in Jet's.

Indi scrunched up her nose and sniffed in and out. When a gust of air hit Jet's face, she jumped straight up in the air with a loud meow. Indi fell back in a full out belly laugh as Jet settled back down and started licking her paw as if nothing happened. Raven went over and sat Indi back up again, laughing herself as her daughter continued to snicker. "Little monkey. You're lucky that cat loves you so much." She tickled Indi's belly.

"Come in," she called at the soft knock on the door.

Simone stepped in and closed the door behind her. "Hi. I just wanted to apologize for the surprise party. We didn't think that it might traumatize you."

Had her reaction been that bad? "No, it's fine. I don't know why I freaked out."

Simone raised her brows with a slight smile. "Don't you? I can guess."

Yeah, she so didn't want to go there.

"Do you really not celebrate your birthday, Rave?"

Raven shrugged. "No, not for a long time."

"Why? Do you mind me asking?"

Raven shrugged again and set a toy in front of Indi. "It was just always something I celebrated with Ena. When I turned sixteen, I was still pretty raw and hurt that Ena hadn't come for me, so I told Adara that I wasn't interested in celebrating my birthday and she respected my wishes."

"Mmm." Simone's eyes narrowed, but she said no more on the matter. She pointed to Raven's legs. "Kiran and Rauri are on their way up to see you."

Raven looked down at herself. She was wearing a tank top and panties. "Thanks for the warning." She grabbed the jeans she'd taken off from the back of the rocking chair and slid them on just in time for another knock on the door. She pulled it open to allow Kiran and Rauri to come in. "Hey."

"Hello, love," Kiran and Rauri said in unison.

Kiran handed her a black silk robe, neatly folded. "Your mother wanted you to have her robe because she hoped you'd become the new High Priestess, but she had more than one robe, aye?"

Raven clutched it to her breast. "Oh, wow." It was another one of her treasures that she'd thought was lost. "Thank you. I was just trying to figure out what the heck I was going to wear."

"You're welcome."

"And this one is for Indigo," Rauri said, handing another black silk robe to Raven. This one was tiny and instead of *HPS* embroidered in gold and purple, it said *High Princess*.

She wasn't originally going to bring Indigo to the celebration, but the fire the night before had convinced her it was safer. She couldn't bear to leave her behind. "It's gorgeous. And hilarious. Thank you."

"Your Gran made it herself," Kiran said.

Raven hugged Rauri. "And that makes it even more special. Thank you."

"Aw, you're welcome, love."

* * *

Simone and Kiran had prepared the clearing in the woods, sacred ground to the Solstice Coven. Kiran built the bonfire at dawn then went back throughout the day to add more wood. Caleb had been given the responsibility of supervising the fire and, at seventeen, he'd been remarkably diligent. The altar was set with the usual tools and Simone had added a cauldron of bright summer flowers. Baskets of lavender, St. John's wort, vervain, and other fresh herbs were set near the altar for people to throw into the fire with their deepest wishes. Summer Solstice, the longest day of the year, was a time to honour the sun as the source of light. A time for Wiccans to celebrate the fullness of life, raise their energy, regenerate abundance, and manifest their dreams.

There had to be close to three hundred people standing shoulder to shoulder in a huge circle. Simone, as acting High Priestess of the Solstice Coven, cast the circle, much larger than their usual gatherings required, before the arrival of the witches. Those who gathered entered through the northeast portal, which was closed once everyone arrived. She assigned watchers at each of the four quarters to guard the sacred area against the intrusion of any negative forces.

Now Kiran stood in front of the altar with Simone on his left and Raven on his right. Simone was acting High Priestess until Raven was ready to take over, but Kiran asked her to be with him and Simone during this ritual. She held Indigo in her arms because she was too scared to leave her in anyone else's care.

"Welcome, sisters and brothers." Kiran held out his arms. "Before we begin, I've a few words. Firstly, I'd like to introduce our acting High Priestess, Rose Meadowsong," he said, giving Simone's magical name. Simone stepped forward and bowed slightly before stepping back. "And our future High Priestess, my daughter, Raven Sage."

Raven stepped forward and followed Simone's lead, bowing slightly and stepping back. She hadn't know Kiran was going to introduce them, but she supposed everyone probably knew who she was by now, if only from seeing her standing next to Kiran who looked identical to her except for their gender and age.

"Last year, we lost our High Priestess, my wife, Ena Bowen. It was Ena who wanted to hold the Pagan Festival here on her land. Every year she traveled to the council to plead her case. It took sixteen years before she would be granted that right. It's highly unusual for a coven to reveal their sacred space much less invite other covens to that place in celebration. But, this was Ena's dream. She yearned for her brothers and sisters from around the globe to join her here. I believe she's with us now, seeing her dream come to fruition. Blessed be."

"Blessed be," came hundreds of voices.

Raven found herself wishing her mother would appear, as she'd done over a year ago when Adara had made a play to take over the coven and place a love spell on Kiran. But, she'd crossed over to the other plane that night, her earthbound business completed. Raven missed her fiercely, especially at moments like this.

Kiran took Indi from Raven's arms and Raven stepped forward, drawing an athame from her belt and facing east. "All hail the element of air, watchtower of the east. May it stand in strength, ever watching over our circle." She traced the shape of the pentagram into the air with the athame and turned to the south, repeating her words and actions with the elements of fire, water, and earth. "All hail the four quarters and all hail the Goddess. We bid the lady welcome and invite that she join us in witness of these rights we hold in her honour."

Raven returned her athame to its sheath, stepped back, and took Indi from Kiran. He moved behind the altar as Simone stepped forward and addressed the circle. "Great One of Heaven, Power of the Sun, we invoke thee in thy ancient names - Michael, Balin, Arthur, Lugh, Herne; come again as of old into this thy land. Lift up thy shining spear of light to protect us. Put to flight the powers of darkness. Give us fair woodlands and green fields, blooming orchards and ripening corn. Bring us to stand upon thy hill of vision and show us the lovely realms of the Gods."

She turned her back on the crowd, facing Kiran, and, drawing out her wand, traced the shape of the pentagram against him. Kiran stepped around the altar and speared his wand into the cauldron of flowers then turned to face the gathering, holding the wand high. "The spear to the Cauldron, the lance to the Grail, Spirit to flesh, man to woman, Sun to Earth." He saluted Simone with his wand then he and Raven joined the circle.

Simone picked up a sprinkler from the altar then addressed the gathering. "Dance ye about the cauldron of Cerridwen, the Goddess, and be ye blessed with the touch of this consecrated water."

Kiran led the circle as they began to move like a huge wheel. As each person passed by the cauldron, Simone sprinkled the consecrated water on them. As Raven passed, she smiled and the sprinkle of water startled Indi. She jerked in Raven's arms but didn't cry out. Raven kissed her cheek, smiling at her daughter's first ritual.

* * *

They feasted on a buffet set out by Rauri, Jasmine, and Helen, Kiran's brother Alec's wife. The wine was free-flowing. Raven had a huge tub filled with ice and beer brought in for those, like her, who weren't fond of wine. Drums beat their rhythmic sounds as people danced around the fire, some leaping over it. Many had discarded their robes, dancing sky-clad. Raven stayed well clear of the bonfire. She respected fire as one of the elements, but she wasn't feeling up to honouring it this night. The celebration would go on until dawn when they greeted the rising sun, and already she was weary from her lack of sleep the night before.

They celebrated the setting of the sun, bidding farewell to the longest day of the year as Raven's eyes darted around from person to person, standing rigid with her daughter asleep in her arms.

"Surely you don't think anyone would be up to no good

here, during a celebration?" Rauri sidled up next to her, a glass of wine in her hand, in a flowing black robe.

"It wouldn't be the first time."

"Ah. Kiran told me what Adara did to you. And to Ena."

"Let's not speak of her here. Not in this place."

"Understood." Rauri brushed a hand down Raven's arm. "Why don't you and Riley go down for a swim? It might help revive you. I'll watch Indigo for you."

"No, I'm fine."

"Raven." Rauri waited until Raven looked at her. "Walk towards me."

"What? Why?"

A knowing smile snuck onto Rauri's face. "Just humour me."

Raven took a step towards her and bumped into an invisible barrier. Her eyebrows popped up and Rauri grinned.

"Where did you think you got it from, love?"

"I never thought about it."

"Take a break. Go have a swim and let me watch over my granddaughter."

Raven blew out a breath. A swim in the moonlight sounded glorious, but she was still reluctant to hand over her daughter. She stabbed her free hand through her hair, leaving it standing on end. "You'll watch who's around you?"

"Aye, of course. I'll have Kiran watch over the both of us as well. How's that?"

"Alright."

Rauri set her glass on the ground next to a rock and took Indi into her arms. Indi curled into her and continued to sleep.

Raven found Riley near the fire, dancing with Jasmine and Kelly. She tapped her on the shoulder and Riley tried to pull her into the dance. She shook her head. "Let's go for a swim."

Riley's face was flushed from exercise, her eyes bright. "That sounds wonderful."

They walked hand in hand in the moonlight, down a slope that led to the beach.

"You've been awfully quiet tonight," Riley said. "What's wrong?"

"Nothing really. Just being a cop, I guess."

"Ah, doing surveillance, are we?"

"Something like that."

"Do you think someone would try something with all these people around?"

Raven threw her free hand up in the air and let it drop to her side. "I don't know, Ri. I didn't think someone would burn my friggin' house down."

Riley stopped walking and Raven turned to face her, stabbing her fingers through her hair. "Shit, I'm sorry. I'm tired and cranky, and you didn't deserve that."

"Maybe we should just go back."

"I'm sorry. Please, I didn't mean to upset you."

"It's not that, Rave. You're right. We don't know what length someone is willing to go through to get to you. And right now, it's just the two of us here."

Raven stepped into Riley, threading her hands around Riley's waist. "I assure you, we're safe."

"You've got that protective barrier up?"

"Yes."

"I envy some of your superpowers, Rave."

Raven laughed. "Do you know how Adara was stealing my powers?"

"Not really, no."

"The more time she spent with me, the more she was able to soak up my powers."

"Okay."

Raven laughed again. "Riley, over time, you'll absorb some

of my powers."

Riley's mouth dropped open then snapped shut. "But, I thought you could block that from happening now."

"I can."

"I don't understand."

"I choose to share them with you."

"But why? Won't that diminish your powers?"

"Some, but why do I need all that power?"

"To protect yourself and Indi."

"And you." She tapped her finger on the tip of Riley's pert nose. "I'll have plenty of power for that."

A piercing scream sliced through the air from above them, followed by shrill shouts. Raven grabbed Riley's hand and ran, pulling her along the path. Her ears pounded with the blood rushing through her veins, her breaths coming fast and ragged. *Indi. Oh, shit.* She never should have left Indi.

She ran every day, yet her legs burned with each step like they were weighted down. They burst into the clearing where a crowd gathered near the fire. Raven pushed her way through, dragging Riley behind her. When she reached the centre, Kiran lay on his back and, behind him, a black-cloaked figure lay unmoving on the ground. Rauri stood guard over him, hugging a screaming Indi to her chest. She could nearly see Indi's tonsils. Her little face was red, her bottom lip quivering with every intake of breath.

A man dressed in black with a black hood over his head jumped onto Kiran, straddling his hips. He cocked his arm back and slammed his fist into Kiran's face. Kiran's head bounced off the ground and the man cocked his arm back again.

Raven pushed Riley towards Rauri. "Stand with Rauri. Don't leave her side." Her eyes met Rauri's and Rauri nodded her understanding. Raven pushed Riley towards her and sprinted towards Kiran. She launched herself into the air, hitting the man straddling Kiran in the mid-chest, knocking him back. Using her momentum, Raven somersaulted and sprung back to her feet. Spinning around, she bent her knees, balancing on the balls of her feet.

The man jumped up and started towards her. Raven shot her hand out, blue sparks flying from the tips of her fingers. The blast of energy hit the man in the centre of his chest, sending him flying back into the mob. Raven raced towards him, but the crowd grabbed his arms and legs, pinning him down. "Someone call 911," Raven yelled. She sprinted for the altar and grabbed a length of red rope from a basket next to it then used it to hogtie the man before pulling his hood off. She'd never seen him before. He had dark brown hair, brown, nearly black eyes, and a thick scar over his right eye that cut his eyebrow in half.

She turned to check on Kiran and found him sitting up, his hand cupping the left side of his face. Behind him, Rauri was kneeling next to the black-robed figure who still lay motionless. Riley knelt beside him, pressing two fingers against his neck.

Raven went to Kiran first. "Dad?"

"Alec, Michael, and Caleb went after the other one." He started to push himself up, but Raven held him down.

"Just sit for a bit." There was no way she was going to let him run off into the woods in the state he was in. She went over to Rauri and Riley and realized it was William, her grandfather, unconscious on the ground. "How is he?"

Riley glanced up at her. "Stable, but unconscious."

"He was protecting me," Rauri wept. "They tried to get Indigo. I couldn't bring him inside my protective barrier without opening it up and putting Indi at risk."

Raven wrapped her arms around Rauri and whispered in her ear. "Thank you. May the Goddess bless you." She kissed her cheek then leaned down next to William as Indi continued to wail. The clearing lit up with warm light and Raven directed her golden orb towards William's head. It glowed bright, surrounding him, then faded away to nothing. William opened his eyes and sat up. "Is everyone okay? Did we get the men?"

Rauri let out a weeping laugh and sunk to her knees next to her husband. "Oh, blessed be, you're alright."

"Of course, I'm alright. Is the bairn okay?"

"Aye, well, her lungs are working fine, aren't they?" Rauri laughed.

Raven lifted her wailing daughter from Rauri's arms, hugging her, rocking her, cooing to her. She went over to Kiran as Riley kneeled next to him, checking his face. "I'm going to heal you," she whispered to Kiran. "But, I want the cops to see your face first."

"Aye, that's fine. I'm alright, love. I would have had him in another few seconds."

Raven bit her lip to suppress the grin that desperately wanted to spread across her face. "Oh, I'm sure you would have."

Mick Warren, dressed in her impeccable police uniform, led Grayson LaCroix, Alec, Michael, and Caleb into the circle, the latter three covered in scratches. Caleb had leaves and burrs stuck to his pants, the knees caked in dirt.

"We found these three wandering in the woods," Mick reported. "Said they were trying to find their way back here."

Jasmine and Kelly rushed to Michael as Helen and Elly rushed to Alec and Caleb. They all hugged like they hadn't seen each other in years.

"We lost him in the woods," Alec reported.

"Aye," Michael said. "He knows the area much better than we do. We had a job finding our way back. Is everyone okay?"

"Aye, we're fine," Kiran said, still pressing a hand to the

side of his face.

"Want to tell me what's going on?" Mick asked Raven.

"I wasn't here at the start of it. Riley and I were on our way down to the beach for a swim."

Mick raised her brows and grinned.

Raven ignored her. "They must have been lying in wait for an opportunity. Rauri said they went for Indi."

Mick's grin died, her big brown eyes going cold. "If they were lying in wait, you could have picked them up using your psychic abilities." When Raven just stared at her, Mick's mouth dropped open. "Oh, my God! You're afraid to open yourself up to your psychic powers because of what Tate did to you."

It was true. Raven had scanned for Tate and he mentally attacked her, paralyzing her with a sharp, throbbing pain in her head like it was in a vice. She was afraid if she opened herself up like that, she'd be attacked again. There were far more powerful witches out there than Darren Tate.

"But, you know how to block an attack like that, Rave."

"I know." She didn't need or want Mick pointing out her weaknesses.

"Raven's not the only one with psychic abilities here. We were scanning." Rauri stepped up to Raven and Mick. "None of us detected anything untoward."

"So, they used some kind of block?" Mick asked.

"Aye, it appears so."

"Can you tell me what happened?" Mick took out her notebook and pen.

"I was standing there." Rauri pointed to a tree near the edge of the circle. "Speaking with William, my husband, and Kiran. They rushed in from different sides. One came from there." She drew a line in the air from the altar to the tree where she'd been standing. "The other from that side." She pointed behind the tree. "They rushed me, but they were reaching for Indigo."

"Who's they?"

"Oh, I'm sorry, love. Two men dressed in black wearing black hoods over their heads."

"We've got one in custody." Raven motioned to the man lying on his side near the altar with red rope binding his arms and legs. "The other was chased into the woods by the three men you found trying to find their way back here."

"The same guys who burned down your house?" Mick asked.

"Yeah. Maybe."

LaCroix used his foot on the man's shoulder to push him so he could get a look at his face. "Derek Michael Branson. Good job, Rave. This guy's wanted all across the country."

"Who is he?" Raven asked.

"Hired thug. He'll do anything if the price is right. And has."

"Shit." Chances were this guy wouldn't talk and, unless they knew who hired him, they were out of luck.

"What happened next?" Mick asked Rauri.

"Well, they couldn't get Indi, could they? I had a protective shield around the baby and I. William tackled one of the men. They fought and William was knocked out. Kiran fought the other one, the one on the ground over there. He was sitting on Kiran, punching him, when Raven dove into him, knocking him off Kiran. They both got to their feet and Raven zapped him. Then she got the rope from the altar and tied him up."

Mick's lips were pressed tightly together, her eyes twinkling. She looked over at LaCroix. "How do you want me to write this up, Sarge?"

LaCroix shook his bald head, scratching the light growth of beard on his chin. "You might want to paraphrase, maybe find alternative words for protective shield and zapped. Or omit them altogether." He sighed and pulled Derek Branson to his feet.

Chapter 15

Raven walked back to the house with Mick. Indigo stopped crying, but was still wide awake and clinging to Raven as if her life depended on it. Raven convinced Riley to stay behind and enjoy the celebration. It was Riley's first experience with the coven, and she could certainly use some frivolity after the past twenty-four hours.

She warned Kiran that she was placing a protective dome around the entire house and anyone returning would need to phone so she could open a portal.

She saw Mick off, then fed and changed Indi. Every time she tried to put Indi in her crib, she began wailing again, so she settled into the rocking chair with Indi snuggled into her breast, her little fist gripping Raven's t-shirt. "I promise it won't always be like this, my little angel," she whispered. "We'll figure something out."

One question kept repeating itself over and over in her mind - why would they want Indi? There were only two answers that she could come up with. One was holding her for ransom, in which case they were after Ena's money. The other was that it was Indi's powers they wanted, not Raven's. Even at six months of age, it was evident that Indi had great powers, but no one knew that except those very close to Raven. Unless they were taking a chance. Raven's witch blood was about as pure as it comes. Indi's father, Jaxon Lang, was a hereditary witch, but Raven didn't know how pure his blood was. She wasn't even sure if his father or his ancestors were witches. Maybe whoever was behind the attempted abduction knew more about Jax's bloodlines than Raven did. Or perhaps someone was bargaining on the fact that Indigo would be a powerful witch and more malleable than Raven.

None of it mattered, she thought. What mattered was finding out who was behind it and taking them down. Unfortunately, being off on maternity leave, Grayson LaCroix was never going to let her become involved in the investigation.

She spent most of the night rocking Indi and spinning things through her head and was no further ahead at dawn than she'd been the night before. She got up and laid Indi in her crib, grateful when she didn't stir. Taking the baby monitor, she went downstairs to watch the sunrise and wait for the Hayes crowd to return.

The sky was a brilliant kaleidoscope of purples, pinks, and oranges before the sun breached the horizon, all of it reflected in the glossy surface of the lake. It never ceased to amaze Raven that the view was different every morning. No sunrise ever seemed to be precisely the same. It was beautiful, awe-inspiring. She imagined everyone at the celebration honouring the sun and, as it peaked over the horizon, she whispered, "Hail, Sun." She wondered if she'd timed it to coincide with the many who'd made it through the night issuing the same greeting.

It was nearly an hour later when the crowd of Kiran's houseguests staggered across the field towards the house, laughing and bumping into each other. Raven grinned. A good night was had by all by the looks of it. The only ones missing from the bunch were Kiran and Simone. They would have stayed behind to clean up. Raven should have been there helping them, but she couldn't bear to leave Indi, even with a house full of witches.

They climbed the steps to the deck and Raven rose to greet them. Riley threw herself at her and Raven braced herself.

"Rave! You missed a great night."

Her arms flung around Raven's neck and Raven wrapped her arms around Riley's waist, holding her up. "Yeah, it looks like you enjoyed yourself."

"She's all yours now," Jasmine said. "We got her this far."

Rauri ran her hand down Raven's arm. "Good luck." She chuckled and followed the others inside.

"Let's get you up to bed." She hung on to Riley's waist and steered her into the house.

"Oh, it was marvellous. I danced all night." She threw her arms in the air and danced through the great room, nearly falling over a chair before Raven could grab onto her again.

"Okay. That's lovely, but I think the time for dancing is over."

Getting her up the stairs was an effort. She helped her brush her teeth and wash her face then supported her as they stumbled into Indi's room. "Shhh. Don't wake Indi. She didn't sleep very well last night."

"Okay," Riley whispered loudly. She stumbled over to the crib, gripping the railing, and stared down at the innocent little angel sleeping soundly. "She's so beautiful, isn't she? Looks so much like you."

"Yeah. Let's get you undressed and into the sleeping bag."

Riley spun around and fell onto Raven. Raven had to brace herself again to stay upright.

"Do you know what would be the perfect end to this night?" Riley slurred in Raven's ear.

"What's that?" Raven pushed her upright and started undoing the buttons on Riley's blouse.

"Mmm. Making love with you. There's nothing in the world like being with you." She tugged on Raven's t-shirt, dragged her nails over Raven's sensitive belly, and fused her mouth to Raven's.

It was like taking a sip of wine. Raven started giggling and couldn't stop. Her giggles sent Riley into fits of laughter and they ended up on the floor.

"Shhh, you'll wake Indi."

Riley rolled on top of her, her thigh pressing between Raven's legs and her eyes nearly rolled back in her head. It was hard enough trying to subdue Riley without her having to fight her own out of control libido. "Ri?" Riley's mouth crushed down on hers. The kiss was wild, demanding, and Raven couldn't help but respond. Sharp pangs of arousal shot through her like dozens of pinballs let loose in a frenzied game. Her back arched of its own volition when Riley's hands found her breasts. Then she replaced them with her mouth and used her hands to work on Raven's pants. She needed her to slow down. She was out of control, her body screaming out for release already.

Raven grabbed for Riley's hand as it plunged into her pants and found her centre. "Ri ... slow down."

"No." Riley popped her head up, her bloodshot eyes gazing into Raven's. "Take it. Just shut up and take it." She grabbed Raven's wrists, using her body weight to pin them over her head as Raven bucked and squirmed beneath her.

"Riley, stop." This didn't feel right, despite her raging libido. Her body was betraying her as her mind repelled what was happening. "Stop." She couldn't scream for fear of waking Indi, but she needed Riley to hear her.

Riley worked Raven hard and fast as Raven continued to buck and twist away. "Take it and let me watch you. This is what you want, isn't it? This is what you like?"

"No ... Ri, no." Pleasure surged through every cell in her

body until she couldn't take it any longer. Raven's muscles went taut. She threw her head back and bit her lip to stop herself from screaming out. She detonated like a ton of C4 going off. Every muscle shuddering, shaking, quivering with the force of her orgasm. Raven panted like she'd just run a marathon, and she felt like she had. She closed her eyes and a warm tear slid down her temple.

Her muscles were still quaking when Riley laid her head on her breast and whispered, "You're welcome."

Why she was saying you're welcome, Raven had no idea. Despite the spectacular orgasm, she felt like she'd been terribly used. She laid there for a moment, stroking Riley's back, threading her fingers through her hair, trying to get her breathing back to normal. Her legs were like jelly, trembling and weak. "Ri?"

Riley didn't answer, didn't move.

Raven rolled them both, so she ended up on top of Riley, staring down at her. Her eyes were closed, her breaths slow and deep. *Damn you, what the hell was that?* She pushed back onto her haunches, the tears flowing freely now, and buried her face in her hands.

* * *

By the time she got Riley into bed, grabbed a quick shower, and changed, Indi was awake. She got her changed and dressed and went down to the kitchen to heat up a bottle then got a call from Kiran that they were nearly home. She carried Indi out the back to open the portal for them.

Kiran and Simone walked with their arms around each other's waists like they were holding each other up. They climbed the deck stairs wearily. Simone dropped her arm from around Kiran's waist when she saw Raven waiting on the deck for them.

"Good morning," Raven said. Indi babbled her own good morning.

"Morning." Kiran kissed Raven's cheek then reached for Indi. "How's my wee love this morning?"

"Better than last night."

Kiran raised an eyebrow. "Rough night? You don't look like you got any sleep, love."

"Neither do you."

"Ah," he grinned. "But it was worth it, aye? Everyone had a brilliant night."

"So I heard. Riley certainly seemed to have enjoyed herself."

"Oh, aye. Riley got into the wine a wee bit too much, but we didn't see any harm in it. She's had a bad few days." He popped her on the end of her nose with the pad of his finger. "So have you."

Raven shrugged and turned to go back into the kitchen before the bottle on the stove got overheated. Kiran and Simone followed her in.

"Sorry I didn't come over to help clean up." Raven turned the stove off and lifted the bottle out of the pot, setting it on the counter.

"Not to worry, love. We had lots of help from some of the other covens." He pulled a couple of bottles of water from the fridge and handed one to Simone. "You can leave the protective dome down now, aye. The event planner's going to be dropping some things off later this morning and I'd rather not have to get up."

"Yeah, sure." She figured they were safe for the time being anyway, between the house full of witches and the fact that these guys seemed to be striking at night.

"Alright then." He handed Indi back to Raven after kissing both of her cheeks. "We're off to bed." He reached for Simone's hand, but she didn't take it.

"Simone," Raven said. "I'm a big girl. I can handle the fact that you're sleeping together." To Raven's surprise, Simone blushed.

"I just don't want you to think that I'm … I don't know."

Raven went to her and kissed her cheek. "I don't." Sleep well."

The doorbell rang as they made their way to the stairs.

"Shite!" Kiran said. "Who the bloody hell would be ringing the doorbell at this hour?"

It was nearly nine o'clock, but Raven didn't say that. "I'll get it. You two go and get some rest."

She opened to door to Nick Stokes, the fire inspector. "Hey. Good morning."

"Hi. I was told you were staying at this address. I hope you don't mind me stopping by."

"No, it's fine. What can I do for you?"

"We found something at your place that we thought you might want." He waved towards the dolly at the bottom of the porch steps.

"Oh!" Raven ran down the steps to examine the steel safe strapped to the dolly. The keypad had melted, but she'd find some way to get it opened. "Oh, wow! This is great."

"I can't guarantee what's inside hasn't been damaged by the heat. Is there someone who can give me a hand lifting it up the steps?"

"Yeah, me. Just let me put Indi in her highchair."

"Here, give her to me," Simone said from the doorway. She came out and took Indi from Raven while Raven and Nick hauled the safe up the steps and set it inside the front door.

Nick brushed his hands off on his navy pants, then pulled his wallet from his pocket. "I wanted to give you my card as well. If you have any questions or any more information about the fire, give me a call."

"Well, actually." Raven took the card. "We arrested one of the arsonists last night."

"You did?"

"Yeah. They tried to abduct my daughter. One of them got away. The other one should be in lock-up at the detachment."

Nick nodded. "I'll give Grayson a call." He saluted with two fingers off his brow and jogged down the steps.

Raven closed the door and turned to Simone, taking Indi back. Her bottle was ready and the poor thing was probably starving. "I thought you were going to bed."

"I just wanted to make sure you were okay."

"I'm fine." She grabbed the bottle from the kitchen counter and tested it on her wrist. Indi had her mouth open before the bottle got close. She grabbed it in her fists and shoved it into her mouth, sucking furiously. "You'd think I never fed her."

Simone smiled down at Indi. "Maybe she needs more than just formula."

"I'm giving her pablum, too."

"Well, she's definitely got a healthy appetite." She pressed a kiss to Indi's brow. "But, what about yours?"

"What about mine?"

"Raven, you're barely sleeping and you've hardly eaten the last couple of days."

Raven narrowed her eyes. "It's been a rough few days."

"I know." Simone brushed her hand over Indi's silky hair. "Raven, the reason I worry about what you think about me being with your father is that I care about you. You matter to me."

The last thing Raven needed was another mother figure in her life, another person who might betray her. "I'm fine with you being with my father, but I don't need another mother."

"And I don't want to be your mother, so we're good there." She smiled. "How about we just be friends?"

"I thought we were."

Simone laughed. "Yes. We are." She kissed Raven's cheek, then Indi's. "On that note, I'll say good night. Or good morning." She started for the stairs then turned back. "Just promise me you'll take care of yourself. That little baby in your arms needs you healthy."

"I will." Raven stared down at Indi. "I promise."

* * *

Raven spent the better part of the morning trying to break into her safe with Indi sitting next to her in the car seat she'd pilfered from Kiran's SUV. "I don't know, Indi. We may never get this thing open."

"Of course you will," Rauri said from behind her. She stood on the bottom stair in her black housecoat. Her jet black hair perfectly coiffed. "Use your powers, Rave."

"How?" Raven scowled.

Rauri rolled her eyes and sat on the floor next to Raven. "Watch carefully. You may learn something." Rauri pointed her finger at the edge of the door next to where the melted keypad was. A blue spark shot out and the safe door popped open. "It's not just good for zapping people into the air." She blew on the tip of her finger and grinned.

Indi babbled something then pointed her finger at Raven. A blue spark shot out and zapped Raven in the shoulder. "Ow! Holy fu… Holy crap!" She clasped her hand over her shoulder, sure she smelled burnt flesh.

Rauri doubled over laughing and had Indi belly laughing with her. "Good thing you're a healer," Rauri spurted.

"Yeah, good thing. Thanks for teaching her that." Raven pulled the safe door open. The first thing she pulled out was the metal lockbox containing her service weapon. Then she realized the key for the box was on her keyring. The one that had been on her kitchen counter when the cottage burned to the ground. She pointed her finger at the lock and sent a blue arc into it. The box popped open and she drew out her SIG Sauer. It looked fine, but she'd have to take it to the firing range to make sure it wasn't damaged.

"Oh, my." Rauri leaned over for a look at the gun. "Do you

carry that for work?"

"Yeah. I'm a cop."

Rauri laughed. "I know that, love. But, our cops don't carry them for the most part."

She'd known that. She didn't understand it, but she'd known it.

"What else have you got in there?"

Raven blushed. "Nothing of value."

"Oh, I don't believe that for a minute. They may not have monetary value, but they have value for you. Why else would you keep them in a safe?"

Raven pulled out the long, thin piece of willow, smooth as Indi's bottom, the handle wrapped in soft deerskin. Rauri gasped as Raven ran the tip of her finger down its length, feeling the power in it.

"It's Ena's wand," Rauri said. "Oh, Rave. That is definitely a thing of value."

"Yeah." It was certainly something she treasured. And it had survived the fire undamaged. Thank the Goddess.

"Do you mind me being here? Is this something you want to do in private?"

"No, I like that you're here." As long as she didn't teach Indi any more tricks. Her shoulder still throbbed.

The next item she pulled out had also belonged to Ena. It had a curvy blade, sharp on both sides. The black handle featured the three moons in silver at the hilt and a silver pentagram at the base. Ena's athame, her ceremonial knife, used mainly for casting circles.

"I always loved that athame," Rauri said. "It's quite beautiful."

"You've seen it before?"

"Of course. This isn't my first visit to Solstice, love."

Of course, she would have come to visit Kiran. The twelve years Raven had been estranged from her mother was time stolen from her. Adara had taken Raven in when she left home at fifteen and prevented Raven and Ena from reconciling to keep Raven close to her so she could steal her powers. If they'd repaired their relationship way back then, Raven would have had ten years of knowing her parents together and knowing her father's family. Instead, she hadn't met her father until after Ena's death at Adara's hand the year before.

"I miss her, too," Rauri said softly.

Oh, damn. Raven bit down on her bottom lip and squeezed her eyes shut.

"It's alright to feel, Raven. It's alright to grieve and be sad and be angry. It's alright to cry."

"I just … have so many regrets."

"You know what they say about regrets? There's nothing you can do to change the past, so take it as a lesson learned and move on."

Raven snorted and swiped at her wet eyes. "Now you sound like my therapist."

"Well, doesn't he sound intelligent? He? She?"

"She."

"Well, yes, I suppose it would have to be."

"Why do you say that?"

"You don't trust men, Raven. Or, very few of them."

Three - Kiran, Jax, and Grayson. They were the only men she'd trusted in her life. "Is that a bad thing?"

Rauri guffawed. "No, I suppose not."

"Great. Glad we've had this little chat."

"It makes you uncomfortable."

"Not really." It made her miss all of the uncomfortable chats she didn't get to have with Ena.

"You know, Ena talked about you all the time. Her greatest wish was that you would one day forgive her."

"There was never anything to forgive. It wasn't Ena's fault.

It was mine." She swiped her hand over her eyes again. *Damn, Rauri. Why did she have to bring all this up?*

"And there is it," Rauri sighed. "You blame yourself. Oh, Rave. Whatever it was, it takes more than one."

"I blamed her for not seeing what he was doing to me, but I should have told her the first time it happened. I should have trusted her to protect me." The thought of someone doing that to Indigo and Indi not telling her brought a completely different perspective to how she'd handled that time of her life.

Rauri's hand slid into hers and held on tightly. "You never should have had to live through that, love. No one should. But, I can understand you resenting Ena for not knowing it was happening. I think that would be a natural response."

Indi began to fuss and Raven thought, saved by the whine. Rauri lifted her out of the car seat, but Indi stretched her arms out for Raven with a half-hearted cry. Raven took her and pushed to her feet. "I'll make her some pablum."

Rauri got herself off the floor with a grunt and a groan then pressed her hand to the small of her back. "I can feed her if you like. You look like you could use a few hours of sleep." She stroked the pad of her thumb under Raven's eye.

Raven wasn't sure if she was brushing away a stray tear or pointing out the dark circles under her eyes. "I'm fine. I'll take a nap when she does."

Her bangs feathered up with the breath she exhaled as she began to walk away, silently thanking Indi for getting her out of that conversation.

"Raven." Rauri caught Raven's wrist, bringing her to a halt. Her warm brown eyes stared directly into Raven's. "You found it in your heart to forgive your mother. Now you have to find room to forgive yourself. I don't know how old you were when he first hurt you, but I know you were young. A child. Find a place in your heart to forgive that child. She was too young to be making the very adult decisions you blame her for. Things were happening that she had no control over."

Eyes burning, breath hitching, Raven pursed her lips tightly together to hold it all back. "I'm trying." Her lip quivered as she spoke. *Damn, Rauri really was sounding like her therapist.* "I'm just not there yet."

"Oh, come here, love." Rauri wrapped Raven and Indi in her arms and Raven's body went rigid. "It's okay to let it out, especially when you're around those who love you."

But Raven didn't let go. Wouldn't let go.

Rauri leaned back, meeting Raven's gaze. "I know you've carried all of this on your own for a long time, but now you have a bloody big family at your back. It's okay to lean on us, to let us support you."

Raven nodded, not trusting herself to speak without losing control.

"Oh, you're a stubborn one, Raven Sage." The edge of her lip curled up slightly. "I've one more thing to say, then I'll leave you to feed the wee one."

Goddess help her. At least it was nearly over. Raven nodded again.

"There's one more person you need to forgive, aye? You need to forgive Adara Kirby."

Raven's nostrils flared, her eyes narrowed. Until that moment, she hadn't realized how much anger she still carried around towards Adara.

"Not for her sake, but for your own healing."

Raven closed her eyes and nodded. She was right. Of course, she was right. Why did her grandmother have to be such a wise woman? "I'm not there yet, either."

"And that's okay, love. But, the longer you hold out, the longer you suffer for it." She kissed Raven's cheek then Indi's and walked away.

Raven stood there, closed her eyes, and breathed. Damn it,

she wasn't ready to forgive Adara for all of the horrible things she'd done, especially killing Ena. She wasn't sure she ever would be.

Chapter 16

Pablum sprayed across the highchair's table and all over Raven's face as Indi blew a raspberry. "Honestly, kiddo. We're going to have to figure out a better way to do this."

Riley stepped into the kitchen and groaned. Her hair looked like she'd stuck her finger in an electrical socket. She stood in an old pair of boxer shorts and a faded grey t-shirt looking around the room as if lost. "I need Advil. I feel like I've been hit by a train."

"You look like a train wreck," Raven snorted, wiping the pablum from her face. She nodded to her right. "In the cupboard next to the stove."

Riley retrieved the Advil and a bottle of water from the fridge. She sank into a seat at the kitchen table, spread her arms out over the table and rested her face against its cool surface.

"That bad, eh?"

Riley groaned again in response. "What have you been doing all morning?"

"I had a lovely chat with my grandmother." Raven spooned another mouthful of pablum into Indi's mouth. This time she gobbled it up while banging her hands on her table.

Riley pushed herself up, threw three Advil into her mouth and chased them down with a swig of water. "What kind of chat?"

"A grandmotherly one, I guess." She'd never had a grandmotherly conversation, but she supposed that was exactly what it was. "She basically told me it was senseless to keep what-iffing myself to death."

"Pfff." Riley lowered her head to the table again. "You're not the only one with what-ifs, Rave. What if my father wasn't a monster? What if my mother didn't abandon me because she couldn't stand the sight of me? Get over yourself already."

Raven felt like she'd just been slapped in the face, except the pain went much deeper. "Okay, you're in a sour mood." She wanted to lift Indi out of her highchair and run from the room, but Indi sat there with her mouth wide open, waiting for the next spoonful. Raven obliged her.

"I'm just not feeling great, okay? What are you doing with the rest of your day? I think I need to go back to bed."

She was planning on putting Indi down for a nap and taking one herself, but that plan didn't sound so appealing now. "I need to go out and get a new cell phone." And a new car. That should keep her out for a while. Away from Riley's sour mood.

"Fine. See you later." She pushed up from the table, leaving the bottle of Advil and the water behind and shuffled back upstairs.

"Don't worry," she said to Indi. "She'll feel better after she sleeps it off." Trouble was, she'd never seen Riley lash out like that. Maybe she just needed to be more sensitive to what Riley was going through right now and how she was feeling about the way she came into this world. It couldn't be easy learning you were the product of a rape. She just wished she knew what to do or say to help her through it.

* * *

Luckily, she lived in a small town where everyone knew

her and had heard the news about her cottage. It made getting a new driver's licence without any identification that much easier. With a temporary licence in hand, she was able to get a new bank card. The cell phone came next and then she headed to the Land Rover dealership. They didn't have a Range Rover with all of the options she wanted, so she was going to have to wait for them to have one shipped in from somewhere else, but at least she'd gotten the ball rolling.

Instead of heading back to Kiran's, she drove over to her cottage, or what was left of it. She got out of the car and walked down the driveway with Indi sleeping in her arms. Someone had taken the empty shell of her car away. She stopped at what used to be the side of her house and stared at the pile of ash, broken glass, and burned wood. Some of the beams protruded out of the ash like blackened spears reaching for the sun. It was so senseless. Why did they have to burn down her home? Did they hate her so much because she supposedly had powers?

She walked to an undamaged patch of grass and sat with Indi under the shade of a great oak tree, surveying the damage. When she couldn't stand to look at it anymore, she turned her gaze to the lake that had always brought her comfort. The sunlight danced across its surface, sparkling brightly. Her kayak still sat on her dock, undamaged. At least she'd still be able to enjoy that.

"Oh, Indi. What are we going to do?" She didn't want to stay at Kiran's for long and she wasn't sure she wanted to stay at Riley's apartment. She needed to be near the water where she could walk outside whenever she wanted and be surrounded by nature. Without that, she worried she'd completely lose it. This was her grounding place, her sanctuary.

She didn't know how long she'd been sitting there when she heard a vehicle coming up the road. It stopped at the top of the driveway and a door opened and closed. She couldn't be bothered to look up to see who it was. She just wanted to be alone with her sleeping angel snuggled into her.

"I thought I might find you here," Mick said. She sat down next to Raven and crossed her tanned legs. "I called the house and no one seemed to know where you were."

"I just needed some time."

"I know."

Mick knew her well. In the beginning, it was because Mick kept invading her mind with her own clairaudient powers and then because they'd become friends.

"Did you get anything out of Derek Branson?"

"Not really."

"Yeah, I didn't think so."

"We're talking to his known associates, looking for the second guy."

Raven turned her head to Mick. "I know this is a lot to ask, but would you keep me in the loop?"

Mick grinned. "I thought that's what I was doing?"

The edge of Raven's mouth curled up. She lifted her head to the breeze and closed her eyes.

"So, what are you going to do? Are you going to rebuild?"

"Yeah."

"Good. I know what this place means to you, Rave. Why don't you rent an RV to live in while you're rebuilding? You've got the land. That way, you could still be here, in the place you love."

Raven smiled and opened her eyes. "I've gotten a lot of advice today, from forgive myself to get over myself, but I like yours the best."

"I agree with the forgive yourself part, but I feel sorry for the person who told you to get over yourself. Are they still alive?"

"Ha. Barely." She didn't say that it was for self-induced

reasons and nothing Raven had done.

Mick shifted as if she was trying to get comfortable sitting in the grass. "I have some news."

Raven lifted a brow and waited.

"I wrote the detective's exam last week."

"Congratulations, detective." Raven grabbed Mick's hand and gave it a quick squeeze. "That's great."

"I don't know if I passed yet. I'm still waiting for the results."

"You passed. You're an excellent cop, Mick. You'll make an even better detective."

"Thank you for that." She shifted again, running her palm over the blades of grass that shot up from the earth. "I wondered if you'd…" She blew out a breath. "Um …consider taking on a partner when you come back to work."

Now Raven blew out a breath. Mick knew she worked alone. Everyone at the detachment knew she worked alone. She'd been forced to partner up with Mick the year before when they'd been working the murder of a young woman and ended up investigating Raven's mother's death, too. She liked working with Mick, but did she want to take her on full time? "I don't know, Mick. I'll think about it." To work closely with a partner, you needed to be able to trust them and that was something she wouldn't have been able to do, even a year ago. But, she had to admit to herself that she did trust Mick. Somewhere in the last year, she'd developed trust in her. It helped that Mick was so reliable. "I'll definitely think about it."

Mick grinned. "That's … awesome. Thank you."

* * *

Half the household ran out to the driveway when Raven pulled in, headed by Kiran, who looked furious. He stood by the car with his hands on his hips and a cold stare aimed at her. Raven took a deep breath and opened the door.

"Where the bloody hell have you been? We've been worried sick."

She took another deep breath. She should have considered that they'd worry, but she still wasn't used to having this big family worry about her. "I'm sorry. I needed some alone time."

"You've been gone for near on six hours, Raven. You said you were going out to run a few errands. Did you even take a bottle for Indigo?"

Raven opened the back door and removed her cranky daughter from the car seat. She didn't have a diaper bag, so she'd loaded up a plastic bag with wipes, diapers, a couple of baby cookies, and two bottles, just in case. "Of course, I did." Indi slept most of the afternoon, but Raven had sent Mick down to the Solstice Café to heat up a bottle when she woke up. She didn't like nuking them, but it was either that or come home and she hadn't been ready to leave her houseless plot of land. And, bless her, Mick had returned with a warm bottle and two coffees.

When Raven turned, Kiran reached out for Indi, but Indi wailed and clung to Raven. "Sorry, she's been clingy all day."

"Aye, well, she had another fright last night. The poor wee soul." His eyes softened as he took in his granddaughter then hardened again as he looked at Raven. "Are you going to tell us where you've been all afternoon then?"

She was a grown-ass woman, not a freakin' teenager coming home past curfew. "Look, I appreciate you taking us in, but don't think that means I'm going to give up my independence and only do what you want me to do."

"Is that what you think this is? Bloody hell, Raven. You were all nearly killed in a fire and someone tried to abduct Indigo last night. I think that gives us the right to worry."

Raven stabbed her fingers through her hair. "I'm sorry. I didn't mean to worry you. I ran my errands and then I went to sit by the lake." She didn't want to tell him that she'd spent most of the afternoon sitting next to the ruins of her cottage. "And I was perfectly safe. Mick was with me."

Riley stood on the front porch, leaning against a column in faded blue jeans worn to white strings at the knees. They hung low on her hips, exposing an inch or two of toned belly below her t-shirt. She must have had a shower because her hair was no longer wild. It hung in soft curls over her shoulders. She was simply beautiful. She didn't smile at Raven the few times she met her eyes, but then neither did Raven.

"First thing in the morning, you're getting a new cell phone."

Raven rolled her eyes. "I picked one up this afternoon. Same number."

"And you didn't think to call to let us know you were okay?"

"Okay, enough already. No, I didn't think to call. I'm perfectly capable of protecting Indi and myself. I didn't realize I had to check in every five freaking minutes."

"Kiran," Rauri said softly.

"What?" He turned to Rauri, stabbing his fingers through his hair. "I'm bloody entitled to worry."

"Yes, you are. But if you keep this up, you'll just push Raven away."

He threw his arms up in the air and stormed into the house, mumbling something that Raven couldn't hear.

Thanks," Raven said to Rauri.

"Next time, just give him a call, so he doesn't worry."

"Yeah, sure." First thing in the morning she was going to see about renting that RV. Mick had helped her find the perfect spot for it, a few hundred yards up from where her cottage had been, right beside the beach. At this point, she couldn't get out of Kiran's house fast enough. She didn't want to go in there now with the whole gang of them having witnessed Kiran interrogate her. She stood there for a few minutes while the hoard filtered back into the house. Riley remained on the porch, watching her.

She walked over to the steps and looked up at her. "Hey."

"Hey."

"You okay?"

"Hungover, but otherwise fine."

Raven looked down at the ground as she raked her fingers through her hair then looked back up at Riley. "Look, I don't know what to do or say to help you with what you're going through, but I thought maybe it might be a good idea if you saw a therapist to help you process everything."

"Where's this coming from all of a sudden?"

Raven lifted her hand out to her side then dropped it. "What you said to me earlier today."

Riley's brows drew together. "What did I say to you?"

"About having what ifs." She didn't want to repeat the rest of what Riley had said.

"It's you that has the what-ifs, Rave."

Had she still been drunk and not remembered? "Okay, fine." What was she supposed to say if Riley didn't even remember?

"You promised Jenny you would do a cleansing of Solstice this morning."

Shit, she'd forgotten all about that. "What was I supposed to do? Wait around all day for everyone to get up?"

"We were up all night, Rave. Everyone needed to get some sleep."

Lucky them, Raven thought, then admonished herself for the self-pity. That wouldn't get her anywhere. "Fine, we'll do it tonight."

She climbed the steps and went into the house, straight up to Indi's bedroom. She closed the door and sat with Indi on the floor. All she wanted to do was climb into the sleeping bag and sleep for about twenty-four hours, but Indi was wide awake. Just another few hours and she could put her down for the night. "What am I going to do with you, little angel?"

Indi looked up at her, scrunched her nose and sniffed in and out. Her little arms waved up and down as she laughed. She supposed that was better than shooting sparks at her mother.

Raven had hoped that Riley would come up and join her, but she didn't come. She wasn't sure what had happened between Riley aggressively jumping her bones that morning and the defensiveness in Riley when she'd only tried to answer her question about her chat with Rauri. Now things were definitely strained between them. She wasn't sure if it was something she did, or just Riley being in a sour mood.

Raven glanced up at the knock on the door, hoping to see Riley, but Simone popped her head in.

"Raven, why don't you let me look after Indi for a while so you can get some sleep?"

"It's fine. Another few hours and I'll put Indi to bed, then I'll sleep tonight."

Simone sighed. "Will you at least come down and have some dinner?"

Raven's stomach rumbled as if in answer. "Yeah, I'll be down." She had to talk to everyone anyway and organize this cleansing Solstice of negative energy for Jenny.

"Good. I'll see you in a few minutes then."

The door began to close and Raven said, "Simone?"

Simone pushed the door open again and popped her head in. "Yeah?"

"I'm okay. You don't need to worry."

"But, you're not yourself, are you, Rave? It's like you're withdrawing from all of us."

Damn it if she wasn't right. She had been pulling away,

putting her walls back up again. She stared up at the ceiling and blew out a breath. "I'm scared shitless, Simone." Her breath hitched. "They tried to take my baby." She lifted Indi into her arms and hugged her to her chest.

Simone came into the room and sat next to Raven, her arm extending around Raven's back. "Of course, you're scared. We all are. And it's all the more reason for you to let us in. Let us help."

Raven nodded, pushing her nose into Indi's neck and breathing in the baby-fresh scent.

"And it's also why you need to make sure you're taking care of yourself. You won't be any use to Indi if you're sleep-deprived and malnourished."

Raven only nodded again. She was going down to dinner and she planned on going to bed as soon as they'd cleansed the town. Letting everyone help her was going to be a little more challenging, but she'd try.

* * *

Raven stood at the east end of Solstice with Rauri and Jasmine, each holding a burning stick of sage, representing the element of air. Indi was asleep in her stroller at Raven's side, perfectly safe inside her protective dome. She spoke into her cell phone on speaker mode. "Everyone set?"

"Aye," Kiran's voice came through the phone. "Ready in the south." He was with Alec and Helen, each of them holding a lit silver candle, representing fire.

"Ready in the west," Simone said. Her companions were Michael and Elly. They each held a small bowl of sea salt, representing earth.

There was a long silence as they waited for those in the north to check in - Jenny, Rebecca, and Riley. Raven was about to ask if they were there when Rebecca's voice came through. "Aye, ready in the north." Each of them held a chalice of water, representing the element of water.

Raven led them on a short meditation of deep breathing, relaxing their bodies, and ridding themselves of negative energy. Then they began to chant.

"Negativity that invades our sacred place, we banish you away with the light of our grace. You have no hold or power here. For we stand and face you with no fear. Be gone forever; for this, I will say: this is our sacred place and you will obey."

They repeated the chant over and over. Raven had requested Jenny to be the one to stop the chanting when she felt the cleansing had succeeded. So they continued, twelve voices connecting the four points of Solstice. The three chanting from the north dropped away first, then the others followed slowly. Raven waited a moment then said, "As we will, so mote it be."

Chapter 17

The only light in the room when Raven woke up the next morning was the soft glow of a night light plugged into one of the wall sockets. When they got home after the cleansing, she'd put Indi to bed then climbed straight into the sleeping bag. She'd barely spoken to Riley all evening, or Riley had scarcely spoken to her, and she hadn't been sure if she'd join her on the floor of Indi's room or find another place to sleep. But, Riley's body hugged hers, her head resting on Raven's shoulder. So, she couldn't be that mad at her, but Raven still felt like something was off between them.

She pressed her nose into Riley's hair and breathed in, the scent of lavender and jasmine calming her. Maybe everything was fine now. Perhaps Riley had forgiven her after organizing the cleansing ritual. Had that been the cause of the angst between them? In the past, she probably would have let it go. Now, she knew they needed to talk and sort things out before it festered into something more.

She kissed Riley's hair and closed her eyes again. She must have dozed back off because the next thing she knew, Riley's cell phone alarm blared an annoying tune and Indi cried out.

"Shit." She pulled herself out of the sleeping bag and went over to the crib.

"Sorry," Riley moaned. "I have to get up and get ready for

work."

Jet was curled up next to Indi in the crib. Raven lifted Indi into her arms and turned to Riley, who sat up, still half asleep. "You're going in to work?"

"Yeah."

Raven took a deep breath as she bounced Indi in her arms. "Just because the festival is over doesn't mean the threat is. Riley, you'll be exposed at work." Exposed and an easy target.

Riley stared up at her with heavy-lidded eyes. "I have to, Rave. I have to work."

"I know, but...you'll be careful? Use your protection spells? Be aware of who's around you? Call me if you sense anything suspicious?"

Riley got out of the sleeping bag and went to Raven. "I'll be careful." She pressed a kiss to Raven's mouth, quick and chaste.

"We should talk. After work."

"I promised Jenny I'd help her and Rebecca look for a place after work."

"Oh." She knew she should be happy that Riley was getting to know her mother, but it hurt that she'd made plans without her. Stupid, she told herself. Just because they were back together didn't mean Riley had to spend every waking moment with her. "After that, then?"

"Yeah, sure." Riley gathered up some toiletries and a clean set of scrubs then headed off to the shower.

"Well, I guess that leaves you and me," she said to Indi. "What will we get up to today?" She had a mid-morning appointment with her therapist and she needed to contact her insurance company about the car and the cottage. After that, she was going RV shopping. She'd call Mick and see if she was off today, both to get an update on the investigation and so she'd have company. She hadn't told anyone else about getting the RV and, for now, she'd keep it that way. The fewer people who knew where she'd be living, the better.

* * *

All in all, Raven had a productive day. She dealt with the insurance company before leaving the house, met with her therapist and made a consultation appointment with Dr. Shoal for Jenny Gallagher. Mick had worked the night shift, so she'd gone to the RV dealership on her own and quickly found a suitable RV. Instead of renting, Raven opted to buy it. She figured she could sell it once her and Riley's new cottage was built. She arranged for the RV to be delivered then contacted a contractor to hook up water and electricity. Unfortunately, the power lines had been damaged in the fire, so it was going to be at least a few days to get it all sorted out. She bought wood to build a deck, arranged for its delivery, and then realized she also needed new tools, so she bought those, too.

With Rauri's words fresh in her mind, she'd talked to Dr. Shoal about blaming the child she'd been for not reconciling with Ena. For not telling her what was going on with Gregor Paigo, for suppressing her powers and rebelling against Wicca, which caused her to blame herself for Ena's death. She hadn't realized until Rauri had told her to forgive the child that she'd been blaming the child version of herself all this time. Her criticism softened. She hadn't completely forgiven herself, but she wasn't quite as critical of her decisions and actions back then.

Of course, Dr. Shoal had heard about her cottage burning down and talked to her about the grief process. Who knew you could go through the stages of grief for a home? She figured she was still in shock, a sort of denial. She had anger to look forward to next and just wished she knew who was behind the whole thing so that she could direct that anger towards them.

She had one more stop to make before heading home. She walked into Mystique and found it empty save for Alana MacKinney, sitting behind the counter reading a book. Alana jumped up and crossed the shop when Raven stepped in the door. "Raven. I'm so glad you came. Where's that darling daughter of yours?"

"Sorry. I was out doing some errands and just stopped in on my way home." She wasn't comfortable saying who she'd left Indi with. Not with all that had happened over the past few days.

"You bring her with you next time. You know how much I love babies. Especially little girls because I only had boys." Alana grinned and took Raven's hand. "Now, tell me what you need and we'll get you restocked."

"Actually, I just want a Book of Shadows."

A crease formed between Alana's eyes and she patted Raven's hand. "Oh, dear. I never thought about losing that in the fire. You'll have to start from scratch."

"It's not for me. It's … a gift."

Alana showed her three different styles and she chose one bound in soft leather of deep browns and golden reds. It kind of reminded her of the colour or Riley's hair. The three moons graced the front with a pentagram in the centre of the full moon. "I'll take this one."

As she was paying, the bell above the door chimed and she turned to see Jade Storm in a tight pair of skinny jeans and a flowy green blouse carrying a leather messenger bag over her shoulder. Raven narrowed her eyes. She figured Jade Storm would have left town after the festival.

"Hello," Jade smiled.

"Hello," Alana greeted her with a smile of her own.

"Hey." Raven took her bank card back from Alana and stuffed it in her back pocket, waiting for Alana to put the book in a bag.

"I've taken a cottage on Fairy Lake for the summer. It's just so beautiful here that I couldn't leave yet. Kind of a working holiday. I've found several shops to take some of my jewelry on consignment and I was wondering if you'd take a few pieces here, Alana." She set the messenger bag on the counter and pulled out a blue velvet box.

"I've got quite a bit of jewelry here already," Alana said. "But, I'll take a look at what you've got."

"That would be great. Thank you."

Raven took her bag from Alana. "Thanks, Alana. See ya later." She turned and walked out, leaving Alana and Jade to their business. It was time to take a closer look at Elizabeth Jane Thompson.

As soon as she got in her car, she took out her cell phone and looked up the phone number for the Royal Canadian Mounted Police in Lake Louise, Alberta. She identified herself as Detective Constable Raven Bowen of the Ontario Provincial Police and asked if they knew an Elizabeth Jane Thompson.

She already knew that she didn't have a police record, but sometimes the local police knew a lot more than she could find out on a standard run. It turned out that they did know Elizabeth, or Jade, as she had helped them with a few of their investigations as a psychic. Interesting, but it didn't help Raven in figuring out why Jade Storm remained in Solstice.

* * *

Raven pulled into Kiran's driveway just ahead of the bus that was picking up his family to return them to the airport. Kiran would have lectured her if she hadn't made it back on time to say her goodbyes. She helped load luggage then stood dutifully by the door while Kiran's family and members of Rauri's coven boarded the bus.

Instead of getting on the bus, Rauri was hugging her family goodbye.

"You're staying?" Raven asked.

"Aye, love. My work isn't finished here." She ran a hand down Raven's arm as she watched the bus door close.

"What work?"

"We'll talk about it," Kiran said, waving as the bus started along the road.

"You're worried there's still a threat."

Kiran's expression was grim. He stared after the bus even after it disappeared around the bend in the road.

"Did Jasmine see something?" Her eyes darted between Kiran and Rauri. "Well?"

Rauri took Raven's hand in both of hers. "We don't believe the threat is over, love. There's still negative energy in and around Solstice, and those men went to extremes to try to get to you and Indi. They won't give up this easy."

That wasn't news to Raven. She'd known it. Felt the negative energy. "But, you don't know anything concrete?"

"No," Kiran answered. "And that's the problem, aye?"

"I'll touch base with Mick again tonight. I ran into Jade Storm at Mystique. She's rented a cottage on Fairy Lake."

Kiran braced his hands on his hips and pursed his lips. "Can you do some digging on her?"

"I already have. No criminal record. In fact, Storm worked with the RCMP in Lake Louise a few times to help them solve cases."

"Worked with them? How?"

"As a psychic."

Kiran shared a glance with Rauri.

"She's clairvoyant," Kiran said.

"Aye. It would seem so."

"What does that have to do with anything?" Raven asked. She was getting frustrated with their cryptic glances, sure they were withholding information.

"We have a theory," Kiran said. "Whoever is behind the

attacks had the power to block us from detecting these two men. We should have picked them up in the woods."

"And a clairvoyant could do that?"

"Not necessarily," Rauri answered. "It would take a powerful spell."

"Okay, so we're talking about a hereditary witch? One with better than average powers?"

"Aye." Rauri nodded. "And a clairvoyant powerful enough to help the police solve crimes may have other powers."

"This isn't good." Raven turned and stared out over the lake behind the house. "If they're able to block us from detecting those two goons, they're sure as hell able to block us from detecting them. And their intentions." She turned back to see Kiran and Rauri share another look. Kiran nodded at Rauri.

"We have another theory, love," she said. "The powers we've seen you display are all powers you've inherited from the Hayes line. We think you may have untapped powers from the Bowen side." She took Raven's hand in hers again. "We think maybe Ena blocked you from those powers in an attempt to keep you safe."

Raven's eyes darted between them again. Kiran looked away and stabbed his fingers through his hair.

"I don't understand." Why would it matter if she had untapped powers?

Kiran huffed out a breath, his eyes meeting Raven's. "We believe whoever's behind this has the power to sense others' powers. Perhaps that's why they want Indi."

"I still don't uderstand what that's got to do with me possibly having undiscovered powers."

"What do you know about Ena's powers?" Kiran asked.

All her life, she'd heard stories of how powerful the Bowen women were, but she'd never thought about what their specific powers were. She couldn't think of any that Ena exhibited. She spent her time making oils, potions, spells, and whatnot, which she sold through Mystique or online.

"Nothing." Raven raked her fingers through her hair, staring down at the ground as she tried to think. "I don't know anything about her powers."

"Aye, that's what I thought." Kiran placed a hand on Raven's shoulder. "Come inside, love. There's much we need to discuss."

* * *

Rebecca stepped into the foyer when they walked into the house. "The baby is waking up from her nap. She's just started making noises on the monitor."

"Okay, thanks," Raven said and headed up the stairs. As she got Indi up and changed, she ran through the times she'd spent with her mother in her youth, trying to remember any sign of her powers and couldn't remember any. She thought about Ena and Kiran saving her on the cliff when Adara attempted to shake her off of it, but that was a spell they used and not a specific power. Then at the coven gathering on the full moon when Adara attacked her, Ena hadn't appeared until after Raven put Adara down.

There was tremendous power in Ena's wand, but that didn't tell her what specific powers Ena had. So she started going over what she did know about her mother. She knew that Ena had hidden her paternity from her, from Kiran, from the Wiccan community, because she feared precisely what was happening now. She feared that someone would try to get to Raven for her powers. Ena hadn't challenged her when she decided to rebel against witchcraft and Wicca because she thought it would help keep her safe. But, Ena continued her training, coming to Raven secretly in her dreams, to prepare for the day when she could no longer protect her daughter.

Raven came down the stairs with a sleepy-faced Indi in her

arms. Rauri and Kiran sat at the kitchen table, sipping tea. She caught a glimpse of a red car through the kitchen window pulling out of the driveway. She leaned over the sink to get a better look, but the car was out of sight. "Was that Riley?"

"Aye," Kiran answered.

"She didn't come in?"

"Jenny and Rebecca were ready and waiting at the front door when she pulled in and out they went," Rauri said. "Is everything okay, love?"

"Yeah." Why wouldn't Riley have at least stopped in to say hello? She'd texted her several times throughout the day and each time Riley had texted back that she was okay. That was it. Raven passed Indi off to Kiran and put a pot on the stove to heat a bottle. When it was ready, she handed it to Kiran and took a seat at the table. "Was Ena clairvoyant?"

"Oh, aye. Very," Kiran said.

Raven flopped back in her chair and exhaled loudly. "She saw what's happening now, didn't she? That's why Ena tried to hide my powers. That's why she was so worried about anyone finding out I was yours. Something horrible is going to happen."

"Oh, love." Rauri placed her hand over Raven's on the table and patted. "We don't know that. The thing about visions of the future is that they're only one version of what could happen. Our choices, our actions can change the outcome. It's never set in stone."

"This blocking us from detecting those goons? He or she can block us from reading their thoughts or seeing a vision of what's going to happen? Is that what you're thinking?"

"That's one of our worries," Kiran said. "Jasmine wasn't able to get a vision of the fire or the attempt to take Indi and that's unusual."

"What are the other worries?"

Kiran leaned forward, closed his eyes, and kissed Indi's brow. When he looked up at Raven, his forehead was wrinkled and the lines around his eyes were more pronounced. "We're worried that it's not just energy and psychic powers that this person can block."

It took Raven a moment, but when it clicked, her eyes popped wide open. "You think they can block all of our powers."

"We don't know that for certain. It's just a possibility at this point." Rauri turned her teacup in a circle, gazing down at it. "If that's the case, we need to figure out what powers you have from the Bowen side."

"Why, if they can block them?"

Kiran set Indi's bottle on the table and lifted her to his shoulder, rubbing his palm over her back in circles. "I need to tell you a story," he said.

Chapter 18

Raven sat out on the deck with a cold beer in her hand and the baby monitor at her side. The sun had set and Riley still hadn't returned. Jenny had called the house to say they were going out for dinner, but that was all she'd heard. With so much uncertainty about the person responsible for burning down her house and going after Indi, Raven didn't like not knowing where Riley was. At the same time, she didn't want to crowd her when she was just getting to know her mother.

The story Kiran told her took place not long after he and Ena started seeing each other, a few years before Raven's conception. A negative energy had descended over Solstice, very similar to what they were experiencing now. No one was able to pin down a source. At the time, Ena shared the Bowen house with her mother, Beatrice, who was the High Priestess of the Solstice Coven. Ena tried to convince her that they were being watched, but Beatrice thought she was paranoid. She was a powerful clairvoyant and hadn't picked up anything other than the negative energy.

The story sounded so similar to what was happening now. It was eerie. The coven had gathered at their sacred ritual space in the woods where they'd been attacked by three men. Beatrice attempted to stop them and protect her coven, but her powers were blocked somehow. Ena was able to use her powers to take down and subdue the three men, but not before Beatrice was killed by a knife to the heart. They'd used her own athame to kill her.

The three men never talked. They'd been hired thugs and were sentenced to life for murder. The person behind the attack was never found. The reason they'd killed Beatrice was still unknown.

It had to be the same person behind the events taking place today. That told Raven the person responsible had to be at least fifty years of age, removing Jade Storm from the running. Unless Jade was a descendant of the person responsible for killing Beatrice and had taken up the cause on their behalf. She couldn't completely rule her out as a suspect.

Kiran's point to the whole story was that Ena was the only one at the gathering who was able to use her powers. They hadn't been able to block her. Kiran and Rauri thought there was a possibility Raven inherited that trait from Ena. Raven prayed they were right. If she couldn't protect her daughter, she didn't know what she would do. But, she didn't know how to find out one way or the other. They had no idea how this person was able to block others from using their powers, so they had no way of testing it.

She took a long sip of her beer then leaned her head back, closing her eyes. The men that burned her house down and tried to get to Indi hadn't been able to break through her barrier or Rauri's. They hadn't stopped Raven from zapping the one guy. Had they tried? Were they testing to see just what Raven could do? "You're a coward," she yelled into the darkness. "Hiding behind your blocks. You want me, or my daughter? Show yourself. Meet me face to face."

The wind picked up. Leaves rustled in the trees. The whoosh of waves hitting the rocks on the cliff became louder, more intense, as if the weather was mirroring her mood.

"Rave?"

Raven turned her head to see Kiran standing in the doorway.

"Jenny and Rebecca are home. They need a portal through your shield, love."

"Right." Instead of going through the house, Raven walked around to the front. Riley's car was pulling out of the driveway. She stopped and stared after it, forcing herself not to chase the car down the street. She opened a portal for Jenny and Rebecca then followed them into the house. "Where's Riley going?"

"Home," Jenny said. "She has to work early in the morning and she was tired."

Raven clenched her teeth and fisted her hands at her side. She wanted to lash out at Jenny, blame her for whatever was up with Riley. "It's not safe for her to be out there on her own."

"It's you they want. You and that child of yours. Riley is perfectly safe."

"You don't think they'd use Riley to get to me?" Foolish bitch. If it wasn't for Riley, she'd tear a strip up one side of this woman and down the other.

Jenny paled slightly. "No. She's safe."

Rebecca feathered her fingers down Jenny's arm. "Jen?"

"She's using protection spells and we've added our own. We wouldn't leave her unprotected."

Raven's eyes met Kiran's, who stood in the kitchen doorway with Simone at his side. "That may not be enough." She stomped off and went out to the deck to retrieve the baby monitor and her empty beer bottle. She dropped the beer bottle off in the kitchen and started for the stairs.

"Are you okay?" Simone asked.

"No, damn it." She spun around, facing Simone and Kiran. "That woman pisses me off. She's known Riley for all of five minutes and thinks she knows what's best for her. I bet she spent all evening trying to convince Riley to stay away from me. She's barely spoken to me since yesterday morning and now she's gone to her apartment alone. If anything happens to her, I'll kill Jenny Gallagher myself." She stabbed her fingers through her hair and fisted it in her hand.

Kiran crossed the kitchen to her and wrapped a strong arm around her shoulders. "I thought she'd had a change of heart about you and Riley, love. Maybe Riley just wanted her own bed. It couldn't have been comfortable sleeping on the floor."

"But we've got one of the spare rooms now. How am I supposed to protect Riley if she's putting distance between us?"

"Why don't you go up and call her?" Simone said. "It sounds like you two need a good talk."

* * *

Raven closed the bedroom door and placed the baby monitor on the nightstand. She drew out her cell phone and dialed Riley's number. It rang twice before Riley picked up. "Hey," Raven said.

"Hey."

"I thought we were going to talk this evening."

"Oh, sorry. I guess I forgot. Jenny and Rebecca wanted to go out for dinner after we looked at a few places."

It sounded like Riley was unloading her dishwasher. A drawer opened and closed and there was a clash of cutlery. "Ri, it's not safe for you to stay at your place alone."

There was a loud sigh and a moment of silence before Riley spoke. "It's not safe for me to go to work. It's not safe for me to stay at my apartment. I'm sorry, Rave, but I'm not going to live like that."

"What's that supposed to mean?"

"It means I'm not going to run scared and change my life because you're worried about something that may or may not happen." She wasn't yelling, but her voice was raised. She sounded frustrated.

"Riley, what's going on here? I mean, a few days ago, you were down on your knees, practically begging me to take you back and now you're barely talking to me. When we do talk, it's like I'm a pain in your ass."

Riley huffed. "All this stuff that's been happening has got me on edge. I just need some time to process everything."

"So, what, we're breaking up?" Pain, sharp and intense, sliced through her chest. She closed her eyes and pressed her fist over her heart while she waited for Riley's answer.

"No, not exactly. Just putting getting back together on hold."

"That's breaking up, isn't it?"

"Whatever. Listen, I have to go. I've got work in the morning. I'll stop by tomorrow after work to pick up the rest of my stuff."

The line went dead. Raven dropped the phone to her lap and stared at it. What the hell just happened? Jenny freaking Gallagher is what happened. She had to be putting Riley off of her. What happened to working through things together and being there for each other? *Damn it!* She surged to her feet, her cell phone dropping unnoticed to the carpet, and began pacing the room. She needed to run off the anger coursing through her veins. She changed into her running gear, grabbed the baby monitor, and went back down to the kitchen.

Simone and Kiran were still sitting at the table. "Would you listen for Indi? I haven't had a run in the past few days."

Simone stood, pushing her chair back. "Raven, what's wrong? You look awfully pale."

"I just need to go for a run, okay?" Her voice cracked. She had to get out of there before she broke down in front of them. She left the baby monitor on the counter and charged out the door. Kiran called out her name, but she didn't look back. She cleared the porch steps with a leap, arms and legs pumping as soon as she hit the ground. When she was far enough away from the house that they couldn't hear her, she let out a rip-roaring primal scream. She told herself that the tears dripping from her eyes were from the wind in her face. A storm was blowing in. The sky was starless and the wind whipped through the trees. Thunder roared in the distance.

She kept running, going over the past few days with Riley in her head, trying to figure out what she'd done wrong this time. Riley seemed fine at the Summer Solstice celebration, but then she'd gotten drunk, which wasn't like her. Her behaviour the next morning wasn't like Riley either. Raven still cringed when she thought of the way Riley had taken her. Then the comment about getting over herself. Since then, they'd barely talked. But what caused the change in behaviour? The only answer Raven could come up with was Jenny Gallagher and she cursed herself for not staying at the celebration.

Chapter 19

With her head supported in her palm, elbow on the table, Raven spooned another mouthful of pablum into Indi. She'd tossed and turned all night, often waking to reach for Riley and finding nothing but cold, desolate sheets. Her chest ached with the loss, the gaping hole inside her back with a vengeance. Like she was empty. A vast void.

She barely noticed Rauri come into the kitchen. She made herself a cup of tea and sat down across from Raven. Indi blew a raspberry and laughed as the pablum spattered over Raven's face. Raven just spooned up another mouthful and shovelled it into Indi's little bow mouth.

"Will you tell me what happened?"

Raven lifted her head wearily, looked at Rauri, then leaned her head against her hand again. "Nothing to tell."

"Alright. But, if you change your mind, I'm here."

Raven closed her eyes, swallowed the emotions clawing their way up her throat. "Would you watch Indi for me this morning? I've got a few things to take care of."

"Aye, of course. But, you look like you could do with going back to bed."

No point, Raven thought. She'd just toss and turn.

After feeding Indi, she bathed her then hopped in the shower. She put the Book of Shadows she'd bought with

Riley's things, thought about putting a note with it and decided she didn't know what to write.

She was out the door ten minutes later and went straight to her land. The wood for her deck had already been delivered and the RV showed up five minutes after she got there. She directed them to position the RV where she wanted it, then she went and sat next to the pile of ash. The ground was damp from the rain the night before, but she didn't care.

She supposed Dr. Shoal was right about grieving for her home. Damn it all to hell, she wanted her little cottage back, wanted to turn back the clock to the night she and Riley had snuggled all night and Indi was safe in her crib. She wanted to freeze time at that moment so that nothing changed. Her body shook as she let rip another primal scream, then dropped her face into her hands and wept.

"Why, you son of a bitch? Why destroy my home? What have I done to you?" She screamed until her voice was hoarse then she got to her feet, stepped into the ash, and began tearing through the debris. Her vision was blurred by tears, her wild digging spurred by anger. "Why?" she screamed. She wasn't sure if she was asking why destroy her home or why Riley left her. She lifted a length of a charcoaled beam and launched it across what used to be her living room with a wild growl. Fists clenched and shaking, she leaned back and screamed at the sky, "Why?"

"Raven!"

Arms circled her waist and she was lifted into the air, kicking and screaming. She pushed at the arms, but they wouldn't budge.

"Stop it! It's not safe." Kiran set her down once they reached the driveway and clamped his hands around her biceps as she struggled to get free. "Stop it, Raven."

Her shoulders heaved and she collapsed into him, ugly crying into his chest, her blackened hands clenched into tight fists in his shirt. His arms circled her, holding her close.

"Damn it, Raven. I know how much you're hurting? Why do you have to suffer alone when you have your family to lean on?" His breath hitched. "It kills me to see you like this, love."

Oh, damn. Raven had totally lost her shit. She couldn't stop the sobs wrenching out of her and she didn't want to. Kiran held onto her, rocking back and forth until finally, finally, she cried herself out.

"It will be alright, darling. The house can be rebuilt."

"It's not … just the house."

"I know, darling." His hand brushed over her hair and he pressed a kiss to her temple. "It's Riley, isn't it?"

She nodded into his chest, squeezing her eyes tightly shut against another onslaught of tears. Goddess, she was a mess.

"Let's get you home and cleaned up."

She turned and started towards the car, but her legs were like jelly and she wavered. Kiran's arm circled her waist and he threw the other one behind her knees, lifting her.

"I can walk," Raven croaked. She'd tossed a beam a few minutes ago and now she barely had the strength to lift her head.

"Bloody hell. Just shut up and let me get you in the car."

He put her in the passenger seat of his SUV, which Raven had driven there. Simone's car was parked behind it. "I can drive." She pointed behind her. "Simone's car."

"I'll come back for it. Where are my keys?"

She dug in the pocket of her jeans for them, but it was an enormous effort. She was utterly exhausted, her strength zapped. She dropped the keys before she could hand them off. Kiran caught them up and got in the driver's seat. Raven was asleep before he hit the end of her road.

* * *

Raven awoke disoriented and groggy. The sun was bright

outside the windows. The last thing she remembered was Kiran lifting her into his car. How had she gotten into bed? She lifted the sheet and stared down at her body. Except for the cute boy shorts she'd bought at Walmart, she was naked. She didn't remember coming into the house or getting undressed. There was white gauze wrapped around her right hand and halfway up her forearm. Black soot was caked under her nails and around them.

She turned her head and looked at the clock on the nightstand. Six fifteen. *Oh, shit. Indi.* How could they have let her sleep all day? She threw the sheet off and jumped up, only to drop her butt back down to the bed when the room spun. She waited for it to settle, then tried again, getting up slowly this time. She made it to the dresser and pulled on a t-shirt just as the door opened.

Simone entered carrying a tray. "Back in bed," she said with a stern look.

"I need to check on Indi. It's after six. I've been sleeping all day."

"And you'll continue to rest. Get in the bed."

"No." Raven fisted her hands and glared at Simone. "I'm going to go find my daughter."

"I'll have Rauri bring her up, but you're getting back in bed. Doctor's orders." Simone set the tray on the nightstand and turned to Raven with her hands on her hips. "You had a stress-induced breakdown this morning, Rave. I had to give you a sedative so you'd get some rest. Now get your ass back in that bed, or I'll have Kiran come up here and put you in it."

Raven snorted. "As if."

"I'd be surprised if you had the strength to resist him."

She couldn't argue. If her hip hadn't been resting against the dresser, she'd probably be on the floor. "You'll bring Indi up?"

"Yes."

Raven swallowed her pride and walked back to the bed on rubber legs. She got in and Simone fluffed the pillows at her back then set the tray on her lap.

"Eat."

"I'm not hungry."

"Damn it, Raven. Eat." She walked out and slammed the door behind her.

Raven rolled her eyes, then studied the bowl of chicken noodle soup on her lap. She hadn't had chicken noodle soup since she was a kid. Ena used to make it for her when she was sick. Tears welled up in her eyes. *Damn it.* What was wrong with her? She blinked them away and picked up the spoon. Her stomach roiled, but she sipped some of the broth then waited to make sure it wasn't going to come back up again.

"There she is. There's mummy." Rauri came in with Indi in her arms. Indi grinned and reached out her arms. Her little cheeks were rosy, her chin wet with drool.

Raven lifted the tray to the nightstand, her arms shaking like she'd done too many reps with a heavy weight. Rauri set Indi on her lap and Raven wrapped her trembling arms around her.

"We think she's cutting another tooth. She's been a bit grumpy all day."

Raven kissed the top of Indi's head. She'd been asleep all day and still missed her little angel. "That'll explain the drooling."

"Aye."

Raven would have stuck her pinky in Indi's mouth, but she still had soot all around her nails. She looked up at Rauri, wondering how much she knew. "Did Riley stop by to pick up her stuff?"

"Aye," Rauri said softly. She sat on the edge of the bed. "I'm sorry, love."

"You didn't tell her ..."

"No, of course not. Jenny may though. She was here when Kiran carried you in."

"Great." Heat flushed up from Raven's chest and bloomed over her face.

"Hmmm." Rauri glanced away then slowly brought her eyes back to Raven. "Kiran asked Jenny and Rebecca to leave this morning. They packed up and left in a taxi. I'm not sure if they went to a hotel or Riley's."

Oh, man. Raven wished she hadn't missed that. "Why?"

"Oh, they had words when Kiran brought you in."

She could just imagine what Jenny had said. Indi gripped onto her index finger and Raven smiled down at her. The strength of her daughter's grip was stronger than Raven felt at the moment.

"I'm sorry for the trouble she's caused."

"It's not your fault, Gran."

Rauri smiled and patted Raven's leg. "No, but I brought her here."

"How long do you think Simone is going to force me to stay in bed?"

Rauri roared. "Oh, I imagine until you're feeling better."

Raven rolled her eyes. "Have you seen my cell phone?"

"Aye, it's in the kitchen. Kiran didn't want you to be disturbed."

"Would you bring it up for me?" Stupid, but she wanted to see if Riley had called or texted.

"Alright." She got up and went to the door then turned back. "This has been hard on him, aye? Simone nearly gave him a sedative as well."

Raven blew out a breath, her bangs fluttering up. "I'm sorry. I didn't mean to upset him."

"No, of course not. Kiran loves you, Raven. And he's worried sick."

"I know. I'm sorry."

"I know you're fiercely independent and I ken why, but it would be easier for him if you could talk to him more. If something's bothering you. I think it would be better for you both, aye?"

Raven nodded. Could she possibly feel any worse? She knew Kiran was an empath and anything she was feeling would affect him. Goddess, was there anything more embarrassing than your father being able to tune in to your emotions?

* * *

It was Mick who walked into the room a few minutes later with Raven's cell phone. "Hey, we came by to see you and Indi. Kiran said you're not feeling well."

"No, not so great."

"What's wrong?" Mick set the phone on the nightstand and sat on the edge of the bed. "What happened to your arm?"

Raven glanced down at the white bandage. Simone hadn't said what was wrong with her arm and she didn't remember injuring it. She must have cut it when she was digging through the ashes. "Ah, I cut myself."

Mick's eyes narrowed. "What's going on, Rave?"

There was no way she was going to explain what had happened that morning. She narrowed her eyes at Mick. "Drop it, okay?"

Mick grabbed her hand and studied her nails for a moment. Raven pulled her hand away, but not before Mick had gotten a good look at the soot surrounding her nails.

"Okay," Mick said, her eyes softening as if she understood.

"Any news on Derek Branson?"

"Not much. Branson's been charged with assault, but he's wanted by the RCMP for murder in Vancouver. He's being picked up tomorrow morning. LaCroix is going to have another run at him tonight, but we're not hopeful."

"Anything on those cigarette butts or the lighter fluid?"

"Oh, yeah. Some of the butts had Derek Branson's DNA. The other ones were a sibling, a brother." Mick grinned. "Derek has one brother. Erik James Branson. We've got a warrant and a BOLO out on him."

And that would be like finding a needle in a haystack, especially if he knew his brother was in custody. Erik would be in the wind. "Younger, older?"

"Younger. Twenty-four, I think."

"Hmmm." They might get a lot more out of a twenty-four-year-old than they would thirty-year-old Derek. If, and it was a big if, they could find him.

"Hear anything on your exam?"

Mick grinned again. "Aced it."

"I knew you would. Congratulations."

"Thanks," Mick blushed. "There's going to be a little ceremony next week. I was wondering if you'd come."

Raven gave Mick a weak punch to the shoulder. "I wouldn't miss it."

"Really? That's great."

"Hey," Jax said as he walked into the room and reached his arms out for Indi. Indi giggled and lifted her arms. He was tall and muscular with nordic good looks - straight blonde hair and bright blue eyes. He dropped kisses all over Indi's face, making her giggle harder. "Hello, sweetheart. How's my darling today?"

"Cutting another tooth," Raven said as if she'd been there all day to see her fussing.

"Is that why you've stopped breastfeeding?" he asked.

Raven's head shot up, their eyes meeting. "You knew I wasn't breastfeeding?"

"Kind of obvious."

He nodded towards her small chest and Raven looked down at herself. She supposed her breasts *had* shrunk since she stopped breastfeeding. "I know I should have told you, but ..."

"It's alright, Rave. It's your choice, your body."

"It wasn't a choice. I, uh ... my milk dried up."

"And you were scared to tell me?"

She cringed. "Sort of."

He leaned over and kissed her cheek. "You're cute."

"Yeah, sure." She rolled her eyes at him.

"You want us to take this little one off your hands for a while so you can rest?"

No, she didn't. She hadn't seen Indi all day. But, she couldn't deny that she was exhausted and Jax was entitled to time with Indi, too. "You'll stay here with her?"

"Yeah." He glanced at Mick. "We'll make sure she's safe, Rave."

Of course, Mick would have kept him updated on what had gone on. "Hey, Jax? What do you know about your lineage? You know, witch wise?"

His father left when he was a baby and his mother passed away when he was in college. He didn't talk about either of them much. His mother had been a member of the Solstice Coven as far back as Raven could remember. That's where she'd met Jax and they'd become quick friends.

"You know my mom was a witch, Rave."

"Yeah, but was she a hereditary witch and do you know how strong her bloodlines were? Was your father a magus?"

"Why are you asking?"

Raven swiped her hand through her hair. "It's just a theory. I don't know why someone would try to take Indi unless they had some idea of the powers she'll have or they wanted to hold her ransom for Ena's money."

"I don't know much about my father. My mother didn't talk about him much after he left. My mom's side is all witches, although I don't know how far back the line goes. I could give my aunt a call."

"Yeah, would you?" She could have asked Alana herself when she was in Mystique the day before, but she hadn't even thought of asking her.

"Just how powerful do you think she'll be, Rave?" He asked while staring at his daughter.

"She's already displaying some magical powers, but they seem to be from the Hayes side."

Jax laughed. "That's not a surprise. Just look at her." She was her mother and grandfather through and through with the jet black hair and ice-blue eyes framed in thick black lashes. Indi scrunched up her petite nose at him and sniffed in and out, giggled, then repeated her funny face. Jax lifted her into the air, blew a raspberry on her belly and Indi broke out in a full belly laugh.

That got everyone laughing and Raven silently thanked the Goddess for the blessing of her daughter.

"Come on, little angel. Let's give your mother some peace." He started for the door and Mick got up to follow him.

"Hey, could you do me a favour before you go? Could you bring that book on the dresser over for me?" She didn't have the strength to lift the Bowen Grimoire and she wanted to have a look to see if she could determine what powers her ancestors had.

"Sure," Mick said. She lifted the book with a grunt and brought it over, laying it on Raven's lap. "A little light reading?"

Raven laughed. "Yeah." She flipped open the cover and then through the first few pages. Skimming through page after page, she found a lot of the early entries were written in the Runic alphabet. Not a big deal, she thought. She had a book with the Runic alphabet in it. All she had to do was decode it. Then she remembered she no longer had that book.

It had burned with her house. She picked up her phone and texted Kiran. Surely Ena had something in her library with the Runic alphabet in it.

He walked into the room a few minutes later with a paperback book in his hand - *The Grimoire of Lady Sheba*. "How are you feeling, love?"

"I'm alright. Are you okay?"

"Aye. You gave me quite a fright." He brushed his hand over her bed head as if he could tame her unruly hair.

"Sorry. I don't know what got into me. I was just so angry all of a sudden."

"It's okay to be angry, Rave. I'm sure I'd feel the same. What's worrying us is you're not taking proper care of yourself. You're not sleeping or eating."

He must have been talking to Simone. "It's not like I'm not trying. I just toss and turn."

He pointed to the neglected bowl of soup on the nightstand.

Raven scrunched up her nose. "It's hard to eat when you don't have an appetite. In my defence, I did eat a few spoonfuls."

"Well, then. That's brilliant. You should be up and running again in no time. That'll really build your strength."

"Have you read this thing?" She patted the Grimoire on her lap, hoping he took the change of subject bait.

"Not all of it. I didn't translate any of the entries written in the Runic alphabet." He placed the paperback on top of the Grimoire. "Which you'll find in here."

"Thanks. Did you find anything in it that might be relevant?"

"Not really. I was mostly interested in what your mother had written." Kiran stood and reached over, giving Raven's hair a tousle. "Don't spend too much time on it, aye? You need your rest, love."

Raven didn't even get through the first page before her eyes were struggling to stay open. The first entry was dated September 17, 1867, and was written by Eloise Bowen. She told the story of their journey from England to what she called Canada West and settling into a remote town her mother, Lady Moira Bowen, had dubbed Solstice. Eloise stated that her mother thought them finally safe in this secluded area surrounded by forests and lakes, noting that Lady Moira finally seemed at peace and content. It sounded like they'd been running from something, but Eloise didn't mention what it was, at least in the first entry. Raven had to close the book and slide it off her legs. She was asleep as soon as she scooted down the bed and got comfortable.

* * *

Raven looked around the room. It was her mother's kitchen, but it didn't look nearly the same. The walls were papered with a floral print instead of painted. There was no fridge or stove. Only a large hearth with a hearty fire. She looked out a window to the cliffs and Fairy Lake. It was the same view, except where the great room should have been, there was a garden. Across the lake, she couldn't see any of the cottages that should have dotted the shoreline.

She turned and went to the window on the other side of the room, looking out over the town of Solstice. The driveway wasn't paved and there were no cars. She could see a couple of buildings dotting the main street, but it certainly wasn't the town she knew.

"Well, hello."

She spun around to stare at the girl standing in the entryway to the kitchen. Her long russet brown hair waved down over her shoulders and she wore a floor-length blue dress with long sleeves and a high collar. The bodice was tight, like a corset, and the skirt looked like a bloody bell, wider at the floor than the doorway. "Hey."

The girl smiled demurely. "Why, you must be our Raven Sage. We wondered when you would finally visit." She spoke with a posh English accent, musical with her lilting voice.

"Who are you?" And how did she know who Raven was?

The girl's eyes widened. "You don't know?"

Raven shook her head.

"I'm Eloise. Your five times great grandmother."

Raven snorted as a woman stepped up behind Eloise and laid her hands on the girl's shoulders. She stopped laughing when she got a better look at the woman in the dim light. She wore a pale yellow dress in a similar style to the girl's. For a moment, Raven thought she was looking at Ena. Her hair was the same colour as the girl's, but her features were all Ena.

"Mother, Raven Sage has come."

The woman laughed and covered her mouth with her hand. "You look like you've seen a ghost." She stepped around Eloise and took Raven's hands in hers. "Forgive me my terrible sense of humour. Hello, Raven. You've finally come into your Bowen powers. Merry meet."

"Merry meet," Raven repeated automatically. "What do you mean, I've finally come into my Bowen powers?"

"Why, dream travelling, of course."

"Dream travelling?"

"It's one of the Bowen blessings. Will you have tea?" She turned back to Eloise. "Eloise, dear. Would you mind?"

"Not at all, mother." She hastened to a large metal pot and hefted it over to the fire, setting it on a hook. "It shan't take long, Raven Sage. Although we don't have your modern conveniences."

"I don't understand," Raven said. Dream travelling? She must be dreaming, that's all.

"You've come from your time to ours," the woman said.

"I'm sorry. I don't know your name."

The woman's hand covered her mouth again as she laughed. "But, of course, you do. I'm Lady Moira, High Priestess of the Silver Star Coven and your six times great grandmother."

"Lady Moira, I think I'm just dreaming."

"You see, Eloise. I told Ena she never should have hidden Raven's

blessings from her. She doesn't believe."

"If she doesn't believe, how can she be here?" Eloise asked.

"Now, there's a question." Lady Moira pulled Raven to a scarred rectangular table with benches at either side. "Please sit and tell us about your journey."

"My journey?" Raven dropped her butt onto the bench.

"Yes. Why have you come to us now?"

"I don't know. I'm sleeping." Wasn't she? This was the weirdest dream she'd ever had. It seemed so real yet unreal at the same time.

"Well, of course, you are." Lady Moira laughed again. "We dream travel when we've a need to visit our ancestors or others. Sometimes we dream travel to the future, but mostly the past. We've been to your time, although we prefer the quiet solitude of our own. You have questions you need answered, Raven Sage."

"I suppose I do. I guess I need to know what powers I've inherited from the Bowen side, if any." What had Moira said - I told Ena she never should have hidden Raven's blessings from her? "Ena blocked me from them, didn't she?"

Eloise set a cup of flowery tea in front of Raven then curtsied. Curtsied. Weird. "Thank you."

"My pleasure." She got a cup for Lady Moira and herself then sat across from Raven, staring at her with a dreamy smile on her face. She put her elbows on the table and rested her chin in her palms. "You're magnificent." She sighed and blushed a rosy tone.

Raven nearly spit her tea across the table. She snorted and cupped her hand over her mouth and nose to prevent her tea from spewing. "You're my great, great, great, great, great grandmother!"

"Please forgive her," Lady Moira said with a reprimanding look at Eloise. "She's like a rabbit. Anything with a heartbeat has her loins stirring. It's her age, you see. And the Bowen genes." She took a sip of her tea, her eyes gleaming as she gave Raven a knowing smile.

It brought the ache in Raven's chest into sharp focus.

"Oh, dear." Lady Moira reached across the table and patted

Raven's hand. "Not you, too? Ena suffered greatly with her lost love."

Was she that obvious? Yeesh. Time for the change of subject tactic. "Would you tell me why you left England? What brought you to Canada?"

"Dark times. We weren't safe." Lady Moira rose from the table and scurried from the room.

Raven stared after her with her mouth hanging open.

Eloise watched her mother retreat then turned sad eyes on Raven. "It's difficult for her still. She can't talk about it."

Raven didn't want to know the answer now. As bad as things had been in her childhood, in the time that Moira and Eloise lived, she knew things could be and probably were much worse. "That's alright. I don't need to know."

"No, you've lived through your own dark times, haven't you?"

She still was. Raven rubbed the ache in her chest. She hadn't gotten any answers, but she wanted to leave this place. The trouble was, she didn't know how to wake herself up.

Chapter 20

Raven sat bolt upright in bed with a gasp. Dream. It had just been a dream. She'd never heard of dream travelling. Yet, Ena had come to her in her dreams for years, secretly continuing her Wiccan training. Was that the same as dream travelling? Were Lady Moira and Eloise dreaming, too?

Oh, man. She really must be suffering from stress if she thought her dream was real. But, if it was … on the off chance that she really could dream travel, did it mean she could visit Ena in the past? Her breath hitched. What she wouldn't give to have a conversation or ten with her mother.

She pulled the Bowen Grimoire onto her lap and flipped through the pages until she found Ena's first entry. Like Eloise, she'd begun with a sort of journal entry, but hers was more of a bio. It was dated the day of her sixteenth birthday. She described herself, her likes and dislikes. She mentioned half a dozen boys that she had her eye on. Well, that hadn't changed. At least, until Kiran had come back into her life. Near the bottom of the page, she found what she was looking for.

Lady Beatrice finally allowed me to experience my first dream travel and we visited my great, great, great, great grandmother, Eloise, and my great, great, great, great, great grandmother, Lady Moira. I was shocked when we met. It was like looking into a mirror and seeing myself in the future. We sat at the table to sip herbal tea in the same kitchen where I ate breakfast and dinner every day, except it wasn't the same kitchen at all.

It hadn't been a dream.

Raven flopped back onto the mattress and stared up at the ceiling. "Holy shit." She could visit Ena. She didn't know how it worked, but somehow she'd figure it out. She wanted to go now and sit with Ena at the kitchen table sometime during the years they'd been estranged. Heck, she'd even sip flowery tea.

She closed her eyes and tried to will herself to sleep, but she was too wired. There were too many thoughts running through her head about what she could talk to Ena about. What if she could warn her about Adara? Would it change what happened? Could she stop Adara from killing Ena? Could she heal Ena while dream travelling? Oh, the possibilities were astounding.

Her heart sank with the realization that if she stopped Adara from doing all the horrible things she'd done, she wouldn't have Indigo. She'd gotten pregnant when Adara had put a spell on her and Jax so that they'd sleep together. It was her way of breaking up Raven and Riley so that Raven would spend more time with Adara. She needed to keep her close to soak up Raven's powers.

Could she dream travel to Ena and warn her about Adara and risk never having her baby girl? Was life so cruel that she'd be forced to decide between her mother's life or her daughter's?

She glanced over at the clock and decided she'd probably had more than enough sleep for the day anyway. She sat up and dropped her legs over the side of the bed. She got up slowly, testing the strength in her legs. She definitely wouldn't be going for a run this morning, but she managed to get a shower and change. She headed for Indi's room. Resting her forearms on the rail of the crib, she watched her baby sleeping peacefully in the soft glow of the night light with Jet curled at her side and realized there was no decision to make. As much as she wanted a second chance with her mother, she couldn't do it at the risk of not having Indi in her life.

She went back to her room for the Bowen Grimoire and settled into the rocking chair in Indi's room with it to see what other family secrets she could glean.

She started with the first entry that wasn't written in the Runic alphabet. In 1925, on her sixteenth birthday, Moira Bowen, Lady Moira's namesake, and Ena's great grandmother wrote her first entry. She, too, described herself and her life before detailing her spells and rituals. She spoke of the swell of the population during the summer months and the growing number of cottages being built.

Mum says our safety is paramount and insists I be leery of every person I meet. I can't imagine, after all these years, that he would still be looking for my ancestors. Surely he must be dead by now. But, mum says his revenge was passed down to his son and his son's sons. Maybe we'll never be safe, us women of the Bowen clan. Or, maybe, we always have been and my ancestors are simply overly paranoid. Or, perhaps it's wishful thinking on my part. I have no desire to be leery of the handsome young men driving through Solstice in their parent's fancy cars. Ah, but they are enticing. And that's a story for my diary, my beloved descendants. Sorry to disappoint.

Raven laughed. The Bowen hyper-sexual gene certainly didn't seem to skip any generations. She moved on to Moira's daughter, Amaris Bowen's first entry on her sweet sixteenth in 1944.

They come in droves, carting their wounded to our serene shores and why shouldn't they? This is the perfect place to heal, body and mind, and there are so many broken souls. Mother and I advertised a healing day camp, not knowing whether anyone would come. So many are not open to natural healing rituals, though it would do them good. To our surprise, it was an enormous success. At least, it was until Mother abruptly ended the program. She won't tell me why, but it had something to do with a man who registered with the program as Randall James Parker. Handsome he was, with wavy brown hair and lovely hazel eyes. Haunted, as were so many, but lovely. When he gave his name, Mother looked terrified. She's secluded herself in her rooms and has become overly protective. Still, I've been sneaking out to see the twins and she doesn't seem to have noticed my absence.

Raven snorted. Why settle for one when you can have two? She rushed back to her room for a pen and paper then wrote down the name Randall James Parker. It was her first tangible clue.

The next to write her story in the Grimoire was Raven's grandmother, Beatrice. Her first entry was written in the year 1966.

It happened on the one-hundredth anniversary of Lady Moira and Eloise's flight from England. They came to our sacred ground and desecrated it with fire and steel. One hundred years they waited to exact their revenge! We were powerless, as if our abilities had been stripped from us. It was like being paralyzed. They forced mother and grandmother to their knees, then wrenched poor Siobhan from her mother's grasp and forced her down next to them. Goddess help me, I don't know how they knew about Siobhan. We'd been so careful, my lover and I. I couldn't look at her as all three took their turn with me, forcing my loved ones to watch their debauchery. Goddess help us! For I fear they are not done.

* * *

Raven slammed the book closed, tossing it to the floor as she shot to her feet with her fists clenched at her sides. She paced the room like a caged lion, wishing she could punch something, someone. It was bad enough that Beatrice had been gang-raped in front of her lover, her mother, and her grandmother, but Ena had been born nine months later. Whoever those men were, one of them was her grandfather. She had an inkling for how Riley must feel. She'd just had a shower, but she wanted another one, as if she could scrub away the horror crawling under her skin.

"What it is, love?" Rauri stood in the hallway in her black robe. It wasn't even dawn, yet her hair was styled to perfection.

How could she explain everything she'd read? Her hand waved in the direction of the Grimoire. "I thought I could learn something about the powers of my ancestors."

"Ah." Rauri stepped into the room and put her arm around Raven's waist. "Come down with me. I need a cup of tea, then we can sit down while you tell me what you've learned."

Raven turned to the crib. "Indi…"

"I've got the monitor here, darling. She's fine." Rauri lifted her hand to show Raven the monitor.

Raven nodded and let Rauri guide her down to the kitchen. She felt numb, like she was in some kind of stupor. Like she was in shock and maybe she was. Raven slumped into a chair at the kitchen table and dropped her head onto her folded arms. "I don't have all the answers, but something happened in England before Lady Moira brought Eloise to Canada and whoever she wronged waited a long time to get their revenge." She told Rauri what she'd learned from reading Moira, Amaris, and Beatrice's stories.

"They blocked their powers like they did when Beatrice was killed. You know why they couldn't block Ena's powers, don't you?" Raven didn't wait for Rauri's response. "Because Ena is one of them, she's of their blood. As am I."

"Oh, Rave."

"No, don't you see? I'll use that to take them down. To rip them to pieces."

"You have the right to defend yourself, but there's a fine line between defence and offence. Be very careful, Raven Sage."

Both hands dove into Raven's hair and formed tight fists. "I don't even know who they are?" She shot to her feet, nearly knocking her chair over backward, and paced the kitchen. Funny how anger gave you such energy, such strength. She didn't feel weak at all. "But, I have one lead to follow up on."

Rauri looked up at her with a wrinkled brow. "Just promise me you won't do anything alone and you'll be very careful. We don't want to lose another Bowen, Raven."

"This has been going on for a hundred and fifty years. It's time to put an end to it." She just needed to figure out what *this* was and how to stop it once and for all.

"Good morning," Kiran said as he walked into the kitchen and put the kettle on. "Feeling better today?"

The baby monitor sounded with Indi's cry and Raven threw up her arms and shrugged.

"I'll fill him in, love," Ruari smiled weakly. "You go see to Indi."

Raven got to the top of the stairs and shook out her arms and legs, trying to dispel some of the ire rushing through her veins before she picked up Indi. Then she took several deep breaths and walked into Indi's room. Indi looked like she was doing a push up then she rolled to her side and onto her back. Raven leaned over the crib rail, grinning down at her. "Look at you doing your morning exercises."

Indi grinned up at her with one sparkling tooth and babbled. Then she shoved her entire fist into her mouth. Raven tugged gently on her wrist until Indi's goobery fist popped out. Lifting her into her arms, she cooed. "Good morning, angel." She kissed her cheeks, her nose, her forehead, her chin. Indi leaned forward and smushed her slobbery mouth to Raven's cheek like a little suction cup. Raven lifted her out in front of her, holding her at arm's length. "Thank you for your kisses." Then she pulled her in and peppered her face with kisses again. She couldn't imagine anyone hurting this sweet child. Goddess help them if they tried. Her blood was beginning to race through her veins again, so she put thoughts of the Bowen tragedies aside and concentrated on her daughter. "What are we going to wear today?"

Kiran stepped into the room, kissing his granddaughter before brushing and hand down Raven's arm. "Maybe now's not the best time for you to be reading that Grimoire."

She laid Indi on the changing table and grabbed a clean diaper. "I don't think there will ever be a best time, but I need to know what happened all those years ago if I'm going to be able to protect Indi."

"I just think you should give yourself some time to recuperate before you get into this."

Sometimes she had to remind herself that Kiran was an empath and what he had experienced with her yesterday morning could have been more traumatic for him than it was for her. She slid her hand down his arm and gently clasped his wrist. "I feel better. Besides, how do we know if we've got any time to waste. They've already attacked twice."

"Well, someone has. You don't know that it has anything to do with your ancestors."

Raven finished changing Indi and lifted her into her arms before facing Kiran. "I still need to investigate what happened."

He pursed his lips. "Maybe Ena had good reason to keep you in the dark, Rave. She must have felt it was necessary to protect you."

The edges of Raven's mouth curled up. "I think I might have an opportunity to ask her."

His brows drew together. "How's that?"

"Dream travelling."

Kiran sighed. "And so it begins. How did you figure it out?"

"You knew about it?"

"Ena was always full of stories in the mornings after her travels."

"Why didn't you say anything?"

"Because there had to be a reason she didn't want you to come into your Bowen powers and I didn't know what that reason was, but I know it was to protect you."

"We could keep hiding, keep suppressing my powers, but trouble's coming and I'd much rather have every advantage possible when it arrives."

Kiran raked his fingers through his hair and huffed. "Aye. You're right, of course."

Raven nodded. Step one complete. "I want to have a look through the attic for diaries or journals."

"Bloody hell," he sighed. "Full steam ahead."

* * *

It took a lot of digging through boxes and all of the morning, but Raven found diaries belonging to most of her ancestors. The only ones she couldn't find diaries or journals for were Lady Moira and Ena, and those were the ones she most wanted.

She put Indi down for her afternoon nap and sat at the kitchen table with Rauri, Kiran, Mick, and dozens of diaries. She split them up amongst the group. "Here's what we're looking for - any mention of what happened in England before Lady Moira and Eloise came to Canada and any reference to a Randall James Parker."

Rauri's head shot up from the diary she was leafing through. "Randall Parker?"

"You know the name?" Raven asked.

"I've heard it before, aye." She narrowed her eyes, looking off into space. "I can't put my finger on it, but I think he's a figure in magickal history."

"Google him," Mick said.

Raven stared at her blankly, then smiled, leaned forward and kissed her on the mouth.

Mick screeched, wiped her mouth and turned bright red.

Raven got up to go grab her laptop then realized she didn't have one anymore. She turned to Kiran. "Could I borrow your iPad?"

"Aye, of course. It's in the office on the desk."

She retrieved the iPad and entered Randall James Parker in the search bar. Of course, about fifty million Randall James Parkers popped up. Raven slumped back in her chair with a sigh.

"Try adding the year Lady Moira left England," Rauri suggested. "That ought to narrow it down."

Raven added 1866 to the name and hit enter. "Bingo." She clicked on the link for Wikipedia and leaned forward. When everyone leaned over her shoulders to peer at the screen, she decided to read it out loud, skimming through for the relevant pieces. "Randall James Parker, High Priest of the Silver Star Coven from 1858 through 1866 when his wife, Lady Moira Gwyn Bowen, disappeared along with their daughter Eloise Amaris Bowen and the entire coven. It is said that they absconded with Parker's fortune and a rare magickal amulet of the Goddess Cerridwen. Parker went mad and was committed to an asylum until his escape in 1871."

"Bloody buggering hell." Kiran raked his fingers through his hair at the same time Raven did.

"The Sacred Moon," Rauri whispered.

"The what?" Raven asked.

"The Sacred Moon Amulet," Rauri repeated. "It's imbued with the powers of Cerridwen, Welsh Goddess of the Moon and Harvest, Keeper of the Sacred Cauldron. The amulet brings great psychic ability and metaphysical powers to the bearer. It's been missing for … well, I suppose you know how long it's been missing."

Raven's eyes drifted up to the ceiling. "It's in a freaking box up in that attic, isn't it?"

Mick, Kiran, and Rauri all followed her gaze. "I suppose we should go and have a look," Kiran said, but no one moved.

Raven dropped her face into her hands and scrubbed. "Shit. That's where the Bowen money came from. It's stolen."

"They must have had good reason," Rauri said. "Most of the coven left with them. Besides, he was her husband, so was it really stealing?"

Raven lifted her head and stared at Rauri. "It's still stealing."

"Such a copper." Rauri winked with a sheepish grin on her face.

Chapter 21

Weeks passed with no more attempts on Raven or Indi. It was as if the threat left with the festival, yet a lingering negative energy hung over Solstice. It wasn't anything Raven could put her finger on and, at times, she wondered if she imagined it. Or perhaps it was the soul-deep pain that engulfed her again after losing Riley. Riley hadn't called, not even to thank Raven for the Book of Shadows, but she may not even know that it was from Raven. Or, she did and threw it out or something.

She'd spent days reading through dozens of diaries, searching boxes for the elusive Sacred Moon, all to no avail. Mick was working on tracking down info on Randall James Parker after he escaped the asylum, but it was as if he disappeared off the face of the planet. Raven figured he changed his name, started a new life, and probably spent it searching for his wife and daughter.

Raven and Indi moved into the RV and Raven hired an architect to design a new cottage and Jax's company to clean up the debris and build the house. The first few days that they were working at the site, they found a few salvageable items. Some of the weights she had in her home gym had survived, but not much else. They'd found Riley's crystal ball, shattered into pieces with the copper base melted into a wad of blackened metal. For some reason, losing that piece bothered Raven. She'd called the artist and arranged a commissioned piece to replace it, although she had no idea if she would give it to Riley or if Riley would even want it. It was just something she felt compelled to do.

She sat out on the deck she'd built while Indi was having her nap inside the RV and gazed out over Fairy Lake. The heat and humidity left a light sheen of sweat over her entire body, but Raven didn't mind. She preferred this to the long, cold winter.

At least she still had this view and the nature surrounding her. The RV was cramped, but it had quickly become home. She'd made her altar on the kitchen island. It didn't offer a lot of privacy, but it was the best she could do. She was content, she thought, except for the gaping hole and the constant thoughts of Riley, wondering what she was doing, reaching for her in the night. It was like starting all over again. All the work she'd done on herself in the past year seemed to have gone out the window.

She caught a movement out of the corner of her eye and glanced down the beach to see Jade Storm walking along the shoreline in bright purple shorts and a lime green tank top. Jade waved and Raven just sat watching her. She started up the lawn towards Raven and a smile slowly spread across Raven's face. Wait, she thought. *Wait for it.* Her grin grew with each step Jade took towards her then *whap*. Jade hit the protective shield face first and Raven burst out laughing.

"Holy shit!" Jade's hand flew up to cover her nose as she glared at Raven. "What the hell was that?" She reached out and touched the invisible barrier then banged on it with her fist. "That wasn't funny. It hurt, damn it."

Raven had to force herself to stop laughing. Just when she thought she had herself under control, she'd snort and giggle again. She really had to start hanging around with adults more or do something for entertainment.

Jade rubbed her nose. "Are you going to get rid of this thing so I can sit down?"

Raven shook her head. "Nope."

"I'm no threat to you, Raven Sage. You have incredible psychic powers. You should know that by now."

Raven didn't feel like laughing anymore. She narrowed her eyes.

Jade narrowed hers right back. "You haven't read me, have you? Why not? You called the RCMP in Lake Louise to check up on me."

And the sergeant she talked to probably called Jade right away to tell her an OPP detective was sniffing around. That told her Jade was pretty tight with the sergeant at least, maybe the whole detachment.

Jade threw up her arms, her hands slapping her thighs when she dropped them again. "Read me now, then."

"What do you want, Jade?"

"Nothing. I'm just neighbourly." She pointed down the beach. "My cottage is just down the road."

"You rent that particular one because it's next to my land?"

Jade laughed. "Man, you're paranoid, aren't you?"

Raven just glared at her.

"Okay, fine." Jade sat on the grass and stretched her long legs out in front of her. "Seems to me you could use a friend. I'm getting sick of watching you sit out here by yourself every evening or standing in your window for hours on end staring out into the dark. You look so damn lonely. I can feel your pain from way over there." She swung her arm towards a massive white cottage and matching boathouse sitting at the end of a point.

"You spying on me, Jade?"

Rolling her eyes, Jade leaned back, planting her hands in the grass behind her. "If I have to sit here all day until you figure out that I'm just trying to be a friend, so be it. If you weren't so stubborn and pig-headed, no pun intended, maybe you'd realize that I can help you."

Raven got up and walked into the RV. She was tempted to leave Jade sitting out there to see how long she'd last. Instead, she grabbed two beers from the fridge, twisted off the tops then went back out. Raven passed one of the beers to Jade and sat down, taking a long swig from her bottle.

Jade eyed the beer then got to her feet. She took baby steps forward, feeling for the barrier with both hands. "Thank you," she said as she stepped up onto the deck. If I'd known all it would take was insulting you, I would have done it a long time ago."

"I don't need a friend."

"Yeah, right. Because you've got them coming over in droves to hang out with your bad self. What happened to the pretty red-head?"

Raven sipped her beer and stared out at the lake.

"Touchy subject?"

Raven flicked her head to the side and pinned Jade with a narrow-eyed glare. Jade smiled, batting her eyes, and Raven turned her gaze back to the lake. *Should have left her on the friggin' lawn.*

"You know, whoever's responsible for burning down your house is using one hell of a powerful cloaking spell."

Raven turned her head again, searching those emerald green eyes for … something. A hint of guilt, maybe? Jade met her gaze and let her search. Raven didn't find what she was looking for. "How would you know that?"

"It's like I can sense their energy all around us and nowhere at the same time, but I can't get a read on them at all. They've been here. Stood over the ashes of your cottage. And still, I can't get a sense of them."

"How do you know they've been here?"

"I came here a couple of days after the fire and I could feel that elusive energy. It was strong, suffocating." Her hand brushed over her throat.

"You'd know if you were near it again?"

"Oh, yeah. Definitely."

"What are you really doing here, Jade Storm?"

Jade took a long haul on her beer then stared into Raven's eyes. "This is what I do, Raven. It's what my mother did, what my grandmother did. I chase down and banish negative energy, negative entities. I'm here to help you."

Her first thought was that she didn't need Jade's help. And that was her stubbornness kicking in. If Jade indeed was who she said she was, she should accept her help. Any advantage she could get in the battle she knew was to come, she should grasp. She was leaning towards trusting Jade and that was so unlike her. There were unanswered questions still. "You told me you were a member of the Shadowmoon Coven."

"You did your homework," Jade smiled. "Except for reading me." She sighed and said, "The Shadowmoon Coven isn't technically a coven as it only has one member. I'm a solitary witch and some have a problem with that."

"Why would anyone have a problem with it?"

Jade shrugged. "Maybe it's my problem. I don't like people looking down their nose at me when they find out I'm a solitary witch as if they're better than me."

It made sense to Raven, so she dropped it. "They haven't made another move against Indi or me since the Summer Solstice."

"No. Perhaps they're regrouping after you arrested their hired hand. Or they're waiting for something."

That's exactly what Raven's gut was telling her, although she still didn't trust it. They were waiting for something - a specific time or for Raven to let her guard down. "There's nothing I can do until they make their next move."

"Mmm. Well, I can think of ways to pass the time." She reached over and skimmed the tips of her fingers up the inside of Raven's exposed thigh.

A sharp pang of arousal shot straight to Raven's core. Her muscles clenched, her breaths sped up. She clamped her hand around Jade's wrist and jerked her hand away from her tingling skin. "I'm not interested in a relationship."

Jade laughed, low and sultry. "Who said anything about a relationship? I'm only here for a short time, Raven. There's no reason we can't enjoy each other until I leave."

"I don't do casual." She'd seen Ena bring too many men home over the years Kiran had been absent from her life and she didn't want that for herself.

"So, what? You're going to remain celibate until your girlfriend realizes what a fool she was for letting you get away?"

She was still throbbing, arousal pulsing at her centre and spreading out in waves. Who could blame her? Jade was a striking, sexy woman and Raven had been sex-deprived for the better part of the last year and a half.

Indi's voice cooed out of the baby monitor followed by a wild, screeching meow and then Indi's belly laugh.

"Shit." Raven jumped up and ran into the RV. When she got to Indi's room, she was still belly laughing, lying on her back in the crib. Jet was on the floor, licking her hind end and there was a slight scent of burnt hair. "Did you zap Jet?"

She bent down and rubbed Jet's head then went over to the crib. Indi's laughing slowed and she grinned up at Raven. Raven shook her head. How did you stop a seven-month-old from using magick? "You're a little monkey." She lifted her daughter to her shoulder and Indi curled up her little body and burrowed her face in Raven's neck. Turning her head, Raven pressed her lips to Indi's hair and just held her like that for a moment, feeling the joy surge through her heart.

"Monkey," she repeated and pictured Jet shooting straight up in the air when Indi zapped her.

* * *

Raven laid in bed that night staring up at the ceiling. Her body hummed with the memory of Jade's touch, but it was Riley that monopolized her thoughts. She didn't want to think about Riley. She wished there was a switch that she could flip to turn her feelings for Riley off. Hell, maybe if she slept with Jade, it would help her get over Riley, but she didn't want to sleep with her for that reason. She didn't know if she was attracted to Jade or if it was just her raging Bowen hormones.

Crap. Now all Raven could think about was sex. She threw off the sheet covering her and swung her legs over the side of the bed, dropping her face into her hands. It wasn't sex with Jade she was thinking about, but sex with Riley.

She threw on a t-shirt and went to the living room, staring out the window. She could see Jade's cottage on the point in the moonlight. Exterior lights shone from the main cottage and the boathouse, twinkling prettily on the lake. None of the interior lights were on, but that wasn't a surprise since it was after two in the morning. The last time she'd slept peacefully through the night, Riley was in her arms. Did Riley lay awake at night, thinking about her, missing her touch? When was she going to stop torturing herself?

She went to the fridge and drew out a bottle of water, guzzling down half of it before wandering through to Indi's room and watching her daughter sleep in the soft glow of the nightlight. She lay on her belly with her little legs pulled up at her sides like a frog. Jet, ever faithful, was curled up at her side, one paw draped over Indi's arm. She smiled and rubbed Jet's head, eliciting a blissful purr. "I guess you've forgiven her for scorching your ass."

She lifted Indi, careful not to wake her, and snuggled her

into her chest as she reclined in the rocker. "Your mother's a mess," she whispered and thought of Ena and the years she'd spent broken-hearted over the loss of Kiran. She hadn't dream travelled since the night she'd visited Lady Moira and Eloise. It wasn't that she didn't want to, but she still wasn't sure how it worked. There was no mention of dream travel in the Grimoire or in the diaries, no step by step instructions to follow. She wished she could go that moment to her mother's kitchen sometime after their falling out. She longed to bask in the glow of her mother's love. She'd had a taste of it after Ena's death only to lose her again when she crossed over. Raven sighed, closed her eyes and breathed in her baby's fresh scent.

The sunlight streamed into Ena's kitchen, the herbs hanging above the window a silhouette against its brightness. Raven turned with Indi hugged to her chest to see Ena sitting at the kitchen island, the light beaming down on her like a spotlight. Her face rested in her hands, her elbows on the island with her tools spread out around her.

"Mom?"

Ena's head shot up, her eyes red-rimmed and puffy. Her mouth dropped open and she quickly covered it with her hand as tears formed in her eyes. "Oh, Raven. You're dream travelling."

Raven nodded.

"My block has been removed. Or did I do it?"

How did she tell her mother she was dead? "You ... you're not able to block my Bowen powers anymore."

Ena rose so slowly it was as if she was levitating. "It's not safe, darling angel. We're not the only ones who can time travel."

Of all the reactions Raven thought Ena might have to seeing her, this wasn't among them. "I thought you'd be happy to see me." Especially at this time. The kitchen was exactly as it had been the night she'd run from this house.

"Oh, I am, darling angel. I am."

She walked to Raven and Indi's legs began pumping, her little arms reaching out to Ena, the grin on her little face showing off her two bottom teeth. Ena's arms came up, her eyes meeting Raven's. "May I?"

Raven nodded and passed Indi over. Indi scrunched up her body and pressed her face into Ena's shoulder as Ena rubbed her back. "Merry meet, Indigo Amaris Rauri Bowen. Blessed be."

"You know her name."

"I do." Ena wrapped her arms around Indi and closed her eyes, her cheek rubbing back and forth over Indi's hair. "I suppose you came because you have questions."

"I came because I wanted to see you, Mom. I came because I miss you."

A fat tear slipped out of the corner of Ena's eye and dribbled down her cheek. She moved Indi to her hip, opening her free arm. Raven stepped into her embrace. Goddess, this was what she needed. Her breath hitched and Ena's arm tightened.

"Oh, sweet angel. You're hurting. Tell me what's happening."

That wasn't why she came. She didn't want to talk or think about Riley. "There's been a lot happening. My house was burned down to flush us out and then they tried to take Indi."

Ena went still in her arms. "They?"

"We arrested a hired thug. We don't know who's behind it, exactly."

"We arrested? You're a police officer?"

"Detective."

Ena leaned back, her eyes wandering over Raven's face as she laid her hand on Raven's cheek. "You're even more beautiful than you were as a child. And Indi ... she's all you and ..." Ena's words dropped away and deep anguish filled her eyes.

"And Kiran," Raven finished for her.

Ena's eyes darted from Indi up to Raven. "So, you know."

"Yes. He helps me a lot with Indi."

Ena's eyes filled again, but her smile was reflected in them. Then they filled with anguish again. "It was only to protect you, Rave. There is enough of a target on your back without people knowing your lineage."

"I know."

Ena's hand brushed down Raven's arm and clasped her hand. "Come and sit. Tell me what you know."

They settled onto the couch in the great room with Indi in Ena's arms. She fell asleep there, her little fist clenched in Ena's hair. Raven chose her words carefully, avoiding any mention of Adara Kirby. She told Ena all that she knew of her ancestors beginning with Lady Moira and Eloise and of the strange negative energy around Solstice. When she was done, Ena lifted Indigo into Raven's arms, disentangling her hair from Indi's fist, and left the room. She came back with a black marker and wrote a number across Raven's palm.

"There's a safe behind the Robert Bateman in my office. You'll find the answers to your questions in the notebook on the top shelf." She leaned in and kissed Raven then Indi. "Be careful, angel mine. The death of every Bowan dating back to Lady Moira has been at their hands."

"Not yours," Raven said before she could stop herself.

"Don't be so sure. Even if it wasn't at their hand, they were in it."

Raven woke with a start. Indi was fast asleep against her chest and Jet sat on the dresser staring at her. "What? You want to come with us next time?"

Jet meowed and it sounded remarkably like *'yeah'*.

Raven grinned and lifted her palm to study the black numbers written across it. She glanced up at the clock. The sun would be up soon. A few more hours and she could go over to Kiran's.

* * *

The Robert Bateman depicted a great blue heron standing in the water surrounded by marsh grasses. Kiran, Simone,

Rauri, and Raven stood in front of it. Kiran hadn't even known about the safe behind it. Raven wondered if anyone would ever have discovered it if she hadn't dream travelled to see Ena.

"Do we just lift it off the wall?" Raven asked.

Kiran stepped forward, grasped either side of the frame and tried to lift it, but it swung out to the left on hinges. A black wall safe of approximately one foot in width and two feet in height was revealed. Raven looked at the number on her palm, then stepped forward and entered it onto the keypad. There was a click and she pulled the door open to find three shelves. The lower shelf was filled with old leather-bound journals. The middle shelf held a deerskin pouch and several more journals. On the top shelf sat one lone notebook.

Raven pulled one of the journals from the bottom shelf and opened the cover. Printed in an elegant scroll inside the cover was 'Lady Moira Bowen - 1865'. "Jackpot," she said. "This is exactly what I've been looking for."

Rauri pulled out the deerskin pouch and pulled out a large pendant. "The Sacred Moon," she gasped. A large, rough black stone with iridescent greens, blues, and purples shimmering throughout was surrounded by an engraved oval of sterling silver and attached to a silver box chain. The stone itself was mesmerizingly beautiful.

"We should leave it in the safe," Raven said. Who knew what it would do to the bearer? Rauri had said it would give them great psychic and metaphysical powers, but how could they be sure?

"Aye, you're right, of course." She gently replaced the pendant in the pouch and set it back on the shelf, picking up one of the journals next to it. "This one is Ena's."

"We'll need to read those, too."

"Do you want to take them all out?" Kiran asked.

"No. Let's each take one of Lady Moira's. When we finish

with it, we can replace it for the next one in sequence." They checked the inside cover of the journals and took the first four into the kitchen. Raven also brought the notebook from the top shelf.

Raven took the 1865 journal and began reading. Towards the end of the year, Lady Moira began writing of Randall turning more and more towards the dark and that she feared for their safety.

We cannot leave without the money that I brought into our union. He holds that and the Sacred Moon as ransom over me. Somehow, I must figure out a way to obtain what is rightfully mine.

Raven speared her fingers through her hair. "She didn't steal the money. Or, not exactly. It was hers when they married."

"Aye," Rauri said. "And Randall Parker was going mad long before his wife and daughter made a getaway. He was practicing black magic and wanted to use Eloise as an altar, letting the men have their way with her. When Lady Moira refused to allow it, he made her the altar in Eloise's stead."

"Holy shit." Raven dropped her face into her hands. She knew it was bad, but to have your husband use you that way?

"This is all well and good," Kiran said. "But it doesn't tell us how Randall Parker or whoever is behind this gained the ability to block powers and cloak their presence. Nor does it tell us who we're up against."

"For that, I'm going to need to dream travel," Raven said. She picked up the notebook and skimmed through its pages. About a quarter of the way through, she found the heading 'Dream Travelling'. The first few paragraphs told her the process and then there was another heading - Rules and Responsibilities. Under that heading, she found some very stern warnings about altering the future during time travel.

Rauri abruptly closed the journal she was reading and held

it in her lap between tight fists. Her brow drawn, she pursed her lips. Her eyes lifted and met Raven's with such sorrow that Raven felt her pain.

"You must promise me, Raven, that you won't read Lady Moira's journals."

"Why?" Of course, she was going to read them. There were things she needed to know to protect her daughter and the future Bowen's. This threat against them had to end.

"Because Lady Moira used these journals to process what she suffered at the hands of Randall Parker. It wouldn't do any good for you to read what she experienced."

Raven's nostrils flared, her eyes narrowed. "Oh, but it's okay for you to read it. Or Simone. Or Dad."

Rauri's eyes softened. "We haven't been through what you have, love."

Raven fisted her hands to prevent herself from slapping her grandmother. She spoke through gritted teeth, her voice low and rough. "What I went through doesn't make me damaged or weak or unable to handle the hard stuff. I'm a cop, Gran. I've investigated rapes and worse."

"I only meant to save you the pain of reading what was done to her. Lady Moira was your kin, Rave."

"Yes, she was. And I'll read whatever I need to if it helps me find who's responsible for everything that was done to her and the rest of my ancestors. This has to stop now because I'll be damned if I let them harm my daughter in any way." Her fists clenched at her sides and the veins in her neck pulsed. "Ena said that they were responsible for the death of every Bowen woman dating back to Lady Moira, including her own. She said it may not have been at their hand, but they were in it."

"You think they helped Adara?" Kiran asked with narrowed eyes.

"I don't know. Ena was adamant that they would have

been involved in her death."

Kiran blew out a breath and crossed his arms over his chest. "We need to know who they are."

"Can I spend the night here?" Raven asked. "I'm worried if I dream travel that I won't hear Indi if she wakes up." Ena had said that it wasn't safe. That they weren't the only ones who could time travel and Raven feared that she was talking about whoever was behind the threat. She wanted Indi safe in her bed.

"It's your house, love," Kiran said. "You're always welcome here."

Chapter 22

Raven set up an altar in the spare room and cast a circle. She lit white candles, performed a protection ritual, then settled into bed. She chose a date that was mere weeks prior to Ena's death, just before Adara began to poison her with arsenic, and set her intention as she dozed off.

She wondered if the kitchen of the Bowen house was some kind of portal. This was her third time dream travelling and she always seemed to begin it at the same spot. The kitchen was much as it was when she'd come here after Ena's death. The kitchen island was Ena's altar, the place she spent most of her time, mixing oils and potions and spells to sell online and at Mystique. It wasn't until that moment that she realized this kitchen in the present day had lost the floral aroma of those oils and potions and that tugged at her heart.

"Mom?" she called out, but she knew the house was empty.

She went into the great room and looked out to the cliffs, hoping she'd find Ena in one of her favourite spots, standing sentry over her cliffs. The landscape was snow-covered and the lake beyond the cliffs frozen. A well-worn path had been cut in the snow out to the cliffs, but Ena wasn't there.

She went to check the driveway for Ena's car next and found her standing out on the road in a long black cloak, looking out over the town of Solstice.

Raven grabbed a parka from the hall closet and exited the front door. "Mom?"

When Ena turned, her eyes were drawn, her face pale except for the twinge of red at her cheeks. When she saw Raven, her eyes brightened and she grinned. She took two running steps toward Raven then drew up. "Oh, Rave. Is it you or ...?"

"I'm dream travelling," she answered and her heart ached as Ena's face dropped. She jogged the rest of the way and embraced her mother. "I'm sorry."

Ena hugged her back then drew away and took Raven's hand. She led her back to the spot where she'd been surveying the town below. "Can you feel it?"

The same negative energy suspended over Solstice in the present-day hung like a heavy weight in the air. "Yes."

"I'm not long for this world, darling angel."

"I know," Raven whispered. Raven closed her eyes and breathed in the cold, crisp air. "I'm sorry for getting so angry that night and for running away. I sat in that park and all I wanted was for you to come after me, for you to choose me."

Ena pressed her fingers to Raven's lips. "The dark energy was here that night, too, Rave. It wasn't your doing."

"I don't understand."

"There was nothing either of us could have done to change the outcome of that night. Or the past twelve years for that matter. There were dark forces at play." She turned and looked back out over Solstice. "As there are now."

"Who's behind it? Whose energy is it?"

Ena's sighed. "Come inside. It's cold and I fear this won't be a short conversation."

Ena made a tea for herself and a coffee for Raven and they settled into the great room again.

"Is Indi okay?" Ena asked.

"Yeah. You said it wasn't safe, so I left Indi with Kiran and Rauri." She didn't want to tell Ena about Simone and Kiran.

Ena smiled. "Rauri is with you?"

"Yeah, she's staying with Kiran for the summer."

"Is he okay?"

"He's grieving, Mom, but he's getting better."

"Is he ... has he found someone?" Ena twisted her hands in her lap. "I want him to be happy and not to spend his life grieving for me the way that I grieved for him. It's no way to live."

Cripes! This wasn't a conversation she wanted to have. Ena already seemed distraught. She didn't want to make it worse. "Yes, he found someone."

"Simone?"

Raven's eyes widened. "Um ... yeah."

"Good. Simone is a beautiful soul who's been alone for too long."

Raven breathed a mental sigh of relief. "She is and she's been very loyal and good to him since your passing. She was a friend, nothing more, until very recently."

"She always was the most loyal and loving friend to me as well. Will you tell them I'm happy for them?"

Raven squirmed in her seat. "Yeah, sure."

"And will you tell me what's hurting you?"

"It's a long story." Raven picked up her coffee and sipped. Just the thought of Riley amplified the constant pain in her chest.

"I know heartache when I see it, darling angel. Is it Riley?"

Raven squeezed her burning eyes closed.

"I'm sorry," Ena whispered. "I always thought you two would be forever."

"Yeah, me too." She set her coffee back down on the table. "Can we talk about whose energy we felt?"

"Yes." Ena took Raven's hand between both of hers. "But, I want you to know that you can come and talk to me anytime you need to. I'm here for you, angel mine."

"Do you know how many times in the past year and a half I've wished we could have those twelve years back? I missed you every day, Mom. Every single day during that time, I wished you'd come

for me. I thought ... I thought I didn't matter."

Ena scooched closer to Raven and wrapped her arms around her. "You matter, angel. More than you'll ever know. I love you so much."

"I love you, too."

Ena's breath hitched, then her shoulders heaved as she sobbed into Raven's shoulder. Raven clasped her hand at the back of Ena's head and held her, fighting her own tears.

When she got her weeping under control, Ena said, "I'm sorry, Rave. It's just that I never thought I'd hear you say those words again. You see? I also thought I didn't matter."

"I never stopped loving you." Goddess, how she wished she could explain without risking changing the future.

"But, you hated me for something."

"I...I didn't hate you. I resented you. I...I, uh..."

Ena brushed her finger over Raven's lips. "It's alright. You've forgiven me for whatever it was and that's enough for now."

Raven nodded. When she lifted her head to meet Ena's gaze, it felt like it weighed a ton. "Do you forgive me?"

"There's nothing to forgive, Rave. I just wish you had talked to me about what was causing you so much pain instead of lashing out and running. That was my fault for not making it easier for you to feel comfortable talking to me. I was so wrapped up in my own heartache that I wasn't a good mother. For that, I am deeply sorry."

"No, you're right. If I had just talked to you ..." She shook her head and swiped at a tear that managed to sneak past her defences. "Everything would have been different."

"Well, hindsight is twenty-twenty, isn't it?" They both smiled.

Raven took a deep breath to shake off the straggling hurt, regret, sadness. "I need to know who's targeting us, Mom. I need to put an end to this to protect Indi and the future generations of Bowens."

Ena turned and stared out the window. "I don't know that that's possible, Rave."

"The hell it isn't. Everyone keeps telling me what a powerful *witch I am because of my bloodlines. What's the point of having that kind of power if I can't use it to protect the people I love?"*

Ena sighed. "You're not going to let it go, are you? There's nothing that I could do or say that would convince you to run, to hide?"

"They'd just find us anyway. Besides, I'm not the running and hiding type." She smiled, but Ena didn't return it.

"We don't know who's behind it, exactly. They almost always use others to do their bidding. What we do know is that it stems back to Randall Parker's quest for revenge. Revenge over something that didn't belong to him in the first place. We suspect he had another child after his escape from the asylum and that his quest was handed down from generation to generation."

"Any suggestions on how I might find them?"

Ena pressed her palm to her chest as her eyes glassed over. "For so long, I've tried to keep you sheltered, Rave. To protect you from all of this. Do you understand how difficult it is for me to see you want to dive headfirst into it? It terrifies me, sweet angel."

"I'd rather die trying to take them down than sit quietly waiting for them to take me out."

Ena looked Raven in the eye. "You're such a warrior. Such a protector." She nodded with short, quick jerks of her head. "We believe that it's Parker's descendants who are behind this and we think they may be members of the coven and have been for generations."

Raven flinched back, her eyes popping wide open. "You can't be serious?"

They know too much about us for them not to be close or at least be getting information from someone close to us. They know where to hit us where it hurts the most ... keeping Kiran and me apart, keeping you and me apart. Those were the two things that could have destroyed me."

Was Gregor Paigo raping her part of their plan? Was Riley breaking up with her part of it?

"Rave?"

She was starting to question every bad thing that had ever happened to her. She looked back up at Ena.

"If you think there is something they may have had a hand in, believe it. They know what would hurt us the most."

"Riley breaking up with me. Going after Indi. Burning down my home, my sanctuary. Those are the things that hurt. But, I have to look at what else I have that would destroy me. Kiran." And she supposed Simone as well. "Rauri. My job."

"I've kept records of every member of the coven since I became High Priestess. Our ancestors did the same. I've been through them over and over. Someone in those files, or someone close to them, is the one we seek."

That gave her a lead. Something tangible she could do to try to pin down who was at the core of this. "Thank you."

"Well, hopefully, your cop instincts will find something that I missed."

Raven leaned over and hugged Ena. "Thank you," she repeated and she meant it from the depths of her soul. "Nice chat." They both laughed.

"Look at members with repeated generations in the coven. If my computer is still intact, you'll find my notes in a Word document titled Grocery List. *But, be warned, Raven Sage. Your best friend is on my shortlist."*

* * *

The room was bright with the morning sunshine when Raven blinked her eyes open. She sat up, rubbing her eyes and glanced at the bedside clock. It was after seven. She thought she'd wake right up after the dream travel, but she'd slept right through the night. Now she'd have to rush to get Indi dressed and fed, go home to shower and change, and then get to Huntsville for an appointment to select some of the materials for her new cottage. And all she wanted to do was search through the coven records.

She got up, pulled on her jeans and went through to check on Indi. She wasn't in her room, so she went down to the kitchen and found Kiran and Simone feeding pablum to her daughter.

Simone slid her chair out of spitting distance. "Oh, no. I have to work this morning. I don't have time for another shower."

Kiran laughed. "That's fine, darling. I'll do it." He shovelled a spoonful of pablum into Indi's waiting mouth, but she didn't blow a raspberry or smear it all over her face. She swallowed it eagerly and opened her mouth wide for more.

"Someone's hungry this morning," Raven said as she headed straight for the coffee pot.

"Aye, it appears so." Kiran fed her another spoonful and grinned when she swallowed the lot. "Or, she's finally figured out what to do with it."

"Wouldn't that be a blessing?" Raven said.

"How'd it go last night, love?" Kiran asked.

Raven brought her coffee to the table and sat next to Simone. She filled them in on what Ena told her about suspecting the person or persons responsible may be coven members. "I've got an appointment in Huntsville this morning, so it's going to have to wait until I get back."

"I'll check Ena's computer for a *Grocery List* file," Kiran said. "Then, I'll root through the boxes upstairs for the coven records."

"You don't have to do all that. I can take care of it this afternoon."

Kiran covered Raven's hand on the table with his. "I want to help, darling. In any way that I can."

"Okay. Thank you." She stole a piece of Simone's toast and took a big bite. Why did someone else's food always taste so much better? She grinned as Simone tsked. "Oh, by the way.

Ena wanted me to tell both of you that she's happy for you."

Simone choked on her coffee. "You … told her about us."

"She asked. She's delighted that it's you, Simone."

"Aye, she would be," Kiran said. "She was very fond of Simone."

Simone leaned over and kissed Raven's cheek. "Thank you."

"Yeah. So stop worrying about being with my dad and just be happy together. That's what she wants. That's what we all want."

Indi bellowed out what sounded like, "Bah!" When she got everyone's attention, she opened her mouth wide.

"You're falling down on the job, Grandda," Raven said with a laugh.

Kiran grinned and filled Indi's mouth with pablum.

* * *

Jade walked up from the beach as Raven was strapping Indi back into her car seat. "I missed you yesterday."

"I wasn't home." Raven closed the back door of the Range Rover and opened the driver's door.

"I figured that out," Jade grinned. "Where are you headed?"

"I've got an appointment."

"You're just a wealth of information. Mind if I tag along?"

"Why?"

"Because I meant what I said about being here to help. I'll share what I know if you do the same."

"Why would I do that?" She didn't mean to sound so defensive.

Jade rolled her eyes. "Are we going to start this again?"

Raven stared at her for a moment, then nodded to the passenger side. "Hop in if you want." She got into the driver's seat, clicked into her seatbelt and started the car as Jade settled into the passenger seat and pushed a pair of aviator sunglasses up her nose. "So, what do you know?"

"The energy is building. Whatever they're waiting for, it's coming sooner rather than later."

Raven's belly tightened. "There's an esbat in a few days." The full moon celebration would take place at the coven's sacred gathering place on the Bowen land.

"Yeah. Do you think your coven would allow me to attend?"

Raven spared Jade a glance as she pulled onto the highway and merged with the summer traffic. "I don't see why not." If Jade wasn't on the up and up, at least she'd have her in her sights.

"So, I've shown you mine. Are you going to show me yours?" Jade fluttered her lashes and made Raven laugh.

"I don't have anything to show, I'm afraid. We've been trying to figure out the source, but we haven't had any luck."

"I have some thoughts on that. If you're interested."

"Anything would help at this point." She wanted to know just how much Jade knew and what those thoughts were.

"I've done some research on your family, Raven. All of your ancestors dating back a hundred and fifty years have died quite young and under suspicious circumstances, including your mother."

"Tell me something I don't know."

"This energy is somehow tied into your family history."

"Again, tell me something I don't know."

Jade blew out a breath. "I thought you said you didn't have anything?"

Raven smiled, her eyes on the road.

"Okay, I get it. You don't have anything you're willing to share." Jade turned and stared out the passenger window.

Raven's thoughts turned to the coven. She knew all of the current members and there were only a few that she thought may have ancestors who were members. Alana, Jax's aunt, was one. Her mother and grandmother were members if she remembered correctly. Simone's family went back generations in the coven as well. She started to tell herself that there was no way Simone could be involved then remembered feeling the same way about Adara. She couldn't believe Adara would murder Ena, but she had. Raven had been entirely wrong about her and it still affected her confidence in her own intuition. Could Adara be the source? Raven didn't know much about Adara's heritage. Her parents and brother had been killed in a car accident when Adara was four. Adara was the only survivor. She'd spent months in the hospital then went into foster care. To this day, she walked with a limp due to that accident and suffered from chronic pain.

Raven blew out a breath that fluttered her bangs. She needed to go through the coven records then trace family trees. It was going to be time-consuming, to say the least. She'd recruit Mick. *Be warned, Raven Sage. Your best friend is on my shortlist.* Shit. Jaxon Lang, her best friend and Mick's boyfriend, was on Ena's shortlist. She couldn't pull Mick in until she cleared Jax. She glanced at Jade. Trust her or not? "Why are you doing this? Why do you want to help?"

"I told you," Jade said with a huff. "It's what I do."

Raven drummed her fingers on the steering wheel. She had hours of research and reading to do, and the faster she got through it, the better. "We think the source could be a member of our coven. We're looking at those who have generations of family who have been coven members." Raven found a parking spot in a lot about a block and a half away from the builder's supply store. She turned to Jade and filled her in on everything. When she was done, she said, "I could use some help going through the files and researching the family trees. What I'm hoping to do is link someone back to Randall Parker."

Jade said nothing but offered her hand to Raven. Raven

shook it.

* * *

It was nearly midday when they stepped out of the builder's supply store onto the sidewalk. Raven pulled a sun hat out of her diaper bag and stuck it on Indi's head then donned her sunglasses. She started up the street towards the parking lot with Indi in her stroller and Jade at her side, scanning the road and everyone on it. It was deeply ingrained in her, not just because she was a cop but because of the abuse she suffered as a child. She was always hyper-aware of her surroundings.

In the café across the street, she caught sight of flaming red hair and focused on Riley sitting across from Jenny and Rebecca. She was talking with her hands and laughing. Raven rubbed the ache in her chest. It hurt to see her having fun, enjoying herself, while Raven continued to suffer.

"Do me a favour?" She took Jade's hand and entwined their fingers.

Jade's eyebrow popped up, but she didn't pull her hand away. She closed her fingers around Raven's then followed Raven's eyes to the café. "Oh, okay." She pivoted on one foot, spinning in front of Raven, then crushed her mouth to Raven's.

Raven stiffened. Jade's lips were soft and full. She meant to pull away, but Jade had skills and her lips seemed to be moving of their own accord. She tilted her head to the side and delved deeper, her body thrumming with pleasure. Her breaths sped up, her pulse throbbing.

Jade pulled back and they stared into each other's eyes. "Wow." Jade touched her fingertips to her lips. "You kiss like a dark angel, Raven Bowen."

Raven grinned, mostly because she could see Riley out of the corner of her eye, glaring at them with an open mouth.

"When I saw you and your girlfriend at the festival, her

head was full of the three of you as a family. That's what she wants. Or wanted. As long as we're giving her a show, let's give her a good one." Jade undid the belt at Indi's belly and lifted her into the air, grinning and laughing. She hugged Indi to her chest then retook Raven's hand, swinging their arms between them as they started down the street.

Riley grabbed her purse off the back of her chair and charged inside the café. Jenny and Rebecca turned their heads, Jenny hurling a death stare at Raven. Rebecca just looked surprised.

Raven didn't know if Riley came out of the restaurant or not. She didn't approach them at any rate. She took Indi from Jade and strapped her into the car seat then got into the driver's seat. "Thanks."

"My pleasure." Jade wiggled her eyebrows.

They were halfway back to Solstice when Jade spoke again. "She's a fool, you know."

"Who?"

"Your lover. Or ex-lover." She reached over and dragged her nails lightly over the nape of Raven's neck and into her hair. "She's a fool to give you up."

Yeah, well, that didn't help. Raven's libido went into overdrive, but her eyes burned. "Maybe I'm the fool." For not being able to get over her.

Jade snorted then very seriously said, "Maybe you are."

Chapter 23

Raven picked up several boxes of files from Kiran's then took Indi home to feed her and put her down for a nap. Once she was asleep, Raven took the baby monitor out to the deck with the boxes of files and set them down between her and Jade. The first thing she perused was Ena's *Grocery List*.

Ena had saved her a lot of work. She'd listed the current members and traced each one with generations of members back like a family tree. Simone's lineage went right back to when Lady Moira and Eloise came to Canada with coven members from England. Her five times great grandmother was among those from the original Silver Star Coven. That, in Raven's opinion, probably excluded her from the list of suspects.

Alana's, and Jax's mother, Kelly's, lineage only went back to their grandmother. When Ena had said that Raven's best friend was on her shortlist, she'd assumed it was through his mother's ancestors. But, it was Jax's father, Jacob Lang, who had ancestors going back several generations of coven members. Jax's grandfather, Rainer Lang, his great grandfather Jac Lang, and his great, great grandfather, Kaleb Lang, had all been members of the Solstice Coven.

"Shit." Raven slapped the documents onto the table and stomped into the RV for a pen and a notepad. When she came back out, Jade was holding the papers. Raven slumped back into her chair, rubbing her temples. This was giving her a nasty headache.

"Isn't Jaxon Lang your …?"

"My daughter's father? Yeah."

"Well, shit."

"Yeah." Raven sat up and opened her notepad. She wrote down Kaleb Lang's name. "We need to trace Kaleb Lang's lineage."

"Got a laptop?" Jade asked.

"Yeah, I'll grab it."

"I'll get it." Jade rose. "Just tell me where?"

"On the kitchen counter."

When Jade came back out with it, she set it on the table, then stood behind Raven and began massaging her stiff neck and shoulders. Raven would have stopped her, should have stopped her if it hadn't felt so damn good. "This probably isn't a good idea."

"Why?" Jade dug her thumbs into the knots in Raven's shoulders and Raven groaned. "Are you afraid it might lead to something else? Last I checked, you were single. There's nothing wrong with allowing yourself some pleasure, Raven. It might even help. Maybe you wouldn't have all these knots if you allowed yourself a good bout of sex now and then."

Jade leaned over and dragged her teeth over Raven's neck, sending shivers down her spine and a spear of arousal shooting straight to her core.

"It can be very healing," Jade whispered into her ear.

"Rave?"

Raven jumped out of her chair at the sound of Riley's voice. She spun around to see her glaring with a red face at the edge of the deck. "Hey."

"Can we …" She started to raise her hands, then dropped them. "Talk? In private?"

Raven looked at Jade. She smiled seductively and pressed a kiss to Raven's lips. "Why don't I come back later, lover?" Jade started down the lawn to the beach, walking towards her cottage, hips swinging and a bounce in her step.

Raven stared after her, not sure if she wanted to turn to face Riley. She wondered how long she'd been standing there watching them.

"It didn't take you long to move on."

If only she knew. "You're the one who broke up with me, Ri." She sat back down in her chair so she didn't embarrass herself when her legs gave out.

"I said I needed to put us on hold."

"Why? One minute you were saying that we would get through our difficult path together, then the next, you could barely look at me and you broke things off."

Riley stepped onto the deck with her fists clenched at her sides. "Because my mother told me about the Bowen curse. Everyone in your family has died young, Raven."

"And that was enough for you to walk away?"

"So, you don't deny it?"

"There's no curse on the Bowens, Ri. Jenny's first tactic to break us up didn't work, so she tried a new one. And, hey, you fell for it."

"She's seen your death, Rave. In a couple of months, you'll be gone."

"And instead of sticking with me, getting through it together, you decide to dump me to save yourself the trouble?"

"Ugh! You're impossible!" Riley stomped off the deck.

Raven jumped up and followed to the edge of the deck then stopped. "Hey, Ri? The thing with visions is they're only one possibility of what could happen. So, don't write my eulogy yet."

Riley skidded to a halt but didn't turn around. "What are

you talking about?"

"She didn't tell you that her vision wasn't set in stone?" Raven huffed out a laugh. "That figures." If Jenny even had that vision. Raven highly doubted it. Jenny just wanted Riley away from her.

"I don't understand."

"Even if she did see my death, it doesn't mean I'm going to die. Visions can be interpretations, have a different meaning. Death often signifies a new beginning. Or, if it was my actual death, it still doesn't mean it's going to happen. Our decisions, our actions can change an outcome. If the vision is based on me making a certain decision and I choose a different option, the outcome changes."

Riley turned slightly, looking at her out of the corner of her eye. She looked more confused now than angry. "Why are you with her?"

Raven's heart pounded in her chest. The pain there was excruciating. She should tell Riley the truth, but did it matter? "Because I can't do us anymore, Ri. It hurts too damn much." Her voice cracked and she rubbed her fist over the pain in her chest. "I can't take it."

Riley stood there, nodding, half looking over her shoulder, her fiery hair glinting in the sunlight, but she wouldn't meet Raven's eyes. Raven wasn't sure what she wanted. If she wanted her to walk away or turn around and run into her arms. It was like sitting in that park, praying that her mother would come after her, choose her. She didn't think she could stand to see Riley walk away. "Ri?" she croaked, the pressure in her chest ever-increasing until it felt like a dump truck was sitting on it.

"I … I'm sorry for the pain I've caused you." Riley took one step then broke into an awkward jog, her legs stiff and jerky. She ran down the road towards the empty plot that used to be Raven's cottage.

More than anything, Raven wanted to run after her, but she couldn't leave Indi alone in the RV. She dropped down to the deck and threw her arms over her head, sobbing. She'd done the right thing, right? Eventually, her heart would begin to heal, to feel normal. Except, she was pretty sure that she would never get over Riley Gallagher.

Jade stepped out of the trees and crossed the deck, sitting behind Raven. She wrapped her arms around her and whispered, "I'm so sorry." Raven leaned back, clutching her chest, and Jade brushed her fingers through Raven's hair over and over again. "She still wants your little family, Raven. That's her dream."

"Oh, Goddess. Don't tell me that." It had been her dream, too. Just a few short weeks ago, she'd envisioned the three of them together in her cottage, pictured them at their handfasting, raising Indi together, and maybe even having more kids. It may have even happened if Jenny Gallagher hadn't interfered.

* * *

The rumble of a diesel engine roared up the road and Raven stiffened in Jade's arms. "Oh, shit. It's Jax." She jumped up and ran for the boxes, shoving Ena's Grocery List inside one of them.

Jade grabbed one of the boxes. "Where do you want it?"

"My bedroom closet." The truck's tires crackled and popped over the gravel driveway. "Quick." She ran into the RV with one box and Jade on her heels. They stuffed the boxes into the bedroom closet just as the knock came at the door.

"Rave?" Jax called.

Raven opened the door to Jax and Mick. Jax was setting a cooler next to the barbecue. "Hey."

"Hey," Mick and Jax said in unison.

Mick narrowed her eyes, studying Raven's face. "You've

been crying."

Raven stepped out onto the deck and Jade stepped out behind her. "Riley was just here."

Mick's gaze cut to Jade then back to Raven. "Bet that went over well."

"Yeah, great."

"Jade Storm," Jade said, offering her hand to Mick then Jax.

They introduced themselves as Raven stabbed her fingers through her hair.

"We brought some steaks. There's enough for four," Jax said.

"Great." Raven sat down in a deck chair just as Indi started giggling through the monitor then stood again. "I better get her before she zaps Jet again." She escaped into the RV. When she got to Indi's room, Jet was rubbing her head against Indi's cheek, purring madly, and Indi was giggling. "Come here, monkey." She lifted Indi and cuddled her, swaying back and forth.

"You okay?" Mick asked from the doorway.

Raven nodded, not trusting herself to talk. She was right on the edge of losing it again.

"Are you and Jade …?"

Raven shook her head and pressed her lips to Indi's brow. She took a deep breath and said, "Riley thinks we are."

"And you didn't set her straight?"

"What's the point?"

"Um, repairing your relationship."

"I'm done, Mick. I can't stand the pain. I just … I can't do it anymore."

Mick huffed and took Indi from Raven. She laid her on the changing table, changed her diaper and dressed her in a little sundress while Raven sat in the rocker. "Where's her sunscreen?"

Raven pointed to the shelf right next to Mick's face.

"Have you found out any more about who's behind the fire and stuff?" Mick asked as she slathered the lotion over Indi.

"Nope."

"Do you think they left after the festival? I mean, nothing seems to have happened since then."

"Maybe." Raven reached over and turned the baby monitor off. "I don't want to talk about it, Mick. I don't want to talk about Riley. I just … don't want to talk."

"Okay." Mick lifted Indi into her arms. "Want a beer?"

Raven pushed herself out of the rocker. "Yeah, that sounds good."

Kiran, Simone, and Rauri showed up next. Raven loaned Jade one of her bathing suits and they all ended up in the water. Indi loved it. Her legs kicked and her arms waved, splashing everyone who got near. Every time she splashed water on her own face, her little body went rigid and shook. Indi's eyes popped wide open and her little mouth formed an o. Then she belly laughed. Everyone was in hysterics at the expressions on her little face. Goddess, it was precisely what Raven needed. She didn't know what she'd do without the comic relief provided by her little angel.

When everyone headed back into shore, Raven turned and swam out into the lake, legs kicking hard, arms windmilling. The water got colder the further out she swam. It was a nice contrast to the sun beating down on her shoulders. She swam until she was nearly exhausted, then turned around and headed for shore at a more leisurely pace.

Jade was waiting for her with a towel when she got out. "Thanks."

"That was some swim."

"Better I expel that energy in the water than somewhere else."

"Would that energy be sexual frustration?" Jade grinned,

her eyes drifting slowly down Raven's body then back up again.

Raven shook her head but couldn't help but laugh. "You ever give up?" she asked as she rubbed the towel over her hair.

"After the way you kissed me today? Not a chance."

Raven dropped her hands, clinging to the towel. "Look, Jade. That was just …"

"What? A mistake?"

"No. I don't know."

"Look, I get that you're hurting. No pressure. Honest." She smiled and started up to the deck where Kiran and Jax flipped burgers on the barbecue and Rauri bounced Indi in her lap.

Raven slung the towel around her neck with a huff. What was she doing? She followed Jade up and sat quietly watching Jax in swim shorts, displaying his golden tan over taut muscles. Jax's straight as a ruler blonde hair was still damp from his swim, his deep blue eyes twinkling at Mick. Could she have been so wrong about Jax? Like she'd been about Adara? Her gut told her Jax was a good man, but she couldn't trust her gut.

* * *

As soon as Mick and Jax left, Raven and Jade pulled the boxes out of her closet. They sat in the RV's living room with Kiran, Simone, and Rauri and got to work. Kiran brought a few more boxes of coven records in from his car.

Raven pulled out the Grocery List again. "We need to pull the files on Kaleb Lang. Ena has him listed as a coven member from 1929 through 1956."

"Lang? As in Jaxon Lang?" Kiran asked with a creased brow.

"Yeah." Raven stabbed her fingers through her hair. "That one."

"Well, then. I'll take care of pulling files." He shuffled around the five boxes, looking at dates, then pulled one over in front of his seat and began flipping through the files.

Raven watched him for a moment in awe. There was no hesitation, no questioning her, just calm acceptance. "I don't know how we're going to trace his ancestry. There must be something online we can use."

Jade grabbed Raven's laptop from the table and opened it on her lap. "That's where I can help. Have we got a middle name?"

"Here." Kiran pulled a folder from the box and flipped it open. "Kaleb Manus Lang, born the sixteenth of February, 1913." He handed the file off to Simone to read through.

Jade's fingers began to fly across the keyboard.

"What are you using?" Raven asked.

Jade smirked. "Public records."

Raven's mouth dropped. "Are you hacking into government sites?"

"Do you want it fast or legal?" Her fingers continued to tap away at the keyboard.

Raven opened her mouth, closed it again, and frowned. *Shit.* "Fast. How likely is it you'll get caught?"

Jade's head cocked, her fingers stopped moving, and she stared at Raven from under thick lashes.

"Okay. Just asking." *Yeeesh.* She turned her attention back to the Grocery List. The next name with multiple generations of ancestors in the coven was a close friend of Simone's. But all of the names were people that were close to them, especially Simone because she'd been with the coven continuously since she was very young. "Esmerelda Erickson. Coven member between 1895 and 1913."

Simone's head shot up from the file folder on her lap. "Maddie's ancestors?"

Raven dropped the papers onto the coffee table. "Look,

everyone we're looking at is someone close to at least some of us. They've been coven members for generations. That means it's people we know and care about."

"I understood that," Simone said. Her hand slid down her thigh as if pushing her snug dress down. "I just never thought …" She dropped her head to the file folder again. "Never mind."

Kiran's hand covered Simone's thigh and she looked up into his ice-blue eyes. "They have to be checked, love. It doesn't mean she's involved in anything untoward."

She offered him a closed-lipped smile and nodded. "I know. Thank you." She leaned in and gave him a chaste kiss.

They were so sweet together, it brought Raven's chest pain back into sharp focus and that gaping hole inside her seemed to swell. She picked up the list again as Kiran began rifling through boxes.

"Let's add Kathryn MacKinney to the list." She had to look at Alana's and Kelly's grandmother. Ena had put her on the shortlist for a reason and the name set Raven's hair on end for some reason. "Coven member from 1950 to 1971."

"Alana?" Kiran said. "That puts Jax on the list twice, Rave."

"I know," she whispered, lowering her eyes. Alana was Jaxon's aunt, Kelly his mother. Why did she feel guilty for putting Jax there? Kiran was right. They had to check, but it didn't mean Jax was involved in any of this.

Jade sighed, looking up from the laptop. "Kaleb Lang is going to take a little more work. He was an immigrant from Sweden."

That explained Jax's nordic blonde hair and blue eyes, Raven thought. "Can you access records over there?"

Jade only smiled then went back to typing.

"Esmerelda Serenity Erickson. Born the twenty-first of September 1879," Kiran said and handed that folder over to

Rauri.

While he rooted through another box for Kathryn MacKinney's file, Simone closed Kaleb Lang's folder and set it on the coffee table. "There's nothing suspicious in there that I can find."

"That's fine. I didn't expect there to be," Raven said. "I'll take a look through them all later anyway."

"That's it? Just the three?" Simone asked.

"Yeah."

"Raven, you don't have my ancestors on your list."

Raven met Simone's gaze. "Your ancestors came over from England with Lady Moira and Eloise. I figured that ruled you out."

"That doesn't exclude me. If you're investigating someone like Maddie. You have to look at me as well."

The corner of Raven's mouth lifted. "Are you saying there's a need for us to investigate you, Simone?"

"No, but ..." She sighed, rubbing both palms down her thighs. "In the interest of being thorough ..."

"What we're looking for here is a tie to Randall Parker. Another son or daughter, a brother or sister. Someone who may have continued his quest for vengeance down through their descendants."

"Yes, I know."

"Is there any reason you believe your ancestors may be linked to Parker? Do you think if your ancestor had links to him, Lady Moira would have brought them here with her?"

"No, but we can't rule it out just because my five-times great grandmother came here with Lady Moira."

Raven blew out, feathering her bangs. Simone was right and Ena had put her on the list. She picked up the Grocery List again. "Emma Kathrine Wells. Silver Star Coven member from 1862 through 1867. Solstice Coven member from 1867 through 1875." She threw the list back onto the coffee table.

"Those are the lines we need to trace." She felt like Simone's was a waste of their time. Who knew how hard it would be to trace ancestry a hundred and fifty years ago and on a different continent?

When they had the full names and birthdates of all four on their list, Jade closed the laptop. "Can you write the names and dates down for me. I'll continue this at home. The wifi is spotty here and I have better equipment at my cottage."

"Yeah, sure." Raven began writing a list for Jade and Kiran packed up the boxes.

"Would you like a lift?" He asked Jade.

"Yeah, that would be great. Save me a walk in the dark down the beach."

Kiran hung back as Rauri, Simone, and Jade went out to the car. "Are you alright, darling?"

"Yeah, sure."

Kiran stepped up to her and tapped the pad of his finger against the tip of Raven's delicate nose. He laid his palm over her heart. "I feel your pain and it's breaking my heart, Rave."

Her eyes burned, but she refused to let her tears fall. "I'll get over it. Eventually. Won't I?"

"I can only tell you from my experience with your mother that when it's true love, when it's a soul mate connection, either you find your way back to each other or you never heal."

That wasn't what she wanted to hear.

"Can't you talk to her? Patch things up?"

"I don't want that. I can't keep putting myself through this. It hurts too damn much every time I lose Riley."

"I know just how much you're hurting. I know how much you were hurting when I first met you last year. What worries me is that it isn't going to get better, that you'll spend the rest of your life alone and in pain."

"Well, according to Riley, I don't have long to live

anyway."

Kiran dropped his hand, then clutched Raven's. "What are you talking about?"

"That's the reason she gave for breaking up with me. Jenny told her she had a vision of my death and that I only had a couple of months to live. Oh, and that the Bowens were cursed."

A storm began to brew in Kiran's eyes. They narrowed, his brow creasing, and his mouth formed a tight, white line. "Bloody buggering hell. I could murder that bloody woman. You know that even if she did have that vision, it doesn't mean you'll die."

"I know that. I told Riley the same thing."

"Still, it's worrisome, aye?"

"Yeah." It certainly wasn't a comfortable feeling when someone predicted your death.

Kiran raked both hands through his hair. "I'll be glad when we get this whole mess sorted out, aye?" He kissed Raven's cheek and went to the door. Turning back, he added, "And we bloody well will sort it out."

Raven stepped out onto the deck behind him and watched them all get in the car and drive away. She stood there for a long time, staring off into the darkness, asking herself if she was making the biggest mistake of her life by pushing Riley away. Raven turned in the direction of Jade's rental and saw the lights come on inside the main cottage. She wished she could just move on, take comfort in Jade's arms and forget about Riley. What Jade was offering was no strings attached, no broken hearts. Just fun and pleasure for the time they had together. Why couldn't she just take that and be happy?

She went back into the RV, grabbed a beer and took it back out to the deck, knowing sleep wasn't going to come easy this night.

Chapter 24

The cottage on the point was a three-storied monstrosity with floor to ceiling windows facing the lake on each of the levels. White clapboard siding gave way to granite stones on the bottom floor. A flagstone patio held a fire pit surrounded by Muskoka chairs. Jade stepped out onto the deck on the second level and waved. "Breakfast is almost ready. Come on up."

Raven climbed the steps up to the deck with Indi strapped to her chest in a baby carrier and a diaper bag slung over her shoulder. She stepped through the glass doors into a massive great room and kitchen with wide-planked pine floors, clean, crisp white walls, and eclectic artwork. A grand stone fireplace rose out of the pine, two white couches perched in front of it as if paying homage.

A pharaonic island separated the kitchen from the great room. Jade had set two place settings on it and heaped bacon, eggs, toast, and hash browns onto the plates. "Coffee?"

"Yeah, please." Raven set the diaper bag next to one of the couches and removed Indi from the carrier. She slid onto one of the stools at the island and settled Indi on her lap.

Jade poured coffee and orange juice and set them next to the plates, then took a seat next to Raven. "You look like you got about as much sleep as I did."

"You stay up all night doing that research?"

"Pretty much. I'll show you what I've got after you eat."

Raven looked at the heaping plate and hoped she'd be able to stomach at least some of it.

"I know you're hurting, Raven, but you need to take care of yourself. Especially now."

It was bad enough having Simone on her about taking care of herself. She didn't need Jade doing it, too. "Why especially now?"

"Because something bad is coming."

"The esbat?"

"I don't know. I just feel that energy building and I don't like it."

Raven picked up a piece of dry toast and took a bite, washing it down with coffee. It had been a long night of trying to process her thoughts and she was no further ahead than she'd been at the beginning of the night. Kiran's words kept repeating in her head and she was trying to decide if she should stay the course or try to get Riley back. "Do you think you could give me a reading?"

Jade's dark brows rose. She swallowed then took a sip of orange juice. "If that's what you want."

Raven stabbed her fingers through her hair. "I don't know what I want. That's the problem." But, she wanted to see if Jade would see her death and, if not, what she saw in her future if things stayed as they were.

"Riley?"

"Yeah."

They finished breakfast, or Jade did. Raven managed half a slice of toast and one egg. Then they sat side by side in the great room and Jade asked Raven to remove her pendant - the pentagram that Kiran had given her for protection. Raven laid her hand over it. She hadn't removed it since Kiran had given it to her over a year ago.

"It's the only jewelry you're wearing and it will allow me to read you."

Reluctantly, Raven removed the pendant and handed it over. Jade clasped it between both of her palms and closed her eyes. Raven watched her face. She could see her eyes flickering behind her closed lids, but her expression never changed. Then she blew out a breath.

"You're destined to a difficult life, Rave. There will be challenges, primarily because of who you are or what you are."

At least she didn't say it would be a short life, Raven thought.

Jade opened her eyes and studied Raven for a moment. "You know that there is always more than one path to choose and the future is malleable in that sense."

"Yeah."

"On your current path, you won't find happiness in this life."

Which was just what Kiran had told her. "Yeah, I figured. What if I choose the other path?"

"There will be ups and downs, as there always are, but you'll find happiness and contentment. Does that help?"

"No." It wasn't what she wanted to hear, but maybe it was what she needed to hear. Was she just being stubborn because she couldn't stand this pain? "Yes. Maybe."

"You know the decision you want to make, Rave. It's why you won't sleep with me. You're still loyal to her. You still love her. You always will."

Raven blew out a breath and flopped back into the couch. "I don't even know if she'd want me back. Or if I want her back."

"Oh, she wants you. She's just confused right now."

And that made Raven feel like a real shit. Instead of focusing on her own pain, she should have been there for

Riley. "Did you see anything else? Anything to do with this negative energy?"

Jade's brows drew together. "Remember, there's always more than one path."

Raven nodded.

"Your life is in danger."

"Tell me something I didn't know."

"This energy, this negativity, it's directed at you. I'm sorry, I don't know how to explain it. It's more of a sense than anything that I'm getting."

"What about Indi?"

As if on cue, Indi clapped her hands and babbled a story. Then she screwed up her nose at Jade and sniffed in and out. Her cute giggles followed.

Jade laughed and brushed her knuckles down Indi's plump cheek. "You've got a real ham there, Raven."

"Oh, don't I know it."

"She's safe. For now."

"What do you mean, for now?"

"If we don't manage to stop this cycle, it will continue as it has done for the past hundred and fifty years."

"Well, either we stop it, or I die trying. That's what is going to happen, right? We may not know the outcome, but it's going to be one of those two."

"I think so." Jade sighed. "Let's go into the office and I'll show you what I've got from my searches."

Jade pulled an extra chair over to the modern, cherry wood desk with a massive iMac sitting on its top. Raven sat next to her as Jade opened a spreadsheet. "Let's start with Kathryn Ainsley MacKinney, Jax's great grandmother and Alana MacKinney's grandmother because I've hit a dead-end with her. Kathryn's mother is listed as Elizabeth Gayle MacKinney, born May fourteenth, 1906. She was thirteen when she gave birth to Kathryn and the father is listed as unknown. I traced the mother's ancestors, but there's no link to Randall Parker."

"Thirteen?" The hair on the back of Raven's neck stood on end. She didn't even know where to start looking for information on a possible rape that took place in, what, 1918? *Cripes.*

"She would have conceived in late September 1918, if she delivered full term."

Raven grabbed a piece of paper from the printer on the desk and wrote down Elizabeth MacKinney's information. "Okay, next?"

"Let's speed things up by saying that I found no connection with Simone's ancestors or with Maddy's, whoever she is."

"Alright. That leaves Kaleb Lang."

"Okay." She opened another tab of the spreadsheet. "Kaleb Manus Lang was born to Eric and Rebeka Lang. Eric's father is Randall Lang, born 1873, two years after Randall Parker escaped from the asylum. Randall Lang's father is listed as Randall James Lang, senior. His birth date coincides with Randall James Parker's - April ninth, 1827."

"Bingo." Raven wanted to be excited, but they'd just confirmed that Randall James Parker was Jax's ancestor. "Shit." She stood, pacing the room with Indi in her arms. She swiped her hand through her hair, leaving it standing up in several directions. All of this ancestor stuff was starting to get mixed up in her head. If one of Jax's ancestors, or several of them, raped her grandmother and conceived Ena, how did that affect Indigo? The little she'd eaten for breakfast roiled in her belly.

"We need to talk to your Jaxon," Jade said quietly.

"How the hell do I ask him about this?" She spun around and shot daggers at Jade, even though she knew this mess wasn't her fault. "How do I ask the father of my child, the man who's been my best friend since we were toddlers, if he's involved in killing my mother, my ancestors?" If he was involved, did he put Adara up to making her sleep with him? Had he planned the whole thing? She slumped down into a chair by the window and Indi began to fuss.

"I could talk to him if you like." Jade rose from her chair and came to stand by the window. She looked out at the lake with her arms wrapped around herself. "Or, we could not talk to him and just keep an eye on him."

"You ever pick up on any negative energy coming from him?"

"No, but we know they're good at blocking us from detecting that sort of thing."

"Yet, we can detect a negative energy around Solstice."

"Because of its strength. You can't block that high of an energy. Not completely."

Raven dropped her face into her free hand while she bounced Indi on her knee. She just couldn't see Jax involved in this, but that's how she felt about Adara and look how wrong she'd been. Still, there was another option that needed to be investigated further, even if that one also pointed back to Jaxon. "I need to dream travel back to 1918 and find out who knocked up Elizabeth MacKinney."

* * *

Raven put Indi to bed at Kiran's that night and, because she was exhausted, got ready for bed right after she'd put her down. She cast her circle, lit her white candles, and performed a protection spell then slid into bed.

In 1918, her three times great grandmother, Beatrice, was the High Priestess of the Solstice Coven and her daughter, Moira, was nine years old. She set her intention to visit in mid-October 1918 and laid there wide awake, her body humming as her thoughts drifted to the few nights she'd spent with Riley snuggled beside her just weeks ago. It wasn't even the sex she missed so much as Riley's presence, the feel of Riley's body against hers, Riley's heart beating against her chest, her warm breaths caressing her skin.

A knock at the front door had Raven's eyes fluttering open. A moment later, Kiran's voice drifted up, but she couldn't make out what he was saying. She got out of bed and started to pull her shorts back on when a familiar voice, loud and demanding, reached her.

"I know she's here. Her car is parked in the driveway."

Kiran responded, but again she couldn't make out his words.

"I'm not leaving until I speak to her."

"Riley!"

Footsteps pounded up the stairs and Raven quickly did up the button on her shorts. She took one step towards the door when Riley nearly flew past. She skidded to a stop and entered the room with Kiran on her tail.

"I'm sorry, darling," Kiran said.

Raven waved him off. "It's alright."

He met her eyes and she nodded, then he turned and went back down the stairs. Raven waited for Riley to say what she wanted to say. They stared at each other while Riley breathed heavily with her fists clenched at her sides. "I've been thinking about what you said yesterday and I wanted to talk to you."

"Now you want to talk?"

"What's that supposed to mean?"

"Ri, lower your voice. You'll wake Indi."

Riley took a deep breath and rubbed her hands over her face. When she looked back up, she looked drawn and tired. "When you asked me for time, I gave it to you. Yet, when I asked for it, you just moved on."

"When I asked you for time, I explained why I needed it and you agreed. You didn't ask me for time, Ri. You went from 'we'll get through it together' to pulling away from me.

I tried to get you to talk, but you just pulled away more. You didn't come to me and give me a chance to confirm or deny what Jenny was telling you or even just to talk about it. You just left."

Riley stared at her open-mouthed, her cheeks flushing a rosy pink.

"That hurt," Raven said with her voice cracking and unshed tears burning her eyes. She tapped her fist against her chest. "You accused me of being closed off. I've been trying my best to open up to you ever since. But, you closed yourself off to me the minute you started listening to Jenny's bullshit."

"She's my mother, Rave. I've wanted nothing more than to get to know her since I found my adoption certificate. You knew that, but you wouldn't give me time to figure things out."

This was getting them nowhere. Pointing fingers and accusing each other didn't help a damn thing. "What happened to figuring things out together? I wanted to be there for you through this, Ri."

Riley's eyebrows popped up and her mouth dropped open. "Oh, that's rich. You can't see beyond yourself to help anyone through anything. It's all about you."

Ouch, that hurt. Was she really so self-involved? Raven stabbed her fingers through her hair and turned to the window, staring out over the cliffs and Fairy Lake. "What are you doing here, Ri? What do you want from me?"

"I want you to give me what I asked for and stop sleeping with that woman!"

Raven snorted out a laugh and turned back to Riley. She was sure that Riley had slept with other women when she lived in Toronto last year after they broke up. Raven was the one who hadn't slept with anyone else, yet Riley didn't know that. She didn't know whether to tell her the truth or not.

"Why is that funny? Do you know how much it hurts to

see you with someone else? I waited for you for six months while you worked out your shit. You couldn't wait five freaking minutes for me to work out mine?"

"It wasn't giving you time that was the issue, Ri. I would have given you all the time you needed if you had just talked to me about it first. It was how easily you walked away without a backward glance that tore me to shreds. I either have to move on, or we get back together and promise to stop hurting each other. The problem is, I don't know if that's possible."

Riley walked to the bed and sat, dropping her face into her hands. "Have we hurt each other to the point we can't get past it? Is that what you're saying?"

Raven sat rigidly next to Riley, her hands firmly on her thighs, and stared straight ahead. "I don't know. I can only tell you that I can't stand the pain anymore." Riley's angry speech to Jenny in the first few days of her visit kept running through Raven's head.

That woman *is the love of my life, my soul mate. I don't care how difficult a path she may face in the future. It'll be less difficult because we'll be forging it together, helping each other through it.*

What she'd said was beautiful and Raven had thought it meant they would work through anything together. "I'll give you the time you want. Just try to keep in mind what Jenny said to you in the office that day."

"What was that?"

"That she didn't come here to be your mother. She came here to warn you away from me."

Riley's back straightened and she clenched her fists in her lap. "You don't know what you're talking about. She does want a relationship with me. We're getting to know each other and it's good."

"I hope that's true, but you can't deny she's doing her best to tear us apart."

"I asked her about what you said about her visions, Rave. She said you're just in denial."

"I guess we'll find out soon enough." She was even more motivated to take down whoever was behind Randall Parker's revenge. She'd love to shove her finger in Jenny Gallagher's face and tell her *told you so*. Petty, but hey, it would feel pretty damn good. "In the meantime, do me the courtesy of running anything she tells you by me before you believe it."

"I'm not going to run to you and tell you every conversation I have with my mother."

Raven took a deep breath. "That's not what I'm asking. I'm asking you not to believe anything she tells you about my family or me without talking to me first."

Riley unclenched her fists, stretched her fingers out, then clenched them again. "Why did my mother and Rebecca move from here to a hotel?"

"Kiran asked them to leave."

"Why?"

What had been said when Kiran brought her home after losing it in the ashes of her cottage, Raven didn't know. She only knew that Kiran had had enough. "He was fed up with her insulting me in his house."

"What did she say?"

"I don't know, Ri. I wasn't exactly present. You'd have to ask Kiran."

They sat in silence and the longer it stretched out, the more awkward it felt. Raven got up and went back to the window, wondering what version of events Jenny had given to Riley. She didn't want to ask. Raven wanted Riley to tell her. She could just imagine what Jenny must have thought seeing Kiran carrying her into the house covered in soot. Raven hadn't asked him what Jenny had said. She figured he wouldn't tell her anyway and she wasn't sure she wanted to know.

Riley stood and walked to the door, then stopped. "You'll stop sleeping with her? Give me some time?"

Raven turned, facing Riley's back. "As long as you keep me in the loop and don't shut me out."

Riley's hair bounced down her back as she nodded. "Alright."

She walked out without looking back and ran down the stairs. Raven heard Riley's voice and Kiran's and was tempted to go out to the railing so she could listen to the conversation. She sank to the floor and dropped her face into her hands instead, feeling like she was just prolonging her misery. Riley wanted a relationship with her mother so bad that Raven was sure she'd be loyal to Jenny. And that didn't bode well for a future between the two of them.

* * *

Kiran hit the mute button on the TV remote when Raven walked into the great room. He was sitting between Simone and Rauri on the couch watching a rerun of Criminal Minds, Rauri's favourite American show.

"Alright, love?" He asked gently.

"Yeah." Raven stuffed her hands in the back pockets of her shorts. Sleep was not an option after her talk with Riley, so she'd come down here to keep her mind from constantly repeating images of Jenny winning and Riley walking away from her for good this time. "Did Riley ask you what Jenny said that made you kick her out?"

"Aye, she did."

She stood waiting, but Kiran didn't offer up an answer. "Will you tell me what she said?"

"I'll tell you what I told Riley," he said. "It doesn't do any of us any good to repeat garbage."

Raven looked up and blew a puff of air at her bangs. "The thing is, Jenny has probably said at least as much to Riley. I don't think Riley's going to tell me what she's saying and I have no way of defending myself if I don't know what I'm defending against."

The three of them were like the hear no evil, speak no evil, see no evil monkeys lined up on the couch. They all looked at each other then back up at Raven.

"Am I the only one who doesn't know what's being said behind my back?"

Kiran bent forward, rubbing his hands over his face. When he looked up, his eyes were pain-filled. "I'm your father, darling. One who loves you very much. Do you think it's easy for me to repeat ugly lies about you?"

"No, and I'm sorry. But I need to know." She braced herself as she saw the defeat pass over his face.

"She said you're … depraved. She said that the things that Gregor Paigo did to you caused you irreparable damage and she's had visions of your depravity."

Raven took a step back, feeling the punch to her chest. "I don't understand why she hates me so much. How could she say things like that?" Riley must know that's not true. The morning after the Summer Solstice popped into her head. Is that why Riley was so aggressive? Had Jenny told her that's what she wanted? It would explain why Riley had gotten so drunk that night. She dropped into a chair, her hands still fisted in her hair.

"You've said that whoever's behind hurting you and your ancestors used others to do their dirty work," Rauri said. "Is it possible, they're using Jenny to hurt you?"

Raven's hands slid out of her hair and down her face. "If that's the case, and their goal is to mess with my head, it's working." She shot to her feet. "Can you listen for Indi? I need to go out for a bit." She grabbed her keys from the kitchen island and was out the door before anyone could say another word.

* * *

She pounded her fist on Riley's apartment door. "Riley? Open up."

Footsteps approached and the door swung open. Riley gaped at her and pulled the door closed as she stepped out into the hall, but not before Raven got a look at Jenny and Rebecca sitting on the couch in the living room.

"Rave? What are you doing here?"

"Did she tell you I was depraved? Is that why you were so aggressive with me the morning after the Summer Solstice?"

"Aggressive? What are you talking about?"

"You were drunk and very aggressive. I asked you to stop, several times, but you wouldn't listen. You said that's what I wanted. Did *she* tell you that?"

"Oh, my God. Are you saying I tried to rape you?" She lowered her voice to a teeth-clenching whisper. "She said you'd say something like that, accuse me of being the one in the wrong."

"Oh, for cripes sake, Riley. Listen to yourself. How many times have we slept together over the years? Have I ever given you any indication that I wanted to be forced? That's what she told you, isn't it? That I wanted to be held down and forced?"

The colour drained out of Riley's face. "*Is* it what you want?"

"No!" *Damn it all to hell and back.* She wanted to get inside that apartment and strangle Jenny. "How could you even think that?"

Riley's eyes focused on the floor. "I ... It made sense when she explained it."

"Don't trust anything she tells you about me, please. I don't know if she's making this shit up or if someone is giving her these visions to hurt us. Just promise me you won't believe anything without talking to me about it."

"What do you mean, someone is giving her these visions?"

"It's a long story and I don't have time to explain. I need to get back to Indi." And, she didn't want Riley spewing everything she told her to Jenny.

"Fine." Riley turned the handle and started to open the door.

"Are they staying here?"

"Until they find a place, yes."

She couldn't very well tell Riley to kick her mother out, but she wanted to. "Just be careful, okay?"

"Okay." She slipped inside and shut the door.

Shit, shit, shit. How the hell were you supposed to defend yourself against someone playing these kinds of games? Because whether it was Jenny or someone messing with her visions, that's exactly what was going on. Someone was playing sick games with her.

Chapter 25

Raven woke to Indi's giggles over the baby monitor. She groaned and threw the covers over her head.

"Good morning, wee love."

Raven couldn't help but smile at her father's Scottish lilt coming over the monitor.

"Shall we get some breakfast and let your mummy have a lie-in?" He grunted. "Oh, you're getting to be a big lass, aye? Let's change your nappy then."

Baby babble followed. It must have been a good story because she went on for minutes.

"Aye, is that so? You'll be wanting to learn to drive soon, aye?"

Raven's eyes popped open. "She's seven months old."

"Don't worry, wee love. Grandda will teach you. Your mummy's liable to write you a ticket."

Raven snorted. "I'll write Grandda the ticket."

She was awake now, so she got up and took a quick shower before heading downstairs to make sure her father wasn't giving her daughter a driving lesson. She found him in the kitchen feeding Indi something that didn't look like pablum. "What's that?" She leaned over the bowl and sniffed. It smelled like apples.

"Apple sauce." He spooned a mouthful into Indi's mouth.

"It's good. Isn't it, wee love."

Indi gobbled it up, arms waving up and down, and grinned then opened her mouth wide for more.

"At least she's not spitting it all over the place." Raven leaned over and kissed the top of Indi's head. "What's this about teaching her to drive?"

Kiran's eyes flicked up to hers, a sheepish grin on his face. "You weren't supposed to hear that."

The coffee pot gurgled and Raven poured a cup for herself and Kiran. She brought them to the table and sat across from him.

"Thanks, love. What's the plan for the day then?" He asked as he spooned more apple sauce into Indi.

Raven shrugged and sipped her coffee. "It's the esbat tomorrow night."

"Aye. Are you worried?"

Not worried, she thought. She wanted a showdown with whoever they were up against. The problem was, they probably wouldn't come themselves. "No, not really. I just wish I knew what the hell was going on."

"You're not the only one."

Rauri stepped into the kitchen, said good morning, and headed straight for the kettle to make her tea. "I've just been on the phone with Jasmine. She's had a vision, aye?"

The legs of Raven's chair screeched across the wood floor as she turned to face Rauri. Rauri finished filling the kettle and put it on to boil before turning to them.

"Trouble's coming. Jasmine thinks it's going to happen at the esbat and that it's going to be the source, not hired thugs."

"What's she seeing, exactly?" Kiran asked.

"That's the problem. She's not getting a clear vision, more of a sense."

"Morning." Simone glided in ready for work in a tight-fitting royal blue dress and matching pumps. She leaned over

Kiran and gave him a quick kiss.

"Morning, love." He grinned up at her. "You were right about the apple sauce. She loves it."

Just as he said that Indi blew a raspberry and sprayed him with said apple sauce. Everyone burst out laughing. Indi clapped her hands and laughed with them.

"Don't laugh. You're just encouraging her," Kiran said, wiping his face with a tea towel. Rauri, Simone, and Raven pursed their lips then burst out laughing again when they all looked at each other.

"Oh, Goddess bless you," Raven said and kissed Indi's cheek. "I think you're the only thing keeping me from losing my mind this week."

Simone cleared her throat and had Raven studying her, Kiran, and Rauri. "What's up?"

"Did everything go well with Riley last night, love?" Kiran asked.

"What? Are you worried I'm losing my mind?"

"Did you get some sleep?" Simone asked.

"Oh, for crying out loud. Stop it. I'm fine."

Rauri's hand came down on her shoulder and she whispered in Raven's ear. "We're here, love. Lean on us."

Raven closed her eyes and leaned back in her chair. "I just went over there to try to get her to see the truth. She knows me. She knows I'm not depraved. But Jenny sure had her convinced."

"Is she still convinced?" Kiran asked.

"I think she realizes it's bullshit." It sure seemed like she was questioning it. Raven hoped she'd look back at all the times they'd been together and realize how ridiculous it was. "Jenny and Rebecca are staying at her apartment."

"Where they can have the most influence over her," Simone said.

"Yeah." That had been Raven's thought when she saw

them inside the apartment.

"But, she's far from given up on the two of you," Rauri pointed out. "She's come to see you twice in the last couple of days."

"Yeah, because she thought I was sleeping with Jade."

"Are you?" Rauri asked.

Raven snorted. "No, but I sort of made it look like we were, so Riley thinks so."

Three pairs of eyes stared at her as Indi spread apple sauce around the highchair table.

Raven rolled her eyes and explained seeing Riley, Jenny, and Rebecca laughing at the café in Huntsville and she just wanted Riley to feel an ounce of the pain she was feeling.

"You should probably tell her the truth," Simone said. She set her coffee cup in the sink and picked up her purse. "I've got to get to the office, but if you need anything, call." She kissed Kiran again and rushed out the door.

"She's right," Kiran said. "If your relationship is going to work, Rave, you need to be open and honest with each other."

"She's not open and honest with me. She's listening to all the shit that woman is telling her and believing it without talking to me. How could she have believed the crap Jenny said about me being depraved? She knows me. The least she could have done was talk to me about it. Instead, she …" She trailed off. So not going there. No one needed to know what happened the morning after the Summer Solstice.

"She what?" Kiran asked.

"Nothing. It doesn't matter. We need to make a plan for the esbat to keep everyone safe. Either that or cancel it."

"I'm not bloody cancelling." Kiran shoved a spoonful of apple sauce into Indi's mouth. Most of it ended up spread over her face and in her hair.

"Then, we need a plan." Raven leaned her forearms on the

table. "Even after all the research, we know nothing about the source of the threat or what they're planning."

"I thought Jaxon was identified as Randall Parker's descendant." Rauri brought her tea to the table and sat next to Raven. "I thought we were going to have a wee chat with him."

Shit. "Yeah, okay. I'll invite Jax and Mick over to my place after work."

"We'll bring dinner," Kiran said with a smile. "And apple sauce."

"Better bring lots of beer," Raven huffed. This was a *wee chat* she didn't want to have.

* * *

The afternoon sun beat down on Raven's RV deck. She fed Indi, just up from her nap, in the shade of the awning. Out on the lake, a speed boat shot around with tubers bouncing on the wake behind it. She could understand people wanting to tube, but she preferred a sedate pace in her kayak, taking in the views from the lake.

Jade walked up the beach in a huge straw hat and sundress, waving. Raven waved back, watching her as she came up the lawn. She stopped before the deck and reached out with her hand.

Raven laughed. "You're okay."

"I thought I'd check and see how everything's going?" She took the seat next to Raven and brushed her fingers through Indi's hair. "Hello, sunshine."

Indi pulled the bottle from her mouth and babbled at Jade.

"Well, aren't you full of stories."

"She seems to have a lot to say today," Raven said with a grin for her daughter. "I think she said Mum this morning."

"That wasn't Mum. It was ummm," Kiran said as he stepped up onto the deck with a cooler. He placed it next to the barbecue and pulled a beer out of it. "Beer, anyone?"

"Yeah, sure," Jade and Raven said in unison.

He twisted the tops off and handed them out. "The apple sauce was so good she was trying to say yum."

Raven laughed. "Yeah, you looked good in apple sauce."

Kiran grinned, leaning back on the deck railing and sipping his beer. "You just wait. You'll be wearing it soon enough."

Raven didn't doubt it.

Indi used one hand to hold her bottle and waved the other at Kiran, babbling away.

"See," Kiran said. "She said, that's right, Grandda."

"What? Now you can interpret baby talk?"

"Of course. One of my Goddess-given talents."

"I don't know why you'd need an interpreter," Jade said to Raven. "You're clairaudient. All you have to do is read her."

"Not going to happen," Raven said. "I won't intrude on my daughter's thoughts. She's entitled to her privacy."

Jade laughed. "Tell me that when she's a teenager."

Raven rolled her eyes. She had years before she had to worry about that. Thank the Goddess. "Where's Rauri?"

"Shopping with Simone. They should be along shortly."

Mick and Jax arrived next, with another cooler. Jax set it next to Kiran's and reached out his arms for Indi. "There's my girl." He lifted her, kissed her cheek, and settled her on his hip as she babbled to him. "Can I change her into her swimsuit?"

"Yeah, sure. It's in the bottom drawer of her dresser."

"Want to go for a swim, sweetie?" He went into the RV as Mick stared after him with dreamy eyes.

"I can't wait until we have kids of our own," Mick said. "He's such a good dad."

"Yeah." She wouldn't look so dreamy once she heard what they had to say, Raven thought. She was dreading it. She was hoping Rauri and Simone would take their time shopping when she heard another car coming up the lane. *Crap*. Maybe Jax would get in the water with Indi before someone opened up the conversation. She could only hope.

It wasn't Rauri and Simone that came around the corner from the driveway, though. It was Riley, Jenny, and Rebecca. Riley took one look at Jade sitting next to Raven and spun on her heel. Raven jumped up and went after her. She grabbed Riley's arm as she got to her car and said, "Take a walk with me."

Riley spun out of her grasp. "Why should I?"

"Because I've never slept with Jade. Walk with me. Talk to me."

Riley huffed and began to march up the driveway towards the lane.

Raven caught up to her in a couple of long strides. "There's never been anything between Jade and I. She's just been helping me investigate the fire and stuff. When I saw you laughing and having fun with Jenny and Rebecca at that café in Huntsville, I wanted you to hurt as much as I was hurting, so I asked her to kiss me. It was all a show."

Riley stopped and glared at her. "Why would you do that?"

She'd just explained why, hadn't she? "I was hurting, Ri. And seeing you having a good time like nothing had happened hurt even more."

"When I came here the other day, she was kissing the back of your neck."

Jade had dragged her teeth over the back of Raven's neck, but she wasn't about to point that out. "Yeah, she came onto me a few times, but I didn't do anything with her."

"How am I supposed to believe that after what I saw with my own eyes?" Riley's hands waved in front of her, her hair bouncing with the ferocity of her words.

"Fine. Believe whatever the hell you want." Riley believed

Jenny without question, but she doubted Raven. Enough of this freaking bullshit. "I'm done. Done." Her arms flew out to the sides like she was calling a runner safe at home base. "You can tell Jenny she won. And stay the hell out of my life." She spun around and stomped back to the RV.

"Raven!"

She threw her arm up like she was swatting away an annoying fly and kept going. Riley clamped onto her wrist with both hands and pulled until Raven stopped. She didn't turn to face her but stared straight ahead, waiting for Riley to let her go.

"Stop. Please, listen to me." Riley's breath hitched, her voice cracking. "I don't know who to believe anymore. I'm so confused. I don't know what to believe."

"You do, Riley. Listen to your heart, look at what you know from experience, listen to your gut. You know the truth." She pulled her arm out of Riley's grasp and walked away. When she stepped up onto the deck, Jenny and Rebecca were sitting in a couple of her deck chairs sipping from plastic wine glasses. Raven stormed over to Kiran. "I need to speak to you inside." She turned and went into the RV and paced the kitchen. When Kiran stepped inside, she growled, "What are they doing here?"

"I thought it was best to get everything out on the table. Everything. That's the only way we're going to figure out what's going on."

"And you didn't think to let me in on it?" She wanted to scream and yell at him, but she also didn't want Jenny to hear her, so she gritted her teeth and tried to keep her voice as low as she could. Her entire body shook, vibrating with the adrenaline pumping through her.

"You wouldn't have allowed them to come."

"You're damn right, I wouldn't have."

Riley's voice screamed from outside. "Why are you doing

this? Why are you telling me all these horrible lies about Raven?"

Raven couldn't hear Jenny's response, so she stepped over to the door. Tears streamed down Riley's red face, her hands were clenched so tightly her knuckles were white and she shook them at Jenny.

"What the hell is wrong with you?"

Jenny stared up at her, her face as red as Riley's and her lips pursed tightly together. Jax was down in the water with Indi, looking up at them. Mick stood against the deck railing, wide-eyed. Jade tried to disappear into her chair. Rebecca dropped her head, refusing to look at anyone. Raven held her breath.

"I didn't lie to you," Jenny said. "I told you what I saw in my visions."

"Then your visions are as fucked up as you are," Riley yelled. "If anyone is damaged because of what Gregor Paigo did to them, it's you."

Rebecca shot to her feet. "That's enough."

"You're just as bad, going along with her sick predictions. You both make me sick." She turned on her heels and ran.

Raven shot out the door and ran after her. She caught her just as Riley pulled her car door open. "Ri, don't drive in the state you're in." Riley turned and flung her arms around Raven's neck, burying her face in Raven's shoulder.

"Oh, God, I'm sorry. Please, forgive me." She sobbed, shoulders heaving, and clung to Raven.

Raven just held her, her cheek resting on Riley's head, and let her cry it out. She continued to hold her after Riley's shoulders stopped heaving and her breaths slowed.

"The things she said about you, she made it sound so plausible."

"It's alright, Ri."

"No, it's not. I got drunk that night because I couldn't

stand the things she said. I laid awake last night thinking about what you said and I had flashes of memory from the next morning. I … I held your wrists down, didn't I?"

"Riley, don't." There was no reason for Riley to punish herself further, Raven thought. It would do no good.

"You said, Ri, please stop, and you were crying. Did that happen?"

"It doesn't matter."

"Oh, God. I'm sorry, Rave."

Raven closed her eyes, cupping the back of Riley's head and holding her close. "It doesn't matter."

* * *

They went for a walk to give Riley time to compose herself, then walked back to Raven's deck. Simone and Rauri were there, although Raven had no idea when they'd arrived. Jenny and Rebecca were still sitting there, to Raven's surprise, and everyone else sat around the deck, quietly sipping drinks. Indi sat in her father's lap, babbling to Mick.

Riley sank into a vacant deck chair and buried her face in her hands. Raven sat on the arm of the chair with her hand on Riley's back. Kiran met Raven's gaze with raised brows. She nodded, silently telling him Riley was okay. She wasn't. It would take her time to heal from all of this.

"The reason we've asked you all here," Kiran began. "Is because we believe the strange goings-on are connected to a long-standing issue with Raven's ancestors. We believe whoever is behind all of this is using others to do their dirty work. One of the things we think they may be influencing is Jenny's visions."

Jenny, Rebecca, and Riley's heads popped up. Jenny glared at Kiran. "You think to save your daughter's reputation by disputing my visions."

"My daughter's reputation is impeccable. It's your visions that are disturbing and disreputable. I don't know what all you've told Riley, but I think Riley knows Raven well enough to discern the truth of your visions."

"I do," Riley said. "It wasn't until Raven told me I knew the truth, that it was in my heart and my knowledge of our past experiences, that I realized what a fool I'd been to believe Jenny."

Raven raised a brow. Riley had gone back to calling her Jenny instead of her mother.

"I don't know why she told me such horrible things, but I know in my heart they're not true."

"Jenny, love, if you saw these things in your visions, then we have to assume someone is giving you false images," Rauri said. She laid a hand on Jenny's thigh. "You haven't been the Jenny I know since we arrived here. We think maybe we can help resolve the issue if you'd allow Raven to give you a healing."

Rauri's gaze met Raven's icy glare. "And, if Raven will consent to it."

Raven's gaze shifted to Jenny, who sat rigid and red-faced.

Rebecca's hand slid into Jenny's. "Please, Jen. Do this for us if nothing else."

Jenny whipped her head around and burned Rebecca with her flaming glare. "For us? What has this got to do with us?"

"I can't keep going like this, Jen. Either something changes, or I have to leave you."

Jenny's flames shot around the deck. "You all think *I'm* mad. You think *I'm* the crazy one."

"No," Rauri said, patting Jenny's thigh. "We think you're being influenced by negative forces."

Jenny sniffed and shot her nose in the air. Rebecca released her hand and pushed to her feet. "Would someone call me a taxi, please?"

Jenny rose stiffly. "What are you doing?"

"I love you, Jen. But, I can't stand watching you self-destruct and hurt good people. It goes against everything we believe in."

"Even if I agreed to this … this … healing, do you think she would do it?" She waved her hand in Raven's direction. "She wouldn't."

"I would," Raven said.

Jenny shot her a shocked look. "Why? After everything you think I've done to you, why would you want to help me?"

"For Riley. All she's ever wanted is to find her mother and build a relationship with her. Maybe if you saw that I'm not this deranged person that you think I am, you'd try to develop a healthy relationship with your daughter."

Jenny looked up at Rebecca.

"Please," Rebecca said. "You've got every reason to at least try it."

"Alright. Fine." She sat back down, rigid and stiff, her mouth a fine white line.

Riley looked up at Raven and mouthed, "Thank you."

Raven cupped her hands and generated a ball of golden light. Indi laughed and clapped her little hands. She formed her own ball of energy, a beautiful glowing white light. As Raven sent her ball of energy towards Jenny, Indi gave her's a little push. It collided with Raven's twisting and forming into one pale yellow light before it washed over Jenny's body. Jenny's back arched and she shuddered then sank back into the chair as if her muscles relaxed for the first time since she'd stepped foot in Solstice.

Rebecca grabbed Jenny's hand. "Jen? Are you alright?"

Jenny's heavily lidded eyes lazily drew up to Rebecca's. "Yes, I'm fine. Tired. I just feel drained."

Rebecca's eyes shot to Raven, her brows drawn in.

"She's fine," Raven said. "A good night's rest and she'll be fine."

"I'll get her home then." Rebecca glanced at Riley then dropped her eyes. "Would someone call us a taxi, please?"

"I'll take you," Riley said, rising from her seat.

Rebecca smiled. "Thank you." She helped Jenny up and led her towards Riley's car.

Riley turned to Raven. "Would it be alright if I came back after?"

"Yeah, sure."

Riley took Raven's hand and squeezed. "Thank you. For everything." She pecked her cheek and walked off to her car.

Raven slid into the seat vacated by Riley, tilted her head back and took a deep breath. She was exhausted from the emotional roller coaster ride of the past hour or so.

"Did you see what Indi did?" Jax said with a wide grin on his face. "Did you see my daughter?" He lifted her into the air. "Aren't you amazing, sweetheart? Can you believe that? She's only seven months old." He laughed and hugged Indi to his chest, kissing her cheek.

"Don't get too excited," Raven mumbled. "You're not going to like the next act."

"What?" Jax asked.

Kiran stood. "I've got a pizza coming. How about we eat first, then we'll move on to the rest of our business."

* * *

With the dishwasher loaded and the counters gleaming, Raven had no excuse to stall going back outside any longer. She wasn't looking forward to this conversation with Jax. She picked up a rag and began polishing the granite counter again and Riley stepped in the door. Raven stopped cleaning and took in Riley's quiet beauty. The sun streaming in the door behind her made her look like an angel.

"Hey."

"Hey." Riley stepped up to the island and placed her palms on its surface. "I wanted to ask if you're still open to giving me some time."

For the first time in weeks, Raven thought they may have a chance at repairing their relationship. She also knew that Riley had some healing to do. "Yeah, whatever you need."

Riley looked up at her with those soft green eyes from under her lashes. "You mean that, don't you?"

"I love you, Ri. I always have and I always will. I'm here for you, so yeah, whatever you need."

Riley reached across the counter and laid her hand over Raven's, curling her fingers around Raven's palm. "I love you, too. I just … I don't know. I feel like I have a lot of processing to do."

"Would you consider seeing Dr. Shoal or someone like her? She's helped me a lot, Ri, and I think it would help you, too."

"I see the changes in you, Rave." Riley squeezed her eyes shut. "I do. I don't know how I let myself believe those horrible …" She hiccupped and her free hand covered her mouth. "What I did to you …"

Raven came around the island, her hand still clasped in Riley's. "Hey, it's alright." She hugged Riley to her. "It's done, Ri. Over and forgotten." Rauri's words from her grandmotherly chat came back to her. "Try not to be so hard on yourself. I know from experience the hard part is forgiving yourself, but know that I have no hard feelings about what happened. It really is done and over, Ri."

"How could you forgive me after what you've been through, after what my father did to you?"

"Hey." Raven's fingers sank into Riley's hair at the nape of her neck and she kissed her temple. "That man is not your father. Nothing he's done is a reflection on you." She could tell Riley that until she was blue in the face, but it was going to take a long time before Riley got over the fact of who her father was.

"What I did was nearly as bad as what he did."

"Bullshit. You were confused, drunk, angry with me. You were hurting, Ri. Please find a way to forgive yourself. You're nothing like him. Believe me." She rocked back and forth like she would if she was trying to soothe Indi. "I know it's going to take some time, but I'm here and I love you."

"Rave," Kiran called from outside.

Raven sighed but didn't loosen her hold on Riley. "Yeah, I'll be out in a minute." Riley pulled back and Raven brushed the pads of her thumbs under Riley's eyes to clear away the tears. "You can stay in here as long as you like. There's wine in the fridge. The bathroom is the second door on the left down the hall."

Riley nodded. "Sometimes, I don't think I deserve you."

"And others you wish you could trade me in for a better model," Raven grinned.

"Oh, I think they broke the mould after you."

"Yeah, well, once you achieve perfection ..." She laughed and Riley slapped her shoulder.

"You just keep right on thinking that."

At least she'd gotten Riley to smile and laugh a bit.

"Rave!" Kiran called again.

Raven winced. "Sorry."

"It's alright. Go ahead. I'm just going to freshen up my face a bit."

* * *

Little arms reached out to her as soon as Raven stepped out onto the deck and she took Indi from Mick. She curled up and burrowed into Raven's shoulder. "I should probably put her down."

"Give us a minute, aye?" Kiran said with a stern look.

Raven huffed out a breath and stood rocking back and forth with Indi.

"You all know we've been trying to trace Randall Parker after his escape from the asylum." Kiran began.

"Yeah," Mick said. "I've tried every route I could think of and haven't found any trace of him after his escape in 1871."

"Aye. Because we believe Parker changed his name and started over in Sweden."

"Sweden?" Jax sat with his forearms resting on his thighs and swivelled his head to Kiran. "My ancestors are from Sweden on my father's side."

"Aye, we know. We believe we've traced your ancestors back to Parker. Or, at the very least to one Randall James Lang. His date of birth coincides with Parker's."

Jax frowned. "That would mean that Rave and I are related."

"Don't worry, love," Rauri said. "It's a distant enough connection that you needn't worry."

"The thing is…" Kiran ran his fingers through his hair and looked up at Raven.

She raised an eyebrow at him. Call her a coward, but she was going to let Kiran take this one.

"The thing is that Raven's ancestors believe that Parker may have had offspring after his escape from the asylum and passed his quest for revenge down through his ancestors."

Jax stared at him, nodding.

"They also believed that those ancestors have been members of the Solstice Coven for generations."

Jax continued to nod. "Okay."

"And that they've been carrying out their revenge against the Bowen women."

"You think my father and his ancestors have been responsible for hurting Raven's family?"

Kiran looked up at Raven pleadingly.

Raven rolled her eyes. "We need to ask you what you know about it, Jax?"

Jax straightened in his chair and stared open-mouthed at Raven. "You think I know something about it? Honestly,

Rave, don't you think I'd tell you if I had any information that you or our daughter were in danger?" He went to Raven and cupped her cheek with one hand and placed the other on Indi's back. "I love you both, Rave. I would never allow harm to come to either of you. I haven't seen my father since I was a kid, but if he had anything to do with the fire or the attempt to take Indi, I'll kill him with my own hands."

The look in his eyes was so fierce, Raven believed him. It hadn't even clicked with him that they were looking at him as a suspect. "That's all I need to know. Will you come to the esbat tomorrow night?"

"I haven't been to a coven gathering for years, Rave."

"I know. But, I need you there for Indi."

"You're taking Indi? Are you mad?"

"The only way I can protect her is if she's with me, Jax. But, I need you there in case anything happens to me."

"In case anything happens to you? Like your death, you mean?" His hand rubbed his head, leaving his hair standing on end. "Damn it, Rave. What are you asking here?"

"I'm not planning on it, but if it comes down to it, I'll give my life to save hers. If that happens, you get her the hell out of there and protect her. Do you understand?"

There was a gasp behind her and she cursed herself for forgetting Riley was in the RV. Jax's glassy eyes remained locked on Raven's. "You expect me to watch you die and run with our baby?" He turned to Kiran. "Is this some kind of sick joke? We all have powers. We can't let harm come to Raven or Indi."

"They may be able to block all of our powers. We think Raven may be the only exception," Kiran said.

Jax sank to one knee and took Raven's hand in both of his. "Please, Rave. Leave Solstice. Get on a plane. Don't go anywhere near the gathering tomorrow."

There were tears in Raven's eyes now. "I can't do that, Jax.

If I run, they'll just catch up with me eventually. If I can end this now, then we can live in peace. I'm not going to spend my life running, scared shitless that they'll get to Indi." It struck her then that that's how Ena had lived her life and look where it got her. "I'm taking these bastards down tomorrow night."

"How? How are you going to do that? You don't even know who or what you're up against."

She hadn't worked that out yet, but she sure as hell wasn't going to give up. "I don't know, but I'm not letting them win."

Jax bent his head, his brow touching the back of Raven's hand. "Damn you, Rave. You better not fucking die on us."

Chapter 26

Every time Raven got the spoon near Indi's mouth, she fake cried and pushed it away. She'd tried pablum, banana, and organic green beans pureed to mush. All to no avail. "Okay, I give up," Raven huffed. She set the bowl aside and got Indi out of the highchair. "Are you cutting another tooth, angel." Her cheeks were flushed, but she didn't have a temperature and she was drooling like crazy. Raven wet a baby washcloth under cold water and handed it to Indi. Indi wailed and pushed it away. "Alright, alright." The washcloth went into the sink and Raven went to the window, rocking Indi back and forth in her arms. "Full moon tonight, sweet angel." Maybe Indi was feeling the same anxiety about what was to come or perhaps she was picking up on Raven's trepidation. Who knew?

A wheezing cough behind her had Raven spinning around. Ena stood bent over near the kitchen island, hacking up a lung. "Mom?" She looked as she did in the videos she'd taken just before her death. Raven ran to her and wrapped her arm around Ena's waist. There was nothing to her but skin and bone. Goddess, help her. "What can I do?" Raven asked as she led Ena to the living room.

Ena sank into the couch, holding up a hand until the hacking subsided. "Sorry, angel. I don't have much time. I don't have the energy to stay here long."

"Let me heal you." Why hadn't she thought that dream travelling could work the other way as well and Ena could visit her?

"You can't, Rave. We can't change the future."

"Please, Mom." Her eyes burned at seeing Ena like this, wasting away to nothing.

"It's too late for me, angel mine. Please, let me talk. There's not much time."

Raven sat Indi on a blanket on the floor and placed a couple of toys in front of her. She eased onto the couch beside Ena. Ena leaned over and grasped Indi's little hand and Indi gave her a two-toothed grin, babbling away.

"She's a storyteller, Rave. She's beautiful, so like her mother."

"In more ways than one. She's already conjuring healing light."

"You were at a young age, too. Be mindful of who knows of Indi's powers."

"How do I stop a baby from using her powers?"

"You'll find my notes in my journals, angel. It took me ages to figure out how to control yours. You conjured your beautiful golden light in the middle of the grocery store one day. I was horrified."

Raven laughed because she could imagine Indi doing just that.

Ena continued to hold Indi's hand and laid her other hand on Raven's thigh. "Listen to me, Rave. Until today, my visions of your future were always the same. That's why I tried so hard to protect you. But, this morning, I saw another possible outcome and it requires you to have all your powers, every advantage you can find. You have the power to stop them, Rave. You and only you. In the past, we ensured the Sacred Moon was in a safe place when we felt their energy. That's what they've always been after and we've kept it safe. We are the guardians of the Sacred Moon of the Goddess Cerridwen. It has been our duty to ensure its safekeeping. If it gets into their hands, unimaginable horror will ensue. It's the key. Do you understand?"

"Yes."

"You must wear it to the esbat, Rave. Wear it and save yourself as well as the future generations of Bowens. You'll find it in -"

"The wall safe. I know."

Indi bent forward, bracing her hands on the floor in front of her and pulled up onto her knees. She rocked back and forth, her little bottom bouncing up and down. Raven and Ena laughed and Indi squealed in delight.

"She looks like she's twerking," Raven snorted.

"You used to do the same thing just before you began crawling. Once she starts going, you won't get any rest."

"I've already got the place baby-proofed." Raven was sure she'd find things that still needed to be done, but she'd prepared the best she could.

"You're a wonderful mother, sweet angel."

"Thank you." That meant the world to her. She was terrified that she'd screw up.

"I must go. My energy is fading, angel. After the esbat, will you dream travel to see me, before my death, and let me know you're okay?"

"Yes." She threaded her fingers between Ena's and held on. She wanted to squeeze, but Ena's fingers seemed so fragile.

"They'll know your powers, Rave. They can sense them. You won't be able to surprise them with your powers and you won't know they're there until they want you to know. Hit them with everything you've got as soon as you can."

Raven nodded.

Ena reached up and ruffled Raven's hair. "And get a

haircut, sweet angel."

And she was gone. Raven ran her fingers through her hair, flopping her bangs from one side to the other. Then she blew up. Her bangs feathered up then flopped down over her eyes. Yeah, probably needed a haircut.

She looked down at Indi and she was right in front of her, her little hands reaching up to grasp onto Raven's shins. "And so it begins," she grinned, lifting her daughter into the air. She hadn't crawled very far - less than two feet - but she'd done it. Raven placed Indi in the middle of the floor on her hands and knees and took out her cell phone to get a video. Indi plunked herself down on her bottom and picked up a plush toy, stuffing it in her mouth. "Figures," Raven huffed.

* * *

Rauri encircled the box chain around Raven's neck, the weighty stone of the Sacred Moon nestling between her small breasts. Raven looked down at it, resting against the silk of her black robe. "Maybe we should put it on the inside, so it's not so glaringly obvious." She lifted the heavy stone and slid it under her robe. As she withdrew her hand, Rauri clasped it between her palms.

"You're shaking, love."

Raven took a deep breath and tried to relax her tense muscles. "It's a bit intimidating when more than one source has predicted a less than optimistic end to this night for me."

"We have every faith in you, darling Raven." Rauri's warm brown eyes looked deep into Raven's as if she was trying to fill her with inner strength. "You will end this senselessness tonight."

"I hope you're right, but I have to be realistic, Gran. My will is in the junk drawer in my kitchen."

"Pfffft." Rauri waved her hand at Raven. "Don't be ridiculous."

"No, listen. Please." She took another deep breath to ward

off her rising emotions this time. "Jax will get custody of Indi, but I need you to watch over her and teach her to use her powers. There are provisions in my will for her to spend time with you and with Dad."

Rauri spun on her heel and went to the window, but not before Raven caught the glimmer of tears in her eyes.

"I won't hear of this, Raven Sage." Her breath caught as she spoke. "Tomorrow morning, I'm going to give you a good cuff upside of that thick head of yours. The time is here for this absurd vengeance to end. You, my dear granddaughter, were fated to be the one to end it. You are more powerful than any witch I've known and we've only seen a fraction of your gifts. I refuse to contemplate any outcome other than victory." She turned back to face Raven, tears flowing down her rosy cheeks. "We believe in you, Rave. You must believe in yourself if there's any chance of success this night."

"Oh, I'm freaking well going to end it tonight, but I still have to prepare for a worst-case scenario." She stepped forward and closed the safe door then swung the painting back into place.

"Bloody stubborn witch, you are."

Kiran popped his head in the office door. "Everyone's here. We can go over the plan again when you're ready."

"We'll be right there," Raven answered. She went to Rauri and cupped her face in her hands. "I'll be calling down the moon tonight. Will you do me the honour of guarding Indi while I'm doing that?"

"Aye, love. I'll guard her with my life."

Raven was counting on it. She gently placed a kiss on each of Rauri's cheeks. "You won't tell Dad about the will until it's necessary?"

"No, love. It won't be necessary."

"Bloody stubborn witch, you are," Raven said in her best Scottish brogue.

* * *

When she walked into the great room and saw Riley sitting on the couch next to Jax and Mick, Raven's blood began to boil. "You shouldn't be here, Ri."

"I'm a member of the coven. You can't keep me from attending."

"You haven't been initiated in yet."

"You can't keep me from being there, Rave. Being there for you."

How was she supposed to argue with that after going on about getting through their trials together? "I don't want to risk your safety, Ri."

"I won't sit home, safe and sound, waiting to hear if you've been harmed. I can't. Please don't ask me to."

Raven speared her fingers through her freshly cut hair, leaving it spiking up in several directions. Her hands were shaking, so she crossed her arms, burying her hands under her arms. "Okay, fine." She squeezed onto the couch next to Riley and scanned the grim faces seated around the room - Kiran, Simone, Riley, Rauri, Jaxon, Mick, and Jade. Indi was on a blanket on the floor, banging two blocks together. Raven closed her eyes for a moment and said a quick prayer to the Goddess to see them all safe through this night. She had to be there for Indi after this was all said and done.

There wasn't much they could plan, not knowing who or what was coming or *if* it was coming. The basic plan was to be hyper-alert, continually scanning for anything out of the ordinary, especially the negative energy that they'd all been sensing around Solstice.

"The priority is to protect Raven," Kiran said.

"No," Raven objected. "As far as we know, I'm the only one whose powers they can't block. I can protect myself. Your priority is to protect Indi,. At all costs."

"I still think she'd be safer if you let me take her from here,

Rave," Jax said.

"And if it's Indi they're after? If they go after you and Indi instead of coming to the esbat?" It was a risk she couldn't take. Especially if she was wrong about Jax and he was involved in this mess. She needed Indi near her.

"I get it," Jax said. "I don't like it, but I get it."

Mick would be nearby in the woods with several other police officers. They'd be outside the protective barrier that Raven would place over the gathering and unable to enter until Raven or Rauri opened a portal for them. If their would-be attackers were outside the protective dome, they wouldn't be able to harm the coven. That was the best-case scenario. Raven hoped they'd tip off their presence and she'd be able to take them down outside of the gathering. If they were inside it, they wouldn't be able to escape, but every coven member would be at risk.

Raven picked up Indi's black robe from the coffee table and went to her, slipping it over her head and feeding her arms into the sleeves. Indi patted her chest and babbled.

"That's right," Raven laughed. "You're Lady Indigo Amaris Rauri Bowen, High Princess of the Solstice Coven." And guardian of the Sacred Moon of the Goddess Cerridwen, she added silently.

"Ba," Indi said.

"That's quite a handle for a seven-month-old," Jax said and lifted his daughter into his arms.

Raven just prayed Indi wasn't going to be the sole guardian of the Sacred Moon come morning light. Only Rauri knew she was wearing the Sacred Moon. She figured the fewer that were in on that piece of information, the better. Jade, Jaxon, and Mick didn't even know about the Sacred Moon unless Jax knew about it from other sources. As much as she trusted him, the self-doubts in her intuition forced her to not be able to completely rule him out. The family connection was too much to ignore.

"I arranged for paramedics to be on standby," Mick said and dropped her eyes when everyone looked at her. "Just in case."

Raven went to her and took both of her hands in hers. "Thank you." She kissed her cheek. "Blessed be."

"Blessed be," Mick repeated. "Stay safe, or I'll never forgive you."

"That's the plan." She smiled and squeezed Mick's hands, hoping to reassure her, but it felt like she was saying goodbye.

Chapter 27

They walked seven abreast, with Indi in her father's arms, across the field towards the woods that would lead them to the sacred ritual grounds of the Solstice Coven. Raven, Kiran, Simone, Rauri, and Jade all wore black silk robes with red ropes around their waists, signifying their status as third-degree priest or priestesses. Riley wore a black silk robe but had yet to be initiated as a first-degree priestess, so she wore no rope around her waist. Jaxon hadn't practiced Wicca since his mother's passing years earlier, so he wore faded jeans and a white t-shirt stretched across his muscular chest and shoulders.

Before they stepped into the woods, Raven turned back and looked out over the cliffs and lake that had offered her comfort throughout her life. Under the full moon, the lake sparkled brilliantly. She absorbed its beauty, letting it calm her. Her tense muscles relaxed and the trembling in her hands faded away. She whispered her thanks to Mother Earth and turned to follow the others.

As she entered the woods, she bent over and pulled off her sandals, preferring to feel the earth's energy through her bare feet as she navigated the well-worn path to the ritual grounds. Every one of her ancestors, dating back to Lady Moira a hundred and fifty years ago, travelled this path at least a couple of times a month, their energy co-mingling with the earth's. Raven felt like she was gathering their strength with her as she journeyed towards the clearing. She stretched out her arm and let her fingertips brush the rough bark of the trees and the soft leaves of ferns and natural plants. She breathed in the fresh night air and tuned into the sounds of leaves rustling in the trees, the long hoot of an owl in the distance, the soft footsteps of her friends and family.

When she reached the clearing, she felt energized and ready to take on their foe. There was much to do before the rest of the coven arrived. Simone, as acting High Priestess, cast the circle then began the preparations for the Full Moon esbat with Kiran's help.

Raven sat in the middle of the circle in the lotus position facing the altar, her upturned hands resting on her lower thighs, forefingers and thumbs touching. She closed her eyes, breathing deeply, and envisioned herself conquering their enemy.

Once preparations for the esbat were complete, Simone purified the seven of them plus Indi, then they gathered to perform a powerful protection ritual. Then Raven invoked the Gods and Goddesses to watch over and protect the coven.

"Someone approaches," Jade said.

Raven turned to the path leading from the Bowen house, seeing no one.

Jade smiled. "Lovely energy. Raven, I believe you have some visitors."

A figure wearing a black robe appeared down the path, her long russet brown hair flowing with her movement. Behind her, more figures appeared until eight women entered the circle. The first in the line Raven recognized immediately. Lady Moira walked to Raven, where she stood in front of the altar. Facing Raven, she said. "We are forbidden from interfering in the events this night, daughter of the Bowen line, but we came to offer you love and positive energy. She took Raven's left hand and slid a silver ring with a large purple stone onto her forefinger. "Amethyst for protection. She kissed Raven's cheek and moved off, allowing her daughter, Eloise, to approach Raven.

She wasn't the sixteen-year-old who Raven had met but a beautiful woman in her mid-twenties. Her eyes sparkled as she smiled at Raven and pushed what Raven thought was a spiral-shaped bracelet onto her left wrist. Eloise pushed it up her arm until it circled Raven's bicep. "For the warrior," she said with a cheeky grin. "Lady Raven, protector of all."

As Eloise moved off, her daughter Emelia stepped up to Raven. She also was in her mid-twenties. Her eyes were like a cat's, glowing golden yellow. She smiled demurely as she tipped a small bottle on the pad of her finger then touched it to Raven's breasts then her pubis. "Sandalwood, for protection. Blessed be."

Four more Bowen women bestowed her with gifts of protection before Ena stood in front of her. Raven's breath caught and she bit her lip, fighting back the tears. Ena was vibrant and healthy, her eyes glowing as she smiled at her daughter. She laid her palm over Raven's chest and smiled knowingly when it covered the Sacred Stone. She nodded, then took Raven's right hand and slid a ring of silver encasing a brilliant, rough stone of reds, oranges, yellows, greens, blues, and purples. "Fire agate," she began. "For protection and courage. Be well, Lady Raven of the Solstice Coven. I'm so very proud of you."

Ena turned and joined the line of eight generations of Bowen women facing Raven. They joined hands and lowered into an elegant curtsy. It was a greeting bestowed upon a High Priestess, which Raven wasn't. She glanced at Simone to see how offended she was, but Simone only grinned at her, her eyes glowing. The Bowen women rose as if one and, in unison, said, "Blessed be, Lady Raven, warrior, protector, guardian of the Sacred Moon. Blessed be."

Raven took a step towards them and faced empty space.

Kiran stepped up next to her and wrapped his arm around her shoulders. "Alright, love?"

No. Raven wanted her ancestors to come back. She wanted Ena to be in the here and now, healthy and vibrant as she'd just seen her. But, she just nodded as a single tear spilled out of the corner of her eye.

* * *

Once all of the coven members arrived, Simone closed the magic circle and Raven placed a dome of protection around the clearing. Raven took her sleeping daughter from Jaxon and snuggled her across her chest. Then she took her place next to Kiran and Simone in front of the altar. The coven members stood in a circle and walked past Simone, one by one, as she purified them with holy water.

Just as Simone began the Full Moon ritual, the wind picked up as if a vicious storm was brewing, but when Raven glanced out at the trees beyond her protective barrier, they weren't moving and the full moon still shone brightly in the sky above them. She ran to Rauri and pressed Indi into her arms. "Protect her," she commanded, glancing between Rauri, Riley, Jaxon, and Jade. "At all costs."

She turned back to the altar and a towering figure in a black cloak and black hood stood between her and Kiran and Simone. She began to thrust her hand toward him and Riley stepped in front of her.

"If you want her, you'll have to go through me."

"Riley, no!"

The man in the black hood laughed, rough and raspy, as he cocked his arm back. "As you will, so mote it be."

Raven dove and pushed Riley out of the way. Something hit her side, just below her left arm, with great force. It was like a cement block had been shot through her ribs and into her chest. She landed with an oomph as all the air was forced from her lungs. She couldn't get her breath back, but she staggered to her feet and shot her hand towards the man. She was so weak, the sparks that flew from her fingers sputtered and died before they met their mark.

Something hard hit her right temple and pain exploded through her head before everything went black.

Raven came to lying face down on the granite altar, her hips digging into the sharp corner and her legs dangling down the side. Her arms were stretched out in front of her with two big fists wrapped around her wrists like steel bands. The rest of the body attached to the meaty fists was covered in a black cloak and hood. A few feet in front of the altar, Kiran, Simone, Rauri, Jaxon, and Riley knelt with their hands palm down on their thighs, facing the altar. Another looming figure in a black robe and hood stood behind them. Behind him, the rest of the coven stood in a circle, unmoving and gazing straight ahead.

Indi was on the ground in front of Kiran on her knees with her little hands on Kiran's forearm, wailing with her little face red and her lip quivering.

Raven's head jerked back when someone behind her grabbed a fistful of her hair and yanked. The deep raspy voice said, "You have one chance, Raven Sage. Take us to the Sacred Moon now or suffer the consequences."

They didn't know she was wearing it. Raven wanted to laugh at them, but she gritted her teeth and growled, "If you haven't figured out after a hundred and fifty years that you're never going to get your filthy hands on it, you're dumber than I thought."

He laughed and shoved her head, cracking it off the granite altar. Her head was already pounding, as was her side and chest. She ached everywhere. It was like she had shards of ice running through her veins. Except, she realized, for the heat pulsing over her chest. The Sacred Moon.

Indi's wailing pierced the air and the deep voice shouted, "Shut that thing up."

Raven roared a primal scream and shot blue arcs into the crotch of the man clasping her wrists. There was a loud shriek and he released his grip. Raven threw her arms back behind her and shot out another pulse of energy. A thump sounded on the ground behind her and she pushed herself off the altar, stumbling back a few steps before she found her balance. The man with a deep voice pushed to his feet. She shot her hands towards him, fingers curled like long claws. The veins in her neck and forearms corded and pulsed, her teeth gritted, and her mouth formed into a snarl. Her entire body shook.

She raised her arms and the man began to levitate into the air. Five feet, ten feet, fifteen. Raven threw her arms down to her sides and his body was thrust to the earth. It bounced with a great thud, then settled back onto the ground and lay unmoving.

Raven spun to the man standing behind her family. She thrust her right hand towards him, then curled her fingers into a tight fist. He grabbed his throat, clawing at it as he lifted into the air.

The man that had been holding her wrists got to his feet and stumbled towards her. She thrust her left hand out to him and closed her fingers into a fist. He mimicked his partner and Raven raised them both up into the air until they were dangling, grasping at their throats, their feet jerking and kicking below the hem of their robes.

"Cease! Release them!" Alana ran forward and the rest of the coven members began to come out of their stupor. Kiran immediately lifted Indi into his arms and began to comfort her.

Raven could see Mick on the other side of the barrier,

banging it with her fists and screaming, but she couldn't open the portal yet.

"You'll kill them," Alana yelled. "Release them."

They'll know your powers, Rave. They can sense them.

Ena's words came to her as she realized Alana had been the only person who could detect her protective shield. She drew her fists into her chest then thrust out her arms, sending the two men into Alana. She was knocked off her feet and the two men landed on top of her. Raven held out her hand, holding them in place while she used the other to open the portal for Mick and the other officers. They ran towards the pile of black robes lying on the ground and began to secure them.

Mick pulled the hoods off the two men and Jax swore. "They're my cousins. Brandon and Landon MacKinney."

Raven took a step towards Kiran, reaching her arms out for Indi. A loud crack resounded through the clearing and Raven dropped like a stone. Pain shot up her neck into her head. Like she didn't have enough of a headache already. She tried to push herself up and couldn't move. Black shoes and a black robe moved towards her. She glanced up to see the man she'd slammed into the ground hunched over with his left hand hugging his torso. His right hand hung to his side, the moonlight glinting off the silver gun in his grip. He raised his arm and the barrel of the gun came up, aimed right at Raven's head.

Damn it. Why couldn't she move? Why couldn't she be facing the other way? She wanted to see her daughter, to see Riley, just once more. There was screaming and shouting behind her, but she couldn't make out what anyone was saying. Bright lights danced in front of her eyes, then there was nothing.

Chapter 28

The incessant beeping drove Raven mad. Someone jackhammered inside her head when all she wanted was to sleep. Her throat hurt and she tried to clear it, but it just made her gag. *Shit!* There was something in her mouth and down her throat. She tried to reach up to pull it out, but nothing happened. *Shit! Shit! Shit!* Her eyes flew open, bulging like a spooked horse, and darted around the brightly lit room. There were machines all around her and a glass wall in front of her. Was she tied down? Why couldn't she move? Something was wrapped around her neck. A C-collar? She couldn't even move her damn head.

"Rave?" Riley's face appeared over her. "You need to calm down. There's a tube in your throat and a machine breathing for you, but you need to remain calm and let it do its job."

Calm down? Was she out of her freaking mind? *Get this damn thing out of my throat for cripes sake.*

Riley's hand stroked her forehead, her fingers feathered through her hair. "You're alright, babe."

No, she bloody well wasn't. *Help me! Help me for cripes sake!*

A sliding glass door in the wall in front of her opened and a nurse dressed in bright pink scrubs came in.

"She's panicking," Riley said. "She needs a sedative."

No! I don't need a fucking sedative. I need you to take the fucking thing out of my throat! She tried to yell Riley's name and gagged on the tube in her throat.

"Rave, you need to calm down. If you aspirate with that tube in your throat, we'll be in trouble. Don't try to talk. Just relax, babe."

The nurse pushed a needle into the IV line and hit the plunger.

Stop telling me to fucking relax. Why the fuck can't I move? Why can't I talk? What the fuck is happening? Where's Indi? Is my baby okay? Oh, fuck. What happened? Her head grew fuzzy and her eyes fluttered closed.

* * *

She didn't know how many times she woke up in an all-out panic. Every time, a nurse ran in and shot something into her IV line that put her out again. This time her eyes fluttered open and she stared up at Kiran, his eyes red-rimmed and puffy.

Fuck. It's bad. Kiran's face blurred as hot tears ran trickled down her temples. *Tell me. Tell me how bad I'm hurt.* She still couldn't move and that damn tube was still stuck down her throat.

"Hello, love."

She tried to answer and gagged.

A chair leg screeched against the floor and Riley's head appeared over her opposite Kiran. "Don't try to talk, Rave. You're alright."

Goddess, she wished Riley would stop saying that. She damn well knew she wasn't alright.

Kiran's hand ran over her hair. "Raven, love, you're the only one who can heal yourself, aye?"

"You can answer by blinking once for yes, twice for no," Riley said.

She blinked once.

"Can you conjure your healing energy?"

Why hadn't she thought of that the first time she woke up? Blink. She concentrated on generating healing energy in her hands. Nothing happened.

"Are you trying it now, love?"

Blink.

A gush of air escaped Riley's lungs and her face dropped out of sight. Raven stared up at Kiran as he lowered his head, shoulders heaving. Tears streamed out of her own eyes.

The sliding glass door opened and a dark-skinned man with salt and pepper hair wearing light green scrubs and a white lab coat entered carrying a clipboard. "Hello, Raven. I'm Dr. Singh." He drew a tissue from a box on the table next to her and dabbed at her eyes. "Has anyone explained your injuries to you yet?"

She blinked twice. *About freaking time.*

"You came in with a gunshot wound to the back of your neck. Do you remember getting shot?"

She blinked once. She remembered the gunshot and dropping to the ground, staring at the man walking towards her with the silver gun. Had he shot her again?

"The bullet crushed your C2 vertebrae and caused extensive damage to your spinal cord. It's what we refer to as a complete spinal cord injury or tetraplegia, in your case."

What the hell was he saying? Her eyes darted to the right, looking for Riley. She came back to the side of the bed with a grim look on her face. "You're paralyzed from the neck down, Rave."

Goddess, she couldn't live like this and never hold Indi again, never touch Riley or feel her touch, never walk in the woods or go for a run. She couldn't even conjure her healing light. *Oh, shit.* Indi could. She started blinking her eyes rapidly. How the hell was she supposed to ask them to get Indi in there, fast?

"She wants to say something," Dr. Singh said.

Isn't he just freaking brilliant?

"If you start saying the alphabet, Raven can blink when you get to the letter she wants and spell out what she wants to say."

Okay, maybe she was a little harsh. That was very helpful.

Riley started saying the alphabet and Raven blinked when she got to I. Then N. Then D. Then I. Goddess help her, this was taking forever.

"Indi's fine," Kiran said. "She's in Solstice with Rauri, Jax, and Mick."

Raven stared up at them. If Indi was in Solstice, where the hell were they? She glanced around the room and settled on the name tag on Dr. Singh's lab coat. Sunnybrook Medical Centre. How did she get to Toronto? She'd gone off-topic. She began blinking rapidly again and Riley called out the alphabet until Raven spelled out, "Bring her here."

Kiran shoved his fingers through his hair. "I don't know if that's such a good idea, love. It's a long drive and …"

Raven blinked rapidly. There had to be an easier way to communicate. Riley rhymed off the alphabet again and Raven spelled out, "Indi heal."

Kiran and Riley stared at each other over the bed. Riley's hand shot up to cover her mouth and tears streamed down her face. Kiran headed for the glass door, pulling his cell phone out of his pocket as he went. "I'll call Jax."

* * *

Over the next five days, Jaxon brought Indi into the hospital for a few hours every morning, but all she did was reach for Raven and cry. They wouldn't even let Indi onto the bed with her because they were afraid she'd cause Raven more damage. How much more freaking damaged could she get?

Every day when they left, she lay there thinking about spending the rest of her life unable to move and hooked up to machines to keep her alive. For hours on end, she listened to the rhythmic hiss of the ventilator and the constant beep of the heart monitor. She hated those sounds with a passion. It was like listening to a faucet continually dripping. Goddess help her. She couldn't live like this.

On the sixth day, after two hours of Indi squirming in Jax's arms, crying and reaching for Raven, he said, "I can't do this anymore, Rave. I can't bring her in here every day and watch this. It's killing me."

What the frig did he think it was doing to her? She wanted to hold her baby. She wanted them to put Indi on the bed with her and let the poor thing snuggle with her mom.

"The only time she's ever conjured her healing light was when she's seen you doing it, love," Kiran said.

For about the millionth time, she tried to generate her healing light. When nothing happened, she closed her eyes and wracked her brain for something that would look like she was conjuring healing energy and came up empty. She began blinking rapidly and Kiran started calling out the alphabet. She spelled out, "Put her on me."

"We can't, love. You know we can't."

Damn it, if they weren't going to bring Indi in again, she damn well wanted to at least feel like she'd hugged her. Or tried.

When Mick walked in the door, Raven looked up at the ceiling and thought, thank the Goddess. It's about damn time. She blinked rapidly and spelled out, "Read me," and stared at Mick.

Mick nodded.

Finally. Where the hell have you been?

"Working. I'm sorry. This is the first chance I've had to come to see you."

Tell them to put Indi on my lap.

"Um, she wants you to put Indi on her lap."

"Rave," Kiran sighed.

Who the hell cares if she does more damage? What freaking difference will it make at this point?

Mick's mouth formed an O and she blew out. "Wow. Um, she says, what difference will it make if Indi does any more damage?"

"I can't do this anymore. I'm sorry, Rave. It's just too hard." Jax rubbed his head as Indi squirmed in his arms, still reaching for Raven and crying.

Hot tears flowed from the corners of Raven's eyes. *I can't do it either. Do you understand? I can't live like this. Not like this.*

"Oh, Rave," Mick said as tears flooded her eyes. "I'm sure it won't always be this hard."

If you unplug that machine, I'll be gone in a few minutes. This is not how I want to live. I can't even hold my child, Mick.

"That child needs her mother."

Not like this. What kind of a mother will I be like this?

"What's she saying?" Kiran asked.

Mick looked up at him with horror in her eyes.

Tell him.

"She … she wants the plug pulled." She burst into tears and her voice rang through Raven's head. *Damn you for making me tell him that.*

Kiran stabbed his fingers into his hair and spun around, staring up at the ceiling. Jax buried his face in Indi's neck and kept sniffing.

Get the doctor in here, Mick. I need you to translate.

Mick wept into her hands.

Please.

"Oh, for fuck sakes. Alright." She stormed out of the room and Raven could see her at the nurses' station, pulling tissues out of a box on the counter.

Mick rarely used profanity. The worst she usually said was, "Geez." She knew this was hard on all of them, but for cripes sake, how did they think she felt? How would they feel if they were stuck in a bed in this state, knowing it would never get any better?

Kiran leaned over and pressed his lips to her forehead. "Please don't do this, love. Please. We'll be here to help you." He covered his eyes with his hand and wept. "Please, love."

I'm sorry. Raven squeezed her eyes shut. *I'm sorry, I can't.*

"You wanted to see me?" Dr. Singh said as he walked in the door with Mick on his tail.

Riley stepped in after her and scanned the wet faces. "What's going on?"

Tell him I want a DNR.

Mick looked at Riley, then dropped her head. *Damn you, Raven.*

Tell him.

"First, let me explain that I'm clairaudient. I can hear Raven's thoughts. She wants a DNR. She wants the plug pulled on the machines."

Riley released a keening wail and dropped to her knees. Kiran ran to her and lifted her into his arms. "Nooo," she wailed. "Rave, nooo."

Dr. Singh stepped up to the side of the bed. "Is that true, Raven. Do you want a do not resuscitate order?"

Blink.

"You're a young woman, Raven. You have your whole life ahead of you and although it seems insurmountable now, it will get easier."

It's my right as a human being to request and be granted a DNR. If I don't want machines to keep me alive, it's my right to request they be turned off.

Mick repeated Raven's words through her tears.

Dr. Singh nodded. "I'll make the note in your chart. We'll schedule for the ventilator to be turned off at ten o'clock tomorrow morning." He squeezed her hand even though she couldn't feel it and left the oppressive room.

Raven closed her eyes again as Riley wailed, setting Indi off, and all Raven wanted was to comfort her daughter.

I want Jax to bring Indi in the morning. Please. I want to say goodbye to my daughter.

Mick relayed the message to Jax and he nodded with his head still burrowed in Indi's neck.

When they all began to file out, Raven panicked. *Mick? Will you stay for a while?*

Mick turned back and looked at her with miserable eyes.

You're the only one I can talk to and it's either that or I lay here all night listening to those fucking machines and staring up at the damn ceiling.

Mick touched Jax's forearm. "I'm going to stay for a while and keep Raven company. I'll see you back at the hotel."

He nodded and gave her a quick kiss. Mick pulled up a chair next to the bed and lowered the side rail.

Will you tell me what happened after I passed out?

"You didn't pass out, Rave. You weren't breathing. Riley performed CPR until the paramedics got there."

Did the guy shoot me again?

"No. He didn't live long enough."

Did you shoot him?

"I heard the gunshot and saw you on the ground. I drew my weapon and took a few steps to get a clear shot, but Jade Storm got him before I could get a shot off. I wish it had been me, even if it was Jax's father."

Raven raised her eyebrows. At least she could still do that. *Jade shot Jax's father?*

"No, she's a freaking warrior. She threw a blade from about thirty feet and hit him dead centre of the heart."

I wish I'd seen it. Is Jax okay?

Mick nodded. "He hadn't seen his dad since he was little. It's the guilt over what his family did to you that's hurting him."

Tell him it's not his fault.

"I do."

Is anyone talking?

"Alana sang like a little bird, trying to cut a deal, but they've all been charged with attempted murder, attempted murder during the commission of an offence, forced confinement, blah, blah, blah. You know the deal. Anyway, she's saying that Jax's mom refused to allow his dad to teach him black magic, so he left. Alana was happy to provide him with offspring that he could train in the dark arts. He trained her, too."

Where did they get their power?

"They've been collecting powerful amulets going back generations, even before that Randall Parker character. They were all wearing them. LaCroix has them locked up in evidence right now, but he figures since you're the Guardian of the Sacred Moon that maybe you could guard these amulets, too, and make sure they don't get into the wrong hands."

He doesn't know how badly I'm injured?

Mick's eyes filled and she looked up at the ceiling. "We all figured you could heal yourself and then we thought Indi could. She still could, Rave. If you hang on for a while, she could heal you."

Raven closed her eyes. *She's only ever done it when I was conjuring healing energy. Indi was probably just feeding off my energy. She may not be able to conjure it on her own.*

"You don't know that. She zaps Jet when you're not around."

That's an entirely different thing, Mick.

Mick swiped a couple of tissues from the box on the table and dabbed her eyes.

Tell me about Indi. What's she been doing?

"Ha." Mick sniffed and smiled. "She's crawling all over the place. We're constantly chasing her down, making sure she doesn't get into anything. She's eating all kinds of different foods now. We purée it. You know, so she's not eating artificial preservatives and crap. That's what you wanted, right?"

Yeah. Thank you. You'll take good care of Indi, protect her? Tears flowed down her temples in little rivulets.

"Damn it, Rave. I don't want to have this conversation."

Rauri knows where my will is.

"Stop it, damn it." She stuffed the tissues against her eyes and wept again. "You're supposed to take me on as your partner. This isn't supposed to be happening." The legs of the chair scraped across the floor as Mick lurched to her feet. "You're giving up and it's not fair. It's not fair, damn you."

She ran from the room and Raven was left with hot rivers flowing out of the corners of her eyes, listening to *hiss, beep, beep. Hiss, beep, beep. Hiss, beep, beep.*

* * *

The lights had been turned off in her room, but Raven could see all of the little nooks and crannies in the ceiling tiles with the light shining in the glass wall. Her eyes were heavy, but when she closed them, her thoughts turned to dark memories. Not being able to move set off a panic that was akin to Grego Paigo holding her down all those years ago. Sort of like claustrophobia only different.

Her eyes itched, probably because it was so damn dry in the room, and she couldn't freaking scratch them or ask someone to do it for her. She couldn't even ring the damn call bell for the nurse. She blinked her eyes open and closed a few times, relieving the itch for about three seconds.

When she got tired of staring at the ceiling, she looked at the clock on the wall of the nursing station out in the hall. Two o'clock in the morning. She only had eight more hours of this nightmare to endure. Why she had to wait until ten in the morning, she had no idea. Couldn't they have just turned the machines off when she'd asked for the DNR? Why did they have to be so damn cruel, making her wait? How could Riley and Kiran and Mick ask her to live like this? She'd never be able to sip a cup of coffee or a beer. Or eat a slice of pizza. She'd never be able to work again or do the things she loved, like running and working out. Kayaking on Fairy Lake. She wouldn't be able to get herself out of bed, showered, dressed. Someone would have to do all of that for her and more. She couldn't brush her teeth or her hair, not that she fussed over her hair or anything. She rarely remembered to run a brush through it.

She'd never be able to touch Riley again. She'd never feel that pang of arousal thrumming through her body every time Riley was near or every time she thought about her. She'd never be able to hug Riley close to her at night, feel the heat of her body against hers.

The worst, absolute worst, part of the whole thing was the thought of never being able to hold her daughter again, never being able to hug her, pick her up when she falls, never be able to kiss her or tousle her hair or hold her hand. Not only couldn't she take care of herself, she couldn't take care of her daughter. And that's what had fuelled her decision to pull the plug. She couldn't bear it.

She closed her eyes against the sudden flood of tears then forced them open again when she started to drift off. She looked at the clock. Two minutes past two. Why was time moving so damn slow?

She hadn't dream travelled to let Ena know how the esbat had gone. She didn't know how to tell her mother what had happened and she was scared to death that she'd end up on Ena's kitchen floor, unable to move and without the damn respirator breathing for her. *Fuck.* She repeatedly wondered if

Ena would dream travel to see her, but she hadn't come. Maybe she didn't know where to find her. Was she trying to? Was she going to her RV day after day, waiting for her to return? *I'm sorry, mom.* She closed her eyes against the tears again and drifted off.

Raven stood in Ena's kitchen, staring down at her hands, flexing them open and closed, then wiggling her fingers. She could move. She turned, expecting to see Ena sitting at the kitchen island, but she wasn't there. A video camera sat on a tripod on the other side of the island. Ena had used it the morning before her death to film videos for Raven and Kiran. "Mom?" she called out. No answer came.

She went to the window, leaned over the counter, and looked out to see Ena's car in the driveway. Of course, it was there. She was in no condition to drive it at this point. "Mom?" she called again as she ran for the stairs. She took them two at a time, revelling in the ability to walk, to run. She ran down the hallway to the master bedroom.

Ena lay in the bed, propped up with pillows. A full glass of water sat on the nightstand next to a handheld phone cradled in its charger. "Mom?"

Ena opened her eyes. A weak smile formed on her sunken face. "You got ..." she took a short, sharp breath. "A hair cut."

Raven ran her fingers through it. Goddess knew what it looked like after lying in a hospital bed for so long. She sat on the edge of Ena's bed. "I hate seeing you like this. It's not fair that I can't heal you." Or myself, she thought.

"Tell me about the esbat. I don't have much time."

Damn. Raven looked away and swallowed her tears. "Good and bad. The good news is that we shouldn't have to worry about them anymore. One of them is dead. The other three are in jail and will be for a very long time."

"Good. Who was it?"

"Jax's father, Alana, and their two sons."

"Alana's sons were Jake Lang's?"

"Apparently. You don't sound surprised about Alana."

"No, not really. She always was a bit off, but I could never put my finger on it."

"Yeah, I guess you're right."

Ena reached for Raven's hand and stared into her eyes. "Tell me the bad news."

"This is the last time I'll be able to dream travel to see you."

"Why, sweet angel?"

Fast and straight up, just like she'd tell the parents of a victim during an investigation. "I'm in Sunnybrook Hospital on life support. They're pulling the plug in the morning."

"Oh, Rave." Tears filled Ena's weary eyes. "Can you not heal yourself?"

"I've tried. I'm paralyzed and haven't been able to conjure the healing energy."

"Indigo?"

"We've tried that, too. The only time she's conjured healing energy is when I've been doing it."

"You think she's tapping into your energy?"

"Yeah, it would seem so."

"Give her time, Rave. She's just a baby."

"I can't bear it, Mom. I feel like I'm trapped inside a dead body." Her breath hitched. "I am."

Ena opened her arms and Raven leaned into her embrace.

"Could one of our ancestors do it?" She knew what Ena's answer was going to be - they couldn't interfere with the future. But, damn it, she had to try.

"Rave, even if we were permitted to change the future, you're the only Bowen with that particular power."

Raven pushed up and stared into Ena's eyes. "But, it's not a Hayes power."

"No."

"Then, where did I get it from?"

"It could be any one of the Bowen mates. We've all bred with magickal men."

Raven cringed, remembering how Ena was conceived. Jax's ancestors on his father's side had raped Ena's mother. Was that where the healing power had come from?

Ena's breathing became laboured and her eyes closed.

"Mom?"

Her eyes fluttered open, her lids heavy. "My time is near, sweet angel."

"No. Oh, please, no." Raven held Ena's cold hand as her breaths slowed. "Mom, I love you."

A faint smile appeared on Ena's greying face. "Thank you. For being here … with me … now. Love … you. Need to rest."

She spoke so quietly that Raven could barely hear her words. This was insane, Ena lying here all on her own. She must be scared out of her mind. Raven picked up the phone and dialled 911, then realized that the dispatcher would recognize her voice. She couldn't be found here, not while there was another one of her running around Solstice somewhere. She wiped her prints from the phone, set it on the floor, and willed herself awake.

* * *

They all came the next morning - Kiran, Simone, Rauri, Riley, Jax, Mick, and Indi. Rauri went straight to Raven, leaned over and kissed her forehead. "Are you sure this is what you want, darling?"

Blink.

"Alright. I support you, love. But, it's damn hard for all of us, too, aye?"

A single tear slipped out of the side of her eye with her blink. She wouldn't put them all through this if she could stand the thought of living like this. *Tell Jax to put Indi on the bed.*

Mick looked up at Jax with her red, puffy eyes. "She wants Indi on the bed."

Jax glanced at Kiran, who nodded. He took Indi over to the bed as Indi wailed, reaching for her mother, and gently set her on Raven's lap. Indi immediately pushed onto her hands and knees and crawled up Raven's chest. Jax grabbed her and started to lift her off.

No! Leave her! Let her say goodbye.

Mick repeated Raven's request and Jax set Indi back down. Indi burrowed into Raven's chest, her little legs tucked up underneath her, bottom in the air. For a change, Indi was the only one in the room not crying.

Raven desperately wanted to wrap her arms around Indi. She tried to get them to at least take off the C-collar so Indi could burrow into her neck like she so often did. They wouldn't do it, damn them. *Tell her I love her.*

"We do," Mick cried. "All the time and we'll keep saying it forever." She leaned over the bed and rubbed Indi's back. "Mommy loves you, Indi. Mommy loves you so much."

"Can I get a moment alone with her?" Riley asked.

Everyone nodded, wiping their eyes, and filed out of the room. Riley moved to the side of the bed and ran the fingers of one hand through Raven's hair and the others through Indi's. "Turns out at least one of Jenny's visions was right. What you're doing is selfish, Rave. I don't know if I can forgive you for this one."

Raven stared up into her eyes, trying so hard to convey what she couldn't say. Mick popped her head in the door and said, "She loves you." Then she disappeared from view again.

Riley's shoulders heaved as she wept over Raven. "I love you, too. I can take care of you, babe. I'll stay home and take care of you. Always."

Blink. Blink. What kind of life would that be for either of them? The lavender and jasmine scent of Riley's shampoo invaded her senses with Riley's hair just millimetres from her nose. She didn't know if it was a memory thing or if she actually smelled it. She couldn't sniff with all the tubes everywhere.

"Ugh! You're such a stubborn bitch." She lowered her head and pressed her lips to Raven's brow. "I don't want to say goodbye, lover."

Indi popped her head up and crawled further up Raven's chest. Her ice-blue eyes, framed in thick black lashes, stared down into her mother's identical eyes and she started babbling. She grinned and two top teeth glimmered. Raven hadn't even known she'd cut them. Why hadn't anyone told her? *I love you, sweet angel. I will always love you.*

Indi lifted her little hand and a soft white light began swirling in her palm until it formed a glowing ball of energy. Riley cried out and everyone pushed back into the room. Tears streamed from Raven's eyes. Indi babbled something as if she was making a little speech, then she sent her glowing white light into her mother.

Kiran threw the curtain across the glass wall. "Goddess, how are we going to explain this to the hospital staff?"

"Get the doctor," Riley yelled.

The white light entered Raven's body, but she felt nothing. She kept her eyes glued to Indi's even though she was all blurry through her tears. Maybe she was just too damaged for it to work.

Then the relentless headache began to ease. The tingling started in Raven's fingers and toes, working its way slowly up her limbs until her entire body was wrought with pins and needles. It felt glorious.

"Her hand twitched," Rauri gasped. "Bless the Goddess, her hand twitched."

"And her foot," Kiran said with a wide grin. "It's working. Bloody buggering hell, it's working." He lifted Indi from Raven's chest and threw her in the air, laughing. "There's my wee love. I knew you could do it, my sweet wee lassie."

Every movement Raven tried was like a spastic twitch, but she was moving. Blessed be, she was moving. Now, if only she could get them to take the damn tubes out of her throat and nose.

Two nurses ran into the room with Dr. Singh close on their heels. "What's happening?"

Everyone turned and stared at them with open mouths as if they didn't know how to even begin. Rauri stepped forward and held her hand out.

"I'm Raven's grandmother, Rauri Hayes."

"Dr. Singh."

"Hello, Dr. Singh. This may sound very strange, but we've just performed a healing on Raven."

He looked over at Raven and she lifted her hand and waved. It was a bit jerky, but she waved. Dr. Singh's mouth dropped open, his big, brown eyes nearly popping out of his head. "What is it you did?"

"Well," Rauri began. "We can't tell you that, now can we? But, if you'd run some tests, I'm sure you'll find that Raven is doing much better."

"Let's get her to CT," Dr. Singh said to the nurses. He looked back at Raven and she pointed to the tube going into her mouth. "Let's get you a CT first. If everything looks alright, I'll remove the tube."

She rolled her eyes at him, then reached her arms out for Indi. Kiran handed her over and Raven wrapped one arm around her, holding her free hand out to Riley. Riley grabbed onto it, then leaned over and buried her face in Raven's chest, weeping.

Chapter 29

A gentle breeze blew off the lake, taking some of the bite out of the hot, late August afternoon. Raven had thought she'd been in the hospital for about a week, but it turned out that all those times she'd woken in full-out panic mode spanned over three weeks. Sitting in a lounge chair on her deck, she stretched her legs out in front of her, grateful she wasn't in a wheelchair. Or still in the hospital. The sun beat down on Fairy Lake, dancing and twinkling across its surface as Raven stared out at it. The leaves rustled in the trees and the waves lazily whooshed up onto her beach.

The RV door opened and Riley stepped out with Indi in her arms. She'd taken a leave of absence from work when Raven was in the hospital, but Raven was fine, and still, she insisted on being there to take care of her. Her spinal cord and her C2 vertebra were perfectly healed. As were her three broken ribs and cracked skull that no one had told her about.

Riley sat on the chair next to Raven and settled Indi on her lap. "Clean bum and full tummy."

"Gimme." Raven reached out her arms and wiggled her fingers as Indi reached for her.

"Rave." Riley stood and gently placed Indi in Raven's lap.

"I'm perfectly healthy, Ri. I can lift her, feed her, change her, have mad monkey sex. Nothing is going to happen." She hugged Indi to her chest then kissed her all over her face. It was so good to be able to kiss her. Indi giggled then plastered her goobery lips to Raven's cheek.

"I know. I guess I just need some time to get used to the idea that you're okay."

Raven understood. Her injury had given them all a horrible fright, including herself. She got to her feet and reached for Riley's hand. "Come on, we're going for a walk."

"We don't have any shoes on," Riley protested.

"We don't need them. We're going down the beach." She hadn't seen Jade since the night of the esbat. She wasn't even sure she was still staying at the cottage on the point.

As they walked along the beach, Indi reached her arms out to the water and babbled away. She loved swimming in the lake, but Raven hadn't brought a towel for her, so she bent over and held Indi in a standing position at the edge of the water. Indi curled her little toes in the sand as the water washed up over her feet. She jolted at the first brush of cool water then laughed, stomping her feet and waving her arms.

Raven sat on the sand, holding Indi in front of her, letting her get her fill with stomping in the waves, cherishing the moment. A moment she thought she'd never have. Riley sat next to her, laughing at Indi's antics. This was how she wanted to spend the rest of her life, however many days the Goddess gave her. Sharing this moment with Riley, soaking up the innocent laughter of her daughter, enjoying the sun and the breeze and the soft lapping of the waves, made her heart soar. She leaned over and nudge Riley's nose with her own before brushing her lips over Riley's and grinning. "This, sitting here with both of you, is bliss."

Riley's pale green eyes glassed over and she touched her brow to Raven's. "Sometimes, you say the most beautiful things."

"Bah!" Indi screeched and clapped her hands, her little legs pumping up and down.

Raven laughed and got to her feet, scooping her daughter into her arms. She extended her hand down to Riley. Riley pushed her hand away and began to push herself up. "Trust me, Ri. I'm fine."

Riley stared up at her for a moment then took her hand. Raven pulled her to her feet and wrapped an arm around her waist, a broad smile gracing her face because Riley finally let her do something more strenuous than a leisurely stroll down the beach. She touched her lips to Riley's, still smiling, and, holding Riley's body against hers, rolled her hips. At Riley's gasp, her smile widened.

"See? Everything's working just fine. Good as new." So good that if she didn't stop, she'd end up backing Riley into the woods for a little privacy.

"You're impossible," Riley whispered against Raven's lips. She pushed away, then took Raven's hand as they started down the beach again.

"You haven't mentioned Jenny. Is she still in Solstice?" Raven hadn't heard one word about her since the healing she did on her.

Riley stared off into the distance. "They bought a cottage, then returned to Scotland while Rebecca waits for her visa. Jenny got her citizenship when she was growing up here, but Rebecca needs a visa to stay."

"Everything okay between the two of you?" It hadn't escaped her notice that Riley was still referring to her as Jenny instead of her mother.

"They're planning on living here, but Jenny hasn't spoken to me since that day on your deck. It's Rebecca who's been updating me on their plans."

"I'm sorry, Ri. Maybe she's just working through her crap."

"Yeah, aren't we all?"

As they approached the big white cottage on the point,

Raven spotted Jade standing on the beach, facing the water with her arms extended over her head. Her white gauze coverup fluttered in the breeze, a bright green bikini visible beneath it.

Jade lowered her arms and turned her head towards them. The edges of her mouth quirked up, then turned into a bright grin. She'd been working on her tan since the last time Raven had seen her, the golden-brown a sharp contrast to her platinum blonde hair that still spiked straight up.

Jade held out her hand and said, "Don't move." She grabbed her cell phone from the arm of the Muskoka chair behind her and held it up to snap a picture.

Riley slipped behind Raven and stood on the other side of her, putting Indi between them, and Jade snapped the picture. She walked over to them and handed her phone to Riley with Raven peering over her shoulder. Both Raven and Riley were pale in the photo after spending a month in the hospital, but they looked like a happy little family. Lush green trees served as a backdrop and the lake sparkled to the side. It was a gorgeous picture.

Jade took the phone back and asked for Riley's cell number then texted the picture to her. Then she stepped up to Raven and bussed her cheek. "So happy to see you well."

"Yeah, me too. I wanted to stop by and thank you for saving my life."

"That was all Riley."

"It was both of you. And Indi. Why don't you come for dinner tonight? I think a celebration of life is in order."

* * *

Despite Riley freaking out because she'd just gotten out of the hospital, Raven also invited Kiran, Simone, Rauri, Jax, Mick, and Grayson LaCroix over for dinner. They went into town and bought what they needed with Riley trying to do everything for Raven.

Kiran, Simone, and Rauri arrived first with Kiran carrying a stack of mail. "I stopped off at the post office, love. There's a crate in the car for you, as well."

"A crate?" Raven handed the mail off to Riley and walked out to Kiran's car. He opened the rear door, revealing a wooden crate measuring about one square foot. The label on the side gave a return address in Massachusetts. "Oh. That's for Riley." She leaned forward to pick it up and Kiran nudged her out of the way.

"I'll get it."

Raven rolled her eyes. "Not you, too. I'm perfectly fine."

"I know, love. Perhaps we just need some time to adjust."

Raven studied her strong, fit father. There were dark smudges under his eyes and he seemed to have a few more laugh lines. He'd also lost his summer tan over the past month. She tried to put herself in his shoes. If she'd spent a month at Indi's bedside, seeing her completely paralyzed and helpless day after day, and then going in expecting to watch her take her last breath, she'd need time to adjust, too. "I'm sorry for everything I put you through."

"It wasn't your fault, love. It's just such a drastic change that it's going to take some getting used to." He set the crate back down in the back of the car and rubbed his eyes. "I'm thrilled that you're well, Rave, but nearly losing you damn near destroyed me, aye?"

"I'm sorry." She stepped into him and wrapped her arms around him. Kiran's arms circled her waist and hugged her to his body. "Maybe it's too soon for this celebration." She was just so damn happy to be healthy again that she wanted to celebrate with the people she loved. She didn't take into consideration how they were all feeling and that it was going to take time for them to see her as whole. She'd just assumed Riley was being her usual nurturing self and maybe a little over-protective, but it went much deeper than that.

"I don't think so," Kiran said. He leaned back and offered her a weak smile. "Maybe it's just what we all need."

"Okay, then. A celebration of life it is." She kissed his cheek. "I love you, Dad."

Kiran pulled her back into his embrace. "Och, darling. I love you, too."

* * *

Kiran set the crate on the table on Raven's deck. "This is for you, love," he said to Riley.

"Me?"

"Yeah." Raven raked her fingers through her hair. "I ordered it for you."

"When?"

"A while back. After the fire." Raven stuck her hands in her pockets, unsure of Riley's reaction. She went into the RV and came back out with a screwdriver and pried the lid off the crate. It was packed with little bits of styrofoam popcorn.

Riley peeked in and then dug her fingers into the styrofoam. Her eyebrows shot up and her mouth dropped open. "Oh, no, you didn't." Her hands dug further into the crate and she lifted the crystal ball out by its base of copper flames, popcorn flying everywhere. She hugged the crystal ball to her chest for a moment, then carefully set it on the table and threw herself at Raven. "I can't believe you did that. Thank you. You know how much I loved that crystal ball. Holy shit. I thought it was a one-of-a-kind."

"It was. I commissioned the artist to make another one. When she heard what happened to the first one, she was more than happy to do it."

"Thank you." She leaned back, grabbed Raven's face, and planted a hot kiss on her lips. "Can I cleanse it?"

"Sure. Why are you asking?"

Riley laughed and threw her hands up in the air. "I don't know. I'm just so excited." She picked up the crystal ball and ran into the RV.

Raven stared after her, grinning like a fool. Goddess, it felt good to see Riley smile and laugh.

"Well, that was a hit," Simone said with a sultry smile.

Phew. "Yeah." Raven cleaned up the popcorn and put the crate inside the RV in case Riley wanted to use it to take the crystal ball home, but she was hoping it would stay in the RV, along with Riley.

Grayson arrived next, hand in hand with a beautiful woman. Raven was a little taken aback at who the woman was - her therapist, Dr. Kirsten Shoal. Grayson gave Raven a one-armed hug. "Glad to see you're doing well, Rave."

"Me, too. Thanks." She took the bottle of wine Kirsten held out to her.

"Welcome back," Kirsten said. "It's great to see you."

"Thanks, Kirsten." She waved her hand between Grayson and Kirsten. "I didn't realize you two were dating."

Kirsten grinned and Grayson laughed. "Rave, we've been together for close to two years."

"Oh." Why didn't anyone tell her these things? Or had she been so self-absorbed she didn't take the time to find out what her friends were up to? That had to change. "Well, come sit down. I've got champagne or would you rather a glass of the wine you brought?"

"Champagne would be lovely," Kirsten said.

"Champagne?" Mick asked as she stepped up onto the deck with her arm around Jaxon's waist and his around her shoulders. "I love champagne."

She'd love this stuff, Raven thought. It cost an arm and a leg. And a torso.

Once everyone had a glass of champagne, Raven took Indi from Jax's arms and raised her glass. "Thank you all for coming on such short notice. I feel like I've been given a second chance at life and I wanted to celebrate it with those who mean the most to me. I know this has been a tough month for everyone and there's going to be a period of adjustment, but I want you to know if you need to talk or whatever, I'm here. I love you. All of you. So." She raised her glass again. "Here's to life. We don't know how long we've got to enjoy it, so let's make the best of it."

"Here, here," Kiran said. He clinked her glass with his, then everyone joined in until it sounded like a crystal symphony.

"Oh," Raven called out. "And one more thing. In the spirit of making the best of life." She dropped down to one knee in front of Riley with Indi balanced on her hip. "Riley Gallagher, would you do Indi and I the honour of becoming my wife?"

Chapter 30

As Raven stared up at Riley, waiting for her response, Riley's gaping mouth turned into a scowl, her eyes narrowed and then pooled.

"How could you do this in front of everyone?" Riley whispered through gritted teeth before she turned and ran into the RV.

Raven was left kneeling on the deck with Indi in her arms, feeling like a complete fool. She dropped her head, wondering if she'd ever learn not to screw everything up so completely. Handing Indi and her glass of champagne off to Jax, she padded into the RV, followed the sounds of sobbing to her bedroom door and knocked. "Riley? Can we talk?"

The sobbing slowed, but Riley didn't answer. Raven didn't know whether to go in after her or give her some time. "Ri?"

Still no response. Raven leaned her forehead to the door. "I'm sorry I upset you. I should have asked you privately." The only sounds coming from her room were the odd sniffle. She tried to slide the door open and found it locked. Obviously, Riley wanted some alone time, but giving it to her would be torture. "Ri? I'm sorry. Please, say something."

She stood there in the silence for a few minutes, then turned and left Riley to her solitude.

Raven stepped out onto the deck to silent stares from

solemn faces. She raised her hands, shrugged her shoulders, and dropped her hands to her side. "I guess that's a no."

This was supposed to be a celebration and now she wanted nothing more than for everyone to leave. Only she couldn't ask them to do that. Not after what she'd put them all through. She stifled her emotions, sitting on the deck in front of Indi with an assortment of brightly coloured toys. Indi crawled through the toys onto Raven's lap.

"Well, at least you still love me," Raven whispered as she pressed a kiss to Indi's soft black hair, breathing in her fresh baby scent.

No one spoke, but Kiran's steady hand landed on her shoulder and gave it a reassuring squeeze as Jax handed her the glass of champagne she'd abandoned.

* * *

Raven put Indi to bed for the night, left everyone laughing and talking on the deck, and wandered down to the water to stare out over the lake. Riley was still locked in her bedroom. She'd accepted a plate of dinner from Mick but still refused to come out.

"You okay?" Jade asked as she joined Raven on the beach.

Raven snorted, although she didn't find the situation funny in the least. "I will be. Seems like one of us is always out of sync with the other these days."

"Yeah, well, maybe she'll change her mind."

"Yeah, maybe." Raven closed her eyes and breathed in the fresh air. She didn't think Riley would change her mind.

"I'll be leaving Solstice in the morning," Jade said, handing Raven a card. "I wanted to give you this. If you ever need anything, my cell number is on there."

Raven took the card and read the business name on the front - Something Wiccan This Way Comes. "This isn't for your jewelry business."

"No, that's the company for the other work I do,

investigating negative energies and paranormal incidents. If you ever decide you don't want to be a cop anymore, I'd love to have you on my team, Raven."

Raven raised a brow at Jade. "You're offering me a job?"

"I could use your many talents, believe me. I'm heading to Pennsylvania next. There are reports of negative energy and strange events near a place called Dublin Mills."

"So, I'd need to travel?"

Jade shrugged. "Unless the negative energies come to you, which in your case isn't entirely out of the question."

They both laughed and Jade gave Raven a quick hug. "It's been a slice, Rave. If you change your mind about a roll in the hay, you've got my number."

Raven watched her walk down the beach until she disappeared around a bend. Something told her this wasn't the last she'd see of Jade Storm.

* * *

Once she'd seen everyone off and cleaned up, Raven took the baby monitor down to the beach and sat there listening to the sounds of night falling around the lake - crickets, cicadas, and frogs singing their songs and the soft whoosh of the waves rolling in.

What had started as an incredible day had turned to shit. She sat there, tracing shapes in the sand only to wipe them away with her hand, giving herself a clean slate to start all over again.

The door to the RV open and closed behind her, but she didn't move or call out to let Riley know where she was. She must have seen her silhouette though, as Raven sensed her approaching. Riley sat down next to her as Raven continued to doodle in the sand.

Somewhere in the distance, an owl cried out its piercing *hoot, hoot* into the night. When Riley finally spoke, it was in a whisper so low that Raven strained to hear her.

"You shouldn't have humiliated me like that."

Raven closed her eyes and drew in a deep breath, absorbing the pain searing through her chest at Riley's comment. Only when she was able to speak calmly did she answer. "I asked you to marry me in front of people we both know and love. I don't understand how that would make you feel that way, but I'm sorry for it. It wasn't my intention to hurt you, Ri."

"What did you think was going to happen, Rave? After everything we've been through this summer, what did you expect?"

With her mouth agape, Raven lifted her head and turned to look at Riley, but she kept her gaze focused out over the lake, refusing to meet Raven's eyes. "A couple of days ago, you pledged to spend your life taking care of me, but now that I'm healthy, you don't want me?"

"It's not that I don't want you, Rave. I love you. But, some of the things Jenny told me came true. You very nearly died and the threat to you because of your abilities remains. I don't know if I can live with your recklessness and never knowing if you're going to make it home at night."

Reckless? Was doing what she had to do to protect her daughter and the future of the Bowen line reckless? "You're condemning me for something I cannot change." Now Raven stared out over the lake, soaking up its calmness. She felt like she'd just been tried, convicted, and sentenced to death. "I am who I am. If you can't love me for that, then we're better off ending this now."

Riley drew in a quick, sharp breath. "Ending it? That's a little severe, isn't it?"

"For some reason, the Goddess blessed me with a second chance at life. I'm so grateful and humbled by that. I want to embrace that and enjoy every moment to the fullest. I don't know how many days I have, none of us do, but I'm damn well going to enjoy them.

"The whole time we've been together, Ri, I've had a dangerous job. You didn't hold that against me. It's only since Jenny started getting in your ear that you've had reservations."

"She was right about you dying. If it wasn't for Indi, you wouldn't be here right now. She's right about your path being a difficult one, Rave. That I know in my gut."

Raven couldn't deny that. She felt it herself. "Why do you think the Goddess gave me a second chance?"

Riley turned her head then, locking eyes with Raven.

"There's work for me to do here, Ri. I don't know what or when, but there's work I'm meant to do. And, maybe, just maybe, you're meant to be at my side."

"Is that what you believe?"

"It's what I feel. You told me to trust my instincts. It's what I feel here." Raven pressed her fist to her belly. "In my gut. The warrior and the healer."

With a shake of her head, Riley whispered, "You're the healer. You and Indi. You're the warrior and the healer."

Raven turned her focus to the moonlight twinkling on the water's surface. "Do you remember me saying that, over time, you'll soak up some of my powers?"

"Yes."

"You'll also take on some of Indi's." She turned back to Riley and stared deep into her eyes. "You'll become a powerful healer in your own right."

Those beautiful green eyes widened before Riley broke the contact and stared off into the distance.

"I have a lot to think about. I need some time." Riley pushed to her feet and dusted the sand from her hands. "I'll call you tomorrow."

"Sure," Raven said and, looking down at her doodle in the sand, wondered if it was an omen that she'd drawn a broken heart. She closed her eyes and all she could see was the image of the two of them in the crystal ball, reaching for each other with an unknown force pulling them apart. Raven had no doubts that force was none other than Jenny Gallagher. But, why she was so hell-bent on tearing them apart, Raven had no idea.

* * *

Grayson set four evidence bags on the island counter in Ena's kitchen. Raven carefully unwrapped each with Grayson, Mick, Kiran, Rauri, Simone, and Jax with Indi in his arms circling the island. Each of the medallions held considerable power. The kitchen was nearly vibrating with the energy.

The first medallion was the compass medallion found on Raven's lawn after her house had been burnt down.

"This one belonged to Derek Branson," Grayson said. "He wasn't wearing a medallion when he was arrested, but the shape of it was seared into his chest."

Raven glanced up at Kiran. "A traveller's protection?"

"Aye. It offers guidance and protection to the wearer."

The second evidence bag contained a trinity knot forged out of black obsidian.

"Brandon was wearing that one," Grayson said.

Rauri leaned forward and brushed the tips of her fingers over it. "The Morrigan's Triquetra."

"You know this medallion?" Raven asked her.

Rauri nodded as she traced the shape of the knot with the tip of her finger. "The triquetra represents the triple goddess. The black obsidian clears one's psychic fog and protects against negative energies." She drew in a quick, sharp breath, then met Raven's gaze. "This is the medallion of a warrior goddess. It belongs around your neck, Raven Sage."

Raven lifted her hand and covered the pentagram medallion she wore under her shirt between her collar bones.

She'd much rather wear it than the symbol lying on the counter before her. Not that Raven didn't like the triquetra, but it packed a serious amount of power. She couldn't imagine walking around with that much energy around her neck.

The third medallion looked like a maze snaking around inside the circular gold disk.

"This one was worn by Landon McKinnon," Grayson said.

"Hecate's Wheel," Rauri announced as if everyone should know what that meant. "The power of knowledge and life."

As Raven unwrapped the fourth medallion, a communal gasp sounded. The power in the symbol Raven revealed was both palpable and visible. The golden ankh emitted a warm light as it lay on the counter.

"Eternal life," Simone said on a long sigh.

Grayson laughed. "It certainly didn't help Jacob Lang." When Jax narrowed his eyes at him, Grayson winced. "Sorry, dude. I keep forgetting he was your father."

"Yeah, well. It's not like I really knew him."

Raven watched as Mick wrapped an arm around Jax and drew him in closer to her. She hadn't even thought to offer her condolences. Not only had he lost his father, but his cousins and his aunt had been arrested.

"You're doing the right thing, DS LaCroix," Rauri said. "These are all potent talismans that need to be safeguarded."

"And who better to do that than the Guardian of the Sacred Moon?"

Raven raised her eyebrows at Grayson. She hadn't realized he knew about that.

"This needs to be kept quiet," Kiran said with a grim expression. "If word got out about these medallions and where they were being kept, it would put Raven in danger."

"Not just me," Raven said. "They're being kept in your house, Dad." At least, they were for now. She'd have a safe installed in her new house once it was built and get all five of the medallions in her care out of Kiran's home.

"Not to worry." Grayson laid his hand on Kiran's shoulder. "They've been documented as having been removed from evidence to an undisclosed location for safekeeping. There is no written record of that location and the only people who know it are in this room."

"Then, we'll make a pact." Raven's eyes travelled around the group, meeting each person's gaze before moving on to the next. "We don't talk about them outside of this circle." She got a nod from everyone in turn.

Raven took the four medallions into Ena's office and opened the safe behind a painting. Just as the Sacred Moon medallion had a name, she supposed the other four did as well - Traveller's Compass, Morrigan's Triquetra, Hecate's Wheel, and Eternal Life.

Now it was her job to keep them safe; to keep them from getting into the hands of anyone who would use their powers for wrongdoing. The weight of that responsibility carried with it the responsibility for keeping her family safe from those who'd like to get their hands on them.

She was just closing the safe when Mick wandered in. Raven was glad to get a moment alone with her. In the week since she'd last seen Riley and she'd said she needed time to think, Raven hadn't heard from her.

"How are you doing?" Mick asked.

"Good as new. I'm working out and running every day."

"I wasn't asking about your physical health."

Raven eased the painting back into place and turned to face Mick. "Have you talked to her?"

Mick shoved her hands in her pockets and nodded with her brow furrowed. "Yeah. She went to Scotland."

"Scotland?"

"She went to spend some time with her mother."

That familiar sharp pain was back in Raven's chest. Why wouldn't Riley have called or texted to let her know she was going? That hurt more than her going away. "For how long?"

"She didn't know."

Raven turned to gaze blindly at the painting on the wall with her clenched fist massaging her chest. "Well, I guess that's it then." She'd be damned if she was going to wait around for Riley to decide she wanted to come back. She wasn't about to waste any more time. Besides, the longer Riley spent with Jenny Gallagher, the worse Raven's chances were.

Mick walked to her, put an arm around Raven's shoulders, and stared up at the painting. "Don't be an idiot. Go after her."

Raven shook her head. It wasn't so much that Riley had gone to spend time with Jenny, but that she hadn't confided in Raven about her plans. "That ship's sailed, Mick. Or perhaps the better analogy is that plane's taken off."

ABOUT THE AUTHOR

Wendy Hewlett writes mainly crime fiction with a hint of romance featuring strong female protagonists. She brings a vast array of life experience to her pages having held jobs on cruise ships in the Caribbean, addiction counsellor at a private addictions treatment centre, and years of experience in the security field.

She enjoys learning and holds diplomas in creative writing, forensic sciences, and law & security, to name a few.

When Wendy's not writing, you'll find her engrossed in the pages of a good book, out riding her bike, or spending quality time with her family.

She aspires to empower and inspire women as well as foster their healing with her novels.

Other Titles from Wendy Hewlett

<u>*The Taylor Sinclair Series*</u>

(Must be read in order)

Saving Grace

Unfinished Business

Runed

Trafficked (Coming Soon)

<u>*The Solstice Coven Series*</u>

High Priestess

Guardians of the Sacred Moon

<u>*Stand Alone Novels*</u>

Ailey of Skye

Visit the author's website at: wendyhewlett.com and sign up for her Monthly Newsletter to stay up to date on news, new releases, giveaways, and more.

Follow Wendy on: